The
Blood
Artists

Also

by

Chuck Hogan

The Standoff

The Blood Artists

A Novel

Chuck Hogan

William Morrow
and Company, Inc.
New York

Library of Congress Cataloging-in-Publication Data

Hogan, Chuck

    The blood artists : a novel / Chuck Hogan

       p.   cm.

    ISBN 0-688-15622-3

    I. Title.

    PS3558.034723B58   1998

    813'.54—dc21

                              97-28154

                                   CIP

Printed in the United States of America

First Edition

1 2 3 4 5 6 7 8 9 10

BOOK DESIGN BY DEBORAH KERNER

www.williammorrow.com

For J.A.H.,

a survivor

"We would like to go into the true reasons that brought you here—" he began but she interrupted.

"I am here as a symbol of something. I thought perhaps you would know what it was."

"You are sick," he said mechanically.

"Then what was it I had almost found?"

"A greater sickness."

F. SCOTT FITZGERALD,
Tender Is the Night

The desire for possession is insatiable, to such a point that it can survive even love itself. To love, therefore, is to sterilize the person one loves.

ALBERT CAMUS,
The Rebel

The

Blood

Artists

A virus is a bit of genetic
acid wrapped in protein.
It is neither alive nor dead.
It is small, smaller than
bacteria, many times
smaller than any
animal cell.

A virus has no energy of its
own. It cannot reproduce.
A virus without a living cell
to plunder is helpless and
inert. It must steal life by
slipping into a congenial
cell and tricking it into
replicating viruses.
This is the act of infection.

A virus does not want to
kill. It does not even want
to harm. It wants to
change. It wants that part
of it that is missing.
It wants to become.

Eclipse

*(the barren
early period
of infection)*

The Strange Case
of Dr. Peter Maryk

Everything that begins, begins with blood.

We were at work in a B1 blood laboratory on the third floor of the seventh building of the Centers for Disease Control and Prevention, a network of industrial-looking brick-and-mortar structures located just outside the city limits of Atlanta, Georgia. We were both junior virologists on staff at the CDC, myself and Peter Maryk, and both thirty-one years of age. This was the final week of December 2010.

Peter worked across the lab table from me, standing over a whirring centrifuge, spinning down blood serum. His hair was pearl-white and had been since college, and he kept it short and straight, his angular face and slate-gray eyes set in a mask of severity. He switched off the centrifuge and like a roulette wheel it slowed, ticking to a stop, silence returning to the lab. He crooked his head at a tinny scratching behind him.

"Thirty-seven's going down," he said.

I looked across at the wire cages. Thirty-seven, a large, white, pink-eyed rat, was digging repetitively at the metal floor and shifting back and forth. His hind legs buckled beneath him, and at once he slumped over onto his side.

I crossed to the cage. Thirty-seven kicked sideways at the air, his small-toothed mouth opening and closing. Blood dappled his sugar-white chin. His pink eyes fixed on my face as his body twitched, his tail lashing at the cage floor, *pang, pang*. The jerking became less and less frequent, and Thirty-seven expired staring at me.

There was still a chill. Death made failure real, something I wished not to repeat.

Peter appeared at my side. He opened the top door of the cage with a gloved hand and lifted Thirty-seven out by the tail, sealing him inside a numbered plastic bag.

"It should work," I said. "We've watched it under slides. We know it works. It's just too potent for rats."

Peter said nothing. He returned to his station and set the bag down on the table with a light thump.

"We can't go to primates," I continued. "If we go to chimps we'll have to declare our research, and I'm not ready for that."

Peter and I distinguished each other in our fields of specialization, mine being straight laboratory science, Peter's being field pathology and investigation. I was most at home in a laboratory setting, but Peter was growing restless, and beginning to show his disdain for the project.

Clean human blood was a precious commodity as the first decade of the twenty-first century drew to a close. An onslaught of viral and bacterial disease had depleted the reliable source pool, and patients around the world were dying, stuck on long lists waiting for transfusions of untainted blood. Lucrative black markets had sprung up in every major population center, from New York to Beijing to Cairo, where illicit blood traded at fifteen to twenty times its weight in gold.

Like many medical scientists of the day, Peter and I had dedicated ourselves to the great challenge of developing a safe, synthetic human blood substitute. Yet that achievement alone would not have satisfied me. I was seeking to improve on organic human blood by deriving not merely a perfect substitute, but one infused with enhanced virus- and cancer-fighting properties. Peter was questioning the propriety of our work, and fully half my time now was spent appeasing him. His participation in the project was essential. Peter Maryk's immune system was infallible. He possessed innate immunological qualities beyond the natural ability of any human being known to medical science. When Peter Maryk claimed never to have been sick a day in his life, he meant it as fact. His gifted blood provided the essence of our project. At that time, my goal of conferring some degree of Peter's enhanced immune system to the ill seemed in reach. The potential benefit to medical science and worldwide human health would be inestimable.

We returned to our stations on opposite sides of the wide stainless steel table, Peter to his centrifuge and I to my binocular microscope. I bent over it and looked down upon a small, bustling, crystalline city.

There was a thick popping splash, and I shot back reflexively. Peter was rising from the table, arms out at his sides, blood splattered over his fleshy latex gloves and paper smock and the small beige refrigerator humming behind him.

Peter glowered at me, and I stood. It was a scare, but fortunately the blood was our own. He picked up the dripping plastic pack labeled MARYK and examined the torn eyelet. The rest of the packeted units of blood labeled either PEARSE or MARYK hung from a steel rack over the table. My blood was the project's control. Four small vials labeled PEAMAR4 were the product, to date, of the fourth generation of our efforts.

Peter's spilled blood was inordinately rich in color, oozing over the steel tabletop and seeping in dark parabolas down the walls of the sink. He turned on the faucet and ran water over his gloved hands, then wiped down the sink and counter and untied his bloodied smock, stripping off his gloves. He started toward the door with such intensity that I believed he would walk out and keep going, never to return to the lab or the project, but he merely disposed of his soiled gloves in a red biohazard box set into the wall. He was on his way back for a fresh pair when he slowed to read the flip-up screen of his tablet, a portable notebook computer, recharging in a wall socket and therefore wired into the CDC's central net.

"Stephen," he said.

Every sentence Peter Maryk spoke, even the most benign of phrases, was infused with urgency. His voice was clear and deep, compelling. I went around the table and joined him, struck by the scent of baby powder coming off his bared hands. Peter's hands were never without protective gloves, in or outside the lab. They were pallid and smooth-knuckled, and he held them upturned as though awaiting a towel.

The monitor was flashing an EPI-AID mail message. The epidemic assistance request had been posted over the CDC–maintained LifeLink web from a Dr. André-Dieudonné Kaunda in the central African Congo for vaccine to treat one unconfirmed case of "variola major," or smallpox. I reviewed the symptoms detailed in French beneath the description of the patient, a nine-year-old Congolese girl said to be in the poxing stage.

"Buboes," Peter translated, fancying the antiquated term.

"Can't be."

"The symptoms match. But no request for assistance. Or investigation."

"He's just uncertain," I said. "As well he should be."

But Peter was pulling on a fresh pair of gloves and already heading for the door. I followed him out, across to adjoining Building Six via one of the outdoor wire-encased catwalks linking each building of the CDC. The center was understaffed that week due to the year-end holidays, and our shoe heels scuffed loudly along the well-worn tile steps to the first floor.

Room 161 in Building Six was, considering its duties, an office of modest size. The three desks inside, and the computers they supported, made up a virtual clearinghouse for rare drug and inoculation requests received from around the world. It was in Room 161 in the early 1980s that a CDC doctor first noted a surge in requests for pentamidine, a drug used to treat a rare pneumonia, from physicians in the Los Angeles and San Francisco areas perplexed by an unusual wasting disease afflicting several young, male, homosexual patients.

The door was open. Dr. Carla Smethy stood in relief as I entered. "Stephen," she said, surprised. "I was beginning to think there was no one here at all."

Carla Smethy was in her mid-thirties, black-haired, round-cheeked, and smart. She nudged a curl off her forehead. The Christmas carols jingling out of her desktop computer were an unsuccessful attempt to alleviate the gloom of the rare drug request office.

Peter entered behind me, and Dr. Smethy's smile flickered. In fact, she took one small step back.

"What do you make of it?" I said.

She shook her head. "A first for me. You're the bug experts." She looked to me in an interested way. "How did you get stuck working the holiday?"

Peter sat at her computer. "May I?" he said.

She appeared startled. "Yes—sure."

He ran his gloved hands over the keyboard, first switching off the tinny carols. I kept one eye on the monitor.

"We wanted some lab time," I said in answer to her question. "Thought it would be nice and quiet around here."

She plucked a piece of paper off her desk and showed it to me. "Seen this?"

It was a proof of the cover of *Morbidity and Mortality Weekly Report,* the centers' weekly periodical, featuring the new letterhead logo and initials "BDC." Following public outcry in the wake of emerging and reemerging diseases worldwide, an act of Congress had redrawn the CDC's policy mandates and enhanced its federal powers. As of January 1, 2011, the preeminent health agency in the United States and the world leader in disease prevention would be rechristened the Bureau for Disease Control.

"The end of an era," she said.

Peter had brought up the complete bulletin on the monitor. Delivery of the smallpox vaccine was requested by airdrop west of the city of Dongou on the Ubangi River. A relay trace sourced the sender's tablet coordinates to a location just a few degrees above the central African equator. Peter pulled up a grid map. The coordinates cross-haired into northern Congo, stopping there and pulsing faintly. The bulletin had been dispatched from deep within the rain forests south of the Sangha Wildlife Reserve, west of the Bumba Zone.

"The Congo," Peter said, his strange voice leavened with something like romance. He had worked a year in Dar es Salaam, the port capital of Tanzania, while I had elected to spend my foreign field residency in Calcutta, in a floating pediatrics hospital on the Hooghly River. Acquaintances since our third year at Yale, roommates in med school at Johns Hopkins and rivals in our virology class at Emory, we were now colleagues and research partners at the CDC; it was the only period of time during the preceding decade in which we had worked apart.

"Must be a mistake," she said, looking at the screen. "The wrong request class, it has to be."

I said, "Do we have any variola vaccine in stock?"

"We do, actually. But only because first-year vaccinologists cook it up as part of their training. Otherwise, who cares?"

"But why no medical support?" Peter turned in the chair. He trained his silvery eyes on her. "A call for variola vaccine, but no support?"

She looked stunned. "There's blood on your shirt," she said.

I tried to intervene. "It's all right—"

"It's mine," Peter said. He examined the florid stain.

Peter Maryk was different, innately different, apart from his imposing physical presence. People sensed this. Conversations trailed off when he approached. Rooms changed whenever he entered them. Some people even claimed they could feel him walking behind them in the halls. He was in many ways an irregular human being, which at one time had been a source of great consternation for him. I was the politician of the two, and had taken on the role of social intermediary for him since college, explaining him to some, defending him to others, even apologizing to a few. But every attempt to introduce him into the broader culture of the CDC had failed. Increasingly he seemed uninterested in fitting in any-where.

Dr. Smethy looked again to me. "What do you think, Stephen?"

I looked at the monitor screen. Laboratory space at the CDC was at a premium, and I had been looking forward to Christmastime and the changeover as an opportunity to push ahead on our PeaMar research without interruption.

"We have the lab free and clear for an entire week," I said.

It was part of the alchemy of our relationship that I would temper Peter's morbid enthusiasm. Peter had often questioned smallpox's un-timely fate, distrustful as he was of most of mankind's triumphs, a distrust that now included our PeaMar research. My reluctance here—as there was no question that the distress call required further investigation—was simply an attempt to leverage his renewed participation in the project upon our return.

"Worst case," I said, "it's an orphan," a virus whose symptoms re-semble another, more prevalent disease.

"Even so," Peter said, "there's a very sick little girl out there."

I was stunned. The abject insincerity of his words, known only to me, was shocking. Peter's interest lay exclusively in hunting viruses, and to that end healing people was something of a by-product, the perfume that sweetened and further profited the whale kill. These clumsy words of concern were meant to manipulate me. This was the branch height to which our relationship had evolved.

"How badly do you want this to be smallpox?" I said.

He paged through airline schedules and clicked on a red-eye to Paris. "Our flight leaves in three hours."

In the mid-1760s, a young apprentice surgeon named Edward Jenner was examining a milkmaid suffering from cowpox, an occupational febrile illness characterized by nausea and painful pustular sores on the forearms, when the milkmaid proclaimed that, according to lore, she was now no longer at risk for the dread smallpox. Intrigued, Jenner pursued the milkmaid's agrarian remedy, and on May 14, 1796, came to perform mankind's first vaccination, lancing a sore on the wrist of a milkmaid named Sarah Nelmes and subsequently scratching the arm of eight-year-old James Phipps with the same instrument. The mild case of cowpox this produced in Phipps successfully rendered him immune to future smallpox exposures.

But smallpox continued its wrath, killing sixty million people that century, disfiguring and blinding many millions more. Into the 1950s, the scourge still claimed more than two million deaths each year, a testament to the extraordinary virulence of the microbe, which was transmitted by respiration as well as casual contact. Inspired by the virus's seeming preference for young children and the availability of a secure vaccine, an ambitious multinational campaign to eradicate smallpox was launched in 1967. In September 1976, a three-year-old Bangladeshi girl named Rahima Banu was cured of the last naturally occurring case of variola major, the more severe strain. A twenty-three-year-old Somalian cook, Ali Maow Maalin, cast off the final case of variola minor on October 26, 1977.

Smallpox is the only virus ever to succumb to the efforts of mankind. The sole extant strain remains frozen and archived among tens of thousands of high-risk biological agents in the security containment vault of BDC Building Thirteen.

Edward Jenner deservedly achieved the eminence to which all medical scientists aspire. His contribution to the human species was significant, and in 1823 Jenner died arguably the first global hero.

I, certainly, would not die the last.

I spent our brief Paris layover out on the tarmac at de Gaulle, wrapped in a borrowed orange parka, overseeing the transfer of a hundred pounds of equipment and supplies onto a Swissair jet. The flight to Gabon passed uneventfully. I drifted in and out of sleep while Peter busied himself with his tablet, most likely tapping out some obscure virological missive that would never see publication. We changed planes again and split four matches of computer chess during the final leg of the journey, from Libreville, Gabon, to the sprawling RECI reserve east of Bomassa.

The head of the Rainforest Ecology Conservation International camp was a rangy ex-Californian named Todd. He sported a floppy bush hat and greeted us at the plane with a surfer's smile and a strange look at Peter. "Merry Christmas," he said.

I shook his hand, but Peter was busy watching our Cameroonian pilot, a hajji, kneeling beside the T-tail of the eighteen-seat turboprop, praying his salat. The orange light of the dawning sun warmed the pilot's face and felled a shadow of reverence on the runway behind him.

We declined their offer of breakfast, and four other bright-eyed conservationists helped with the gear transfer into a waiting Pinzgauer Turbo. They argued with one another over the directions, eventually producing a hand-drawn map of cross-outs and jagged arrows.

"Good time to be here," said Todd, his unlaced boot resting on the towing loop of the all-terrain Pinzgauer. "Neat little window on the rainy season right around Christmastime, these next two weeks. Roads should hold. This is Pygmy territory. You two okay with that?"

Peter, tying a white cotton headwrap around his shining white hair, nodded.

"You'll run into them if you're lucky," said Todd. "This is their backyard. And they take francs."

Peter said, "I like your hat."

Todd's eyebrows rose in response. He pulled the hat off his head and inspected it. "Imitation snakeskin," he said, touching the band, as though accused of something. Todd looked a decade older without the big hat, strings of brown hair drawn across his sweat-soaked pate. He seemed to consider making a gift of the hat, then instead replaced it firmly on his head and squinted into the risen sun. "We got some teams camping out there, entomologists, botanists. Should I be calling them in?"

"No need," I said. I pulled down an Emory University ball cap snugly over my brow and climbed into the green Pinzgauer. "We should be back to you in a day or so."

Peter drove us out. The road deteriorated immediately from hard dirt and sandy shoulders to soft gray dirt and no shoulders to encroaching jungle walls and emerald vines sweeping like pennants over the windshield. A light, wavy mist became a driving rain that pattered the massive, thickly veined tree leaves, sloughing rivulets of water into the softening road, and our speed dropped to five kilometers per hour. The road faded and reappeared but the map read true.

I marveled. The vegetation spilled over us as though from a perpetual green fountain, reducing the Pinzgauer to little more than a sturdy beetle scuttling over the ground. We drove like that for hours, and my thoughts returned, as always, to work back home, to PeaMar4.

Peter stopped for the first Pygmy we saw. He was an elderly man with rich brown skin and a short, dusty beard, wearing only a battered navy blue suit jacket and a sheath that covered his groin, holding a whittled staff by the side of the road. Peter got out and approached and exchanged *les salutations* with the diminutive man, whereupon the rest of the tribe emerged from the vegetation behind him, as one. I had remained a few yards back, near the car.

The old man, standing not much taller than one meter, next to Peter who stood just under two, cast a dark eye upon Peter's gloved hands.

"Médecins Sans Frontières?" he said.

Peter shook his head. He spelled out "C-D-C."

Some among the tribe nodded. They were used to intrusions by doctors and scientists. As a race Pygmies possessed extraordinary natural immunities, including a seeming resistance to certain clades, or distinguishing strains, of the human immunodeficiency virus, HIV. Although they had lived for millennia in the remote rain forest region that was the epicenter of the virus that caused AIDS, in the three active decades of the disease no infections had yet been reported among their tribes. This revelation in the early part of this century had led to a resurgence of interest from immunologists hoping to penetrate the mystery of the co-evolution of virus and man.

The old gentleman reassured Peter that we were nearing "the settlement," as he called it. Then at once he grasped Peter's oversized hands and regarded them through their latex shields. "As young as your hands," he said in French, "or as wise as your hair?"

The question seemed to amuse Peter. He glanced back, then looked out at the tribe.

"*Le chapeau,*" he said. One of the tribesmen was wearing a bush hat similar to Todd's, fixed atop a traditional African toque for balance and fit. The snakeskin band appeared authentic.

Peter relieved him of the hat with four hundred of the five thousand francs he had withdrawn on account from the CDC currency office— somehow he had known where to locate the keys—and presented the old man with an appropriate tribute of four blue pouches of Drum rolling tobacco, procured at de Gaulle airport for just such an occasion.

Peter fitted the hat onto his wrapped head as the old man raised his tobacco pouches in appreciation. His tribesmen followed, all raising their hands and whatever tools they held in them. It was something to see, this race of immunologically advanced people saluting Peter Maryk, who was in fact immunologically nearly a race of people unto himself.

I remained behind. In the jungle our roles were reversed, and for one of the few times in my life, I smiled the empty smile of the outsider.

The pitted, sunken road was a courtesy the jungle soon withdrew. The twists and turns of the RECI map led us out beyond the eastern border of the conservation lands, the Pinzgauer surfing a collapsing tsunami of mighty vegetation. The land rose and fell and we rose and fell with it. Roadside bursts of beauty—waterfalls, lagoons—became routine, a whispering palette of emerald and black and olive. In time the rains returned to crash against the steel grille and overmatch the windshield wipers of the Pinzgauer, a fresh sheen of mud slicking the jagged road. The path before us flickered but never quite went out.

The rain pecked at the immense leaves, giving them fitful life as we rolled past. The jungle now seemed antagonistic; my earlier wonder was eclipsed by a mix of respect and fear. In no other place on earth does man feel more like the intruder that he is. Tamed or chased out of the megacities of the world, here resided the fugitive Nature, the artist in exile, stripped of her canvases and finer oils, now hurling paint.

The rain tapered off again and the swirl of the windshield cleared, wipers slowing in relief, the roar of the storm subsiding to a thumping on the steel hood of the Pinzgauer like small rubber mallets pressing out tin. I eased off the grab handle before me and settled back into my seat, and Peter popped his hat back onto his wrapped head. I rolled down my window and the vehicle filled with the dank sweat of the troposphere.

Another thirty minutes and the path began to widen again. Dirt shoulders appeared and the road surface ran smooth. We passed a fallen tree neatly quartered beside the road, and it was a relief to see something touched by the hand of man.

Misty sunlight streamed through gashes in the high canopy ahead, and suddenly the jungle opened on a plot of wet dirt cleared around a large, one-story plantation-style house.

The house was constructed of whitewashed stone. Its clay tile roof glistened from the sunny rain, as did twin pairs of shuttered French windows in front. A fat path of crushed rock led like a white mat to the door. Another muddy car, a Japanese 4×4, was parked near the walk. Above the door hung a sopping flag fashioned waist-to-hem from a tattered, yolk-yellow skirt. It was a homemade flag of quarantine.

We stepped out into light rain and swung out the spare tire hinge to open the rear door. Peter removed his hat and broke the tape seal on a CDC-stamped carton, and we stripped off our gloves, dropping them into a cubic repository emblazoned with the international biohazard symbol. We pulled on two fresh pairs each, first standard latex surgical, then dull green contact issue extending beyond the wrist, sealing them against our skin with adhesive tape. Neither of us had much hair left on his forearms. Peter pulled blue cotton surgical scrubs on over his clothes and I did the same, forsaking the thicker, safer contact suits, selecting for mobility and comfort in the seething clime. It occurred to me at the time that it was always nice to have one higher level of protection to fall back to.

Respirators went on last. I swept my hair in under a surgical cap, then pulled the flexible harness down over the back of my head, adjusting the belt so that the customized black rubber face piece set flush across my brow, behind my ears, and below my chin—again creating a seal. The stubby inhalation valves, extending like insect mandibles forty-five degrees off each side of the chin piece, decontaminated incoming air by exposure to ultraviolet light. UV light destroyed viruses by shattering their genetic material, and was radiation-safe to three hundred and fifty nanometers. A smaller black exhalation valve was set in between.

Raindrops picked at my Plexiglas view. We powered up our respirators, hearing the dull whine emitted by the light source, and lifted the emergency aid kits out of the cargo hold, starting for the house.

The door beneath the dripping flag of quarantine was garnished with a childlike weaving of vines, stems, and berries. An African man answered my knock. He was in his sixties, wearing an agricultural mouth and nose shield tied around his head, his eyes baggy and blinking above it. His open shirt collar exposed pearls of sweat. His gloved hands, one hanging at his side and the other holding the door, were streaked with blood.

"Dr. Kaunda," Peter said through his mask.

The doctor looked from respirator to respirator, then focused on our scrub shirts and the letters stenciled there, CDC. He looked out at the Pinzgauer in the rain beyond us, a dazed expression in his eyes.

"*Parlez-vous français?*" he said.

I nodded, feeling the muzzlelike awkwardness of my respirator.

"*Le vaccin?*" said Kaunda.

Peter held up a small plastic box.

"*Par ici.*" This way.

We entered. A woven mat ran the length of the hallway inside. Dr. Kaunda shut the door behind us and at once the trapped heat of the shuttered house raised pops of sweat on my exposed upper arms. The respirator and twin layers of gloves dulled most of the senses. Taste was lost and touch and smell were well cloaked, though sight remained strong—I could see a light flickering through an opening at the end of the hall—and sounds were muffled but audible over the ultraviolet whine. I discerned a faint cough somewhere within.

Kaunda led us slowly down the hall. The windows were shut in accordance with the rules of quarantine, protecting against the possible introduction of a vector—an insect or rodent or some other conduit of microbial transmission—even though smallpox was passed directly from person to person. A pall of sweat shaded the back of Dr. Kaunda's pink cotton shirt. He felt his way along the wall, moving more like a parent than a doctor.

We turned into a small, flickering bedroom. A fat candle hung unswinging in a ceiling lantern over a stripped bed upon which a nine-year-old girl lay twisted upon a patchwork of towels. She was nude, her arms out at her sides, the swell of her stomach sinking and filling as breath huffed out of her small, blistered mouth. Bulbous pox sores speckled her inflamed flesh, most prominently on her neck and arms, although common also to her torso, upper legs, and groin. The largest ulcerations were swollen to more than a centimeter.

"Elle ne peut pas supporter être touchée," Dr. Kaunda said. She cannot bear to be touched. He stood with the underside of his left forearm pressed against his brow.

Some of the sores were broken and discharging pus, the sand-colored towels under the girl's back showing mixed stains of yellow and red. A rash imbued the unblemished patches of her dark skin with a ruddy glow. Her right eye was swollen shut, the bloated lid poxed and crusting over. Her left eye remained open, and was bursting with veins.

"En feu," she hissed. Burning.

Shed hair lay in wiry, doll-like strands atop her undressed pillow. The bed was soiled with waste and flakes of dead skin.

Peter moved quickly around the foot of the bed. There were trinkets and carved gourds on a wooden nightstand, cleared back from a basin of reddened water. He slid his case onto the table and swiped the gourds and trinkets noisily to the unmatted floor.

Dr. Kaunda said behind us, *"Elle ne peut pas supporter même la pression d'un drap."* She cannot bear even the pressure of a bedsheet.

I said sharply, "She can hear you."

"Maman," said the girl with a cluck of her blistered tongue, shivering, straining up off the bed.

I knelt and set the aid kit down on the floor and fumbled open the clasps. I admit that I did not know what to reach for first.

"Her name," I said behind me.

Kaunda had found a child's wooden rocking chair in the far corner. He was squeezing himself into it.

"Her name," I said again.

"*Jacqueline,*" he answered.

I rose empty-handed and moved to her. The new rubber smell of my respirator had been replaced by the stench of human decay, seeping like a gas down my throat. I fought the odor as I stood over the writhing body of the girl. Peter was preparing an injection across the bed.

"*Jacqueline,*" I said in French. "My name is Dr. Pearse. We have come for you."

Her open eye flickered and fixed overhead. "*La bougie,*" she insisted. The candle.

Peter straightened with the syringe. "Delirious," he said. "Get clear."

Peter popped off the plastic tip protector and readied the needle above the blistered pocket of her left elbow. He located the median cephalic vein and entered it.

She arched and thrust out a low-pitched groan of pain. I kept talking to her in French, partly in order to calm myself.

"It is all right," I said, many times.

Her venous left eye bulged as though straining to see through the ceiling. Peter remained over the syringe and the girl's tensed arm. I realized then that he was not vaccinating her, but was instead drawing out blood.

"Peter!"

He straightened, holding a full red barrel. "We need a clean sample for PCR," he said, never stopping his work, chucking off the needle hub and discarding it, setting aside the full barrel and reaching for a proper hypodermic. He braced her arm at the biceps and stuck her a second time, easing down on the plunger, voiding the barrel and shooting the inoculant into her system. She arched again and cried out shrilly, a cry without human precedent.

He discarded the hypodermic, and we met at the foot of the small bed.

"Abscesses match," I said, mumbling. "The rash, the languor. Odor."

Peter was excited. I suppose we both were. "I don't recall hypotoxicity," he said—the inability to absorb inhaled oxygen, likely the cause of her hypersensitized nerve endings. He listed the classic diagnoses, recalled from text. "If the sores do not touch: recovery probable. If sores cluster: fifty-fifty. If bleeding erupts beneath the skin: death likely."

The girl's sores were clustered. I nodded just to nod. She lay trembling on the stained towels beside us.

"I'll run the blood sample," Peter said. A PCR assay would provide us with a genetic fingerprint of the virus and demonstrate conclusively whether or not it was indeed variola. Before he left, something in the room darkened Peter's expression, and he turned to Kaunda.

The aged doctor was slumped in the girl's rocking chair, his bloodied gloves dangling to the floor. Peter asked him where the parents were.

"Dead," Kaunda said in French, making no effort to lower his voice. "Two days ago. I buried them next to the house."

Peter exited the room without the blood sample. I heard him in the hallway, and he was throwing open doors.

I returned to the girl's side. Her half-open eye was again focused on the candle above the bed. I reached for her small hand and took it in my own, lightly, aware of the rubbery strangeness of her fingers even through my thick gloves, monitoring her eye for distress.

"*Jacqueline,*" I said. "*Jacqueline.*"

Her head rolled slightly and the dark pupil inside her raw red eye settled on me. I warmed my eyes and put forward the smile of a confident doctor. I nodded. Her unwavering stare was one of apparent amazement.

"*Je flotte,*" she whispered. I am floating.

It would be a minimum of six hours before she could be safely evacuated. Six hours before the Pasteur Institute could assemble and fly in a biohazard team with an isolation stretcher—assuming no reluctance on the part of the French government in granting a visa to an African national racked with an unidentified contagion that was perhaps smallpox, a single case of which would, by definition, represent an epidemic. At that point I hoped that it was just that, mere smallpox, the reemergence of the worst scourge in human history, but an entity known and imminently curable.

I was staring at the girl, waiting for her to tell me what to do, as Peter reappeared at my side. "A man's study in the front room," he said. "Mural of a lion hunt on the wall. A rolltop desk full of French pens and empty file hangers. A laser printer. Two unused business ledgers in a drawer, tablet chargers, and a rotary file on the desk stripped to the brackets, even the alphabet dividers. The stove in the kitchen is full of burned paper."

He turned from me to face Kaunda and spoke bitingly, in French.

"Where does the back road lead?"

Kaunda appeared quite aged as he looked up at Peter from the small chair in the corner of the room. He did not immediately answer.

"You are a camp doctor," Peter said.

Kaunda's eyes above his blood-dappled mask showed a prisoner's expression of weary defiance, as that of a man so broken and exhausted that he existed beyond fear. I was still very much in the dark as to what Peter was getting at.

"That is why you requested vaccine only, and not support," Peter said. "You didn't want us here at all." Anger burned brightly in his gray eyes, glowing with each flicker of the candle. "What are you bringing out of the jungle? It can't be ivory. Diamonds?"

Kaunda's latex hands rotated slightly at the ends of his arms in a truncated shrug, and his sad eyes pleaded. "Monsieur Moutouari ordered that help be called only if his daughter became ill," he said in French.

Peter said flatly, "How many more cases like this one?"

"None," Kaunda said. He blinked profoundly, many times. "The others are much, much worse."

The girl's hand slipped from my grip.

Peter told him, "You bring the girl," then picked up my emergency kit and moved out of the room.

I remained, awaiting an explanation from Dr. Kaunda, but the old doctor just sat looking at the dark floor, his head shaking weakly.

The girl was trying to speak. Her tiny, blistered throat was working, but not well. I leaned close and lowered my masked head to her lips as she managed a hoarse whisper.

"*C'est la mort,*" she said fiercely. It is death.

I wondered at the extent of the girl's agony as we crawled along behind Kaunda's muddied 4×4. I chided myself for being too accustomed to life in comfortable, metropolitan Atlanta, having overlooked the significance of the improved jungle road, and failing to question the logistics of constructing such a house in the depths of the African rain forest. And then there was the original **EPI-AID** alert, broadcast by a general practitioner in the middle of the jungle with a state-of-the-art digital uplink. Peter had suspected treachery from the beginning.

On the way out of the house I had looked in through one of the doors opened along the hallway and saw the parents' bed, stripped bare and stained with blood, vomitus, excrement. Outside, a plot of freshly spaded dirt lay on the far side of the house, patted smooth by two days of rain.

The road ran two kilometers longer to a wide opening. We parked behind Kaunda and pulled off our respirators, unpacking the contact suits: bright red-orange rubber jumpsuits with attached hoods and flexible UV face pieces. We stepped into them and pulled them up over our shoulders, sealing them across our chests, waist-to-neck, like the zipper of a plastic bag.

My head throbbed with the danger and the heat. I tugged at the cuff gaskets on my sleeves and the thick black rubber gloves attached, an additional layer of protection for the most vulnerable area of a physician's body. Peter came before me and took hold of my sleeves and coolly double-checked the seal. His thin lips inside his face piece faintly grinned at my distress. "Nobody should be enjoying this," I said. "Not even you."

Kaunda spread a heavy sheet out on the grass. The girl remained curled up inside the backseat, moaning, quaking, nude. I reached in and lifted her out, feeling the fragile puffing of her immature lungs in my arms, and she was lighter even than I had imagined. I lowered her onto the sheet and she doubled in pain, breath pushing through her torn lips like choked laughter. I straightened, immediately drenched in sweat and miserable in spirit.

Behind us, two lanes of shanties constructed of corrugated metal faced off across a wide, sun-bleached band of beaten grass. Heavy stones secured the flat shanty roofs, cooled by leafy tree limbs from the encroaching jungle. This would later become known to us as the heart of the camp town: a kitchen cafeteria, public latrine, small liquor store and bar, general store, Dr. Kaunda's dispensary, and a wide, unwalled market. Farther away, two rows of smaller thatch huts continued around a rightward bend into the trees.

We saw only one person outside. A man was squatting beneath a large woven mat strung up on bamboo stalks near the first of the huts, his shoulders resting against his knees and his hands flat on the burned grass beside his feet. Gourds and pots lay scattered and overturned on a mat before him. He saw us and rose to stand, wearing only a shin-length pair of custard-colored pants, then abruptly turned and disappeared into one of the huts.

A distant wail startled us, and as I turned my head within the hood, a second figure burst from one of the shanties, racing across the grass mall toward the huts. She was a tall, woolly-haired woman unused to running, her slender arms flapping over abrupt strides, wearing a bright, shin-length floral skirt, a tight headdress of the same fabric, and a faded pink T-shirt. Halfway across the grass mall, she saw us, cried out and turned. Her sandals flopped as she raced toward us.

She reached me first and grabbed my rubber arm, bursting out something in a Bantu dialect that I did not understand, and pulling at me to follow her. I loosed her fingers from my sleeve and for a moment held fast on to her wrist, examining her face. There were no sores and her eyes were bloodshot from crying but otherwise clear. I nodded to the woman and started away, but by then she had seen Kaunda. She shouted at him and spat with precision at his feet, and then at the wrinkled sheet of the shivering girl.

I followed inside my bulky suit. The woman clasped her hands as she moved, raising a doubled fist to the dusky carmine sky, leading me past the hanging straw mat and around an old-fashioned, pedal-driven Singer sewing machine set on a table and a ring of stones that was a cooking fireplace, to a hut on the left. She prayed to me to go inside. Sweat ran down my brow into my eyes, which I could not reach to wipe away. I set down the aid kit and motioned to her to be calm, then ducked inside, under neatly trimmed reeds.

A human figure lay still on a small cot mattress. It was a man weighing no more than eighty pounds. His limbs were wasted down to the skeletal architecture of his body, such that each knobby articulation—the ball of the humerus within the scapular cavity of the shoulder, the carpal bones like loose rocks within the fleshy pouch of his wrist—was plainly described. His skin itself was rotting off his body in a fetid stink, marble-sized boils and violet tumorous ulcerations marking the dark map of his flesh. It was less than flesh, a fungus that had grown up over a skeleton. He respired in slow, shallow breaths.

Worst of all was the man's face. His lips were curled back from cracked teeth and dissolving gums in a mummylike sneer, and wrinkled folds of unbound skin were gathered in darkly layered sags beneath his drooping ears. Most expressively, his eyes had found something horrible in the ceiling. They were distended, blood red and fully exposed from their widened orbits, the pupils dilated and floating like compass heads fixed in scarlet spheres—as of a pair of eyeballs plucked from a jar of bloody preserve.

I backed out of the hut. I stood staring at the open black doorway I had retreated through and heard the woman pleading or praying behind me, and I backed away some more. I pointed Peter inside. *"Soyez calme,"* I said to the woman automatically, Be calm, not hearing the words myself until well after they had been spoken.

A figure moved in front of me. It was the man who had been squatting under the mat. He said something in a dialect I did not understand, though it was clearly gibberish. His eyes were sad and scarlet beneath drooping lids, half-open, half-dead, drunk with blood. He made a reaching motion behind him which at first I did not comprehend, and the woman screamed anew.

He produced nothing, and stared at his empty hand in confusion. Peter stood behind him, holding a large unsheathed machete he had pulled from the back of the man's pants. There was blood encrusted on the flat of the blade. The man let out a cry of despair and fell weeping to the ground.

Peter and I looked at each other through our masks. We looked at the machete.

"Christ," I said finally.

Peter flung it deep into the trees. He said, "Come on."

We left the woman. We looked in at each of the more than twenty huts set along the curling pathway. Camp conditions were such that each small dwelling housed as many as six workers, and each hut now contained at least one bedridden infected person, though many contained more. Kaunda rejoined us and led the way to a hastily cleared burial ground in the back trees. At his insistence, the camp workers had dispensed with the traditional washing of corpses. An animal boneyard was similarly arranged nearby.

Kaunda explained that the disease had a peculiar and dramatic effect upon the brain; a few of the infected camp workers had set upon the others with knives, hammers, whatever was handy. The man with the machete was a *sorcier aux crabes*, the camp sorcerer who divined fortunes and, once the deaths had begun in earnest, dispensed *buti* tokens to ward off the fever. Kaunda departed the camp once the sorcerer became ill, in fear of his life.

We crossed a sturdy vine-and-grass bridge hanging over a swift river to a second grouping of smaller huts beyond. The huts were lined around a wide quadrangle of clay-tinged dirt where the afflicted were laid out on woven mats at odd angles, staring with uninterested eyes. Other obviously ill people knelt in grief at the side of loved ones, and still others shuffled about the square in a fevered funk. The recent dead were laid out in rows, their faces fixed in grimace, limbs and torsos emaciated, eyes bloated.

Raindrops bled through the high, dense canopy as Kaunda led us back toward the bridge. He paused near the quiet river, hooking his hand on a low, curved tree branch and blotting his forehead with a handkerchief from his back pocket. "Four days, start to finish," he said in French. "First the headache. Flulike symptoms, a general malaise. Then spasms, chills, and onward." He rumbled a light cough into the dirty handkerchief. He was facing the river. "Four to five days, fever to fulmination. Three weeks now. It set upon the camp like an eclipse."

Peter went around in front of Kaunda. Under his scrutiny, the wizened doctor straightened off the low branch. He swiped at his face with the cloth, standing on short, uncertain legs, but ultimately wilted under Peter's intent, silvery gaze.

"You're sick," Peter said.

Kaunda gestured dismissively with the damp cloth. "Malaria," he said. "It returns now and then—"

Peter shook his head. "You're sick," he said again.

Kaunda looked wearily back at me, a pleading smile, and then again at Peter, appealingly. "A touch of the fever," he explained. "I have quinine in my office."

He tried to move toward the bridge but Peter stood in his way. "Sick doctors," he said.

Kaunda shook his head. *"Non, Monsieur—"*

Peter regarded Kaunda with disgust. "Denying their own disease as they spread it."

"Monsieur." He was indignant now, rubbing at his face with the cloth as though trying to erase it, his balance wavering, "I can assure you—"

Peter turned his back on the man and faced me. "We're on our own here," he said.

For a long time after that I forgot about the heat inside my suit. We unpacked the equipment and immediately began treating people. The metal-roofed marketplace shanty was the only structure large enough to accommodate all of the sick. I drafted the healthier camp survivors—falteringly, in glove-pantomimed French—to help me clear out baskets of grains and meal and burlap bags of spoiled produce, to make room for a trauma center. Peter isolated the area by dividing the camp lengthwise along the center mall, symptomatics to the right, asymptomatics to the left. A dotted row of stones became the borderline between sickness and health. They were all term laborers trucked in from the depressed cities of Kinshasa, Brazzaville, and Yaoundé, recruited by agents of the same illicit concern that had hired Kaunda, lured by high wages too attractive to refuse. Of the roughly one hundred and fifty surviving workers, the two populations at that time were nearly balanced.

After a round of preliminary examinations Peter set up his tablet and bulletined two nurses and seven investigators from the Special Pathogens Section, a division of the CDC that dealt specifically with the epidemiology and etiology of unknown emerging viruses. The aid message read, in part:

Febrile disease characterized by flulike symptoms, delirious sleep, lethargy escalating to dementia, arthritic symptoms, wasting syndrome, endothelioma. Clinical disease includes (prelim): Fever nearing 40°c, epitaxis, weight loss, muscle pain, prostration, allergylike shock, rapid evolution toward death. Agent (prelim): Viral, emerging. Pathogenicity: High.

Advise: Biohazard 4.

There was no international alert, as we agreed that the outbreak was adequately isolated, at least for now. In any event, it was always preferable to establish the disease etiology first, rather than face unanswerable questions that could lead to misinformation and public panic later. Fear was the most virulent disease of all.

Peter backed the Pinzgauer out of the clearing into what became our retreat, abandoning Kaunda's infected 4×4 inside the camp and pocketing the keys. I designated a barrier zone between the two areas, setting out for us a large biohazard box, packets of sterile gloves, and pans and brushes and jugs of Pheno virucidal disinfectant.

We refit Kaunda's dispensary inside the camp, fashioning an operating theater out of an examining table and pump sink that would service autopsies as well. Then we set up shop in the market shanty and began prioritizing the afflicted. The asymptomatic population assembled behind us in a desultory line along the quarantine border, watching us administer to their sick.

Peter broke away around midnight to do the PCR work, and ran the genetic fingerprint of Jacqueline Moutouari's virus through the database at the CDC. It came back exactly as we had feared: UNK, or Unknown. Whatever was eating Jacqueline Moutouari, it was not the smallpox virus. It was something not yet encountered by human medicine.

I visited her later. She was lying on an air mattress in Kaunda's personal hut, behind the dispensary, feverishly reciting what sounded like a child's prayer. The suppurating pustules had merged upon her chest and legs. I could only wait for more antivirals to arrive, in the vain hope that one might click.

I returned exhausted to Peter under the roof of the marketplace.

"The sores have merged," I said. "She's dying."

He immersed his instruments in a pan and ceded the patient to me. "I'm finding tumors in post," he said, meaning postmortem examinations. "It's a retrovirus."

I slid my gloved hands into a bowl of cleansing formalin. Retroviruses were RNA viruses, more complicated than regular DNA viruses, and responsible for a rogue's gallery of diseases including various viral cancers, leukemia, and immune-deficiency afflictions such as AIDS.

"The girl's is different," I said. "Hypotaxia. Range of sores. The symptoms vary victim to victim. There's something to that."

Peter nodded. As he started back to the dispensary I heard again what I had previously taken to be the pounding of my own pulse inside my head. I called after him. "The drums," I said.

Peter looked to the high trees, listening. "Pygmies," he said, before continuing on.

The CDC team arrived by Ford Explorer and Peugeot station wagon at noon the next day. They wore full biohazard regalia and brought with them nearly five hundred pounds of equipment, including surgical supplies and diagnostic apparatus, body bags, nylon restraints, a thirty-liter autoclave, generators, refrigerators, and small transport freezers. The expression in their eyes as they stood among the dying reimpressed upon me the macabre rage of the disease.

Following a short briefing, we left them to string up IV feeds and hang mosquito nets around the trauma center while Peter and I retreated to the barrier point on the edge of camp. We disinfected our suits with a painstakingly thorough Pheno scrub bath, before ripping them open and pushing back the hoods. The pores of my cheeks tingled, exposed to the free-flowing air. We disposed of the suits in biohazard and changed gloves and proceeded to the Pinzgauer outside camp. I broke open a waxed box of distilled water and downed half of it, pouring the rest into a bowl and splashing it on my needy face. Peter, a claustrophobic, strode in wide, relieved circles around the vehicle, happy to be out of his suit. I sat in the open side door of the Pinzgauer and savored the muggy air.

Neither of us had ever seen a virus so devastating as this one was. No one had. A virus with such a high degree of pathogenicity traditionally lacked virulence, just as, conversely, a less debilitating virus achieved wider penetration by virtue of its having a greater number of living, functioning carriers. This African bug would likely burn through the camp inhabitants within one week's time.

All of this went without saying. We still did not know what the virus was or, more important, exactly how it was transmitted. After the meal, Peter waved a mosquito away from his head, and both of us looked at each other with a surly alertness. Silently we withdrew into fresh contact suits.

At dusk anything that could be used as a weapon was confiscated in a hut-by-hut search. The virally induced psychosis had manifested itself in varying degrees among the afflicted, from mere confusion, to stupor, to outright dementia. Only a few became violent and had to be restrained. Psychotic episodes were staggered with brief periods of lucidity, marked by despair and expressions of terror, leading invariably to the final, catastrophic stage of the disease.

That night Peter completed a field assay involving a T cell survey of ten patients in the prodrome, or preliminary, phase of the disease. T cells are the white blood cells that make up the vanguard of the human immune system response. Peter's field test—a simple tally of cells on a microscope slide—found the highest T cell count of the ten prodrome cases to be thirty-four, which was demonstrably low, in fact well below the CDC criteria for establishing a diagnosis of AIDS.

By the end of the second day, thirty-seven more were dead, fifty-one suffered advanced cases, and thirty-two were entering the prodrome phase with severe flulike symptoms. PCR analyses had revealed significant differences in the genetic sequences of the viral strains infecting the population. We were dealing with something unusual, a virus possessed with extraordinary mutative properties.

The CDC team submitted lymphatic samples once daily for PCR screening and adopted a buddy system in order to monitor one another for disease symptoms or fatigue. The virus was almost certainly airborne, and a slipped scalpel or torn glove compromising a suit could lead to a fatal contamination.

Later that evening I began to hyperventilate inside my suit and had to be relieved. A few minutes away from trauma I regained my composure, and on my way out of camp I checked in again on Jacqueline Moutouari. Bleeding had erupted beneath her skin. The sores were now most profound upon her face and torso, many broken open and draining a mustard-yellow discharge. Her decaying body was ridding itself of nutrients and fluids faster than could be replenished. Any attempt at dressing her wounds resulted in cries of pain. The nine-year-old was in agony. I stood over her, daubing some garamycin into her half-open, blood-filled left eye and gently holding her hand. There was no response now, no squeeze or gurgle or twitch of the eye. Nothing had worked. I wandered out to Kaunda's car on the edge of camp and lay back on the passenger seat. I could not fathom the life that was going along blithely back in Atlanta, throughout America and all the world. It was as though the airports we had passed through on the way to this virus had, upon our takeoff, turned to dust. I slept there, fully suited, for two hours.

Peter woke me before dawn and handed me a flashlight. I accompanied him down the dark road, past the camp, ending around a long curve at a natural cave opening in the center of a steep, grassy rise. He approached the cave's wide, dark mouth and stepped inside.

I followed. The walls and the ceiling had been widened and reinforced, our flashlights illuminating work grids painted onto the surface, continuing deep into the dark earthen belly. A fine dust swirled in the bright cones of our beams.

A four-wheeled wooden cart rested on twin rails to the right, containing hand tools and mining implements, pickaxes, hammers. The inside walls of the cart were dented and stained black.

We withdrew from the cave at once. Further exploration was never considered. The chance of compromising our suits was too great, the floating dust itself a formidable potential vector.

We followed the rails along a well-trod path to a long, flat-roofed, pale brick building to the right of the rise. Severed treetops were spaced in large pots atop the roof, and camouflage netting hung halfway down each of the high walls.

The wooden double doors were not secured. Inside, Peter's beam found four more wheeled carts on alternate rails, one filled with broken chunks of brownish-black ore still encrusted with dirt. The main track fed directly into what appeared to be a small refinery. We moved along the length of the left wall, past ovens, stone crushers, smelting vats, and piping, to the end of the line, where beneath a short, iron flume stood a sealed twenty-gallon drum painted sugar white. Peter found a steel rod and pried off the cover, which popped and fell with a clamor against four more barrels behind. It was full of sand-packed chunks of clean, dark, lustrous ore laced with quartz. Peter picked up a small piece and turned it over in the light of his beam.

"Pitchblende," he said. "Uranium ore."

Radioactive material. I backed away from the barrel, and brushed something with my boot. My light found a small bat lying dead in a dried streak of blood. Its brown wing membrane was curled and spattered with sores. I turned my torch up toward the ceiling, pipes leading like steel vines to exhaust portals in the grimy roof. The vent windows along the high side walls were unscreened and open to pest and rodent intrusion. I looked back at the floor; it was fouled with guano.

We exited the infested building and crossed the road to a smaller structure fashioned of the same corrugated metal as the camp shanties, but twice the dimension, and bolted edge to edge. Rats and mice lay twisted along the roadside at our feet, as though having crawled out of the underbrush to die. Peter opened the door on the darkness, and we heard a rodentlike scattering. His flashlight beam swept a long wooden counter where the miners had evidently been served lunch and dinner. We moved behind it to a cramped cafeteria-style kitchen, and there he illuminated four objects set along a high shelf next to a stack of tin food trays. They were flowering plants of some sort, well-dead now, cauliflowerlike eruptions of bunched petals spilling off a broad stalk around medusan strands of horny stigma. The pots holding them were cracked where the root system had burst through the clay and forced out dirt and leggy spindles. The color had since faded off the wrinkled petals, like a comic book bleached by the sun, leaving only shadows where apparently garish streaks of color once rioted.

Peter turned to me, his flashlight hanging down, fallen leaves and crumbs of dirt shining in its puddle of light.

"Four weeks ago the miners broke through the dry gallery wall they thought was the rear of the cave," he said. "They followed a quartz vein of uranite down into a wide cavern running beneath most of the camp, beneath us now. It was a rich deposit. They held an impromptu celebration dinner that night, and some of them brought up a few of the strange plants discovered below. The cavern dips into the water table down there; they had to have waded through it. The ceiling is lower than two meters in places, the stalagmites and stalactites pointed and sharp. They reported large, strange-sounding flying insects. The soil in there hadn't been disturbed for centuries, perhaps never."

"How do you know all this?"

"Kaunda's tablet. He was a camp doctor hired to hand out quinine and Praziquantel tablets to keep the workers working, and got in way over his head. The glass cabinet in his dispensary, stocked with bottles: half are routine medical, peroxide, alcohol; the other half bourbon bottles with the labels soaked off. I found it tucked in there. He began charting the spread after the fifth or sixth incidence. It originated simultaneously in two cave workers and a female cook. The cooks were unmarried women who also accommodated the miners as prostitutes. A fourth case occurred in Kaunda's nurse; the virus spread quickly from there. Animals too. Pigs, sheep, and goats all crashed or had to be put down within days of the first human case."

I took a moment to digest this. "What about the girl?"

"She never came into camp. Neither did her mother. Mr. Moutouari was in charge of the mine and came and went regularly back and forth by bicycle. He led the first expedition down into the cavern after it was discovered. Maybe he brought up one of the more exotic flowers as a present."

I envisioned Jacqueline outside her front door, thrilled with her father's gift of a fantastically queer wildflower, placing it into a small porcelain vase and raising the petals to her nose for a deep breath.

Peter continued, "In any event, someone fronted this excavation. The camp was set up to bring out the pitchblende and clean it off to be packaged and shipped out where it could be milled for uranium. Whoever it is, they've abandoned this place now. The disease scared them off. Moutouari must have warned them. There haven't been any food shipments in more than a week."

"Radioactive ore," I said. "With whatever ancient microbes are sealed in down there. A closed system, mutating, slow-cooking the RNA, selecting and reselecting over time."

Peter agreed. "Over the millennia. A magma chamber of viruses. These people go down there and break the seal, disrupt the ecosystem. That's phase one."

"Then carry it back up here." I nodded. "Whatever they brushed up against, or whatever is in these plants, whatever they breathed, it surfaces and they are infected."

"The cave is clearly the epicenter. The surrounding camp is densely populated. From the incident group to their families, and the nurse to her patients. Then to nonmine workers, the bar owner, the tailor. The far camp was the last to get it."

"Casual contact, then. And aerosol delivery, but with limited capacity. It burns through the camp. Phase two."

"And now phase three," Peter said. "Opportunity for secondary spread must exist. The insect census is a wash for vectors—more species of bug in this tiny camp than in the entire state of Georgia. The river tests clean, no fish washing up yet. But mammals carry it."

Peter saved words by moving his light beam back and forth between us.

"Someone could become infected and vector this virus back to the U.S." I agreed. "There's no physical boundary here, no safe wall we can put up between us and the bug. The sunlight is killing it in the clearing, and keeping it off the trees. But not for long."

Peter nodded meaningfully, looking into the darkness of the diseased kitchen.

I said, "If this has gotten out already, and is showing up anywhere else, we need to know. An international alert. We need entomologists, zoologists."

Peter shook his head distractedly. "Too hot," he said. "Containment is most imperative now. Kaunda's log said there hadn't been any ore shipments out in almost a month—they thought the cave had run dry. We're contained now. More people here means only more meat for the bug."

"But we need support. I'm seeing only limited success in trauma. Fluid management is only marginally effective in slowing the process."

Peter snapped off his light. "Or prolonging the agony," he said. "It's going to burn right through this camp, nine doctors or nine hundred."

He was right, of course. As we left the kitchen I found myself feeling oddly reinvigorated, anxious to get back to trauma. Our challenge had finally taken shape. Peter opened the metal door and we emerged into the apricot dawn of our third day in the jungle.

"A massive cleanup," I said, thinking ahead.

Peter looked around at the cave and the road and the morning trees. A wild plant was growing in the shadow of the cafeteria, its leaves spindly and fevered with overripe color. He uprooted it with his booted heel, and kicked it into the killing light. He said, "Leave that to me."

In the afternoon of the third day I was called away from the marketplace trauma by a young girl in her mid-teens on the healthy side of the quarantine line. She was attractive, even remarkably so, with expressive eyes and a chestnut face almost more sculpted than functional, but inside the charnel house this was just another detail among details, an identifying trait I might have listed along with size and weight on her chart, and in truth a feature not nearly as remarkable as the spectacular disfiguring qualities of the disease. What did distinguish the girl were the stains of vitiligo over her neck and arms, and what I could see of her shins below the hem of her banana-yellow skirt, dappled with depigmented, strikingly pale pink flesh that, in my haze, I first mistook for symptoms of the scourge, and which brought me to her. The young woman's eyes, however, were white and clear.

She began begging me, in quiet, controlled French, to take her away. Save me from this death, she said, her fingers plying at the red-orange fabric of my chest. Her entreaties became more desperate as I continued to decline, but she pleaded and pleaded, even offering herself to me, anything, grabbing on to my suit, until finally I had to wrest her hands and thrust her away. She dropped to her knees in the grass on the healthy side of quarantine, and continued calling after me.

Later that day, one of the nurses brought me Dr. Kaunda. His eyes were bloodshot and glazed, and small lesions had appeared over his body, and he complained of prostrating lower back and abdominal pain. He was still muttering something about quinine. The muscles of his face were lax and formless. The depersonalization phase had begun. I dosed him with Seconal to allow him some sleep, and moved on.

That evening, as I walked in on Peter in the dispensary, working over a corpse, I saw that his head was exposed. He had severed his rubber contact suit at the neck and removed the hood in favor of a respirator and a simple cotton surgical cap. The suit was taped sealed to his thick neck, while the decapitated hoodpiece lay on its side on the floor across the room.

He saw me in the doorway, looking up from his corpse. There was no explanation, no regret. No apology nor even defiance.

Though I strove to return a similarly cool expression, I certainly failed, and finally left without saying a word, proceeding to the hut behind the dispensary.

Jacqueline Moutouari's face was no longer distinguishable. I had seen decomposed bodies before and that was what she looked like now. She was breathing in short, feral breaths with extended pauses in between. Each one seemed her last.

Peter appeared next to me. He was rubbing something sticky off his gloves and looking at her. She clutched at her chest with tiny, crooked fingers.

"End it," Peter said.

The Seconal kit was in my gloved hands. I felt its weight and wondered, as though it were the greatest question in the universe, whether or not I had intended to bring it there. Seconal was a powerful barbiturate sedative, and when administered in significant dosages, was considered a humane instrument of physician-assisted death.

Peter grew impatient. "Give me the kit," he said. He did it himself. Her pulse rate began to fade and, in less than thirty minutes, stopped.

I buried her myself. It was backbreaking work. I buried her behind the dispensary, away from the others.

Peter later abandoned the autopsy room and joined me out in the makeshift hospital, having capped and chilled many more biological samples than we would ever need. His protective gear had changed again, and now consisted merely of a lighter half mask that provided not much more protection than a simple surgical shield, goggles, and half-arm gloves taped to bloody cotton surgical scrubs. He had covered only the vulnerable membranes of his eyes, nose, ears, and mouth. The contact suit was gone. A nurse next to me saw him and gasped but I kept right on working. Peter was able to move more easily than the rest of us, and flaunted this advantage, rotating from patient to patient with breezy dispatch, like a barber inspecting haircuts. Later that evening I asked him for 2 cc of his blood. It came back negative for viral infection. Peter was clean.

When I was first getting to know my third-year roommate at Yale, I ignored Peter's boasting of never having been sick. I was myself descended from a long line of New York Episcopalians who claimed the same, my grandfather having "never missed a day of work in his life," simply by going to meetings ill and routinely infecting half of Wall Street. This was the starched white underpinning of my Protestant Yankee work ethic.

But as I came to know Peter, I watched as he immersed himself in the petri dish of university life without forfeiting a single class to illness; without contracting the case of mononucleosis that kept me, his finals study partner, from participating in the graduation ceremonies; without ever catching so much as a sniffle. I witnessed more of the same as we continued together through medical school: a defiance toward illness that went beyond the bragging of an extraordinarily hardy constitution. In our second year at Emory, in the CDC virology track, each candidate had to submit to a battery of inoculations before being allowed access to the most dangerous biological agents. Peter was the only one to smile through the endless vaccinations—yellow fever, Q fever, Rift Valley, tularemia, anthrax, hepatitis A and B, typhoid, meningitis A type and C type, and multiple flu and encephalitis strains—tolerating each of these and more without any side effects, without developing even the slightest rash or headache.

The clincher came a few months later, when Peter was contact-traced by the CDC's own Crimes of Infection branch as having been seated on a recent flight from Seattle to Atlanta two rows in front of a man infected with multidrug-resistant tuberculosis. Untreatable MDR-TB was the second most prevalent infectious disease in the world, and in the United States it was illegal for carriers to fly on commercial airlines. Contact tracing had turned up all 221 passengers and members of the flight crew, and all were found to have contracted the incurable disease during the five-hour flight, and all went on to secure enormous financial compensation from the airline. All except Peter Maryk. He was the only passenger who did not collect. He had been exposed with the others, and yet somehow had thrown off the incurable disease. A battery of tests proved this. The only sensation of discomfort he recalled was one of exhaustion shortly after landing, which he slept off lying across three chairs inside the airport terminal.

I set to work, initiating a series of laboratory tests exposing samples of Peter's blood to infectious agents both viral and bacterial. He demonstrated resistance to each, and in time and in secret, Peter began exposing himself to some of the more exotic, nonlethal viruses. He cast each one aside without manifesting a single symptom, and with only one unusual side effect.

The more serious exposures were followed by a period of mononucleoticlike languor, the duration of which varied according to the pathogenicity of the infectious agent, ranging from brief periods of sluggishness to deep reenergizing sleep. The effort required to expel invaders from his system prompted an overall energy drain, which Peter termed a "cascade." This typically meant his slumping in a corner chair, following an exposure, as though dawn had found him the last survivor of a wild party with no ride home. When it compelled him to sleep, which was rare, he slept soundly, nearly unconscious. Given his imposing physical appearance and his superhuman immunological strength, these cascades were the only times he ever appeared vulnerable.

Our co-authored findings were published to acclaim in *The New England Journal of Medicine* and entitled, "Noninduced Superimmunoresponse and the Search for the Survival Mechanism: The Strange Case of Dr. Peter Christian." Peter's pseudonymous identity and reputation were however generally known within the CDC and the greater medical and scientific community, and the professional acclaim he enjoyed only exacerbated his alienation from his peers.

The origin of Peter's enhanced immune system could be explained only as an accident of genetics, although a six-generation family history had yielded no clues. His body somehow recognized and isolated unhealthy intruders with alacrity, overwhelming and disabling them profoundly, and dispatching them without any trace of infection—including the production of antibodies. While this latter condition seemed to preclude any direct therapeutic application of his gifts, Peter's blood serum did evince certain benefits in laboratory tests. I determined the reactive process to be CMI, or "cell-mediated immunity," a little-known function of the immune system distinct from the classic antibody response. With CMI, patrolling killer T cells destroy not merely the invading virus, but the infected cell itself, simultaneously ending the virus's bid for reproduction and ridding the body of the threat.

Transfusions of his blood, however, wreaked havoc on laboratory animals. The problem was that Peter's killer Ts attacked without restraint in nonprimates, not stopping at pathogens but going on to devour healthy body cells and eventually whole organs and the blood itself. Still, the prospect of a blood serum enhanced with disease-fighting properties sustained my laboratory efforts over many more months.

Before that day in Africa, I had never seen him be anything but scrupulously careful, or otherwise dare to tax his system in an uncontrolled setting. Peter had the so-called doctor's disease, the compulsion of many twenty-first-century physicians and scientists acquainted with contagion prevalence and modes of transmission to wear latex gloves at all times, even socially. In fact I assumed that Peter went to bed with a pair on. He was conscientious to the point of compulsion regardless of his incredible natural gifts and had never before been one to take any unnecessary health risks. Direct transmission from an unknown virus like this one, such as infective matter gaining entrance into his body through membranes, or a direct blood exposure, such as from a needle stick, still posed a threat. I kept an eye on him throughout that long, hot night, and at one point noticed him working in a vaguely rhythmic fashion, moving in time to the patient drumbeat of the distant Pygmies.

I was being followed. Whenever I started out to the vehicles for supplies, or went to a quarantine hut to isolate an advanced case from their family, or carried a body to the morgue, the girl with vitiligo shadowed me along the quarantine border. As I worked over patients she sat on the grass across the dividing line, hugging her pink-dappled legs, watching me. There were by then only seventeen people remaining on the healthy side. Her time was running out.

At midday I found that I could no longer ignore her, and left trauma suddenly, crossing to the center of the mall. She stood as I started to move, hesitated when I began in her general direction, then rushed to meet me at the quarantine line. I pulled her groping hands from my suit and examined her eyes with a penlight. I inspected her mottled arms and legs, which she displayed proudly, following my gaze with rapt anticipation. She exhibited no signs of the illness. I called upon a nurse to run PCR tests on the remaining seventeen asymptomatics, then wrested myself away again. The girl struggled against me, lunging at my shoulders as I twisted free, stopping only at the quarantine threshold, calling after me as I walked away, *"Docteur! Docteur!"*

By the middle of the fourth day, I knew that all our efforts were in vain. Working in the stifling heat, my body weeping dollops of sweat— I had already lost more than ten pounds—treating patients who only days before had carried me their brothers, their mothers, their children, I struggled to retain some facade of humanity, to make contact with these masklike faces before passing them down the line to Peter to be taken apart and studied. Preventive therapy had failed and supportive therapy was inadequate, and worse, unable to keep up with demand. We had reached the limits of our medical expertise with the resources available.

We were not the cause of this, I reminded myself. But neither were we the cure. We were merely the facilitators.

PCR tests comparing the virus in Jacqueline Moutouari to samples taken just that day showed dramatic changes in the genetic architecture of the virus. The pathogen was incredibly labile, which we attributed to the virus's aeonian radioactive exposure.

The cries came at midafternoon and lasted for several minutes, a feral bellowing somewhere north of camp that halted relief work and commanded our attention, myself and the two nurses, all looking in the same direction as though expecting something to charge out at us through the trees. The sick listened distractedly to the animal screams as though receiving long-delayed news, and a few, such as the strapped-down, wasting figure of Dr. Kaunda, emulated the wild baying, pearls of foam drying at the corners of his broken lips.

Peter left to investigate and later returned to lead me out across the grass bridge, along a macheted path to a high spot outside the camp. It was a ridge overlooking the jungle terrain rolling out to the west. The largest of a thick grove of ancient black trees there had been ravaged, the bottom meter of trunk bark rent to the bare wood and scored with blood and bits of greenish-gray fur. A green monkey lay dead atop a bed of shavings. Its fur was burst with pustules, and black, blood-sodden eyes stared out of its small, drawn, side-turned face. One long arm lay across its belly, the leathery black fingers of both forepaws broken and bloodied. A few paces away, a baboon lay ripped to shreds. The infected monkey had savaged the larger animal before turning its attack upon the tree trunk, then bled to death from its subsequent injuries.

"My God," I said.

Peter opened up the disinfectant pack he had brought along and uncapped a gallon bottle of industrial bleach. He began sloshing it on the monkey carcass.

"A quarter mile outside camp," he said, dousing the tree wound. "The virus is making its move."

Peter often spoke of viruses as though they had motives, as though they were forward-thinking, free-will life forms with plans and hopes for a deviant future.

"Flies are already visiting the kill," he continued. "Whether arthropods can vector this is anybody's guess, but we have to assume for the purposes of containment that they can. It's starting to break."

I looked out over the ridge into the virgin land below. The camp river continued there, a sparkling blue stripe, eventually pooling into a soft clearing that floated hazily, like a mirage, in the emerald distance. Birds arced in slow, careless circles over pink flamingos high-stepping in the shallows.

"We can't quarantine the entire jungle," I said.

Peter nodded his agreement. "That is exactly what I told Krebs."

I turned back and took a step toward him, then stopped. Dr. Martin Krebs was the director of the CDC. "When did you—"

"Earlier today. Reached him in Washington. I told him what we had. It's over, Stephen. We're out of here in four hours."

The caustic smell of the bleach just then began to drift into my suit hood. "What do you mean?" I said. "These people."

"Are dying." His voice was flat, yet urgent as always. "The relief effort has failed. Fifteen minutes after we're airborne, air force jets will fly in and take out everything within five square kilometers."

"Jets?" I moved closer toward him in my suit, as though running underwater. "The Congo government would never allow—"

"The prime minister and the president have already been briefed on the outbreak. They signed off on anything that would avoid the panic of an Ebola-like winter."

"But that kind of disruption would whack out the cave's ecology. We'd only be escalating it."

Peter calmly shook his head. "A few strategic strikes on the top of the rise to reseal the cave for good. The rest, a surface exfoliation. Plants, bugs, animals: every living thing."

"But the camp people. The asymptomatics. How do you propose evacuating them?"

Peter moved on to the baboon, bleach glugging out of the upturned bottle. In the heat and sweat of my contact suit, I felt a bracing chill.

"This is the hottest thing we've ever seen, Stephen. You know that. It's only a matter of time before someone slips up and draws a contamination. This bug could burn through every living thing on this planet if it gets out. That cave is simply too hot to preserve. It is the tumor of the world, never meant to be found. So we bury it. We seal it back up, and work with the samples we have."

"And the asymptomatics?"

He looked at me over his half mask. "You'd bring them back into the U.S.?"

"Murder," I said. "Don't pretend this is humane. It's preemptive, and misguided, and premature. Murder."

"Our job is to protect humans as a species from an extinction event such as this."

"By slaughtering a few? Offering up the remaining healthy ones as sacrifices to the viral god?" I battled to control my breathing. "Going to

Krebs without me. Without even consulting me." Peter's betrayal shocked me most of all.

"I knew what your position would be."

"And so you ignored it? Went around me? Never even considered that you might be wrong and I right?"

"If you have an alternate plan," he said, shaking out the last drops of bleach over the dead baboon, "now is the time."

"We wait."

"We can't wait."

"Let it run its course. Let it burn out. For God's sake, Peter."

He sounded strangely disappointed. "This is Andromeda, Stephen. The Holocaust paradigm: bombing the rail yards to cut the transport lines, martyring those already in the cattle cars to the millions who would die in the gas chambers. That's what disease control is all about: trading the dead for the living. This is no laboratory, Stephen. Categorical imperatives are fine; it's all right to be contemplative on the front porch some warm summer evenings. We're facing world genocide here. Krebs understands that. I am sorry these people are sick. But I am even sorrier they are contagious. *De mortuis nil nisi bonum*." Of the dead say nothing but good.

I watched him recap his bottle of bleach. "What's happening to you?"

"You can't save everyone, Stephen. Not even you. Mercy was right enough for the girl."

It was all I could do to keep from ripping off my suit, as though only my self-destruction would change his mind. "She was dying."

He was kneeling before me now, repacking his disinfectant kit. "If we don't stop it here, cauterize it, now, it's going to slip out of the jungle and march across this continent and the planet."

I saw it all then, the bulletining of Special Pathogens black-baggers, his reluctance to issue an international alert. "You were going to bury this from the beginning."

"No," he said. "Not from the beginning. But early on."

"I'm calling Krebs."

"I told him to expect you. But the jets won't be called back. The uranium mine is in violation of international treaties and the Department of Defense will strike whether we remain here or not."

"Peter," I said. "Listen to me. Burning these people alive . . ."

He snapped the kit shut and stood. "We don't have the supplies to euthanatize everyone. But if you have a favorite or two, be my guest."

He started away with his plastic kit like a salesman moving on to his next call, leaving me standing with the two animal carcasses. Vapor waves of bleach, formerly the essence of cleanliness, of household chores and gym socks in the wash, of pale grout and a gleaming bathroom floor—now and forever the effluvium of disease containment, of ablution.

At once I started after him. The girl with the vitiligo was watching for me at the huts, but I brushed past her grabbing arms to search the camp for Peter. I passed the trauma area and a patient cried out, and I stopped only long enough to treat him. Soon there were others calling for my attention, more than the nurses could handle. After a while I stopped looking over his shoulder. I began treating the doomed as fast as I could.

Steaming rain rang off the shanty roof and pelted into the mud. I had received no satisfaction from my terse conversation with the expedient Krebs, and the rest of the team had been informed of the evacuation and were hurriedly packing up supplies and samples.

Peter reappeared at dusk with jerricans of gasoline from the Pinzgauer and went around burning the huts. With the camp in flames, he joined me in the failed enterprise that was trauma. His head was now completely bare. No mask or shield or goggles, his mouth, nose, ears, and eyes daringly exposed, his white hair glowing under the argent rain-light of the rising moon. Only the latex gloves remained, poreless, wrinkle-free sheaths protecting his vulnerable surgeon's hands.

Fury and despair had synergized into fatalistic resolve, and though my head pounded without mercy, my hands were steady as I worked. I was fighting the clock to treat the untreatable. Death was coming to these people either by nature's hand or by man's, and I was trying to provide some small measure of comfort in place of hope.

Peter was performing agonal biopsies, rapid sampling of the tissues of those closest to death. Heavy rain crashed after nightfall, but no drums, and I understood then where he had disappeared to earlier. He had gone to warn the Pygmies away.

In retrospect, Peter's divestment now seems inevitable. But it was not his claustrophobia—a simple psychological condition, separate from his cascades—that triggered it, as I had then thought. Nor was it Africa itself that drove him to this Kurtz-ian breakdown. I learned its source as Peter worked over the carcass of a middle-aged woman, drawing bloody slush out of her brain where clear cerebrospinal fluid should have been.

"Life, Stephen," he called across trauma, rainfall crashing outside the mosquito net hanging behind him. He set his instruments aside and crossed the corpses toward me. "Eating. Feeding. Consuming, and being consumed. The beauty of decay. All here, Stephen, all the secrets. All the questions and answers, here for the touching but for this thin membrane—" He flexed his fingers inside his gloves. "Warm, stewy. Consumption." He nodded, stopping on the other side of my patient, smiling. "The viscera of our existence. The slime we crawled out of, claiming us back. Creation; destruction. Our endgame peeking out at us from inside a cave—and you and I facing it down. Life, Stephen. In our hands alone. We are the boundary. Death. *Life*."

Blood dripped from his gloves as his hands formed enthusiastic fists. I was terrified.

The girl with vitiligo dogged me through sheets of rain as I rushed along the far shanties to the vehicles. She had been at me all night. "You are leaving," she said, alarmed by all the movement inside the camp. "We will go away now, *Docteur*. You will not leave me here to die."

I stopped finally, the rain smashing at my hood. I turned to her and set my feet in the mud of the narrow walkway, and heard her plead once more. "*La pluie, ça pue la mort*." The rain, it stinks of death. I then grabbed her suddenly with both gloved hands, one on her neck, the other covering her mouth. Her eyes fluttered wide with surprise and I propelled her around to the shaded rear of a shanty, thrusting her up against the metal wall. She was squirming in my grasp, trying to speak. She was trying to breathe. I saw the rain falling in the inches between our faces, smearing my mask and breaking like bits of glass over her nose and lips— and then returned to my senses, and at once let her go.

I stepped back. I looked at my suit gloves and they were clean; I had just come from a formalin soaking. If not for that I would certainly have infected her. "Murder," I mumbled, huffing inside my stale suit, mad with despair and frustration and the unforgiving rain. She regained her breath and came at me undaunted, begging to be saved, her pink-stained hands pulling at my wet rubber chest. "No," I told her, each time with less conviction.

"Stop," I said finally, seizing her thin wrists and holding her arms fast. The downpour rang off the metal roof of the shanty as I scrutinized her clear, desperate eyes. She looked so small and young in the rain. "Wait," I said. "Wait here."

I moved under the branches behind the shanties to the road barrier and quickly disinfected. The seventeen asymptomatics' blood samples had come back dirty—all except hers. Remarkably, for someone living in the tropics of central Africa, she had been demonstrably free of *any* viral infection as of noon that day. I was beginning to think that perhaps I had stumbled upon Peter Maryk's immunological equal.

In my duffel bag in the trunk of the Pinzgauer I dug out my blue thermos and unscrewed the jar top. Dry ice steamed out. I had included with my provisions one 2-cc ampule of PeaMar4, just to have on hand, just in case.

The glass ampule containing the golden sera slid into my hand. The bottle was small and cool and smoking in the heat. I took one of the last remaining clean hypodermics and hurried back.

She met me as I approached. I showed her the hypo and instructed her to make a fist with her left hand and clench her left biceps—"Like this"—with her right. Fumblingly I drew the immunoserum into the barrel.

"The cure," she said brightly.

"No," I said. "But this will help to protect you."

I braced her arm at the shoulder, then paused with the needle just over her skin. I looked again into her eyes. They were clear, and the trust I saw in them was overwhelming.

I jabbed the needle into her biceps. She looked away but did not grimace or call out in pain, and when it was over she released her fist, slowly, and then her hand. She smiled and flexed her arm, gently rubbing the puncture spot. She looked eager and thankful and suddenly quite lovely, and it thrilled me, and I knew then beyond any doubt that I had made the correct decision.

"Now run," I said. "Down along the river, beyond the lake. And never come back here."

She touched the fabric of my chest. "But I am going with you."

I grabbed her other arm beneath the shoulder. "No," I said. Her strewn, dripping hair made her look petulant, and I shook her roughly, once. "If you want to live, go now. If you want to die—stay."

I released her, and after a moment she smiled at me admiringly, and again I hated her. She was like a stray that followed closest when kicked. "If you tell me to do it," she said proudly, "I will." It was as though her blind trust in me were her thanks. I turned and started back toward the mall. "I will go now, *Docteur*," I heard her say behind me, her proud voice drowning in the rain. "I will go."

I went around the corner of the shanty and kept walking.

Their sunken faces stared up at us through the rain, a silent, staring chorus. It was too late for anger and too early yet for regret. I tried to imagine the cymbal crash of immolation and the waves of orange flame, and their drawn faces flaring up, the diseased skin blackening and melting back, and their final revelation: "This is why the doctors abandoned us."

The air force helicopter rose out over the river and the waterfall beyond, pulling away from the hazy clearing and the shrinking pink forms of the flamingos, higher and higher. I looked hard for the girl with vitiligo, as though I might see her there, waving good-bye.

The window was cool against my bared forehead. PCR lymphatic tests had confirmed each of us infection-free, and we seven sat strapped into our seats: malnourished, clinically exhausted, rocking lifelessly with the motion of the military helicopter climbing through the rain. We had shed our contact suits, leaving them collapsed on the mud road with the vehicles and contaminated equipment like so much trash awaiting incineration. We were all finally free of the suits and yet no one could bring him- or herself to celebrate. My own skin felt just as constricting.

Viruses traditionally are named for their place of origin. Ebola River, Democratic Republic of the Congo. Marburg, Germany. Lhasa, Nigeria. Machupo River, Bolivia. Lyme, Connecticut, and Muerto Canyon, Navajo

Nation, USA. I wondered what exception would be made when the place of origin no longer existed.

Peter was strapped in across from me, and I saw that the first stage of his cascade had begun. His sluggish half eyes watched me, his chest emptying and filling deeply. He roused himself awake like a drunk coming to in a strange chair, blinking lazily and licking his thin, red lips.

"Twenty-one days of quarantine on an aircraft carrier," he mumbled. "Doesn't seem so bad right about now."

I saw then something in him that I had never seen before, or perhaps had seen but ignored as I tried to shape his deviance for the benefit of humanity: the monstrous aberrance of Peter's genetic superiority. My eyes opened to his utter inhumanity.

He tipped forward and slurred a few parting words before succumbing to the cascade slumber. "The tumor of the world," he said. "You know I was right."

This was to be his apology. There are chapters to every life, though seldom are we aware at the time of a page being thumbed and turned. This was one of those uncommon occasions.

Zero

I wish my tale of Africa ended there. There is however one more incident I must relate, a brief sequence of events to which, at the time, I was not privy. Even now, with the keenness of hindsight and every fact of consequence available before me, this singular event remains the most strange.

Seven days following the razing of the camp, the rainy season resumed in earnest. Oren Ridgeway, a botanist with Rainforest Ecology Conservation International, was out on the last night of a five-day field expedition into the rain forests of northern Congo, having circled back to within thirty kilometers of the RECI reserve. The night jungle is a haunted place, as I had found, where no man should venture alone. I can picture Ridgeway stretched out on his back, the rain spattering against the roof of his narrow nylon tent, listening to a BBC World Service broadcast on his radio, reporting on the current political climate in the United States, his home.

The pioneering enthusiasm he had arrived with eight months before was by then gone. He had journeyed to the central African rain forest in order to archive and preserve specimens of the tens of millions of uncharacterized species of tropical flora, before population demands and the big boot of human development stamped them out forever. But that night he was facing the futility of his efforts; millions of rare life forms were being willfully exterminated around him, and he was reexamining the merits of his crusade. What was the use, after all, of trying to salvage a representative sample of a species not strong enough to survive on its own? How much should be left to nature? And what of the senselessness of naming something just as it ceased to exist?

The fact that he was even deigning to entertain these questions must have depressed young Ridgeway all the more. The earth was suffocating worldwide under the weight of advancing *Homo sapiens,* and that night, as he lay alone in the pounding rain of the jungle, he must have felt himself its only witness.

Case in point: the jets he had heard streaking across the jungle sky seven nights before; he had reported them. And the black rain, which he at first thought was volcanic ash cycling back through the biosphere; he had reported that too. His reports went out over the airwaves among a million bursts of static, answered by no one, slipping the earth's orbit and pulsing into the galaxies, a lone human voice of protest.

The system had since purged itself, and the rain that night fell again sweet and clear. I see him reaching up and unzipping the tent fold, letting in some of the perfumed forest air, the scent of his smothered cooking fire, its lingering smoke. There would have been faint light from above, threads of silver angling off the waxing moon through the jeweled rain. Perhaps by the light of one of those lunar strands did he notice the branches bobbing in the trees across from his tent. There was nothing unusual about a creature moving through the night jungle—until the creature emerged from the trees on two legs, walking erect. Ridgeway then sat up, repositioning himself to peer through the zipper folds and through the rain.

It was a human figure, too large to be a Pygmy, slipping from the cover of the trees and moving across a muddy path to a tree of surfboard-sized leaves.

Maybe Ridgeway thought it was someone trying to steal something from his camp. Did he turn up the volume on his radio, in hopes of scaring off the intruder? Or did he simply struggle into a plastic poncho and step out into the rain?

"Yes?" he called out. "Hello?"

Not until the silhouette emerged from the cover of the leaves would he have known that it was a female. Ridgeway knew little of the local dialects, and no French, but he was a trusting soul, with plenty of food to share, and would have welcomed friendly company of any sort.

She started across the camp toward him, striding through the strands of silver light, and Ridgeway saw then that she was nude. Her body was young and firm, with branch scratches and other irregular marks covering much of her dark flesh. She walked right up to him, breaching even that radius of personal space generally respected by strangers, breathing deeply, as though after a long run. Her dark nipples brushed against the chest of his poncho with each gust. He opened his mouth to speak then, to ask her what she wanted, and her lips closed on his in a firm kiss. She kissed him full-mouthed and sensually, without otherwise touching his body, and after the initial shock, Ridgeway's neck and back relaxed and he accommodated her passion without resistance. Perhaps he opened his eyes just once, buoyed by his raging pulse, and found her eyes were open too, but dark, her pupils flat and staring. Her tongue then swished the enamel of his front teeth—strangely cold, in his limited experience, colder than any other tongue he had ever tasted—and their lips parted and she stood facing him as before.

He saw more clearly then the dull glow behind her eyes, the thick drops of rain breaking upon her nose and cheeks, and the vague discoloration of her flesh. It was vitiligo, though this meant nothing to Ridgeway. And then at once she turned and started away. She walked not quickly, not even purposefully, the bright glints of moonlight illuminating her buttocks, the sheen of her shoulder blades, and the dimpled small of her curved back, crossing through the rain back into the trees.

She would wander the jungle in this same stupor for some ten more hours before sitting down to rest against a dead tree in the middle of a wide clearing and succumbing to a series of swift, violent, massive strokes. Creatures of the jungle came forward to nibble on her corpse, but did not like what they tasted, and none of them made it back out of the clearing before falling dead. The insects that fed upon the dead creatures also died, so many carcasses cooking under the bright, virus-killing sun. The animals deemed it a sacred place, and all stayed away. The girl's skeleton still sits there, partially intact, slumped next to the rotted tree, its skull fixed in an empty, meaningless grin.

As for Ridgeway, he ran after her that night, but no deeper than the first few forbidding trees. He returned and found her footprints in the soft mud of his camp, small and faint and disappearing in the hard rain—

then gasped out a nervous laugh. She had been real enough, though there was precious little consolation in that. A beautiful woman of the jungle, exotic and nude, had walked out of the trees and kissed him once, as though delivering a passionate message dispatched from the heart of the rain forest, then disappeared again without a word. He shook his head underneath his poncho hood, and smiled.

He looked up and found the swelling moon above the thinning canopy. The warm rain washed his face, smelling of the sky and of the fleeting bare feet of summer, and he stood there, the blood rush still tingling in his veins, perhaps dreaming of home.

This was Patient Zero.

My Own Story, Half-Told

Another page turned.

Stockholm, six years later. December tenth, the anniversary of Alfred Nobel's death, and traditionally the inauguration of Nobel Week, the end of a day that should have been the brightest yet of my thirty-seven years. The diploma and solid gold medal presented me by His Majesty the king of Sweden at the award ceremony at the Stockholms Konserthus lay securely in the safe behind the reception desk in the hotel lobby, while I lay seven floors above, deep in a strange bed like a heavy stone set upon a soft pillow. And for the first time in a long time, I was not alone.

Following clinical trials of varying degrees of success, and in light of Peter Maryk's increasing disdain for the project, I eventually directed our PeaMar research exclusively toward manufacturing a pure, whole blood alternative. The result, PeaMar23, was a certified disease-free, hemoglobin-based, synthetic blood substitute with a storage shelf life of nearly three times the forty-two-day limit of organic human blood.

Coming at a time when worldwide inventories of clean blood were reaching a critical level, news of the discovery was hailed internationally as a triumph on the level of Salk's polio vaccine and, unexpectedly, made me something of a celebrity. PeaMar23 was currently in use in every health clinic in every province of every country in the world, all mass-produced in a plant in Chamblee, north of Atlanta, known as BDC Building Twenty, the Blood Services Section.

For this Peter Maryk and I shared the 2016 Nobel Prize for Physiology or Medicine. My acceptance speech at that day's ceremony had been well received *(The governing principle of my professional life has been that we at the BDC must never let technology overshadow basic human care . . . that we continue to reach out to the afflicted, if only with a gloved hand . . . that we be scientists second, doctors first . . .)*, though as I returned to my seat, flushed with relief amid the applause filling the concert hall, I felt that something was missing.

It was not the ignominy of Peter Maryk's vacant seat next to me. That I could have expected. The breach that first formed between us in Africa had widened during the development of the PeaMar sera, and culminated in the dissolution of our partnership following the unveiling of PeaMar23 four years before. Since our abrupt falling out, Peter had become something of an outlaw among the medical science community, while my professional career had moved in a diametrically opposite direction. For the past thirty months, I had held the dual federal posts of U.S. Surgeon General and Director of the Bureau for Disease Control. Though we both still worked for the BDC, Peter Maryk and I had not spoken to each other for almost four years.

So it was not Peter I was missing as I glanced around at my fellow laureates on the concert hall stage, in chemistry, literature, and economics, all joined on that milestone day by their families. I was unmarried and unattached. Both my parents had passed away that same year, and I found myself alone. When the ceremony ended and I stepped down off the concert stage with one hand in the pocket of my tuxedo pants, making polite conversation with His Majesty who, in an imperial gesture of pity, had seen fit to escort the lone bachelor to the floor, the only familiar face waiting there was Peri Fields's, head of the BDC's Public Affairs Section and my public relations liaison. Her congratulatory kiss as she pressed it into my cheek felt genuine rather than perfunctory, and raised my spirits a bit. Even this spin-weary sorceress of worldwide media was swayed by the authenticity of the Nobel.

Following the royal banquet, Peri and I repaired to the hotel bar for a champagne nightcap, the electricity of the day still coursing through us. My excitement I understood, but hers surprised me, and interested me. For two years in Atlanta, we had shared nothing more than a working relationship. I heard her shoes fall to the floor beneath the table, and watched her mouth as she laughed. I had not been drunk in years. The steady, interested blue of her eyes, moistened by the champagne, caught some of the magic of the chandelier. The clumsy embrace that began in the mirrored elevator on the ride up to the top floor continued more gracefully behind the door to my top-floor suite. There was at first the revelatory exhilaration of intimacy with a close associate, like a hunger choking us both, followed by the fumbling of zippers and buttons and the culminate unveiling of each to the other as we stood beside the high bed. My hands found her warm hair, her neck, her crotch. The preliminary sacredness of touch accelerated to bold groping and grasping, and the sheets tangled around us, twisted and grew warm.

Afterward, I had found the release of orgasm to be rousing rather than narcotizing and lay staring at the thickly papered walls by the light of the city, diffuse through the lace-veiled window, as synapses fired within the charged nebula of my brain. The events of the day came flooding back, but the accolades felt empty again, the honor a cheat. It was Africa, still haunting me. Within every doctor's psyche resides that patient from early in his career, the one who touched him and whom ultimately he failed, and who becomes the secret source of all his healing efforts. I lay there on that strange Nobel night not with Peri Fields, not in a hotel suite, and not even in Stockholm, but a world away, in a camp shanty in deepest Africa, next to the writhing form of a nine-year-old girl corrupted by a pitiless disease.

After a time I did sleep, and awoke to the sound of the door closing. Peri's clothes were gone from the floor, and I sank back against the pillow as remorse seized me all at once. That night seemed a terrible mistake suddenly, a selfish stab at my own loneliness that had perhaps sabotaged a perfect working relationship.

I arose and showered automatically, due that morning at a Nobel symposium arranged early to accommodate my schedule. I dressed alone in the solitude of the hotel suite, the tableau of bedsheets creased and tugged out from beneath the mattress resembling the scene of some passionate crime, to be repaired by the proper authorities in the form of a humming chambermaid.

The symposium concerned the alarming spread of infectious disease around the globe. Before the question-and-answer period, a video program was played on the large screen behind me, entitled *The Disease Dilemma,* a one-hour documentary concerning recent health scares around the world and the Bureau for Disease Control's vanguard role in managing and preventing them. The program had been Peri's brainchild, having debuted on one of the global satellite networks that previous Monday and been available on-demand for downloading since. It was the highest-rated worldwide prime-time broadcast of that week, with tens of millions of viewer hits since, and I was the host.

It had been Peri's strategy, which I had agreed to and signed off on, that as director of the world's preeminent health organization, I was to be promoted to the public as a spokesman for good health and clean living. This was done most expressly in the bureau's numerous Health Promotion campaigns for children, but *The Disease Dilemma* represented a quantum leap forward in terms of popular exposure, and at the time had struck me as a unique opportunity to educate the world about disease prevention. But now, as my voice carried over the heads of the luminaries assembled in the Royal Caroline Medico-Chirurgical Institute auditorium, the program felt dishonest. The role of health messiah seemed to me now a cheap part we could have hired an actor for, or even commissioned a cartoon mascot. I looked down at the day-old Nobel weighing heavily in my lap—it had been suggested that I wear it around my neck, in the manner of an Olympic athlete, which I had respectfully declined—and felt suddenly nothing, which was wrong. It was a significant award, conferred for advancements made in the interests of humanity; for me, there could be no higher praise. Yet the ghost of Africa, like a creeping stain, corrupted all. I was a fraud who had violated my oath by having been complicit in the expedient murders of dozens of camp workers, and though no one ever learned of the firebombing—Peter had seen to that— I felt somehow certain that the more accolades I received, the worse my ultimate retribution would be.

Part of the reason for this was the dark shadow that had followed us back from Africa. The lethal camp virus had inexplicably emerged in the United States fifteen months after our return, achieving worldwide infamy with a massive outbreak in the small town of Plainville, Massachusetts. The Plainville plague was a catastrophe unrivaled in the modern era of disease control, such that the term itself, "Plainville," not only came to denote the name of the virus, but entered the popular lexicon as a site of mass disaster, such as Chernobyl, or Bhopal. Plainville claimed more than twenty thousand human casualties, including entire neighborhoods of nearby towns—though, as far as the public knew, that had been the end of it. In fact there had been four subsequent isolated outbreaks. None was as devastating nor nearly as widespread as Plainville, thanks to the efforts of the BDC in containing the spread of the raging virus, and therefore, with no immediate threat to the public at large, the outbreaks were covered up in order to avoid hysteria and undue media scrutiny. The secret was closely held; even Peri Fields was not aware of the post-Plainville reemergences. Six times since Africa, the Plainville virus had materialized, poisoning every living thing it touched before vanishing without a trace, only to rise up again some months later in another state, with no discernible link between events. Enigmatically, there had been no connecting outbreaks—no other victims of the disease—between the uranium camp in the Congo and Plainville, USA. Its incursion into North America remained a mystery.

Now the program was ending. I listened to myself embellishing the extent of my actual field participation, furthering the superhero image—and cringed, ashamed to know that my hubris had crossed the line into a lie. The truth was, I had not attended the site of any outbreak in the thirty months since I had become director. I had never even gone to Plainville.

The lights came back on and hands went up among the international press assembled in the hall. A British accent: "Dr. Pearse, simply put: Why are so many becoming so sick?"

I nodded, though the question itself was unanswerable. "One of the lessons of what we now call the 'antibiotic era' of the previous century was that as weaker microbes fall away, more resilient ones survive and emerge, and sometimes with a vengeance. We will never eradicate viruses or bacteria from the earth, nor should we. What we as a people must do is to seek to control viruses, as man has learned to control fire, as we control and continue to legislate against crime."

Another question. "Do you agree with your president's statement that 'America is no longer the world's policeman, it is its doctor'?"

"I do, but not as a slight to the other world international-disease-fighting organizations. Our world is shrinking, and the bureau has, for better or for worse—I think for the better—stepped to the forefront of global disease control."

"What do you think it means that your co-recipient, Dr. Peter Maryk, did not attend the award ceremony? Do you consider it a snub to the Nobel Foundation?"

"I can't speak for Dr. Maryk," I said, trying to move along. "You'll have to ask him that yourself."

I recalled *The Disease Dilemma* and its retelling of the Syn-Bank dedication at the White House four years before. Peter and I had both decided that we could not in good conscience profiteer from PeaMar23 and jointly signed over all patents and monetary claims to the BDC. It was perhaps the last thing we ever agreed upon. The revenue filled the bureau's coffers, and in what was known as the "blood dividend" the Bureau for Disease Control became, while still functioning as an arm of the government, a self-supporting philanthropy not funded by tax dollars. The reason I had accepted the more decorative position of surgeon general was to ensure the integrity of the cash-rich BDC, and to preserve its political autonomy.

The news footage of the White House ceremony had shown me at the podium in the Rose Garden, holding forth on my vision of the future of medicine and disease control. Peter, seated in a chair behind me, folding and refolding the event's program repeatedly in his gloved hands, his white hair glowing in the morning sun, declined to speak that day, and each day that followed. After Krebs was forced out, and I was appointed BDC director almost by acclamation, Peter, who could have had anything he wanted, asked only to head the small Special Pathogens Section, with the proviso that he be well left alone.

Another question. "What can you tell us about Dr. Maryk? What is the 'Special Pathogens Section' and why is its work so secretive?"

"Special Path is a separate unit of the BDC," I said, "dealing primarily in disease detective work involving unknown or emerging viruses. There is nothing secretive about that."

"What would you say to those who claim you are putting your own personal agenda ahead of that of the BDC?"

"I would say, 'What personal agenda?' I want to see the world healthy. That's all."

"Where do you go from here, Dr. Pearse?" This particular accent was American. "What's next?"

"Next?" A smile passed over my face. For some reason, the question tickled me, perhaps because of the bad taste left in my mouth from my performance on *The Disease Dilemma*. "Perhaps my resignation as surgeon general," I said, as much for the charm of hearing myself say it aloud as anything else. I hadn't given this any serious thought.

There was a stirring within the press corps. A buzz started throughout the room, and a camera light or two came on, and questions began overlapping—all of which only further provoked me.

"The directorship also," I said. "It may be time for me to get back to research. The Nobel has reminded me of why I got into medical science in the first place, before I got caught up in the parenting of PeaMar23. But only if I can first set up a smooth transition of power at the BDC."

More commotion. I was entertained anyway, and oddly relieved; the announcement seemed to ease some of the pressure that had been building up inside of me that strange night and morning. It was as though my career fever had suddenly broken, and I was waking up, looking around the room with new eyes.

A signal tone sounded above the fray, and I looked off to the side of the dais. There was Peri, looking back at me, troubled by my candor. After some confusion as to whose tablet was going off, she opened her own and then held it for me to see. It could have been an inelegant ploy to get me off the stage, but something in her manner compelled me to stand. She met me at the step, her quick blue eyes anticipating my suspicion.

"It's real," she said. "Dr. Chiles."

Reporters were surging toward us now, and to get away we withdrew through a pair of rear doors into the auditorium control room. Two women looked up disinterestedly from a computer station, then resumed their work. Peri turned her tablet around for me and held it, patiently, as I scanned the header.

It was indeed from Bobby Chiles, my deputy director at the bureau, forwarding an EPI-AID alert originating in a federal hospital in Orangeburg, South Carolina. The disease class caught my attention, listed as UNK, or Unknown.

I pulled the headset out of the tablet and dialed Bobby's office in Atlanta. A window opened in the lower left corner of the screen and Bobby's face, jowly and brown-skinned with a bush of rusty hair on top, appeared.

"Stephen," he said. I saw the familiar black vinyl headrest of his chair behind him. His Georgia accent was strong in my ear, concerned. "No confirmation yet, but it looks like Plainville."

I stared at the screen. The letters "UNK" stood out to me in bold blue pica. "South Carolina?"

Bobby read from a piece of paper. "A tuberculosis ward inside a hospital, burning fast. Eleven down already and we're just now pulling up curbside."

My pulse quickened. "No link to the last outbreak?"

"Nothing so far. Looks like the same deal as the others. Maryk's out in Nevada, chasing down a low-grade hemorrhagic dengue. Protocol's the only reason I'm bothering you. You are both still down as case agents on this thing. Just need your say-so before I call him in."

I was nervous but, moreover, excited. "No," I told him. "I'm taking this one, Bobby. I'm leaving here right now."

Peri said over the top of the tablet, "You are?"

Bobby looked at me across thousands of miles, through the screen. "Come again?"

Peter and his Special Pathogens group had managed the original Plainville outbreak and each subsequent recurrence, shielding the operation from the public eye and, more important, containing the spread. But I remembered my claim on *The Disease Dilemma* broadcast, and thought that now would be a good time to begin living up to it.

"I can be there in a few hours," I said. "They should have the pathogen properly typed by the time I arrive."

I pulled down the headset and signed off, and Peri took back her tablet. "South Carolina?" she said.

"We're heading back. You'll need to clear my calendar for the next few days."

"But the London speech . . ." She broke off, and did not persist. She must have sensed my determination. "I'll extend all apologies," she said.

Her smile brought back some of the night, and in her face I saw again that thing I had glimpsed under the chandelier, that had endeared her to me: Behind the learned cynicism of her profession lingered, like a smattering of character freckles just visible beneath camouflaging cream, the bright liveliness of a small-town girl.

Our shared silence was, rather than uncomfortable, thoughtful. Even encouraging.

"I panicked this morning," she said. "It was stupid. I'm sorry I ran out."

I smiled and shook my head. "Good morning," I said.

I blushed. She didn't.

"Good morning."

Later we returned to the States together, conversing over meals in first class like any other couple, and the time passed pleasantly, but too quickly. After a small kiss inside the main terminal at Dulles International Airport, we departed for separate airplanes, hers back to Atlanta and mine on to South Carolina, that dread feeling in the pit of my stomach returning.

But for now she reached up to swipe a wayward lock of hair off my forehead, then nodded back at the door. "By the way," she said. "Did you actually mean any of that in there?"

The medal weighed heavily in my hand like a gilded ashtray. "All of it, I think."

The chief resident of the Orangeburg Federal Hospital waited anxiously to be introduced. "An honor, Dr. Pearse," he said, and we shook gloved hands, under the ambulance entrance overhang. I was being sealed into a biohazard contact suit, its design much improved in the years since Africa, a lighter, saffron-colored, tear-resistant polymer jumper that was cooler inside and allowed greater mobility of the head and shoulders.

"We've isolated the green zone," he said, "and evacuated all non-exposed patients, support staff, personnel."

"Leaving how many infected?"

The chief resident took a dramatically deep breath. "Sixty-four. Eleven dead already and as many as twenty in the late stages. We would have picked it up sooner, but with the TB patients, it was difficult to tell."

The hood came down over my head. There were many people moving around me.

"The catatonics, Dr. Pearse."

They were pulling tape around my ankles, knees, and elbows, sashing the slack suit material. I nodded my hood at the doctor, prompting him to continue.

"Clinical catatonia, nonresponsive to medication. None of them has spoken or moved in at least the past ten years. They were in the room next to the TB ward, undergoing neurological tests. Dr. Pearse—they're speaking. The infected catatonics. They're waking up, asking questions."

The suit hood smelled of plastic inside, with a lingering coolness like that of a Halloween mask. A Velcro tag labeled S. PEARSE was affixed to my breast, beneath the black BDC logo. I thumbs-upped the Biohazard Containment Unit without enthusiasm and looked again to the doctor.

"The virus we suspect here has been known to have a pronounced effect on the brain," I said. "Now, if you'll excuse me."

I walked alone to the nylon-tunneled entranceway, known as "the umbilical," its pale blue walls rippling in the Carolina breeze. The advance BioCon team had removed the automatic doors to the hospital and installed air locks and negative pressure doorways. I stopped at a steel door papered with safety stickers, checklists, and red warnings, placing my triple-sealed hand upon it. It had been a long time since I'd been inside a suit. I took three deep, filtered breaths, loud inside the hood, then entered.

The second door opened on a hospital corridor and whooshing gusts of air accompanied me inside. The building was sealed under negative pressure so that no microbes could escape to the outside environment; whenever the control doors were opened, air was made to rush inward. The gloomy admitting room and hospital lobby were empty, the talking head on a high monitor still automatically welcoming visitors and issuing paperwork instructions. Hospitals were no longer places where the sick went to be cured. All surgeries, diagnostic tests, and physical examinations were performed at neighborhood-based "parish" clinics under the auspices of the national health care system, at a flat rate surcharge. Federal hospitals had become "managed care facilities," or sanitariums for long-term care of the chronically and terminally ill.

The walls and ceilings were all coated with a white, meringuelike viricidal foam. Eight colored bands ran along the center of the clean corridor floor. I followed apple green where it veered off from the rest.

Around the first corner, other BDC personnel moved about in yellow suits like astronauts burdened by gravity, backs emblazoned with the cardinal red, three-petaled biohazard symbol. One stepped out and approached me, calling to the others in a muffled voice, "Dr. Pearse is on-site." A second suit holding a glassine-shielded tablet, the administrator of the situation log, called out the time in response: "Mr. Director on-site, thirteen-oh-two."

The approaching scientist strode out to meet me, her arms and legs moving naturally inside the baglike suit, the cap lining her forehead and the frame of the Plexiglas shield giving her face a pronounced V shape of dark eyes and slanting cheeks, a sharply tapered chin. The woman's face was striking, but like a sculpture made of glass, her beauty was cold and fixed. Two thin auburn eyebrows arched smartly into an uncreased forehead. Her name tag read U. FREELEY.

Freeley was Peter Maryk's number two in Special Pathogens. She joined me and strode confidently at my side, following the green stripe ninety degrees around another corner. "PCR typing confirms the pathogen," she said. Her voice lowered commensurate with the privileged nature of the information. "It's a confirmed Plainville drift."

"We're absolutely certain?"

"Oligonucleotide mapping will take a day or two, but it's here, and it's hot."

An antigenic "drift" described a slight change in the makeup of a virus. A virus that has "drifted" has undergone a subtle genetic mutation, and can elude previously produced antibodies to successfully reinfect an immunized host. An antigenic "shift" is a wholesale recasting of the virus. Plainville's frequent shifts were as alarming as they were unexplained.

She said, "It originated with the catatonics."

That was meant to surprise me, which it did. "Not the TB ward?"

"Catatonics first. Then immediately jumped to the lungers down the hall."

"No amplification outside the hospital?"

"None yet. Again, a nice, tight environment for containment. We have the hospital logs for all visitors and contact tracing is under way. Quarantine Services should have everyone rounded up within the hour."

"Good. The hospital is locked down?"

"FEMA Biohazard is settled in. Epidemiology is represented by General Investigation, Identification, Host Factors, Pathogenesis—"

"Fine." I cut short the roll call. We had arrived at another air lock bolted to the wall and sealed with drying epoxy, the removed door leaning next to it. The tiles beneath our feet were entirely green.

"Trauma," Freeley said. "We grouped the catatonics here to facilitate treatment."

I nodded and reached for the door handle. I wanted to pick up the old feeling before proceeding with the investigation.

"Just patients inside," she said. "Serology can handle the blood sampling."

"I want to take a look around for myself."

Freeley stepped back, her eyes narrow and steely, like Peter's, and humorless. Her deference to me was forced; she either disliked or distrusted me, or both. I attributed it to Maryk's influence and left her there in the hallway, moving through the portal alone.

The forced air washed me inside the trauma unit. Curtains printed with pharmaceutical advertisements segregated the patient bays, numbered two to twenty-nine around the room. Yellow suits conferred in the central nurses' station, stocking trays and updating computer charts. One nodded to me as he passed, the laminated pages of a small book held in his rubber-gloved hands; the Velcro tag upon his chest read CHAPLAIN.

The fact that the outbreak had not originated with the hospital staff was in itself remarkable. In epidemiological terms, it was the hound that did not bark. The catatonics' incapacitated state seemed to be, at that point, our first solid lead in establishing the epidemiology of the Plainville strain: The disease could have been communicated to them only by a visitor. Thus the vital importance of contact tracing.

An attending serologist passed me wheeling an instrument cart. "Director Pearse," he said, recognizing me, slowing, straightening.

His awed greeting reminded me just how remarkable my presence there was. "I'm here to help," I said.

He gestured to his cart. He was young and thin inside the tightly sashed suit, wearing black-rimmed glasses. "We're just pulling blood," he said.

"Dangerous work," I reminded him, reading his name tag, "Dr. Tenney."

"Yessir. Of course."

"Okay if I accompany you on your rounds?"

"Yessir," he said brightly, and we started across the room.

I discerned the hazy forms of patients through the plastic tent walls, lying supine or sitting up against pillows, doctors and scientists and nurses in yellow suits at their sides. The bays themselves were each roughly the size of an average parking space, and each contained one bed sealed inside an opaque plastic oxygen tent hanging from the ceiling to the green floor. Tenney led the way to a bed near the door, number twenty-five.

He peeled open the tent fold on his side and entered, and I did the same opposite him. Resealed, it was quiet inside but for the hiss of oxygen.

The patient was a woman in her late thirties. The wrinkled sag of her biceps over the bedsheet indicated years of atrophy, though overall the condition of her face and hands evinced care. Her head rolled slightly on her withered neck, illustrating the benefits of dedicated physical therapy.

Her eyes were open and blinking and blushed faintly with hemorrhaged blood. She was early stage, the skin on her face dark and blotchy, her tongue—she was attempting to speak—scarlet and swollen. She looked up at the roof of the opaque plastic tent as though she were falling through the room rather than lying in it.

When she spoke, her unused jaw moved side to side rather than up and down, and her throat rasped hoarsely. "What is happening?" she said.

Tenney was punching up her chart on the bed rail console. "Negative for motor activity and speech functions for eighteen years," he told me. A moment to do the math, then excitement in his eyes. "Since 1998."

"What are you?" she said.

I released and collapsed the railing and sat on the mattress next to her. My suit bunched beneath me, but she was small on the bed and there was plenty of room. Tenney said revelatorily, "She's never seen a contact suit."

I nodded to quiet him. "My name is Dr. Stephen Pearse," I told her. "You are in a federal hospital in South Carolina."

I had to strain to hear her. "Why?"

"Well, you've been asleep for a while."

She swallowed clumsily and raised her quivering right forearm off the bed, high enough that the orange hospital bracelet slid down to her elbow. "See?"

Soft, russet-colored lesions blemished her neck and face, but a bed-sheet covered her body from the chest down, and her hands and arms were as yet free of any Plainville sores. I realized she was in fact directing my attention to her wrinkles.

She said, "Old."

I watched her face as its features, fixed for two decades, shifted slightly with the effect of breaking apart, like ice cracking in warm liquid. They re-formed again in an awkward, lopsided, plaintive expression, and I recognized a teenager's fear in an adult woman's face.

I took her shaking hand and eased it back down onto the bed, and she gazed up at me, patient to doctor. "Parents," she rasped.

"We'll check," I said, and the veneer of her face broke again into another long-unused expression. She wept tearlessly with the fragile eyes of a young girl. I squeezed her hand again. "We're going to need to draw some blood. Then we'll see about getting in touch with your folks."

I motioned for the apparatus and Tenney handed it to me across the bed. It had been a while. I swabbed her elbow and tied and released the rubber tourniquet, drawing out 4 cc as she moaned in pain. Her blood was dark and sludgy. I withdrew and broke off the needle and disposed of it in a biohazard box behind the bed, capping and sealing the syringe barrel. The motions were familiar to me, comfortable. Tenney printed a label from the bedside chart, and we met outside.

"Take care of the blood," I told him, "then see what you can do about her parents."

He appeared confused. "I've got rounds to do, sir."

"Find them," I said. "The hospital will have records. Leave your cart for me."

He went away and I proceeded to a standing pan of Pheno disinfectant—green-hued, like a bowl of antifreeze—to immerse my gloved hands in the sterilizing solution between patients.

Plainville held tightly to its secrets. We could study it in only the most secure laboratory setting, and we could not work with it at all. The virus ate through laboratory animals, fetal tissue, Vero cells, and blood products—any living matter placed in front of it. Only through due diligence on the part of the bureau, as well as some extraordinary good fortune, had the bug failed to achieve amplification beyond the isolated microbreaks since Plainville.

As I was shaking out my gloves over the pan, I heard a muffled voice call my name. I was startled, but not unnerved, and looked around expecting to see another hopeful face inside a suit hood. There were no suits near me. I saw then a small, thin arm moving within a plastic tent, in bay number twenty-six. I went there, unzipping the tent and drawing Tenney's instrument cart in behind me.

Patient Twenty-six was a younger man with a gaunt, collapsing face. I guessed he was in his late twenties, although the disease had aged him significantly. He was mostly bald, with a few patches of wispy silver hair streaming off his pate, as light and thin as spider's thread. Overall, even as compared to the woman in twenty-five, Twenty-six's convalescent care had been superlative. Only his sclera, the whites of his eyes, which were a bright firehouse red, indicated any significant illness. He bore no observable sores, save his badly scabbed lips, which were nearly chewed away, as though he had been gnawing at them throughout his prolonged slumber.

But this man had been in a catatonic state for at least ten years. It was inconceivable that he should know my name.

"Do you know me?" I said to no response or change of expression. Just a hollow stare. The wasting man looked at me across a great distance, as though the center of the hospital bed were quite removed from the sides. I felt no recognition myself. I broke from the man's stare and turned to the chart on his bed rail.

The screen read "Unoccupied." I checked his thin wrists for an admittance bracelet, nor finding one. His left arm was as light as a cardboard tube and I rotated it in search of a needle stick from a previous blood draw. The man did not otherwise move.

"What is your name?" I asked.

"Pearse," he whispered again, in a garbled voice. He was staring at my chest, and I realized that my name tag was there. I turned and surveyed the outer room through the thick plastic tent, where yellow suits moved about hazily. He could not have read my name tag from that distance, and only barely could have made out my face.

"Who are you?" I said again, but his eyes had retreated into a faraway, blood-sodden gaze. I gave up and printed out an Unoccupied label, then proceeded to swab the man's elbow with alcohol. I was still a bit rusty, and it took me three attempts to locate a viable vein for a blood sample. I released the tourniquet and watched the plastic barrel slowly fill with blood.

It happened in an instant. One moment I was finishing off the blood draw; the next, the syringe was falling from my hand, and there was a stinging in the center of my left palm. A shudder or a jerk, that by the laws of atrophy the patient should never have been able to make—and somehow his hand had come up and struck mine just as I was withdrawing the needle from his arm.

Afterward I stood for some time staring at the man beneath me. He had settled back into the mattress, the blood-filled syringe lying alongside his leg. His face was fixed and phlegmatic, his half-open eyes regarding me as though with a blithe red wisdom. All I kept thinking was *He should not have been able to move like that.*

Finally I left the staring patient and broke away from twenty-six. I threw aside the curtain and rounded the crowded nurses' station, entering the air lock leading back out to the corridor. Lamps of deep blue light came on inside the chamber, and doors on either side of me bolted automatically. I had forgotten about the ultraviolet light shower. I tried the second door anyway with my right hand, a wasted effort. It was locked fast. I drew my left hand into a tight fist, and it felt inconceivably warm and heavy; I imagined my glove filling with blood. I closed my eyes and stood for 120 seconds as the blue light cooked the viruses on my suit.

Down the corridor and away from the others I found an examining room with a scrub room inside. I locked the inside door and the light over the sink blinked on, harsh and suddenly blue to my eyes. I turned on the sink faucet. I broke open my warmed suit one-handedly and shrugged off the shoulders and hood, freeing my left arm. There was no blood visible through the gloves. I snapped off the first layer, then the second, and withheld my bare left hand. Still no blood, and no visible breach. I gripped it by the wrist, palm up under the light, and searched for a hole, close enough to see the faint mound of beating pulse in the center of the scoop of my palm. With growing relief, I pressed down on the area with the thumb of my right hand. A single drop of blood squeezed out.

I shoved my hand under the water. It was cold. I needed it hot. Friction was imperative and I rubbed and squeezed at my hand as the water scalded and the sink began to smoke. I forced my hand to bleed. I pulled and prodded at my flesh, trying to open up the meat of the wound in order to irrigate it. I found a bottle of soap and pumped some clear gel into my palm. There was a low-grade antiseptic cleanser on the countertop and I pulled the sink trap and sloshed the green solution into the steel bowl. I thrust my hand into it and expected it to burn, hoped that it would burn. But it did not. I found a scrub brush and scraped at my palm until it was raw.

I pulled out my hand. I slicked away the excess liquid and again held the dripping, reddened palm to the light. In doing so, I caught the reflection of my face in the steamed mirror and was stunned by its look of terror. I moved closer and examined my staring eyes. Wide and un-blinking, a thin orbit of blue circling the dilated black. I knew exactly what was happening. The locus ceruleus, a cluster of nerve cells that is the control center of the brain, responds to stress by releasing hormones that activate the hypothalamus, which in turn triggers the pituitary gland to release adrenocorticotrophic hormones into the bloodstream, which then make their way into the kidneys, which respond by spewing out adrenaline—all of which causes the eyes to dilate, the blood vessels to open wider for increased blood flow, and the heart to pump faster.

It gets into your palm; you could cut off your hand but it's already in your arm; you could cut off your arm but it's already pumping through your shoulder and circulating down into your heart, flooding into the spleen, the liver, the brain. My own body was facilitating the infective process and revolting against me. I felt a gag deep in my throat as though a hand had reached up from my stomach and pulled. I pitched forward with an awful groan and vomited into the sink.

I cleared the trap with my right hand and the sink basin drained. I straightened, choking, one hand gripping the sink edge, the other flat against the wall beside the mirror, holding me up. But then a cooling sensation spread from my spine outward, a sudden, bracing chill of realization, the muscles of my back softening as I faced myself again in the glass of the mirror. I was well acquainted with the horror stories of doctors who imagined themselves into getting sick, and immediately I regained my breath, coughing up a burst of nervous laughter. That passed, and I was sober once again. I washed my face, blotting the sweat from my brow with a paper towel, then wrapped my bleeding hand in a tight gauze cushion. I looked down at the four gloves lying discarded on the floor like pale, strangled birds, and at once disposed of them in biohazard, pulling on two fresh pairs, gathering my suit up around me from the waist and sealing myself back inside. I cleaned the floor and the sink, replaced the soap bottle and the empty jug of antiseptic cleanser, then unlocked the scrub room door and emerged.

I returned to the green zone. The second door opened onto the trauma unit, and my anxiety began again immediately. I needed to see the patient in bay twenty-six. I needed to speak with him, for my own sanity, feeling somehow that he had something to say to me. I found the gaudy curtain pulled aside as I had left it, the tent zipper undone, the Unoccupied sticker peeking out from the bed rail chart.

The bed was empty. The patient was gone. I felt panic welling up, and whirled around to check the adjoining bays.

"Dr. Pearse."

It was Tenney approaching, carrying a printout. "Have they taken any patients out of here?" I asked him.

He was startled. "I wouldn't know, Dr. Pearse—"

"How long was I gone just now?"

"I wouldn't know, sir. You sent me out."

I noticed two patients laid out on gurneys in front of the air lock and hurried over to them. One was an advanced case inside an oxygen tent, a middle-aged woman, her palsied face locked in agony. A black rubber body bag lay on the other gurney. I seized the zipper, pausing a moment for confidence, then quickly drew it down. The seam opened on the wasted, staring corpse of an elderly black man.

I backed away. "How many others have you taken out?" I said to the woman who was attending them.

"None, sir," she said through her hood. "None myself."

"Then there were others?"

"Maybe, Dr. Pearse. A few."

I returned to twenty-six. I drew the hanging curtain around the bay, closing myself off from the prying eyes of Tenney and the rest, and looked at the shrouded bed. I tore aside the plastic tent opening near the cart. The bed linen had been shucked down to the foot of the mattress and I gathered the sheet and blanket in my hands, but my rubber gloves prevented me from feeling any warmth. I shook each out separately, looking for the blood-filled syringe I had dropped there, then pulled up the mattress. I searched beneath the bed and broke apart the plastic biohazard box. I checked the sheet, the blanket, the mattress, the apple green floor for drops of blood. Nothing.

He had disappeared. I backed away to the curtain, stopping there to regroup.

The patient had just awoke from long-term catatonia. He would have had little if any manual coordination, and therefore simply could not have bumped my arm with the intention of infecting me. The entire event was beyond reason. The absence of any admittance records was another mystifying piece of evidence. I had seen people go to pieces inside a contact suit before. Maybe I had imagined the entire thing.

I managed to convince myself of this, even as I knew it was not true. I was trusting that the patient in bay twenty-six was just that, a patient, and not an assassin dispatched in the same way a killer T cell is dispatched to an invading force. Only later would the greater irony be revealed: that this assassin had in fact collected two debts that day, one for Africa, and the other, unwittingly, for himself.

But for now I turned and drew the curtain open again, baring the bay to the rest of the room, telling myself that there was nothing to hide. I crossed the trauma unit back to the air lock with all eyes on me until the bolts clicked again and I was alone, the blue lamps humming brightly and easing the echoes of panic left in my head. Relieved, concerned, mystified: I didn't know what I felt. All I knew was that I was getting away. I stood waiting with my head hung low in the sterile chamber between death and life.

The rest is shameful but I shall tell it anyway.

I returned to Atlanta that evening, traveling home from the airport by taxi. I owned a house in Sandy Springs, just north of the city, a stately five-bedroom brick colonial set upon an incline, overlooking a labyrinthine community of variations upon the same brick colonial. I disarmed the alarm and went upstairs without switching on any of the lights, sitting down at the foot of my bed, relieved and happy to be finally home. Outside the window, trees shifted against the blue-black sky.

I had been among the first to buy into the planned community, named Diver Bridge, a family subdivision of swimming pools and tennis courts, two managed lakes, a shopping center, a Montessori preschool, and twenty-four-hour gated security. The glossy brochure had reminded me of a time and place I was eager to get back to, my parents' seaside retreat in Amagansett and the Long Island summers of my youth, a world away from the fortress of Manhattan. I had bought the house as something to grow into, but three years later remained the only bachelor in a gated neighborhood of families. I had played exactly one set of tennis on the Diver Bridge courts, on a bright Saturday morning two years earlier, and could only recall the *pock pock* of the soft yellow balls being volleyed on the surrounding courts, back and forth. The bureau was my true home.

I stood tiredly and went to the bathroom to change the bandage on my throbbing palm, casually, so as to preclude any examination. Afterward I snapped off the light and stood in the second floor hallway, in the silence and the darkness of the half-empty house.

I forced myself to cook dinner, then sat down to face it. My chagrin and embarrassment at my actions at Orangeburg were peaking. The entire incident now seemed a blur. I knew that the risk of infection from a needle stick exposure was statistically less than two tenths of one percent.

My food was still untouched when I stood again and brought the dishes to the sink. I returned to snuff the candle I had lit, and left my sunken thumbprint in the soft white scoop of wax. That night I slept poorly, thrashing beneath the sheets, dreaming repetitively of soft yellow tennis balls being endlessly volleyed.

Clifton Road began as a leftward fork at Dusty's BBQ restaurant. It was a country road like any other outside the city limits of Atlanta, winding lazily and buffeted with leafy trees and founded upon a clay dirt tinged red as though mixed with rust or Tabasco or old blood. Emory University climbs out of the roadside like a city growing out of sand, a sprawling southern school of old homes and towering white stone buildings. It was the university's donation of fifteen acres in the early 1940s for the establishment of a government agency to battle malaria that planted the seed of what was now the Bureau for Disease Control.

The main BDC campus sloped down from the roadside halfway along Clifton like a fortress founded upon one square block. Old Building One, the brick-and-mortar former entrance, was dwarfed on the right by the bureau's flagship, Building Sixteen, formed of smooth concrete and mirrored glass, its six-story face broadly curved and sky-reflecting. A jumble of smaller, ill-fitting buildings led down to the rear perimeter fence and its posted warnings U.S. GOVERNMENT PROPERTY, NO TRESPASSING abutting the pristine university playing fields and exhausted southern houses of Emory's fraternity row.

Sixteen was the main administrative building of the BDC. Its twenty-first-century face, the horizontal bands of sky-reflecting windows familiar to news viewers, stood out along winding rural Clifton Road like a temple materializing in a field of wheat. Just across the street from Sixteen was the small DeKalb County Firehouse, which was how I always thought of us at the bureau, as firefighters, responding to alarms from around the world and dousing incipient threats.

The BDC had for years been the largest federal agency headquartered outside greater Washington, D.C., and Building Sixteen was its executive seat. Its laboratories were conference rooms, its remedies financial and political. Attachés from other international disease-fighting organizations such as Porton Down, the Pasteur Institute, the Tropeninstitut in

Germany, and the University of Anvers in Belgium, convened there regularly.

The office of the director was the largest in the building, a corner suite, second-floor rear, with a sweeping view across miles of treetops— a lazy current of green leaves in summertime—to the downtown Atlanta skyline. The push of a button activated vertical blinds, and a shadow, like a theater curtain rising, crawled across the room.

It was from there that I oversaw the Orangeburg investigation. Every scrap of information generated on-site was routed through the notebook tablet on my desk, from individual patient case histories and specific treatments prescribed, to hospital ventilation contractor's records and regional disease statistics going back twenty years. All my regular duties were postponed as I consumed each scrap of information, hungrily, drawn in by the devastation of the outbreak as well as its peculiarities. Such as:

An asterisk from a footnoted chart on page seventeen of a poorly written thirty-page report, noting that four of the early-stage afflicted catatonics were on different treatment protocols from the rest. Each had been receiving five hundred milliliters every eight hours of one of three different types of blood sera, code-named, and therefore still in the research stage, MILKMAID, BLOSSOM, and LANCET, with MILKMAID being administered to two patients simultaneously. The names were strange but meant nothing to me, and I posted inquiries on the codes and ran an open search of the BDC net, yielding no answers. None of the sera was registered with the Laboratory Branch, and therefore none had been submitted to or approved by the FDA. This was irregular. I began with Special Pathogens and traced the code names to its Epidemic Intelligence Service under development by a "Dr. Christian," the same pseudonym we had used in the medical journal article detailing the attributes of Peter's immune system nearly a decade ago. Whether he had anticipated my investigation and was flaunting his disregard for procedure, or simply thought I would not bother to pursue the matter, I took his derisive alias for an insult. The case scientist for these irregular blood serum projects was none other than Peter Maryk.

I punched up Bobby Chiles's office down the hall. Bobby was that rare breed of public servant, the brilliant bureaucrat. He had come into the BDC relatively late in his medical career following a brief period of specialization in the family practice of podiatry. He loved medicine and loved science, but was better suited to administration than administering. Bobby was a trusted confidant.

"The Special Pathogens budget," I said. "Did you ever break through those numbers?"

He shrugged a shrug that was a nonanswer. "They balanced."

I did not like what Special Path had become. It was a clandestine service operating within and yet apart from the bureau, accountable to no one except Peter Maryk. Peter did all the hiring and firing and captained every investigation himself, and the loyalty of his people, such as Freeley, was fierce. I had allowed him too much free rein.

Bobby was typing. "I'll punch up the budget numbers and shoot them on over to you."

"Good. Let's meet for lunch, see what we come up with."

Bobby looked out from my screen. "Lunch?" he said. "Stephen, it's after six."

So it was. It had grown dark outside, and my office lights had compensated, coming on dimly without my noticing. The work day had gotten away from me.

I went home and opened the Special Path budget on my tablet, but as intense as my concentration had been at the BDC, I found it nearly impossible to focus at home. I got up and wandered throughout the downstairs area, the dim kitchen, the media room, and then, remembering the exuberance of that night in Stockholm, went to the bar and poured myself a drink. I found my way upstairs and patrolled the empty bedrooms of my unfinished house, pausing before one of the southwest-facing windows overlooking Diver Bridge to Atlanta. Darkness blanketed the glowing halo of the distant city.

Moving lights brightened the tree branches outside the window and directed shadows across the ceiling. Headlights in my driveway, though I expected no one. I left my glass on the sill and walked to my bedroom window for a better view, arriving just in time to see a car back out and pull away.

That second night was longer than the first. Sleep teased but never fully embraced me.

The next day's situation log noted that Peter Maryk had returned from Nevada and assumed on-site command of the Orangeburg investigation. Neither one of us initiated communication with the other. I continued my own multipronged investigation, immersing myself in all aspects of Orangeburg, while simultaneously pursuing the code names and the Special Pathogens budget—which I found to be padded with overruns and blind outlays exceeding $17 million.

I left the office only once that morning, to drop in on Lab Safety in Building Four under some pretense in order to procure a Postprick Kit. In the toilet stall of a nearby washroom, hiding like a junkie in a train station, I administered the preventive HIV and hepatitis series. I was counting on this to relax my mind.

Peri Fields was waiting outside my office door when I returned.

"Hi," she said, and I stopped near. Her light brown hair was done up lightly in a loose bun, run through expertly with a pencil. "You weren't answering my pages, so I thought I'd just drop by."

"Orangeburg," I told her. I was having a difficult time meeting her eyes.

"Were you just out for lunch? We could have—"

"No. Just getting some air."

It was her turn to nod. She crossed one heeled shoe over the other and held her tablet in both hands at her waist. "You know I'm not asking for anything," she said, still smiling. "We can go as fast or as slow as you want."

"I know," I said. "But right now I need to give this investigation everything I . . ."

My words trailed off. She was studying me. She was looking at my hands.

"You're wearing gloves," she said.

I looked at them myself, a worm of guilt starting up my back. "And?"

"Nothing. Except that—you're one of the few here who didn't."

"My image." I nodded.

These words wounded her more deeply than I expected. They warranted an apology which, for some reason, I did not give.

"I'm fine," I said. She reached out to me as I started past her-for my door, her hand brushing my bare forearm, just below my shirt-sleeve. I jerked away.

She turned and stood in the doorway, stunned, as I shut the door.

I did not leave my office the rest of the day. Updates from Orangeburg continued tonguing out of my printer. The White House press secretary had left three messages since my on-camera comments in Stockholm, but I did not respond. Everything else paled next to the outbreak.

My search under the "Dr. Christian" pseudonym led me to case reports corresponding to the mystery code names, buried in an unlabeled Special Pathogens file of year-old interdepartmental performance reviews. The files were encrypted for confidentiality, but all BDC documents were accessible to the director at his discretion.

Downloaded, the case reports contained detailed medical histories of the three apparently healthy subjects, BLOSSOM, LANCET, and MILKMAID, but going back only three years and listing only addresses, no names: Two of the subjects resided in the Atlanta area, the third outside Boston. My thirst for more information, coupled with a reluctance to return to my empty house, compelled me to pursue the matter, without further success, long into the evening.

That night back at Diver Bridge, I paced. My palms and the creases of my knuckles remained cloyingly moist; repetitively, I washed and dried my hands. The bruises on my stuck hand, the ones caused by my first scrubbing out the wound, were not going away. I wandered upstairs, dreading the night that was already upon me.

I discovered an empty bar glass on the windowsill in one of the bedrooms, and for a few frantic minutes believed a stranger was inside the house with me. Headlights appeared in my driveway again, and I rushed down the hallway to my bedroom to look. I watched a car slow nearly to a stop at the bottom of the drive, then strangely pull away.

I remembered my behavior toward Peri, and tried to call her, but had some difficulty using my tablet. A vague sense of uneasiness overcame me like a chill.

I went to bed, and watched the ceiling for headlights. I rolled the Orangeburg investigation over and over in my head, but could not get it straight; fragments from my own life kept intruding, as though like electrical wires the two concerns had somehow become crossed.

I dozed briefly, on and off, each time awakening to the shaded room as though summoned by name. In the dark corners of my bedroom and the furls of the curtains hanging off my windows, faces appeared, watching me, trying to speak. They were the faces of the camp workers. Something terrible was happening to me.

The next day I took care to encounter no one, arriving at work well before seven. Rescheduled appointments were stacking up, jamming my calendar into the weeks and months ahead, but without consequence, as my future now was clear: Once free of Orangeburg, I would tender my resignation to the president. There was relief in this decision—the impending resumption of my life's work, a return to the sterile safety of the BDC labs—which freed me to further indulge the worm of my consuming obsession with Orangeburg, poring over the scores of updates and summaries flowing hourly from South Carolina.

The outbreak once again, by hard work, a miracle, or a combination of both, had been successfully contained. Only two cases had been reported outside the hospital, and both were discovered through contact tracing of recent visitors and duly isolated. Hopes soared, but neither visitor was found to be the source of the outbreak, and rather each had become infected inside the hospital like all the rest. The disease was running its course, and there was still no indication of how Plainville had reemerged among a bedridden group of catatonics.

The virus confounded me. My notes from that morning, scribbled shakingly in black felt pen on the back of a hard copy of an autopsy photograph:

> Latency period between infection and symptom onset 2–4 days; immuno-compromised develop to termination in as few as one day total. Plainville growing more destructive to blood in final stages, breaking down platelets and albumin, flooding organs with mush. *Virus in constant flux*. I.S. excited to overload, profound autoimmune response. Symptomatological spiral w/in 2–4 days, to termination w/in 4–6 days total. Cause of death: grand mal seizure or pulmonary edema, if no opportunistic infection— pneumonia, staph, septicemia, others. Transmission via: blood contact, respiration, urine spatter, w/trace survival in sputum, saliva—even tears.

1. *How,* in limited exposure, do dramatic genetic mutations still occur—all virus-beneficial? (Still no link to previous outbreaks, and no spread outside hospital: Luck?? Missing something??) And 2. How to account for P-ville growing more virulent AND more deadly at same time? Unprecedented.

The only bright points of the outbreak were the prognoses of two of the four patients, the ones receiving the **MILKMAID** sera protocol. Astonishingly, each appeared to be successfully staving off the effects of full-blown Plainville. Equally provocative was the attention paid this development in the reporting materials generated by the Special Pathogens Section: none. I established a new file on my personal tablet, "Investigation.Maryk," and copied into it all information relevant to the mystery sera, including the budget discrepancies and Peter's dummied reports.

At midmorning, a blistering headache overtook me. I medicated myself with caffeine and vitamins and successive half liters of water from my office kitchen suite. It was lack of sleep, certainly; I was exhausted but unable to nap or even sit still. This deficit also seemed to affect my thinking. It was as though time were unraveling. The pain soon faded and I felt much improved; in truth, I felt relieved.

An hour later I experienced a sensation like ice water being poured down the back of my neck. The chills that followed straightened me in my office chair and held me rigid through deepening waves of nausea as papers slipped from my grasp to the floor and my gloved hands began to quiver, the trembling soon spreading to my arms and legs. My neck muscles cramped until I could no longer move my head, and I began to panic. I was tipped back and could only see the ceiling lights, quaking and blurring in my view. I tried to yell for help but the sound was trapped in my throat. Eventually the spasms subsided, releasing me, my tendons aching as though run through with needles. I used my desk to stand. Crushing head pain lingered as I reached for my tablet. At the door I righted myself. I practiced speaking in the event that I encountered anyone, then exited unseen and unmet down a fire stairwell to the parking lot.

I rode out in search of the highway. Steering was difficult but manageable and I sustained a kind of equilibrium by keeping my arms low in my lap and my timorous hands light on the wheel. The joints in my elbows and knees and ankles felt like eggshells slowly breaking open. But overall the driving seemed to help. It was as though I were seated just behind myself, my arms and hands pushed through the empty shirtsleeves of a puppet operating a car. Cruise control was set at sixty miles per hour, and I can remember a red lap-belt light winking at me from the instrument panel. I remained on the highway, not heading home, instead turning north onto Interstate 85 and finding myself soon leaving Georgia, pushing ahead through South Carolina and into North Carolina. I drove on and on, trapped in a dream. I concentrated on the road lines flowing past and found it oddly soothing to be in the middle lane of the great American highway, flowing forth as though on a raft, the cars on either side of me passing and receding, passing and receding.

At one point my tablet chirped on the seat next to me, but rather than answer it, I managed to open the screen and deactivate the Hailing function so that it would not bother me again. I needed only to drive, and not to think.

I slowed only for tolls, which detected the government vehicle and debited the appropriate fee. I feared stopping, certain that it would kill my momentum, but the drive was longer than I could bear. Somewhere in Maryland I pulled off into a service area, parked in the last space, turned off the engine and lay a while sideways across the front seats. I do not believe I slept. After a while I sat up again, feeling watched. I refueled at the service station but did not get out of the car or even roll down my window.

The pain in my head expanded with a force that was nearly crippling, until all at once it was gone, replaced only by a dull ringing tone. The veins in my extremities all throbbed; it had been some time since I had actually felt the wheel beneath my hands. Still, on I drove. I piloted the last leg of the journey slumped against the armrest, too weak to sit up on my own.

Finally I was off the highway and circling Manhattan, its towers looming in my window. I turned off and continued on the road toward Long Island, knowing then that I was heading home.

I reached the familiar town of Amagansett and drifted along the old streets out to the shore. The mailbox and the driveway. Flagstones curling to the brick steps. The door with the golden horse head knocker, and at once I was inside the great house: cavernous, dreamlike, dark. The chandelier was gone from the foyer, a chain and bare copper wire hanging insolently from the high cathedral ceiling. Pale dust outlines of removed frames marked the walls, the remaining furniture draped in thick plastic—all things I should have taken care of after my mother's funeral. I felt my way along the walls to the kitchen, empty and quiet. In the cabinet over the sink, four or five glasses stood mouths-down, orphans of mismatched sets. I reached for a plastic tumbler of swirling colors, which to me signified summertime in the late 1980s, Hawaiian Punch and television laughter from the back porch, sand in my sandwiches and fireflies winking at night. The faucet spat pockets of air, then garbled brown water, then flowed clear. It hurt very much to swallow. There was something wrong with the mechanics of my throat.

I gripped my tablet to my chest and took the tumbler of water and started up the stairs. The task was daunting and I rested frequently, slumping with one knee against the next highest step, the handrail always seeming to twist just out of reach. I gripped the side wall and water shook out of the tumbler and over my gloved hand down to my forearm.

I mounted the top landing and sat there sweating, huffing, leaning on my elbow on the familiar beige carpet. The tumbler was empty now and I let it go. Fatigue overcame me. Something told me that if I did not move now, I might never move again.

I found the railing and hauled myself up, legs bandy and reluctant to respond. I felt sick to my stomach. Bathroom or bedroom: a choice. I lurched toward my old bedroom, striking the doorjamb with my shoulder and knee, and feeling neither. My view of the room faded, a strange pressure behind my eyes sparking silver phosphenes that showered and bloomed. I stumbled inside, fumbling the tablet onto a small writing desk and falling across the twin bed, sizzling against the cold plastic wrap beneath me. I shrugged and pulled and eventually dumped the sheeting out onto the floor, and lay on my back on the bare mattress as the room filled with viscous glitter. The room smelled exactly as I remembered. It smelled of the sea.

Later I awoke to a roaring noise in a room of bare walls, a bureau, an empty bookcase, a child's desk: my old summer room in Amagansett.

Three trophies, small golden boys standing poised to dive, remained atop the low bureau, swimming awards, the smallest for holding my breath underwater the longest.

I looked through the skylight in the ceiling above. This was a wonderfully clear dream with no queer subconscious filters, no anomalous intrusions from other places, or other times. I was a boy again, back in my room at the old summer house, and life was bright and new. Everything lay ahead of me; nothing behind. I closed my eyes and rode out the sensation of somersault after somersault, backward, feet following head, and then changed direction at will, rolling forward and deeper, forward and deeper.

Shooting pain through my thighs, arms, abdomen, neck, thorax, feet, calves, shoulder blades, back. Rockets of pain. I was afire. Thrashing atop the bed, being consumed.

Awake again. Vomit, mainly water coughed from my groaning throat, puddled on the stripped mattress beneath my head. Total apathy at the loss of control over my bodily functions. No embarrassment. No thought to it even. Such extraordinary lethargy, such leadenness, stuporous muscles and sandbag limbs. A wholesale letting-go. Idly I watched as my feet twitched at the end of the bed—watched without the slightest concern. Hours were slipping away, and I knew it, and did not know it.

Night again: or still. My parents huddling outside the door. Mother holding a Dixie cup full of tap water. They were going out. The room and the hallway were dark but my parents were painted with light and faintly glowing. Dressed formally.

"So proud," she said. Over me now, her face before the skylight, smiling down. "Feeling better?"

"A little," I said.

"Just rest. Raisin toast and tea in the morning."

And glasses of flat ginger ale; an uncapped bottle of Canada Dry set out overnight on the kitchen counter. And later, chicken soup.

My father remained on the landing in his tweed overcoat, fixing his collar, waiting to go. Flickering out.

Sunlight struck the trophies on the bureau. I was still in my summer room in Amagansett. Burning up and meaning to do something about it.

Open a window maybe. I was going to get up, soon. It hurt to swallow. It hurt to be lying down.

Peri came to me later. She appeared in the middle of the room with her eyes closed and her arms out at her side, nude. I was terrified she would open her eyes and see me lying there, helpless, but I hadn't the strength to hide. When she did open her eyes, her orbits were hollow and black, and tears of toxic blood poured down her cheeks to her breasts and over her stomach and legs, burning through her spoiling flesh to the meat and bone beneath. She was rotting with her own blood and howling at me as, standing there, she decomposed.

Then she was gone. The bed was trembling.

Vaccine? This way.

She cannot bear to be touched.

Burning

She cannot bear even the pressure of a bedsheet.

Maman

Her name.

The candle

Vaccine. A cure.

Two days ago. I buried them next to the house.

I am floating

You are a camp doctor.

The others are much worse.

It is death

You're sick.

The rain it stinks of death

This will protect you.

I am going with you

If you tell me to do it I will I will go

I looked out at the small writing desk next to my bed and saw the patient from bay twenty-six. Rather than junk the outgrown desk, my parents had moved it to the summer house, and now this wasted phantom sat large in the young child's chair, his flat legs tucked snugly under the desk, gnawing on his lips with destructive precision as he typed. Sideways I watched the ghoulish little man as he keyed through pages on my tablet.

The file he stopped at looked familiar. It appeared to be the title page of "Investigation.Maryk." When he turned his head toward me, his red eyes were kindled by the faint light of the screen and the night glow from the skylight above.

"Pearse," he said, his ragged lips twisted into something like a smile.

Something about this apparition differed from the others, in that something about it was true. The man moved about the room, preternaturally well, dressed in street clothes now and a colorful, brimless cap, his shirt and pants hanging formlessly off his slim hips. He mumbled to himself as he paced, chewing his lips, thinking. Deciding something.

He crossed to the bed, and I heard the plastic sheeting crumpling underfoot. I had forgotten about the sheeting, and the sudden memory of it, an icy splash of reality among the humidity of my dreams, commanded my attention. He leaned over me—his face was cheekless almost to the sinewy muscles beneath, eyes wet and large and boiling red—and I realized I was terrified. He looked me up and down with a flat, sluggish grin, like a deranged artist amused by the incoherence of his own incoherent work.

"Mine now," he told me. "You are mine."

He was right.

Then the room was empty again, and I was waiting for Jacqueline Moutouari. The bed was floating: I was floating. Blackness shone through the skylight as I burned.

The horse head knocker clanked as the front door was opened downstairs. Footsteps wandered somewhere on the first floor, and I imagined she was coming to me now, to take my hand and lead me to the others. The room was beginning to drift again, but I held on, I held on.

A creak on the stairs: I knew the exact spot: fifth step, right side: and the creak again as the foot was lifted. The doorway slid away along the wall, circling the room, everything starting to spin and collapse.

The figure rose onto the dark landing outside my door. There was no disappointment on my part, no feelings either way; acceptance was all. His shadow filled the bedroom doorway, and I saw the zinc shock of hair under the skylight and recalled how in school behind his back they used to call him "Pearse's Lab Rat." Tight pale gloves glowed on his oversized hands. He was like a thing I had created, an ill-considered experiment gone awry and unleashed upon an unsuspecting, unprepared world, now returned to exact revenge upon its master. But like those of the patient from bay twenty-six, Peter Maryk's actions also seemed true, not what I might have fancied or hoped for or feared, but exactly what I might have expected had he actually walked into the room. There was nothing at all like compassion in the severity of his shadowed face, the heat of his bright, gray eyes, the contemptuous slant of his lips. Only absolute, unforgiving disgust.

"You're sick," he said.

Incubation

Maryk

Maryk stood inside the silvered doorway. He looked at the wasting figure of Stephen Pearse lying on the child's mattress. The odor of decay was thick and distinct. He backed out of the doorway into the shadows of the landing. The shock of the moment left him as quickly as it had come. He looked again at Stephen Pearse lying on his side with his right arm stuck off the bed. Stephen's eyes were sunken and crimson and staring.

Maryk returned downstairs. The house was like a museum with each room a closed exhibit. He walked to a glass-walled sitting room off the kitchen in the rear and rooted himself in the memory of his only previous visit. Lace curtains had been sashed along the walls and leather bindings had lined the low bookshelves under the windows. A mayonnaise jar full of buffalo nickels had sat upon the fall front of the cherry wood desk.

Every piece of furniture that remained in the house was shrouded. Maryk set his tablet on an upright Steinway covered in thin plastic sheeting. His black bag balanced on the keyboard and pressed out a dull chord that echoed throughout the cloistered first floor. Outside the windows the sloping backyard was silver and the moon was sprayed over the wrinkling ocean.

He opened his tablet and dialed Bobby Chiles. The deputy director's haggard face appeared in a window on the screen.

"Found him," Maryk said.

Bobby clapped his hands softly once and sat back in his chair. His shirt collar was twisted open anxiously. "Where is he?" he said.

"He's sick."

"Sick? What do you mean?"

"Who else is there with you?"

"I'm alone. Stephen is sick with what?"

"Plainville."

Bobby's eyes held fast to the screen as the rest of his face struggled.

"You need to make a decision," Maryk said.

"—Get him to a hospital."

"Not here. The New York press. Let me bring him back to Atlanta."

"*Plainville?* But how?"

"I am the only one who can get near him without a full suit now."

Bobby's hands were up at his face.

Maryk said, "Listen. We need to act fast. I need all resources placed at my disposal. No restrictions, and no questions asked."

"But if it's Plainville, what can you—"

"I can treat him," Maryk said simply.

Bobby was staring beyond his screen and well beyond Maryk. Maryk told him what he would need and then ended the connection.

He left his tablet glowing atop the piano and took his black bag back upstairs. Stephen lay on the boy-sized bed as before. The things in the bedroom were preserved under plastic except for the bed and a short blond wood dresser with the trophies on it. A cold breath of rot reached Maryk and he looked across at an open and unscreened window. A car passed the house. A city of twenty-five million people waited at the other end of the highway. Maryk wondered if the self-appointed "Health Ambassador to the World" could have already ignited a lethal chain of transmission in the most populated city in North America.

Maryk pulled on a second pair of gloves and tore off strips of adhesive tape to seal his cuffs above his wrists. He dragged the plastic sheeting away from the bed with the toe of his shoe and set to work under the argent glow raining through the skylight above.

Breath swirled out of Stephen's staring face like smoke under the door of a burning house. His eyes were wide and rheumy with blood and gazed at the doorway and the floor before it with an expression of expired longing. Maryk produced a penlight from his bag. Stephen's pupils reacted slowly to the beam like lazy black moons eclipsing blue suns. They were soft and fat. Capillaries had burst behind each lens and blood was flooding the clear vitreous jelly and seeping into the sclera and weeping in dry smudges out of the lacrimal ducts onto the pinches of Stephen's nose. Dots of red and purple petechiae bloomed in a sallow mask surrounding his eyes.

Maryk stood and eased Stephen back onto the mattress with both hands. Stephen's throat gurgled without issue. The mattress was fouled with vomit and excrement and the action of moving Stephen stirred the stench. His bloody stare settled upon the ceiling. He was semiconscious and perhaps aware of Maryk's presence and perhaps even able to see. Maryk reached over with his gloved thumb and middle finger and shut Stephen's eyelids.

Mucus and slime ran down Stephen's upper lip and chin and Maryk collected some in a vial. He unlaced and discarded Stephen's shoe-boots and socks. With a pair of short-bladed bandage scissors he cut along each soiled pant leg and shirtsleeve and up along the buttons of the shirt placket. The heated fabric peeled back like the outer folds of a thing well cooked. Stephen's flesh had the lucent softness of wax. There were visible lesions. Folds of loose skin were beginning to sag off his waist and neck as though he were melting.

Maryk sampled his blood. The puncture wound bled sluggishly and was slow to clot. With tweezers he collected representative hair samples and deposited them in individual glassine envelopes. The follicles pulled easily from Stephen's flesh like candles from a cake.

Lastly he brought out a metal thermos. There was a whisper of release as he unscrewed the cap and tipped the glass ampule of golden serum labeled MILKMAID into his gloved left fist. He drew the contents into a clean hypodermic even as he knew it was too late for the serum to be 100 percent effective. MILKMAID's success depended upon its administration within the first hours of infection. Maryk boosted the serum into Stephen's external jugular. It was a quick trip from there to his heart.

Maryk stripped off Stephen's gloves and noticed tape marks on Stephen's bare left hand. He saw a bean-sized bruise in the center of the palm and a tiny dot breach in the center of that.

Maryk unrolled a biohazard pack from inside his bag. He disposed of his contaminated implements and unwound the tape from his forearms and disposed of his outer gloves. He left the orange plastic bag unsealed in the center of the floor.

He saw Stephen's tablet set upon a child's writing desk. Maryk opened the screen and accessed Hailing/Receiving and found that the digital pulse modem had been disabled. Then he noticed a data entry in the master file list named "Investigation.Maryk." He opened it and paged through the contents. He stopped when he came to the code names, MILKMAID, BLOSSOM, and LANCET. With a keen frown he closed all applications and collapsed the screen.

A team of four Special Pathogens investigators assigned to Batavia, New York, on an E. coli 0157:H7 outbreak were the first to arrive. Maryk illuminated the open bedroom window with a flashlight and ordered immediate aggressive night spraying. Every potential insect vector in the area had to be exterminated before dawn.

The agents regarded Director Pearse's wasting body lying unconscious in a child's bed before filing out.

FEMA Biohazard Containment arrived from Atlanta with more Special Path investigators and Stephen was lifted off the bed and sealed inside a Kurt isolation pod. A Kurt pod was a maintained atmosphere constructed of heavy plastic insulant with two round glove ports on each long side. It was roughly the size and shape of a large box coffin.

Maryk bagged and secured Stephen's tablet himself. He declared a Biohazard 4 and FEMA BioCon initiated a program of full containment ablution.

Blue nylon was stretched over plastic ribbing outside the front door. One of the BioCon agents was inspecting the car parked in the driveway as Maryk exited. Lights were snapping on in the second-floor windows of surrounding houses and across the street a man marched halfway down his front walk in a red silk bathrobe before seeing the BDC insignia on the trucks and hastily turning back.

Stephen's pod was loaded into a BioCon ambulance and the convoy wound quietly through the slumbering seaside town. A BDC transport jet was waiting for them at the East Hampton airport. Maryk contacted Bobby Chiles again from the air and asked about the old B4 lab inside the basement of BDC Building Seven. A state-of-the-art replacement B4 had just come on-line inside the new Bioresearch Building. B4 was a biocontainment research laboratory for safe human manipulation of the most hostile biological agents.

"It's dark," Bobby said. "We bombed the place clean after the move to Nineteen."

"Refit all the fixtures and load in medical and lab research equipment. I need it prepped for surgery as well. You'll have to move fast."

"Containment scrubbed B4 dry to the paint, Peter. With all the bugs we harvested in there over the years, it took them four full days to achieve zero habitat. We're due to turn the space over to Pharmacology."

"They'll wait. I need a workspace. Anticipate everything from PCR typing to glassware needs to full barrier autopsy: Stephen's breeding Plainville now; you don't want samples being shuttled all over the complex. And choose carefully. The equipment has to be small enough to fit in through the air locks, and whatever gets in there won't be coming out again clean."

"But—B4's not meant to hold humans."

"Next, Geist in Engineering. He's the only one there cleared for Plainville. I posted him separately, but he won't cooperate unless it comes from you. I need him to brew up something for Stephen. Tell him it is of the highest priority. I'll also need a nurse with minimum fifty hours full-barrier experience and a strong constitution. We're avoiding Hartsfield International Airport for obvious reasons, so have a medical helicopter ready for transport at DeKalb Peachtree."

"Peter. What do I tell people?"

"Whatever you want, just so long as it's not the truth. I don't want to see anyone when we land on the roof of Building Seven. When we go down through the corridors to B4: no one standing in doorways, no teary spectators. No displays. I don't want to see anyone inside the lab except a security detail, two of my people to help load Stephen inside, and the nurse. And one last thing."

Bobby was scribbling frantically. "Yes?"

"Once these orders are issued, you are to surrender to Quarantine Services. I want every visitor to Building Sixteen since Stephen got back from Orangeburg traced and shuttered up. You're all going to have to sit out at least seventy-two hours."

Bobby nodded without protest. He may even have seen this coming.

Maryk signed off and sat back against the wide hull. He watched Stephen's gaunt body rocking with the motion of the plane inside the shimmying plastic walls of the pod. Maryk called the pilot and instructed him to remain twenty miles out to sea during the trip down the eastern coast. Stephen Pearse was a biological time bomb. The microbial spread from a plane crash on land would wipe out every organic form of life in North America within a few days' time.

Maryk never took an indeliberate step. He collapsed his tablet and closed his eyes and performed a quick self-diagnosis. No cascade. Not yet.

Admittance into a B4 laboratory is an exercise in biological humility. It is a passage from the microscopic carnage of the everyday human environment into a vessel of absolute atmospheric control.

Maryk jacked in his tablet and keyed in his code and the steel latch of the first steel door gave way under his hand. The first room was quiet and small inside with colored pipes running overhead. Air moving into B4 was purged through high-efficiency particulate air filters and exposure to ultraviolet light and high heat sources. Each successive room was negatively pressured so that air flowed into the lab and preserved containment.

Maryk glanced at the computer screens monitoring the unit. All indications were green. He moved past two small windows to a facing oval door and the door opened inward with a breathy *shush*.

He changed into a dull green surgical scrub suit and cap and white cotton socks at the lockers. The third room was small and blue and humming with virus-killing ultraviolet light. The piped ceiling was low and the deep indigo light made Maryk's white hair glow.

Bright blue biological space suits hung from a steel rack inside the fourth room. Maryk bypassed them for a white metal cabinet and pulled on a simple gauze face mask and a pair of goggles. He changed gloves and taped them sealed as the sound of the rushing air grew louder.

The last room was a chemical shower stall illuminated by one dim ultraviolet bulb. Steel spray nozzles nosed out from the walls and a steel grate covered the floor basin. Biohazard warnings and safety checklists glowed on the last door. Laboratory suits were mandatory for admittance. Maryk wore only surgical scrubs, gloves, light face gear, and cotton socks. He threw the latch and stepped over the threshold into airtight B4.

The lab room was a wide gray rectangle. A central work table of sealed glass cabinets had been removed to make room for Stephen's gurney. He was laid out flat and unmoving with IV feeds running to both arms and an oxygen mask over his drawn face.

The nurse stood inside a blue lab suit between a tray of instruments and the monitors near Stephen's head. Her lab suit was hooked to a lime green air coil hanging from tracks that ran along the ceiling. Biological space suits were artificially ventilated for comfort during long stretches in B4.

Her eyes widened inside her hood when she saw Maryk. He had avoided B4 since his first year of training due to his claustrophobia. At that time he had been made to wear a full suit. For decades no human being had freely breathed the air he breathed now. Formaldehyde and bleach tinctured the enclosed atmosphere. Maryk did not smell Stephen yet.

He stepped into a pair of yellow rubber boots inside the doorway. He went past a walk-in freezer around the far left corner to check on the connecting animal room and saw that the monkey cages had all been removed. Biohazard Containment had caulked and gobbed epoxy over the screw holes and scrubbed much of the paint clean off the walls. BioCon was reliably meticulous in its work. The shelves and the wide floor space between were jammed with lab machines and equipment rolled in on movers' casters. In one corner lay the discarded Kurt pod.

Maryk performed the first and most obvious procedure on the long counter between the freezer and the door. It was a standard presumptive PCR test confirming the presence of the Plainville virus in Stephen Pearse's blood.

Maryk returned to the gurney and faced the nurse across Stephen. Her face within the bowl of her suit hood was small and serious. She pointed out a stainless steel rack. "Mistake," she said. Words were at a premium inside her howling suit. "They sent down your blood instead of Director Pearse's."

All BDC personnel submitted blood and other bodily fluids to be banked for research. On the rack near Maryk hung chilled plastic packs of blood labeled MARYK.

"There is no mistake," he said and set about his work.

The biological process of Plainville was a marvel to behold. The virus infiltrated the body's immune system by flipping certain protective T cells against the body's own armed forces. It hijacked the cells' reproductive systems and forced them to breed hundreds of thousands of Plainville viruses. This torrent of new viruses overloaded the immune system and eventually triggered an autoimmune response whereby T cells sent to root out invaders went haywire and turned their attack upon healthy organs. The body's frenzied defensive reaction to Plainville caused the most symptomatic destruction.

Maryk worked to improve Stephen's vital functions before going after the disease itself. He put Stephen under and excised kernel-sized vascular growths and two grossly inflamed lymph nodes and deposited them into a steel pan. He pared samples for biopsy. He opened Stephen's abdomen and the tumors he found were already deeply invasive and metastatic. He went after the most conspicuous masses and scraped away as much as a thimbleful at a time. The largest gripped Stephen's pancreas like a baby's fist. His liver was the color of tapioca pudding and his spleen was inflamed and clogged with curdled blood. There were dead spots on his kidneys, lungs, and intestines where his circulation had failed. His appendix was bloated and threatened to rupture and flood the abdominal cavity with bacteria-rich pus. Maryk removed it.

Maryk went after Stephen's internal bleeding aggressively until the machine choked on the sludge. He repaired abscesses and wrapped damaged arteries and plugged leaking veins with surgical gel before closing. Plum-colored bruising flushed the stitching.

He examined scans of Stephen's brain. There were visible lesions in the thinking center of the right prefrontal cortex, the cognitive behavior and motor planning region of the prefrontal lobe, and the emotional behavior center of the anterior cingulate. But the virus had not yet blitzed the brain stem. Maryk introduced minimal cytokines locally to the brain to excite the immune cells in a bid to preserve Stephen's mind. He required more powerful ammunition but had not yet received his from Engineering.

Maryk's breathing began to deepen and his head and arms grew heavy. The amplitude of Stephen's infection was reflected in the intensity of Maryk's cascade. Maryk knew that he had to get away in order to remain on his feet and see this thing through.

Maryk directed the nurse to draw off as much of Stephen's poisoned blood as she could before transfusing four MARYK blood units. She repeated his orders back to him before Maryk underwent a thorough UV exposure and departed B4.

It was dawn and the aboveground halls of Building Seven were empty. He felt better outside the pressure tank of B4. He found an unlocked office and fell into a chair. He dug a sterile syringe out of his black bag. He drew a measure of clear liquid amphetamine out of a small glass ampule and dosed himself with it. He could not afford the energy drain of a cascade just yet.

The jazz started in his head and he stood and rebuckled his bag. The speed would keep him going a few hours more.

Engineering occupied the bottom three floors of Building Four. There was a bright light shining beneath Geist's office door and Maryk entered and found the BDC's chief genetic engineer balancing number two pencils eraser-down on his desk. The overhead halogens paled Geist's already sallow complexion. Each individual bulb was reflected upon his waxy pate. He had lost every strand of his straw blond hair following a substantial radiation exposure some months before. He previously had suffered degenerative kidney and spleen damage and still occasionally set off sensors in the labs.

Geist looked up at Maryk through round wire-rimmed glasses with the ghosts of his blond eyebrows slightly raised. "Dr. Maryk," he said.

"You know about Pearse."

Geist was inordinately sedate. "From Bobby Chiles. An absolute shame. You know how much I admired Stephen."

"Is that the jizz?"

Between the standing pencils and a photograph of an oily black Doberman sporting a blue show ribbon stood a wire rack containing a single glass tube of clear fluid. Dr. Amory Geist was a pioneer in the field of viral therapy. The retroviral antigen was a genetic smart bomb designed to excite Maryk's killer T cells now roaming Stephen's veins. The tube was capped and safety-taped.

"I'm going to need a patient consent," Geist said. He pulled the tube rack closer to his forest of pencils. "I need a signed consent before I kill somebody. I'd like to know what you're up to."

Maryk said, "Straight viral therapy."

"V.T. isn't cleared for late-stage catastrophic and you know it. If it's Plainville, then Stephen Pearse is dead already."

"He's laid out on a table over in Seven. His cells are dying off by the millions every hour. How long do you want to chat?"

"I am not one of your errand boys in Special Pathogens."

Maryk smiled thinly. "I see," he said.

"And I'm not afraid of you either. I think you know that. My little laboratory mishap relieved me of two things: hope for an average life expectancy; and fear. I don't believe I fear anything anymore. And still, there are rules that I follow. In our game, the rules are all we have. Stephen stood for that."

"Get to the point, Geist."

"I can't stop you from doing this. Bobby Chiles said to give you the juice, no questions asked. But *you* called *me*—that's the catch. You called me in here in the middle of the night to do your bartending for you."

"I could have done it myself."

"Possibly. I don't doubt it. You're very capable, even given your disdain for laboratory science. A few days, a week, maybe longer. Here I have it for you in under four hours. Now I want an audience. I want answers."

"You're the top geneticist in the country."

"Flattery," Geist remarked. "You are desperate, aren't you?"

"I thought you might like the challenge of helping him."

Geist sat back. "When you say things like that, I feel the hair standing up on the back of my neck. And I don't have any hair. Everyone knows how cold-blooded you are, especially Stephen. I would have expected you to be the first to suggest a *quality of life* action, to *relieve his suffering*. Instead you want to prolong it. Why?"

"You wouldn't want to live, Geist? You wouldn't want me to keep you going, even just a few more hours?"

"I told you before: I have no fear. But even I am a little afraid of Plainville."

They regarded each other across the desk under the unnaturally bright office. The pause was long but neither one of them grew uncomfortable.

Maryk said, "You're wondering why I'm still here."

"I'm thinking you're enjoying it. Someone finally standing up to you. Because I know I'm not changing your mind. If you're expecting the 'You Can't Play God' speech, you won't get it here. I play God every day in that glass bell across the hall. I could twist DNA helixes into origami if the mood struck me. But I don't. Because I am a benevolent god. May I offer a theory? I think some doctors love humanity while harboring enormous contempt for actual people. And I think you're one of those— though I may be mistaken about the 'loving humanity' part. Why a retrovirus? Why the brain?"

"I took some pictures. I did a lumbar and a cerebrospinal pull; both were clear. The bug hasn't fully colonized his brain yet."

"So you'd like a chance at that yourself. Circle the genetic wagons, as it were. You realize this retrovirus will run rampant—invading at high efficiency, shooting its genes into the cells' chromosomes."

"Exactly. Only here, you've snipped out the virus gene and recoded it with genetic matter from a beneficial source, fighting bad virus with good virus. I can infect one hundred million cells with good, clean cargo in under two hours."

Geist said, "Transduce."

"Transduce, infect—whatever."

"Not 'whatever.' Viruses infect people; I don't. It is not an infection because it produces no new viruses. A payload has been *transduced*." He sat forward again. "What is this 'beneficial source'? "

Maryk held Geist's gaze without answering.

Geist smiled. "This retroviral antigen will soak him with DNA. It will change him. Not physically, but this is another human being's genetic material. Soup to his brain's saltine. It's dangerous, and it won't hold."

"It will over a limited period of time."

"Which is to say, you expect he'll die before it has the chance. So Stephen Pearse's survival is not your ultimate goal."

"He's too far gone for that."

Geist looked at Maryk as one might observe the artistry of a spider consuming a fly. "The beneficial genetic source is you."

"If it were my DNA, you wouldn't do it."

Geist smiled broadly. "I'll do a lot of things, but plucking the hot stuff out of a live virus and exchanging it for your twisted helix is not one of them. Mengele, in his happiest hour, would still have respected nature enough not to infect an unsuspecting brain with Maryk virus."

"Transduce," said Maryk.

"Whatever."

"Are we through lying to each other yet?"

Geist pointed at the shiny tube. "How do you know this isn't a saline placebo? By the time you figure out it's not working, Pearse would be out of his misery—and there is nothing you can do to me."

"Because I have a theory too. My theory is that you're that other kind of doctor, the bleeding heart kind, and that so long as there is a million-to-one chance Pearse might pull through this thing, you'll take that chance, because Stephen Pearse is the patron saint of your cause. Because you gods in the laboratory are content to leave the practical decisions of death and life to the foot soldiers such as myself. You work in a greenhouse, Geist. I live in the jungle. *Fiat experimentum in corpore vili.*"

" 'Let experiment be made on a worthless body.' Touching. And here I thought you and Stephen used to be friends."

"All I can do is give him a little more time."

"Pardon the non–Ivy League pronunciation: *Corruptio optimi pessima.* 'The corruption of the best is the worst of all.' And one more I know; and then I want you out of my office and out of my sight. The next time you want some chicken soup, open up the can yourself. *Similia similibus curantur.* 'Like is cured by like.' "

Maryk took the tube and returned to the subterranean B4. In a sense he admired the small-focus simplicity of Geist's mind. It reminded him of the half-sad smile of his blind mother when she fumblingly realized some small task.

He injected Stephen with the retroviral antigen. If nothing else his

DNA strategy flooded Stephen's brain with healthy cells that needed killing and this bought Maryk time. Maryk needed time.

He boosted Stephen with another fix of **MILKMAID** serum and charted an aggressive protocol of the same. He ordered monitoring for hyperkalemia due to the massive transfusions and prescribed strict electrolyte and fluid maintenance. He ordered tube feeding into the small bowel and 10 mg perenteral morphine and trycyclics for the pain.

"He's going to get worse before he gets better," Maryk told the nurse, "*if* he gets better. How long can you stay?"

"As long as you need me, Doctor."

The speed was already failing him. Stephen was radioactive with Plainville. "Call if there are any sudden changes," he said.

He dozed in UV. He was a long time changing back into his clothes.

Morning light beat through the windows upstairs as he staggered into an empty break room and dropped onto a bruise-red vinyl sofa. The room ebbed against him as though the entire building had been set to sea. He heard his tablet smack the floor and his breathing became thick and lugubrious. The weight of the cascade fell. He sank heavily away.

The tone did not awaken him. A woman's voice did. He came to hours later in a room full of people eating lunch.

"Hello?" she was saying. A young woman wearing a lab coat. Small nose and large glasses and curled brown hair looming over him. The room smelled of peanut butter and apples.

"Excuse me?" She knew who he was. He could tell by the way she kept her distance. "Your tablet. You're being paged."

He sat up. The others in the room continued to eat and pretended not to notice him. Maryk tasted the roily paste of sleep. His black socks were only half-pulled onto his feet and he realized he had left his shoes behind in the changing room of B4.

The woman backed away. "It's been going off for a while," she said.

He righted his overturned tablet on the floor and opened it and the tone ceased. Stage sighs within the room. The header split in his muddled vision and he concentrated until it became clear. The post was from Reilly and Boone. It was uncharacteristically capitalized.

LANCET IS DOWN.

Lancet

Traffic was squeezed into two lanes on the five-lane Peachtree. Police lights flashed against the orange terra-cotta wall announcing The Groves. Maryk displayed his credentials for a cop wearing lime green gloves and was admitted through the barricade.

Police vehicles outnumbered BDC vans and trucks in the parking lot outside the easternmost condominium building. The structure was fat and frosted with pink stucco and rimmed with Spanish terraces. Evacuated residents sat on a side lawn under trees manicured to look like poodle tails.

Maryk was met by one of his Special Pathogens men wearing a full contact suit at the concierge's desk in the lobby of Groves East. His name was Reilly and he introduced a waiting Atlanta police lieutenant named Cole. The cops behind Lieutenant Cole all wore gloves and police respirators and stood around anxiously. Law enforcement organizations in general hated dealing with disease.

Reilly huffed inside his suit and led Maryk around rather theatrically. Maryk declined a suit with a sideward glance at Reilly but did pull on a simple respirator for appearance' sake. Lieutenant Cole thumbed the elevator button but Maryk walked to the stairwell. Reilly and Lieutenant Cole reluctantly followed. Uniformed police officers in gloves and masks were posted at each landing.

"How bad would you say it all is, the spread?" asked Lieutenant Cole. "We can go wider with the evacuation if it's warranted."

"I won't know what it is until I get in there," said Maryk.

"Helluva job you people do. Tracking this thing, and keeping my boys out of it. Be nice if we knew where crime was going to emerge as it emerged."

"It's like narcotics," offered Reilly. "From the source to the distributor to dealers to the street. Contact tracing. Chain of infection."

White viricidal foam lathered the walls beginning with the eleventh-floor landing. Reilly and Lieutenant Cole slowed there.

Reilly said, "We do appreciate your cooperation, Lieutenant."

"Cooperation, nothing. Damn pleasure. You know I have a son in sixth grade in Conyers who says he wants to be a doctor like Dr. Pearse at the BDC. I tell him he's crazy. That's one hell of a public relations department you got going there."

Maryk was a half flight above. "We can handle next-of-kin notification," he said. "Disease can be a difficult subject, and we've had some experience."

Lieutenant Cole pointed up from the perceived safety of the lower landing. "Shouldn't you be in one of them suits?"

Reilly answered for him. "Dr. Maryk's not so good in confined spaces."

"Lord," said Lieutenant Cole genuinely. He tipped his hat to Maryk. "Luck to you."

The eleventh-floor hallway was foamed wall-to-ceiling. Two suits guarding a door three doors down opened it for Maryk and Reilly. They entered a kitchen area with a larger room beyond. The door closed behind them and they were sufficiently alone.

Maryk stripped off his respirator. Reilly broke open the seal across his chest and with a gasp of relief pushed the hood piece back over his head. The suit collapsed to the carpet and he stepped out of it.

"Seven years of med school," Reilly said. The tension of the situation had short-circuited his usual midwestern agreeableness. "Seven years of med school—for this? We've been going out of our minds here."

"I was detained."

"I thought they'd bust in at any moment."

Maryk moved into the living area. "You should have more faith in their fear. Now what happened?"

Reilly walked inside ahead of him. "Everything's been preserved, everything recorded on disk. The apartment and the hallway, everything."

Rattan shades drawn over the windows glowed brown. The main room was arranged around a media center with a monitor and console set into sturdy wire shelving. There was a black leather couch and a floor lamp in one corner and twin black canvas director's chairs in the other. A large bookcase was built into the near wall. It was full of pop culture memorabilia from the turn of the century—books, posters, glossies, action figures, magnets, mugs, lunch boxes, pins, cels, phone cards, videocassettes. Lancet owned and operated a nostalgia boutique for tourists in the Underground Mall of downtown Atlanta.

"You've never been up here," Reilly said.

Maryk shook his head. "Where is he?"

"The bedroom. We took a liver temp which set death at about midnight, right after he got in from work. Boone's in there now. Haven't touched him otherwise." Reilly was calming down now and the eagerness was returning to his moon-shaped face. "We breezed by his shop at the Underground Mall around eleven and everything was fine. Followed him back home here like any other night and watched him go in. All routine. He put on the lamp and the light in the bedroom window as always."

"That's it?"

"There's nothing missing as far as we can see. He draws his salary every other Thursday and of that takes just twenty in paper, so there's never any hard currency lying around. Everything that isn't tied up in his store he spends on more of the same collectible junk, and obviously, all of that is still here."

"How did you find him?"

"He didn't open the store this morning. We tried a phone call to wake him up. We tried a lot of things before we came in. He was always punctual. Made our part easy. None of it makes any sense."

"Where's the bedroom?"

Reilly led him through the connecting hallway. The bed was queen-sized and neatly made. A rattan shade drawn down over the room's only window lifted and fell against the sill as the bedroom sighed. The breeze stirred the coppery smell of blood.

Lancet was a trim thirty-three-year-old white male with sandy brown hair. He lay facedown across the peach comforter with his head and shoulders falling off the side and the knuckles and backs of his hands curled on the thin white mat covering the floor. He was nude except for athletic socks. Discarded clothes lay in a pile against one wall.

Both wrists had been slit lengthwise. Dry brown blood soaked the white mat and also a wood-handled steak knife lying between Lancet's curled hands.

Maryk stepped back. The shock of the suicide momentarily eclipsed his anger at seeing four years of work thrown away. The instrument choice seemed particularly crude.

"A steak knife," he said.

Reilly nodded. "I know."

The weight of the body upon the mattress had shrugged down the comforter so that the sweat-stained tops of the pillows showed. Maryk went to the heap of clothing across the room and sorted through the pile with his right foot. A vintage pair of black Levi's jeans lay below a white pair of briefs. Both were turned inside out.

"No sign of a struggle, forced entry?" Maryk said.

Reilly said, "None that we can see."

"And no one was following him. You're certain of that."

"Lancet had no enemies," Reilly said. "Not that he had any friends either. He didn't have anybody. Except us, and that he never knew."

Boone rose before the dresser. He was wire-haired and older than Reilly. "This is too much," he said. "We've moved out of the gray area now. Observation, surveillance: fine, okay." He pointed to the bed. "That's a corpse there."

The loss frustrated Maryk as much as it troubled him. "You were to watch him," Maryk said. "You were to monitor him and to make certain that he remained in Atlanta, and that he lived comfortably. But above all you were to make certain, absolutely certain, that no harm came to him. That he remained viable and healthy."

Reilly and Boone looked at each other as men who have worked long hours together will. "What did you expect?" Boone said. "This guy was haunted. He was a ghost, and he knew it. He lived for the past. Look at this."

There were display shelves next to the closet doors and Boone began pulling items off them. A sky blue box reading WINDOWS '95. A *Frasier* mug. An unopened foil pack of *Beavis and Butt-head* playing cards.

A *Lost World* lunch box. An *Entertainment Weekly* guide to *The X-Files*. Stacks of old VHS videocassettes. A red ribbon pin.

"Pull all the phone taps," Maryk said. "Unwire his tablet. Then declare a Biohazard 3 and go through all the motions. Bring him out in a covered pod and get BioCon going on the hallway and the rest of the building. We want the neighbors inconvenienced as much as possible; it will lend legitimacy. Write up a death certificate, nothing too exotic, then contact his sister in Louisiana. Make certain she gets anything of value you find here."

Boone folded open the closet doors and pulled out a vinyl storage bag from among Lancet's personal effects. He drew the zipper down on a green canvas jacket with white sleeves and white snaps and a twilled green-and-white collar. The face of a bulldog was sewn over the right breast and a white capital letter *P* over the left. Script stitching beneath the dog face read: *Plainville Class of '00.*

"How's this for nostalgia," said Boone.

Maryk only frowned. "You may dispose of that."

Quarantine Services had sealed off the auditorium and old cafeteria inside Building One for the sequestration of anyone who may have shared breathing space with Stephen Pearse following his return from Orangeburg. It was a "friendly" quarantine of international health care professionals requiring no ankle monitors and minimal security at each exit.

The shock of the director's illness was still setting in. A moroseness more eloquent than the usual moroseness of enforced quarantine pervaded the old building. Even the QS administrators in their contact suits sat tiredly on folding chairs or leaned dazed against walls. The administrative staff from Building Sixteen sat solemnly in groups and speculated about the future of the BDC.

Maryk strode through quarantine. No one approached or addressed him and no one spoke of him until after he was gone.

Bobby Chiles entered the makeshift examining room and sat down before realizing that Maryk was seated across from him. "Peter," Bobby said anxiously. "How is he?"

Maryk was rearranging the blood-taking supplies on the standing tray between them. "Alive. Blood samples seem to indicate a slowdown."

Bobby's eyes brightened in amazement as he rolled up his shirtsleeve. "Why, that's—that's remarkable, Peter. That's truly remarkable. So there's a chance, then."

Maryk pulled out a Betadine swab and smeared Bobby's exposed brown forearm orange-red. "I can slow the process enough to keep him alive for a few more days. A week, maybe more. Depends on how far gone he is, and how much we can learn about the virus in that time."

"But there's a chance he'll make it beyond that. I mean, there's always that chance."

Maryk broke the skin of Bobby's forearm and entered a vein. "No," he said. "Stephen's not going to make it."

Bobby looked at him blankly as the small plastic barrel began to fill.

"When can I see about moving him out of there?" Bobby said. "B4 is a laboratory, Peter. People will want to visit."

Maryk was firm. "No visitors. Stephen stays where he is. Full rein, Bobby, remember? No distractions."

Bobby nodded distantly. "How could this happen?" he said.

Maryk raised his left hand. He opened it and pointed to the center of his latex palm.

Bobby said, "But he didn't report anything. What was he doing up in New York?"

"Running away. The guilt of infection."

"I knew that, of everyone we had out there, you'd be the one to find him. You two had a history."

"His parents' summer house was a long shot, but it paid off. We're picking apart his tablet now. His bank account shows only one service stop the entire trip."

"He had one of the government fleet. Eight cylinders of compressed natural gas. He could make it there with just one fill-up."

Maryk nodded. "It was a full-service CNG station. A bank account debit through his tablet. Never had to roll down the window."

"No spread, then."

"None yet." Maryk switched to a third barrel. "Except for the publicity woman."

Bobby closed his eyes and nodded.

Maryk said, "And her two dogs. Practically turned them inside out."

"Peri Fields. Public Affairs. You didn't know her."

"A touch, a sneeze, a passed memo, a borrowed pen. It wouldn't have taken much. If she wasn't already out with the flu at the start of it, we would have had a catastrophe on our hands."

"With the bureau at ground zero. We can't be this lucky much longer. It's going to get out."

"That's why Stephen is so important. That's why he stays in the lab. I've got to study him."

"They said Peri had a lot of indoor plants, and that it got into them bad."

"As well as the bacteria in the food. And not just the cupboards—somehow it broke through the refrigerator seal. But the plants were particularly bad. Plainville does something to them, takes longer to kill them. The stalks were growing up through the walls, around pipes, trying to get out. They were even snaking up the birdstand. It was like they were going for her parakeet."

"You aren't saying—"

"It was almost as though the virus couldn't infect it, so it was going to finish off the job by hand. My people have the bird, but it's just like all the rest. Birds don't get Plainville. We still don't know why."

"The parakeet isn't talking?"

Bobby burst into a fit of inappropriate laughter. His head dropped and his shoulders shook as he fought to regain his composure. Maryk left a bandage on the table for him and stood to change his gloves. Bobby looked up sniffling and scooping tears out of his eyes.

"Sorry . . . it's my first quarantine. All the international liaisons and whatnot from Sixteen—I've got plenty of friends here, and at times I'm almost enjoying myself, playing cards to pass the time. But then I remember where I am, and I'm watching these people shuffling the deck and dealing cards in front of me, and all I can think is that, if even just one of them has it . . ."

Maryk opened the door to leave. "Rules of containment," he said. "Same for everybody, doctor or patient. That was Stephen's mistake. No one is exempt."

"Well," Bobby said. He was sober now and rolling down his sleeve as he looked at Maryk in the open doorway. "Almost no one."

The funk was general throughout each building as Maryk moved through the BDC to Building Sixteen. The flags outside were flying at half-mast. He stopped in at the vacant Public Affairs office. He saw an empty box of sterile tissues on one of the assistant's desks and balled up tissues scattered around a tablet keyed to a news server.

The screen image was that of Stephen delivering his Nobel speech at the Stockholm Concert Hall. The log line listed the article as that day's third draft.

PEARSE STRICKEN

BDC Head Infected in Laboratory Mishap
Deadly Agent Unspecified

ATLANTA—Dr. Stephen Pearse, director of the U.S. Bureau for Disease Control and last week's recipient of the Nobel Prize award in Medicine for development of the PeaMar23 synthetic blood, was accidentally infected in an Atlanta laboratory while performing experimental vaccination research . . .

Maryk left the desk and continued inside through a door marked PERI FIELDS but the office had already been stripped down and cleaned out. There was nothing left of her there.

The office of the director remained sealed off from the rest of the building. Maryk stood at the nylon that lined the doorway and watched the yellow suits working inside. One was removing diplomas and photographs from the walls and disposing of them in a carton marked BIOHAZARDOUS WASTE. Another was foaming the brass inlay of the ceiling. A third BioCon agent lifted a large gold medallion off the desk. He briefly inspected Stephen's Nobel medal before depositing it with the rest.

Maryk sat across from Ursula Freeley behind the counter of the gloomy admitting room. Orangeburg had burned itself out. Special Path's biocontainment strategy had denied the arsonist virus the flesh and blood and tissue that was its oxygen. The microbreak had diminished to a few smoldering final-stage terminals.

Freeley sat with her puffed arms relaxed on the arms of the swivel chair and her legs straight out and crossed at the ankles. She appeared more comfortable inside a contact suit than most people appeared outside one. Maryk asked her how Stephen had been when he left the hospital.

"I didn't see him then," she said. "He wasn't here but an hour. Had to see the patients though. Had to touch the sick. I spoke to one of the serologists with him, and he said that when Pearse left he seemed agitated. The hall cameras were all foamed over, so there's nothing to view on disk." She shifted unhappily in her padded chair. "I saw the press release. So now the healer of the free world dies a martyr to his cause. I don't think Plainville victims look too valiant lying in state."

"Better than the panic the truth would bring. What's our status here?"

Freeley crossed her baggy arms. "Not with a bang but a whimper. Survival rate is zero, no surprise there. Again, nothing links the virus to the outside world. No less than two substantive genetic drifts in the virus between the beginning of the outbreak and the end. The lethality of this thing is our one saving grace. It kills so expediently, the infected have little time to infect anyone else."

"Nothing on the vectors?"

"Food, soil, sewage, pests, rodents, vents, air: Nothing stands out. And the catatonics' old blood all tested clean. It was nothing lying latent." She unknotted her arms and stressed her points with a chopping motion on the arm of the chair. "They weren't infected, then they were infected, and now there's nothing to tell us how. It's not nosocomial. This didn't move doctor-to-patient. So how did it get in here? Bugs don't just appear and burn in a limited capacity and then disappear again. There's commonality, footsteps, links. This just doesn't happen—and yet here it is, happening again. This thing is smart and somehow getting smarter."

Maryk nodded and looked sternly off to the side.

"And now Lancet is gone," she added. "That means there are only two left."

Lancet's self-destruction mystified Freeley as well. Maryk was thinking. "Do you ever take off your pants by rolling them down from the waist?" he said.

She looked at him flatly through the mask. "That may be the first personal question you have ever asked me."

"There was a pair of black jeans in a pile of clothes on Lancet's bedroom floor. They were pulled all the way through, inside out."

"You're thinking someone undressed him?"

"I don't know. First Pearse gets stuck with Plainville. Then Lancet turns up dead."

"So? Nothing links the two."

"What if I told you that Pearse had been investigating me? That he was onto the blood project, Lancet and the others. That he had the files in his computer."

Her hard-edged face showed suspicion. "How?"

"Stephen Pearse was many things, but he was never stupid."

She dismissed it. "Who gains by killing Lancet? No one. I don't see it."

"I want you on his post. Reilly and Boone insist there's no sign of forced entry; I need to be certain. We've preserved a number of items from his apartment. Closing Lancet down means freeing up some money, so we'll double security on the others. We've got two survivors left. It is imperative that we protect them."

She nodded at the hospital. "And this?"

"We wait. We prepare, and anticipate. Each time we tell ourselves we've stamped Plainville out for good, and each time we're proven wrong. I'll assemble a rapid response team to cut down our reaction time on the next break, to give us a fighting chance."

"We've got to stop chasing this bug's shadow. We need a viable sample of the pathogen for study. We can't grow it in the lab because it eats through anything we put in front of it, and we can't sustain it safely because of its virulence."

Maryk stood then. "You forget," he said. "We are growing Plainville in a lab now. Stephen Pearse is cultivating Plainville *in vivo*."

Freeley came close to smiling then. Her cunning eyes brightened behind the Plexiglas of her hood.

Melanie

Breakfast, in a whirlwind. Two slices of broccoli and olive pizza pulled cold from her artfully magneted refrigerator, munched in the bathroom as she pulled on clothes from a pile on the floor and simultaneously willed her chopped hair into order. At that speed, it was easy to ignore the blotchy wall stains and flaking white paint, to shirk the general impression that the tiny bathroom was, like so many other things in Melanie Weir's life, collapsing in on her. She had willfully overslept. Responsibility was no longer a viable deterrent to sleep. Each morning she could find fewer and fewer reasons to get out of bed.

She had once worked with a girl who had a scandalous habit of waking up in her bedroom with total strangers. Melanie did much the same thing, except that for her, the lingering scent of a regrettable evening was not cologne and other smells of a man, but turpentine and linseed oil, on her hands and her fingers, and rising out of the coffee cans and mayonnaise jars set on her windowsill like cocktails left out overnight.

She had this weird thing about painting: She had no real love for the art, and no training whatsoever, and yet once every few months, always late at night and often when the moon was full, she answered this inexplicable urge to take brush in hand and fill up a blank canvas. They all started out as masterpieces in her mind, as the painting would reveal all the things about herself she could never understand. But then the next morning she awoke to an unfinished landscape of grotesque images that was incomprehensible even to her.

Each was a variation on a theme. All involved blood, such as lakes or waterfalls of blood, set in lurid but desolate landscapes, populated by tiny people wandering around naked or in torn clothes, and bizarre, wolflike beasts with carrion in their grinning teeth, moving through sunless shadows cast by inscrutably deformed trees. These were not Holiday Inn–quality paintings, she knew. One image common to each work was that of a white-haired man whose face was always obscured. Dead center in her latest garish composition, the man was kneeling without reflection over a boiling reservoir of blood.

Dressed in a crushed velvet jersey and loose jeans, she came back into the bedroom and faced the painting. As a glimpse into her subconscious, this bizarre expression of angst was at the very least unsettling. She took the canvas down off her cheap metal easel and set it on the floor, facing the wall, then went to search for her keys.

Melanie lived in a tiny two-room apartment that was a well of voices. The broad windows of her apartment faced the broad windows of the next building of apartments, linked to her building on either side, three planes of windows and bleached bricks rising. Through her open, breeze-less windows droned the jumbled voices, television clamor, and slamming doors of various other lives. She could make out only a sliver of sky as she looked up from her windows, though she had a terrific view of the accumulated trash tossed from the windows to the asphalt pen below. The Allston-Brighton neighborhood of Boston was a cat box for university students. Many a night she was awakened by the delicate sound of a person or persons relieving themselves off the roof.

It didn't have to be this way. Melanie had been taking one of her fearsome canvases out to the trash one morning when a middle-aged man who struck her as a college professor stopped her at the curb. He saw the painting and expressed an interest in purchasing it, but Melanie gave it to him for free. The man insisted on taking her name and address, claiming that if the painting appealed to his "employer," perhaps some future arrangement could be made. She said sure and gave him a fake address and went on her way. A few days later, a money order drawn on an Atlanta bank in the amount of five hundred dollars was slipped underneath her door, with a note requesting more paintings as they became available. Since that time, whenever she was low on funds and had another canvas lying around, she would contact this gentleman to arrange a sale. Neither he nor his employer ever identified themselves, but if some eccentric wanted to pay for her repulsive paintings—her imagination had conjured a dotty old geezer, like a backwoods Citizen Kane, squirreling her canvases away next to his fishing line collection and carton upon carton of artificial limbs—who was she to turn him down? Twice her secret patron had, in writing, offered to relocate her to Atlanta and install her in an artist's loft there. But Melanie was not born yesterday. Besides, she had no real control over when she painted, or what her mind told her to draw.

The heat rising through the well obliterated most rain and snow, and the depth of the pit defeated direct sunlight, so that the weather, when she went outside, was always a surprise. She found her keys and ran down four flights of stairs, pizza crust in hand, to the glass front door webbed to obscurity with cracks left from a year-old shooting. It was a cold, early December morning.

She glanced up and down her narrow, curving street before starting to the corner, and saw no one suspicious. But the people who were following her rarely appeared so close to her own building.

Her bag slapped against her side as she ran along the Commonwealth Avenue median after a streetcar, catching it and boarding and moving between two empty seats, choosing instead to stand. No one had followed her inside. The train started and she stood holding the overhead bar, rocking along, pretending not to be scanning the faces of the other riders, and resisting the sleeplike pull of mass transit funk.

The B line trolley below Kenmore Square, the one on which she was traveling, ran between the area's two largest universities. She was surrounded by students, all unfinished faces and soft hands, knapsacks slumped at their feet and modishly colored tablets tucked under their arms. The most fashionable kids wore hospital shirts or bruise-colored eye shadow, with plastic hospital bracelets dangling off their wrists. "Ill" was in. "Unhealthy" was the rage. It was evidently a fashion statement about the diseased world they stood to inherit. Melanie had the look herself, in her build and the dark circles under her eyes, only she did not share the sentiment; she came by her disease-chic naturally. One healthy-looking man in the second car, older and well-dressed in a simple suit, stood out from the rest; his only concession was an inconspicuous pair of latex gloves, which, when riding on a public subway, was not a bad idea. The rest all looked like children to her twenty-four-year-old eyes, and she could feel her days of scamming student discounts coming to an end. Four years of being a dedicated dropout, of auditing her life, had earned her no credits, no degrees, no nothing. She was four years' poorer and on the brink of expulsion from the university of her own making.

At the Brighton Avenue intersection the doors folded open and she stepped down with the others, passing in front of the blunt nose of the train to the rail tracks on the other side. The change in acoustics from the trolley to the outside street amplified the ringing that was constant in her head: a flat, mantric tone sapping 60 percent of the hearing in her right ear. At certain times, such as right now, the blare rose so intensely in her head that nothing short of stopping and pressing a hand to her ear would ease it. Others from the streetcar moved around and away from her as she waited. She felt the rumbling of the tracks, but did not make sense of it in time.

She was struck from behind and thrown forward sprawling onto the cement apron. She had been tackled, knocked off the track median toward the street. As she tumbled, she saw a flurry of arms and knees, most of them her own.

Steel wheels screeched as a B trolley burst behind her. The harsh, sudden noise was deafening to her keening ears, and stunned, she jerked back onto her knees.

The well-dressed man from the second trolley car was behind her now, having rolled from the force of his impact half out onto Commonwealth Avenue. An automobile skidded to a stop, curtseying just inches from his right shoulder.

Her handbag had slipped to her side. She groped for the snap and thrashed around inside for her mace, pulling it out and thumbing the trigger. A fine steroid mist escaped. It wasn't her Mace at all: It was her bronchodilator, and with a grunt she flung the inhaler aside.

Then she realized what had actually happened. The well-dressed man hadn't attacked her at all. He had shoved her out of the path of the inbound streetcar. He had saved her life.

"Hey!" she yelled after him. But the stranger never looked back. She saw the soles of his shoes and his gloved hands pumping as he raced away, and by the time she got to her feet he was down a side street and gone.

Very quickly she had her bag back in hand. People were staring at her, and a college kid wearing a powder blue surgeon's cap stepped forward and handed Melanie back her inhaler, asking if she was all right. She snatched it out of his blue-bandaged hand and rushed blindly across the street while the traffic was still stopped.

She went a city block with tears stinging her eyes, apartment stoops and storefronts blurring past her. At the corner she ducked into the doorway of a dry cleaners and she faced her frail reflection in the steamed window as she tried to catch her breath. Cranberry, that was the color she had regrettably dyed her hair, short to her jaw on the sides and flat against her small head like sauce poured over an eggshell. She looked like a punked-out corpse. No combination of clothing or patterns could improve upon her implike frame. She was a mess.

She glanced back up the avenue and no one seemed to be following or staring at her any longer. Her damaged lungs heaved and burned. She took out her inhaler and took a deep, soothing hit, and felt her lungs begin to expand.

Just keep moving, she thought. As long as she kept moving forward, the worst they could do was force her sideways.

The appointment she was running late for was at the Allston-Brighton Parish Clinic, a busy, modern brick office building located across from a Middle Eastern restaurant, half a block down Harvard Avenue. Only a gynecology appointment could round out that most enjoyable morning. Dr. Ursula Freeley's office was not listed in the lobby directory, nor was there a plaque on her second-floor door. But like a horse returning to the corral, Melanie's reproductive organs knew the way.

The waiting room was always empty. The window was open and the receptionist, a different woman than last time, smiled up at her and spoke with a light southern accent. There was never a wait. Melanie was called immediately and shown into the examining room.

Light choral music playing inside did nothing for her, and she remained fraught with the chaos of the street. Water helped to calm her down. As directed, she was drinking glassfuls from two plastic pitchers in order to fill her bladder and thereby raise her pelvic organs for an impending ultrasound. Melanie suffered from endometriosis, a condition whereby stubborn endometrial tissue clung to her insides rather than being voided by her damaged body each month. It had been described to her as "rust" on her ovaries, and could lead to the development of painful cysts which, if untreated, could then lead to tumors. There was no cure, only a choice of two treatments. The first was pregnancy. Melanie's laughing jag at Dr. Freeley's first suggestion of this three years before had prompted a memorable sneezing fit. The other was a laparotomy, a mildly invasive surgical procedure whereby a viewscope was inserted into the navel and a tool was inserted through the abdominal cavity to scrape the uterus clean. Her ovaries were incorrigible and had already demanded the procedure four times. Her pale-as-dough bikini line—"bikini" used in the purest hypothetical sense here—was marked with four slashing pink incision scars facing her indented navel, like the constellation of whatever cursed sign she had been born under. Would the fifth, which she dreaded, cross the first four, thereby completing a set?

She heard the doctor's footsteps out in the hall, the way a deadbolt must feel when it hears keys jingling. Dr. Freeley was businesslike and tall. She was humorless, but as with any good doctor, she had a quiet, confident air that allowed Melanie to tell her things she told no one else. She was also beautiful, with a cool, perfect elegance about her which struck Melanie as fundamentally unjust. Gynecologists, of all women, should not be someone you might lose your date to at a party.

"No examination," Melanie reminded her.

Dr. Freeley set down her chart and wheeled over the blue machine, agreeing with a nod. "Just pictures this time."

Melanie unbuckled her belt and slipped her jeans halfway down over the bony knobs of her waist. She removed her jersey and lay back, sliding her shirt up past her prominent ribs, revealing the scrawny torso of a teenage anorexic.

Dr. Freeley said, "How have you been feeling?"

"Never better," Melanie answered.

"No weight gain, I see. Ninety-two pounds. You're eating?"

"Let's see. Cheeseburgers for dinner last night. Chicken wings for dessert. Pizza for breakfast, and I'm already hungry again. Am I on heroin?"

Dr. Freeley casually touched Melanie's waist with her latex hands, looking merely interested, not concerned. "Just an overactive metabolism," she decided.

Dr. Freeley slathered gel on Melanie's bare stomach and her abdomen bucked against the coolness. Melanie often wondered how much Dr. Freeley knew about her medical past, such as the damage to her lungs. There was something in the way she treated Melanie, much like a child, and in the fact that she had never asked the origin of the other, numerous scars, proud and jagged and slashing Melanie's belly and chest like surgical graffiti, that had gradually raised Melanie's suspicions over time.

"Arch your back more."

The ultrasound examination was mercifully brief. Later, after relieving the swollen balloon of her bladder in the connecting bathroom and toweling off the goop, Melanie noticed dust in the small sink. She ran water which lifted and swirled the grime into dark streaks and whisked them away down the drain, leaving a gray ring. The soap dispenser, she noted, was full; new. That bathroom had not been used in days.

She returned to the greater examining room where Dr. Freeley waited, as always, to take her blood. Melanie's mind ran on as she watched Dr. Freeley work over her arm. Why the need for so much blood? How much did she need for testing? Melanie studied Dr. Freeley as Dr. Freeley studied her, until the room began to spin. Melanie lost count around the sixth or seventh tube.

"Just one more," said Dr. Freeley. "You haven't asked about the ultrasound."

"Right," Melanie nodded. Because she knew the answer already.

"The ovarian adhesions are back again. I don't know why the hormone pills aren't working. We're going to have to schedule another procedure."

Melanie nodded, drifting. "Or else become pregnant. Don't leave out that option."

Dr. Freeley finished and bandaged her arm. "I take it you're between boyfriends?"

"That's a generous way of putting it. But who needs romance when you've got adventure?"

"What about work?"

"A part-time job. With full-time hours. I guess I'm between careers, too. Or between unemployments. Can I ask you a question about these hormone pills?"

Dr. Freeley was placing stickers on the thin tubes of blood. "Yes?"

"Any side effects? Drowsiness, for example? I'm sleeping all the time."

"There shouldn't be."

"Or my inhaler? Confusion, maybe? Paranoia?" The flicker of interest in Dr. Freeley's eyes made Melanie retreat. "Should I worry about operating any heavy equipment?"

Dr. Freeley said, "You seem concerned."

"Oh, no. I guess I'm just between lives."

She held Melanie with a flat, probing gaze. "Sit tight," she said. "I'll get you some orange juice."

She carried off the tray of blood tubes. As soon as the door closed, Melanie grabbed the side of the bed and rolled off. Her shoes clapped against the floor, legs wobbling as she reached out for the examining room counter and pulled herself to it. She swiped the metal basin with her finger. Her fingertip turned gray with cotton-fine dust. An unused examining room sink. No name on the office door. The different receptionist every visit. The always-empty waiting room. Melanie turned and reached back for the bed, waveringly, hoisting herself back on top of it just as Dr. Freeley returned.

Melanie slurped the juice rudely. This was after sniffing it.

Dr. Freeley monitored her blood pressure until satisfied. "Two weeks, then," she said. "For another look. A full examination this time. Then we'll decide."

"What if it's some virus?" Melanie said.

Dr. Freeley looked at her closely. "Some what?"

"A virus. Causing my ovarian rust."

"We know exactly what it is."

There was nothing in Dr. Freeley's face, but instead of backing off again, this time Melanie pushed forward. "I was reading about this hospital in South Carolina," she said. "Some outbreak there that killed all the patients."

Dr. Freeley now seemed impatient. "As I understand it, those patients were diagnosed with Waterhouse-Friderichsen syndrome. Classic acute meningococcal meningitis caused by a bacterium, not a virus. Sudden fevers, neck stiffness, dizziness, a coma within hours, kidney hemorrhaging, and then death. Do you think you have that?"

"You know a lot about viruses."

"One has to these days." Dr. Freeley slowly folded her arms. "We're not heading toward another episode, are we? You trying to check yourself into a clinic, claiming phantom symptoms of some exotic disease?"

These words shamed Melanie. She was much better than that now.

"Things are happening to me," she said quietly, all at once. "I can't explain them."

"What things?"

"People. Watching me. On my way to work. Different places."

"First of all," Dr. Freeley said. "Who?"

"I don't know. My mail too, I think. My phone. I was jumped on my way over here."

"You were what?"

"No, it was okay. One of the people following me around saved my life." Then Melanie thrust out her arms for her gynecologist to see. "Pinpricks," she said. "Small ones, other than yours. None right now, but sometimes I find them—as though I've been jabbed, as though . . ."

The look on Dr. Freeley's face stopped Melanie.

"I'm not just being paranoid about this," she insisted. "Honestly— it's not like my life is so empty that I have to make things up. I mean, my life *is* empty, but I would never . . ." She trailed off. As she shook her head, chemically ruined hair shimmied around her ears. "And then, sometimes, after it happens—after I wake up—I feel as though I've been handled."

"Handled?"

"Tampered with. Examined."

Dr. Freeley watched her with a silent concern that became intimidating. Melanie was starting to feel the table beneath her, and was again aware of the music playing faintly. The blood loss; she couldn't believe what she had been saying. She recalled the gray dust in the sinks and realized she should shut up.

She had never told anyone about having survived Plainville, and by merely considering turning loose this great secret, Melanie realized how truly desperate she was for help—and she was scared.

She talked her way out of the office somehow, not able to think clearly again until she was on the street outside the clinic and trying to figure out which way to go. She eyed the patients coming and going from the lobby, scanning for familiar faces, but soon gave that up. She watched the sky for falling pianos as she picked her way along Harvard Avenue toward work. Ninety-eight percent of the time she was so careful. So why was it that these 2-percent screw-ups continued to define her life?

Blossom

Maryk awoke from his cascade slumber wearing yester-day's clothes. He felt depleted. The cascade was like the digestive torpor following an unimaginably heavy meal.

He sat up on his office couch with his head in his hands. Freeley entered behind a knock. She was used to his cascades. He had only to tell her the cause.

"Pearse," he explained. "Most of the night."

"How bad is he?"

"Improved. But don't look so disappointed. He's dying all right."

Maryk rose and crossed to his desk chair. His office was a small room on the top floor of Special Pathogens Building Fifteen. His black bag rested on a windowsill and his tablet sat alone on his desk. There was no printer. Paper was unsanitary. It was a vector and if handled improperly could break the skin and even breach some gloves.

Freeley's auburn hair was tied back. She wore a beige blouse and cream pants and there was a quiet strength evident in her confident manner and relaxed hands as she stood between Maryk's desk and the door.

"You're here to update me on Lancet," he guessed.

She began. "First, I went through the possessions we kept from his condo and did trace pulls. Nothing there. I ran a laser over all contact surfaces, such as the knobs on the front door. The outside handle was covered with Lancet's prints, while the inside appeared to have been wiped clean. Faint prints remain on the inside door face, however, and are Lancet's."

Maryk stopped her there. "What do you know about fingerprints?"

"From various texts. Lancet's fingertips had some very distinct whorls. It's simple enough if you've got an argon-ion laser."

"Of course," he said. Nothing Freeley did could surprise him. "So if an unknown got inside the condo, they were invited in."

"So it would appear. Still, there was no sign of any struggle, and Reilly and Boone did indicate some level of depression on Lancet's part."

"That's their opinion," Maryk said. "Go on."

"Bathroom floor mat. One partial sneaker impression, common tread, flat and narrow, unisex brand. Size nine for men, eleven for women. Lancet was a nine, but this is a modern tread and doesn't match any vintage pairs in his closet. I followed up with a rather unscientific weight experiment, having different people step on the same mat and then measuring their impressions. Best estimate: one hundred ten to one hundred twenty pounds. I ran it a few times to be certain. Lancet weighed one-fifty-seven."

Maryk was feeling revived now. "What would a one-hundred-and-fifteen-pound person be doing in Lancet's bathroom?"

"Running hot water. I found an unridged smudge consistent with a gloved palm on the faucet handle. We pulled the traps and treated them with a chemical and it came up as Lancet's blood. This means nothing—he could have cut himself shaving months ago."

Maryk said, "You treated the traps with a chemical?"

Freeley shrugged. "Information is the cheapest commodity. You can access everything you need to know about flying to Venus and back. It's having the resources that counts."

"I'm impressed," he said.

"You're supposed to be. Finally, Lancet himself. I believe I've found a pinprick in post. A tiny premortem breach along the base of the hairline, just back of the lateral surface of the neck, and well hidden. But, toxicologically, his system is clean."

"A needle stick." Maryk's mind ran back to the footprint. "Medical personnel?"

"Impossible to tell. Consider the wrist lacerations. Two deep, neat incisions without any hesitation marks. Depressed or not, he was serious about destroying himself and causing some pain in the process. And it is a messy procedure for someone else to perform, with the rest of the place showing otherwise clean."

"But an unmatched sneaker print in the bathroom. A palm print at the sink. A pinprick."

"These are unexplained. And then there is Blossom."

"What about her?"

"I had hoped to resolve this before coming to you with it. We lost her yesterday. This is not unusual, as you know. It's difficult trailing someone who doesn't seem to know where she's going herself. But we activated the trace on her car, and late yesterday pinpointed it in a garage across from the CNN Center downtown."

"Near the church."

Freeley nodded. "Naturally."

The Enterprise Church was a cult movement derived from the works of twentieth-century science fiction writer Gene Roddenberry and popular Star Fleet conventions. Its members awaited the coming Rendezvous whereby an alien landing party would arrive on Earth to mete out justice for their murdered comrade, Jesus Christ. Blossom had been a devoted follower ever since her recovery.

Freeley said, "She wasn't there, but a member said some of them were out recruiting, or whatever they call it, for their church's ten-year Star Date anniversary gathering here in Atlanta, this New Year's Eve."

Maryk frowned. "Then Blossom remains unaccounted for? What about Milkmaid?"

Freeley shrugged dismissively. "Milkmaid is fine, the same."

"You're certain?"

"I saw her yesterday. Mystified as ever. Paranoid, hypochondriacal. She nearly walked into a Boston streetcar yesterday morning. But she is accounted for. Nothing going on there."

Maryk mulled things over. "Tell me exactly how we lost Blossom."

"Early-morning traffic. She jumped a red by accident and wriggled away from her tail, then didn't show up where we had expected her to."

"I've told them a dozen times," he said, "follow the person, not the car." Maryk stood. "I want Blossom located by sight. I want that immediately. I want an exact position on her until we can get to the bottom of this Lancet situation."

Freeley nodded. "I'll get on it myself."

Maryk was alone with Stephen in B4. Stephen's vitals had crashed overnight but his brain activity never flatlined and Maryk had successfully revived him. Stephen had been plateau for vitals since then and was starting to retain some IV meal. Pupil response evinced further improvement.

Maryk had prepped another 500 ml dose of Milkmaid serum. He was administering it when Stephen began to speak.

The nurse that morning had detailed occasional moans and a few instances of trembling in each arm. But nothing could have prepared Maryk to see Stephen stirring beneath him. Stephen's diminished facial features were like the features of a prototype of Stephen Pearse awaiting more cosmetic girth. His hands were the thin speckled hands of a man twice his age. The tube between Stephen's lips drew his head leftward and formed his dry mouth into an emotionless smirk. His lips opened and his whispered voice broke the controlled silence of B4.

"Bobby."

Then his eyes opened. Maryk stepped back and nearly dropped the empty glass ampule to the floor. Stephen's eyes were blood-red around the pale blue irises and distended inside depressed sockets.

Maryk reapproached the side of the gurney. He watched as the word again worked its way up Stephen's gaunt throat like a cartridge sliding into a rifle chamber.

"Bobby."

Stephen's dull eyes reached around the bright lab. He bared his thin lips around the tube as though he were sounding out the letter *e*. His teeth were yellow-gray like cheap ivory and too large now for his jaw. He was staring at the ceiling.

"Where am I?"

His pupils drifted subtly. He was going to pass out again.

Maryk said, "The BDC."

Stephen's throat was raw from the infection and the tubes. The words came out in gasps. *"Sick?"*

Maryk stood stiffly over him. Stephen's revival was nothing short of extraordinary. Maryk's success surprised even himself.

"Peter Maryk is treating you," Maryk said.

Stephen's eyelids closed. His brow went slack but his lips around the tube remained tense. He was still conscious. His blind eyes opened again and gazed up at the piped ceiling. There were full breaths between rasps. He still believed he was speaking to Bobby Chiles.

"Don't. Let. Maryk. Take over. BDC."

His jaw relaxed then and his lips parted with a sigh. His eyes closed again and he was out.

Maryk stood over him smiling harshly.

The console screen behind him beeped twice. Maryk went away from Stephen and turned to the keyboard.

A window opened on Freeley. She was standing before a cement wall under dusky sulfurous light. She was inside a parking garage. She spoke quickly but was otherwise composed. "Blossom is down," she said.

Maryk gripped the console. His gray eyes burned.

Freeley went on, "She was in the backseat of the car the entire time, slumped down. A day, at least. Same way: both wrists."

"Milkmaid," Maryk said at once.

"At work. Just confirmed it. Should I go?"

Maryk glowered at the console.

"Should I go?" she said again.

"No. You stay on Blossom. Tell them to stick tight to Milkmaid and don't let her out of their sight. I'm going up to Boston to bring her in myself."

The Alley

Melanie stood in the doorway to the narrow alley adjacent to the Penny University. It was raining, nighttime, but early still, and too early to be out already on her second cigarette break. Melanie didn't actually smoke. Her scarred lungs couldn't take it. But at the Penny University you had to work eight and a half hours in order to be paid for eight: healthy people were assigned their thirty-minute dinner break in one lump sum, meaning four hours of nonstop customers on either side, whereas nicotine junkies were rewarded for their disgusting habit with a fifteen-minute dinner and three floating five-minute smokers. Smoking breaks were impossible for the managers to monitor, so it was far and away worth the artless deception in order to be able to stretch five minutes of peace and quiet into ten or even fifteen minutes of pure customerless joy. These fake breaks were the only thing that kept her going. The alley was thick with exhaust from the cars on the street, and because of that she wound up sucking in some noxious fumes anyway, but as far as Melanie was concerned, sacrificing long-range health for short-range sanity was really no sacrifice at all.

The Penny University was a four-story brick tower that dominated the wide city corner of Commonwealth and Harvard avenues. It served anything brewed—coffee, tea, beer—and the fare that went with it. Melanie had been employed there as a *barista*—which, she had come to learn, was Spanish for "coffee jerk"—for a record four straight weeks now.

Her foot propped open the heavy door. At least it was only rain, not snow. The hot scent of coffee breathing behind her had seemed pleasant her first week; now it was like the cumulative sigh of a thousand waitresses, rankling the hair on the back of her head. Unseen Harvard Avenue was crowded at the entrance to the alley, and she could hear young voices laughing and tires whispering against the static of the rain, and see the headlights spraying the brick alley walls. Every university student in Boston spent at least one year living in the Allston-Brighton community of trolleys and alleyways and immigrants, and every one of them drifted like *chic*ly-bandaged zombies into the Penny University for a steaming cup of central nervous system stimulant on a drizzling Friday night.

Her breath misted out into the cold alley air as she hugged her chest over her red apron. Her foot had started to cramp, and just as she was repositioning her hip against the heavy black door, she heard a small noise from the other end of the alley. It was a purposeful thump, like a person kicking a wall. A single yellow safety light shone down upon the narrow car path and narrower curbs where the alley veered rightward and out of her view, dead-ending at the dumpsters. She watched the light for shadows, expecting to see some homeless person come stumbling out, zipping up. Something about the noise had sounded human.

Now there was the slightest odor, in itself not peculiar for that alley, but a scent far different from coffee grounds and turned cream. It struck Melanie as oddly familiar, which only magnified her sense of dread. It smelled like sickness. Melanie did something extraordinary then. She went back in from her five-minute nonsmoking break one minute early.

With the fire door closed to the quiet rain and the vats of trendily flavored beer groaning around her, she felt foolish about her fear and shook it off. Cutting short her sanity-preserving break did not bode well for the rest of the night. She wove a path back through the labyrinth of floor-to-ceiling vats to the work area behind the coffee counter, retying her red apron.

Beverly was working to her right, tamping an espresso filter at the rear of the coffee station. Beverly had mousy blond hair and choppy bangs that clung to the lashes of her sleepy eyes. "You're back early," she said over the prep chatter.

"Didn't want to miss anything." Melanie lingered there in the shadows of the twin vats, surveying the main floor. The motif inside was neo-gloom, all red neon and shiny black wood and moody shadow over each floor spun out from a central spiral stairway, with lots of nooks and crannies on the upper levels and plenty of ports for charging up student tablets. Bottom line, the Penny University was a caffeine bordello for the university smart set.

In Melanie's varied and vast work experience, wearing out jobs like they were nylons, she had found the sole redeeming quality of a retail or service-oriented position to be the camaraderie found among co-suffering, co-dependent co-workers. The Penny University, however, stood as the exception to this trench-mentality rule. The microbrewers hated the *baristas* who hated the pastry chefs and so on down the line.

Customers. Constantly customers. If the absentee owners prayed, they prayed to the God of Precipitation on Weekend Nights. Inclemency meant lines out the doors. Melanie watched the kids stamping off street grime onto the spongy entrance mats and could smell, even over the roasted beans, the wet-winter scent of coat sweat and dank wool; fleecy sheep herding together over boysenberry beer, or triple-foam, triple lattes, or super-steeped, hemp-brewed pots of tea.

As she was watching the crowded entrance, a man stepped in from the rain wearing a simple gray suit, standing out from the rest of the young, pained hipsters. The trunk-necked hand-stampers deferred to his flashed ID, and as the man returned his billfold to his pocket, Melanie saw that he wore latex gloves.

She resisted her overactive imagination as she watched from the shadows of the creaking vats. The man proceeded to the center island supply station, rather than straight into the coffee line or up the spiral stairs to the beer floor and beyond, stopping at the recycled napkins and flavored stirrers, eyeing the wide ground floor and allowing Melanie a good, long look.

It was the well-dressed man from the trolley, the one who had pushed her out of the path of the oncoming streetcar. The shoulders and pant cuffs of his cheap suit were dark with rain. She wondered for a moment if it had been him out in the alley, but realized there was no way he could have gotten back to the entrance so fast.

Two other men, whom she recognized as semiregular customers, rose

almost simultaneously on opposite ends of the floor and wandered close
to the man in the suit. They were dressed like students, though as she
now paid attention to them, she saw that they were definitely older.

A wave like a charge of electricity left her motionless and buzzing.

The dark-haired man from the trolley started to move. He crossed
from the center island, scanning the vats as he approached the mess
counter. He couldn't see her there in the shadows. The man appeared
concerned.

The other two fanned back out from the center island. Kids near them,
as though sensing some sort of trouble, moved out of their way.

The dark-haired one from the trolley skipped the line and went
straight to the *barista* well where the drinks were being prepared. Beverly
was foaming up some milk when the man caught her eye. Melanie tried
to whisper to her to wait, but the man was too close.

Beverly started toward him with the milk-frothing pitcher in hand.
Even with wet shoulders and his drowned-puppy hair, the man was dark
and blandly attractive and smiling forwardly, which guaranteed that Beverly would be on her way to help.

They met. Melanie could hear none of it, what with the orders being
taken, the click and clatter of spoons and saucers, and the piped-in blues
overhead. She watched the man produce his billfold—careful, in a conspicuous way, to display his identification only to Beverly, as though letting her in on something. Some sixth sense must have told him he had
an easy mark. Beverly set the hot pitcher on the countertop and pulled
down her mouth guard without taking her eyes from his credentials.

Melanie never saw them near her apartment or her work, only on the
streets. That was how she was able to keep her sanity about being followed.

"Health" something, he seemed to be saying to Beverly, as in "health
matter," or "health emergency." Beverly evidently shared his concern, as
she was nodding slowly. Melanie began her retreat just as Beverly turned
and looked back from the cocoa-powdered counter, her ratty blond bangs
twitching over blinking mouse eyes. She appeared to be alarmed, searching the vat spaces, at first not seeing Melanie. Then she did see her there.
Melanie shook her head, pleadingly, but Beverly jerked back and elbowed

the stainless steel pitcher clatteringly to the floor. The blue tile went white with boiling milk.

Panic, unreasoned and immediate, burst within Melanie, and she turned and took off running. She threaded back through the fat shadows, stumbling and misjudging a turn on the wet floor and careening sharply into one of the vats, her bony shoulder prodding a light *boom* and her bag strap snagging on a gauge. She nearly ripped her arm off freeing herself, lunging between two copper bellies back toward the red EXIT sign over the side door. She hit the disabled alarm bar with both hands and spilled hard into the slick alleyway, flopping over the wet curb outside and almost falling down. Her momentum carried her into the far brick wall, which she pushed off from, fleeing toward the closed end of the alley.

She stopped at the beginning of the turn, seeing the pallid safety light through the rain and realizing she would be trapped in the dead end. She spun and ran back up the alley, fighting the apron tangling between her legs, past the door to the Penny University as it burst open and the dark-haired man from the trolley splashed out.

"Wait!" he said, reaching for her.

But she was past him, running up the alley toward the street. She went ten or twelve steps before headlights swung in front of her, brightly sweeping the slicked walls as a large car bumped over the corner into the alley, bouncing on its suspension, bearing down upon her. She stopped and threw out her hands, and the car skidded to a stop, fishtailing to the brick wall. The passenger door swung open and barred her only exit. The shadow of a large man emerged.

Her bag. She went into it madly, up to her elbow, fumbling for her Mace.

He closed the car door and stepped forward through the headlights. Behind her, the dark-haired man's footsteps scuffed off the wet curb.

"*Mace,*" she whispered crazily, jogging the contents of her bag, and her hairbrush and gum wrappers spilled out onto the tar. She backed sideways from the headlights to the wall, her lungs beginning to contract.

The man from the car strode through the rain-filled beams with a thick, quick leg. He appeared impossibly large before her, his face lost in shadow, the headlights catching his white hair and giving it an odd glow.

White hair.

Her breath left her. Something happened to her then, like a thing opening or unfolding inside her.

She found her inhaler again and flung it away desperately, digging deeper, shaking her bag, backing up against the wet alley wall in his shrinking shadow, dizzy with revelation and a lack of air. She trapped the cylinder in the corner of her bag finally and whipped it out. She fooled with the safety guard over the trigger, fooled with it, *fooled with it,* then got it free as his shadow fell over her.

His hand closed around her hand and the Mace. She looked up and saw his face then, the cool gray eyes, the plunging nose. It was the face that was always missing from her paintings. Something overturned inside her, a revolution of head and stomach. Her neck bucked as her chest contracted, and she pitched forward.

She vomited. She was gasping for breath, sagging, her legs bowing beneath her as his hand remained around hers, the only thing holding her up.

Behind her, breathless:

Where was she? Outside?

Then, from above—deep, strange, stern:

Sloppy. The last thing we needed was a commotion.

Melanie choked on a hollow groan. Her vision swam as her body went limp. The headlights shining on the man's black shoes drifted and twisted, and then abruptly stopped twisting, and the dark rain stopped falling all at once.

The girl passed out. Maryk held her dangling by her hand. "Psychosomatic," he explained to the others. "Put her in the car."

They took her from him. Pasco came off the curb with an explanation. "I lost her inside," Pasco said. "She was hidden in back behind the counter. I thought something might have happened."

Maryk held up a gloved hand to stop him. "We have people taking down plates and VIN numbers?"

"Every vehicle within a three-block radius."

"I want the names and addresses of everyone inside. Then shutter this coffeehouse, or whatever it is, for one week. A health hazard, to cover your blunder. Make it real."

Another Special Path agent nearby looked up from her tablet. "We're into her apartment. Everything's quiet."

Maryk was kicking the vomit off his shoes. "Start packing it up then. Take special care with any paintings. They are to be delivered directly to me."

He was looking into the alley as he said this. He saw a shadow flicker across the dim light at the far end where the alley curved.

Maryk turned to Pasco. "Where does the alley go?"

"Nowhere," Pasco said. "It's a dead end."

Maryk unbuckled his black bag. "Wait with her," he directed.

He started into the alley alone. He passed the door to the coffeehouse and pulled a small syringe from his bag as he rounded the short curve.

The cul-de-sac ended at three high brick walls. A security light was trained down upon the buckled tar. Dumpsters and cracked pallets and flattened cardboard boxes lay in the dull shadows along the slowly weeping walls.

Maryk moved to the center of the light. There was a faint odor of decay distinct from mere waste or spoiled food. The scent was animal. It smelled as though something had crawled in there to die.

A manhole cover shifted as Maryk stepped over it. The *clink* reported loudly off the high walls.

Maryk got down on his knees on the wet tar. He worked a gloved finger inside the hole in the iron disk and tugged. It did not budge. A grunting second effort raised the disk just enough so that he could grip the cover and drag it up and over the lip of the manhole.

It was black space inside and he could just make out an iron ladder leading down. There were scuffs on the top few rusted rungs where shoe bottoms had stepped. Maryk left his bag next to the hole and started down the ladder with the syringe. He had no flashlight. The clank of the rungs echoed as he descended into darkness. He dropped the last few feet to the bottom with a quiet splash.

The echo told him there were widening tunnels on either side. Maryk listened to the dripping water without taking a step in either direction.

He felt the sensation of being watched but then decided he could not entirely trust his senses. His claustrophobia was already narrowing the dim circle of light above him.

He pulled himself one-handedly back up the rusted ladder and out of the dark mouth of the hole. He stood in the open air of the empty alley with the rain falling straight around him. The syringe remained low at his side like a knife.

The Living
Machine

They returned to the BDC that night and Maryk broke off from the rest and made his way alone to Building Seven. He descended to the subbasement and passed through the five staging rooms into the netherworld of B4.

Stephen's gurney was pulled away from the aquarium window to the edge of the work counter. His eyes were closed and the white bedsheet rose and fell between the black straps buckled across his chest, waist, and thighs.

Maryk brought up his chart and inspected the six different intravenous lines. He exchanged bags and feed bottles. Stephen's blood pressure had stabilized and the nitroglycerin drip was no longer warranted. Maryk wondered at Stephen's unexplainable progress. He prepped a dosage out of an upturned ampule and uncapped a y-valve in Stephen's right forearm.

Stephen's red eyes stopped him. He was watching Maryk and Maryk froze with the hypodermic in his hands. Stephen's eyes were bright. He appeared to recognize Maryk.

"Am I dead?" he said.

These were the first words they had exchanged in years.

"You're in the B4 lab," Maryk said. "At the BDC."

Stephen swallowed. Speech was painful. "The lab?"

Maryk nodded. He finished the serum injection. "Safest right now."

Stephen's head turned back and forth on the pillow. His range of movement impressed Maryk. He realized that Stephen was shaking his head.

"Not Plainville," Stephen said hollowly. "Still alive."

134 T H E   B L O O D   A R T I S T S

Maryk held the empty ampule for Stephen to see. The label read MILKMAID. "Only because of this."

"Serum," he recognized. "Code names."

"That's all over now," Maryk said. "Two of them are dead. Murdered. We don't know why."

The muscles in Stephen's depressed face strained against his flesh. "Why straps?" he said. His hands clutched emptily at his sides.

"To keep you still. I operated."

"In a lab?" Stephen struggled to raise his head off the pillow. He was becoming agitated. "What have you done to me?" he said.

Maryk located the bottle of morphine over the bed. He followed the feed line down to the dose administrator and doubled the rate of morphine drip. "I saved your life," Maryk said.

"What have you done to me?" he said again.

Maryk watched Stephen's breathing deepen and his eyes narrow to slits. Stephen was struggling valiantly to remain awake.

"What have you . . ."

Maryk remained looking over him until Stephen fell murmuring to sleep.

Maryk felt the first dragging symptoms of the impending cascade as he made his way toward Building Two. His exposure to Stephen had weakened him but he had one more task to perform that night. The Library and Reports Section was empty. He entered a dedicated user station and logged onto the bureau's Genetech II mainframe.

The Genetech was a "living machine" molecular-based computer that used DNA goop rather than an electronic chip as its processor. A beaker full of properly managed DNA could crunch more arithmetic than the combined circuitry of every conventional computer on the planet. Human DNA was nature's microchip and its capabilities had been harnessed to power the machine that powered the BDC.

What the Genetech did was coordinate genetic algorithms: lines of code that acted like living organisms in competition to evolve to beneficial solutions. The codes mated and mutated to form novel combinations in a Darwinian reserve of ones and zeroes. Less optimal remedies fell extinct as only the fittest survived.

The minivan-sized Genetech brain ran bureau life functions at the highest efficiency in everything from coordinating employee schedules to monitoring experiment conditions. It managed the U.S. Genetic Database and international LifeLink epidemic alert networks. It oversaw security in the pathogen vault freezer of Building Thirteen. Each bureau tablet worked as a low-power satellite borrowing off the assets of the high-capacity digital network the Genetech managed.

Maryk called up the code name files. No one had accessed the reports recently except Stephen Pearse. Yet somehow someone had learned of the existence of the only three Plainville survivors. Everything Maryk had now was riding on Milkmaid.

Maryk initiated a preloaded program "worm" designed to wipe the entire network clean of all records and reports relating to Lancet, Blossom, and Milkmaid. The code name project was terminated. Within twenty-three seconds all records of the project's existence irrevocably ceased to exist.

The Telling

Melanie rolled over and over and finally she broke out of her fitful sleep. She sat up straight in an unfamiliar bed in a small, unfamiliar room. She was alone. She recognized her work apron and black cardigan sweater, but not the wooden chair and desk they were draped over, nor anything else. She threw back the sheets but was otherwise still dressed.

Panic set in. She rushed out of the bed at once, then fell into the wall and grabbed it to keep from collapsing. Her head. She winced against the blinding throb. She was always reeling, always walking into things, always coming to; she was never already there. She tasted acid in her mouth, and the abduction in the alley came back to her at once.

Margarine sunlight poured through the room's only window. It was not the cool December sun of Boston. With one hand shading her eyes, she pulled herself toward its warmth and squinted out the window. She was three or four stories up from grass that was postcard green. She saw immense white stone buildings with lush trees all around, and young people strolling the grounds, satchels tossed over their shoulders. Students, of course. They haunted her. For one roseate moment she imagined she was back at Brown, getting ready to go to breakfast with friends, and nothing had happened yet to her family or her body.

She turned from the window. It was a college dormitory room: the empty bookshelves attached to the tawny-colored wood desk, the thumb-sized strips of missing paint scoring the plaster walls where posters once hung. There were two doors, one open and leading to a closet. She rushed to the other door. The knob turned freely under her hand.

The man from the trolley stood quickly out of a small chair across the hallway. Melanie kept a tight grip on the doorknob, blood beating against her head, while he stood awkwardly still. She didn't think she could make it past him. Even if she did, she had no idea where to go.

"Where am I?" she said.

"Atlanta," the man said.

She looked up and down the hall. It smelled of socks and hair spray. She said, "No, I'm not."

He wore an identification tag on his shirt, with his picture and the name PASCO. "There's a shower down this way," he pointed. "I'm to take you for a meeting in"—he had a tablet gadget in his hand, and tapped a key—"twenty-five minutes."

Melanie closed the door on him. She walked back to the foot of the unfamiliar bed and sat down. Sealed moving cartons were stacked near the empty desk, and she was certain, her intuition commingled with despair, that the clothes hanging inside the closet were from her own.

Her right arm felt stiff. She pushed back her shirtsleeve and discovered a small brown bandage taped over the pocket of her elbow. She touched it lightly, then peeled back one adhesive end, pulling up the pad. There was a fresh needle mark over the largest visible vein.

She did not shower, but did emerge from the room at the appropriate time and followed the man named Pasco outside across a university campus to one of the larger white stone buildings. He walked her squeaking down a waxed floor past closed classroom doors and into a deep, steeply set, empty lecture hall. They descended the blue-carpeted aisle past rounded rows of blue-cushioned seats facing a lectern and a viewing screen on the front wall. A breakfast tray was set before the center seat of the first row, and he showed her to it.

"You were out for ten hours," he said. "We thought you might be hungry."

"Wait." He had started to leave. "What am I doing here?"

His apologetic wince kept the rest of her questions at bay. "He'll be out in just a minute," he said.

He walked back up the aisle, and the click of the door closing resounded throughout the hall. She had no taste for the food, but reached for a tall glass of orange juice and drained it. Only after its coolness had coated her raw throat did she think that the drink might have been drugged. She was setting the empty glass back on the tray when the door beneath the wall screen opened and the white-haired man walked through.

The sight of his hair and black shoes made her feel immediately sick again. He crossed to the lectern in front of her and laid a tablet on top of it and a black doctor's bag underneath. The gloved hands. The pearl-white hair. The white shirt buttoned under the thick neck, the dull black pants. He had walked straight out of one of her paintings.

He was regarding her too, not curiously but clinically, in the manner of an archaeologist coming upon an unusual rock. There was something about the man's face, the squareness of his block jaw, the pride of his nose, the perfect smoothness of his flesh, that seemed to her truer than true. He did not seem real. He seemed wrong somehow, inactual. She looked at his condomized hands, the latex skin stretched tight over thick fingers. She looked at his stark gray eyes, like cold cement tunnels into which his real pupils had withdrawn.

Her stomach turned over and sent up a belch of orange juice that nearly choked her.

"You remember me," he said, a stern voice giving her heart a good quick squeeze. It was not a question or a revelation but a statement, a point of understanding between them. "We remember each other."

His strange voice touched something deep within her, and a memory like a sealed bottle cast not far enough from shore washed back to her. She saw him at the foot of a white-railed bed before a drawn plastic curtain, arms crossed in observation much as he was eyeing her now. She saw his bare, white-haired head as contrasted with the small, silent faces inside the yellow hoods clustered around him. The hospital. She had never forgotten her time in rehab, but he hadn't been a part of that. He had been a part of the fever. He was that doctor.

His presence filled the lecture well, and Melanie felt trapped. "Where am I?" she said.

"Emory University. The Rollins School of Public Health. Just next door to the Bureau for Disease Control."

Disease Control. The words filled her with fear. "I'm going crazy," she said, "aren't I?"

"No, you're not. You have been brought here for your own protection. We were never properly introduced. My name is Dr. Maryk."

She felt woozily sick again. She was grateful for the tray and the imaginary space it put between them. His voice seemed to rise out of her subconscious as much as it did his throat. She could feel her mind opening up again to the sickness, the fever.

"It's"—she didn't like to say the word, didn't like to hear it said—*"Plainville"*—though once uttered, the world had the effect of freeing her, steadying her, like a child's first, daring curse—"isn't it?"

He continued to study her, as though everything she said was being memorized for later evaluation. "You experienced some respiratory distress back there in the alley," he said. He produced her inhaler from his breast pocket. "We'll have to reevaluate your prescription."

"I need that," she said.

His gaze never wavered. She recalled him looming over her face in the hospital, examining her, the pain of the bright light on her eyes.

"I kept quiet," she said.

He nodded. "Of course you did. Who would have believed you? Closure for the public meant no survivors."

She waded through the brutality of his words. "I was the only survivor," she said.

He nodded again. "That was what each of you was told."

She struggled with this, then turned and scanned the coliseum of empty blue seats.

"Just two others," he said. "They couldn't be with us today. We've had some trouble."

Her hands found the hard plastic armrests. She was queasy and scared again. "If I'm sick," she said, "I won't go through that again."

His silver eyes darkened. "You are not sick. Quite the contrary. We need to know if anyone out of the ordinary tried to contact you recently."

"Just you people. Following me around. Whoever you are."

"We are your benefactors." He rested one gloved hand on the lectern. "The other two survivors are dead. Both of them were murdered. It stands that whoever killed them will want to kill you."

A strange smile floated to Melanie's face, and she felt it twist there. "I'm not going to remember any of this, am I?" she said. "I'm going to wake up back in my bed, with needle tracks in my arm from whatever you keep injecting me with."

He stepped away from the lectern. "Those are not injections," he said. He began pacing back and forth, slowly. "How much do you know about Plainville?"

"I grew up there."

"I mean in the current vernacular. The virus, the disease that burned through your town."

She felt herself withdrawing. She realized she didn't want to know any more. She just wanted to forget. She wanted to wake up and not remember. Melanie looked resolutely at the lectern and not at him.

"Central Africa," he said. "Many viruses originate there. The prevailing theory behind this is that man himself originated there as well. Six years ago, two doctors, myself and another, were called upon to investigate a purported outbreak of smallpox in the Congo rain forest. Early-stage Plainville, as we now know it, closely resembles smallpox. We traced the path of the virus back to its source, an illegal uranium mine in an underground cavern rife with latent viruses. It was like a poisoned well in the center of a small town; no one drank from it too long."

Her gaze did not leave the lectern. She refused to look at him.

"The virus the miners brought up had been trapped in that closed system for centuries, its RNA core undergoing constant bombardment from radioactive uranium deposits. It was an ancient agent, in fact the genetic forebear of smallpox. The pathogen was too unstable and too annihilative to combat. We had to cut off the threat at the source. We neutralized the virus aboveground and buried the cave in the jungle. The other doctor with me was named Pearse. I assume you've heard of him."

Of course she knew of Dr. Stephen Pearse. "He's dead," she said. They had all been talking about it at work.

"Dying," he corrected her, resuming his slow pacing. "So. The Congo, New Year's Day, 2011. Plainville, Massachusetts, one week after Easter, 2012. Viruses respect no human boundaries, no walls or checkpoints or borders, only natural limitations, such as temperature, pH, ultraviolet light, and the availability of viable hosts and mobile vectors. But they do leave footprints: the outbreaks themselves. So how does a virus of unparalleled lethality trek from a buried cave in the equatorial jungles of central Africa to a small town in Massachusetts without any traceable link, no intermediate outbreak, or confirmed human carrier? The answer is that it does not. It is essentially an epidemiological impossibility. Viruses do not fly on gossamer wings and can always be traced back to their source. And yet somehow this virus rose up out of the ashes of the African rain forest and seized a small American town.

"The disease appeared simultaneously in the Plainville public school system, its town hall—whose infected carried it to a town meeting held that same night—and the office of a local pediatrician. The pediatrician, Dr. Joseph Weir, unknowingly passed the infection along to his patients over the following three days before manifesting early-stage symptoms himself. While he declined to be examined professionally by another doctor, he did isolate himself from his two children. His secretary, who was also his wife, was fielding calls at home from patients and neighbors with similar illnesses, and just before leaving to bring her dying husband to the hospital—and already exhibiting symptoms herself—she telephoned the BDC hot line to report the mystery illness. With that one phone call Mrs. Anne Weir saved, at minimum, one hundred million human lives. Because Plainville was about to explode."

Melanie felt numb. She hadn't heard another person speak the names of her parents in over four years. "His appointments," she said.

"We checked. He didn't contract it from any of his patients. We determined that much. Plainville was a town of just over twelve thousand, and we reconstructed virtually every resident's whereabouts and movements throughout the town over the days leading up to the outbreak, and still failed to pinpoint the index case: Plainville's 'Patient Zero.' Somehow the virus seemed to have attacked a pediatrician, the town offices, and the public school system all at the same time.

"Plainville is a genetically specialized killer, not just of humans but all animals, reptiles, rodents, and many insects, even and especially plants. Every living thing, except birds; birds in this case are *reservoirs*, and by that we mean that they can host and transmit the disease but are not sickened by it. Like all viruses, Plainville tries to transform the host by slipping into its cells and shooting them full of genetic material—essentially, an attempt to convert the organism into a virus itself. But this conversion is biologically impossible, and so the host sickens and eventually one or the other—the human immune system or the virus—prevails. But Plainville is not a routine DNA virus. It is a retrovirus, an RNA virus, like HIV, infiltrating and disarming the body's defenses; but unlike HIV, which slowly drips into cells, allowing us time to manage and compensate for the AIDS–related complex over the long term, Plainville works with the greatest efficiency. It is uniquely corruptive, riding the bloodlines to every organ as one after another they begin to fail."

Her attention had drifted off, remembering her parents before they were taken away from her. Eventually she realized he had stopped and was waiting for her to notice.

"Boring, hmm?" he said. "Tedious? You didn't get this far in your premed courses at Brown?"

Her indifference fell away, and she looked up at him.

"You'll want to pay attention to this, I think," he went on. "The immune system is your body's monitor. I.S. cells stand guard against invading pathogens—bacteria, viruses, cancer cells—any organism that threatens the health of the body, not only by fighting these attackers, but also by repairing any damage, and even afterward, cleaning up the remnants of a battle. It is a complex, interactive network—your body's police force, its protector.

"Similarly, the Bureau for Disease Control is the immune system of the human species: a vast, interactive network answering distress calls and assigning specialists to investigate and eliminate microbial threats around the world. The disease Mrs. Weir described was one of unknown etiology and therefore assigned to the Special Pathogens Section, which I head. The circumstances were peculiar enough that I traveled to Massachusetts myself to investigate the break. The symptomology was immediately familiar to me, but it was the vegetation about the town, the infected trees and plants, that confirmed my diagnosis. I remember the house-by-house evacuation under the blare of an old civil defense alarm, and our coming upon a luncheon meeting of the Plainville Ladies' Garden Club, and all the old women gathered hysterically, their daffodils and spring lilies— freshly potted, carefully arranged for the affair—all grown leathery and silver-black and wild.

"I communicated the threat back to Atlanta and the BDC responded in force, doctors, scientists, and BioCon troops converging on the town. You might remember this much. We blocked off highways and clamped all arteries into and out of the county. We closed airports in Boston and Rhode Island and called off school for days, effectively throwing a blanket over the entire region. The magnitude of the outbreak had forced us to go public, so we enlisted the media to help us track down carriers. For a while there in Massachusetts it was biological martial law.

"There were more than twelve thousand residents of Plainville, and almost every one of them was wiped out. Another eighty-one hundred satellite cases became infected and also died, most of them residents of surrounding communities. Only four infected people had boarded airplanes before the shutdown; those flare-ups were ultimately contained. Given one more day, the infection would have metastasized exponentially beyond Boston and the East Coast and across the country, and conceivably from there to every neighborhood of the world. A holocaust. To this day, very few people realize just how close we came.

"I set up triage in a hospital in nearby North Attleboro, spending most of my time there, treating the afflicted, learning what I could about the disease. Traditional treatments were unsuccessful, so I began to look into more experimental procedures, all of which failed, except one. Ten early-stage patients were selected for a trial program, each because their symptomatic development appeared to be lagging behind the norm. The trick with Plainville is to get to the infected host as early as possible. Later we learned that one of the ten happened to be the pediatrician Weir's twenty-year-old daughter. Her brother was already dead, his immune system weak from a recent bout with Lyme disease."

As she looked up at him, her stare became harder and harder. Was he dragging her back through all of this just to be cruel?

"Of the original ten, three survived—barely—following extensive surgery, therapy, and subsequent rehabilitation, including massive transfusions of blood. We have tried to repeat this process since, on others, and never succeeded—"

"How?"

Her interruption surprised him. "The blood transfusions were imperative," he said. "But it was more than that. Something about these three patients. They were different. Certain people are born biologically gifted, in ways that under normal living circumstances usually never come to light. Three such cases out of a pool of only twelve thousand was just extraordinary good fortune on our part. Suddenly we found ourselves with three survivors of the lethal Plainville virus. Our next step was to determine whether or not they had built up antibodies to the disease, and lab tests proved conclusively that all three had. Cell samples from these 'long-term nonprogressors' as they were termed, or LNPs, repelled the Plainville virus. This allowed some hope for development of a vaccine, but two problems persisted. First, Blossom."

He went to the lectern and opened his tablet. He tapped some keys and a photograph of a middle-aged woman with short, straight, ready-to-go brown hair appeared on the wide wall screen. Melanie saw that the image had been cropped from a larger, family portrait.

"Each LNP was assigned a code name for confidentiality. Blossom was a homemaker, a mother of two, worked mornings in a local craft store. Her family was 'old Plainville,' and she lost every relative she had to the disease. Her immune system damage was severe, and compromised the quality of the disease-fighting antibodies in her blood."

He cleared the image and replaced it with a snapshot of a young man sitting shirtless in a battered lawn chair on a lawn of gray-yellow grass. His image toasted the empty lecture hall with an open can of Old Milwaukee, and Melanie thought she recognized him, vaguely.

"Lancet, you may have known. He graduated from Plainville High School and returned to work there part-time as a janitor. But his bout with the disease had damaged his spleen, impairing its ability to filter impurities out of his blood."

He changed images a third time, and there on the large screen was a high school yearbook photograph of a chocolate-haired teenager wearing her mother's gold cross pendant and a hopeful smile. Her chin rested on the back of a pudgy hand holding a small, simple violet, and a cheap photographic effect gave her glass earrings a prismatic glow.

"Milkmaid's blood, however, emerged undamaged," Maryk said. "Her blood was optimal."

Melanie's jaw trembled as she stared up, low-eyed, at the photograph of the stocky girl in the pale blue dress. She remembered that day and all the outfits she had brought with her to the session, and how pleased she had been with the result.

"Milkmaid," Maryk said looking up at the screen. "Premed at Brown, following in her father's footsteps. But then, junior year, she ran out of academic steam. Took a leave of absence from school and moved back home. Worked as an assistant at the local pet hospital."

He turned back to her, and Melanie felt her fear turning into hostility.

"So Plainville had been contained. Most assumed it was vanquished, but I was unconvinced. There was also the concern that the virus might somehow reactivate itself in these survivors after a period of latency, and render them infectious once again. Yet I could hardly confine all three in the hospital. There was no guarantee that they would even voluntarily comply with the research, and anyway, I don't favor the closed setting and sterile conditions of a laboratory. Ideal results achieved under ideal conditions are unreal results, and I required a real-world solution. So a campaign was undertaken to monitor the LNPs upon their release. Inducements were made to encourage all three to relocate here, to Atlanta."

He replaced the portrait of the old, forgotten Melanie with a more recent photograph of the woman known as Blossom. She appeared much changed, thinner, harder-looking, handing out leaflets on a street corner. Her hair was cut short and she wore a T-shirt with an small insignia over the breast. Melanie could make out the words on the front of her shirt, "Live Long."

"As I said, Plainville has a varied and pronounced effect upon the brain. Blossom, after her recovery, was not the same person she had been before her illness. She became preoccupied with the future, joining a fringe religious order. She was not employable, and we doubted she could even survive on her own. She was therefore awarded a sweepstakes prize through the mail: a weekly stipend and free rent in an Atlanta apartment complex. She took this to be a religious sign and relocated immediately."

He then put up what appeared to be a kind of surveillance photograph of Lancet: now older, cleaner, shaved, and better dressed. He was conversing with a customer from behind a store counter.

"Lancet also emerged from his illness a changed person. But he became fixated on the past, manifested in a preoccupation with the popular culture of his youth. A poor credit rating from his previous life prevented

145

him from opening a nostalgia retail store in the Boston area, but at a franchise fair there he was offered an attractive deal on some prime retail space in the Underground Mall in downtown Atlanta and accepted without question. For whatever reason, Lancet became a merchant of his past."

Maryk cleared the wall screen.

"But Milkmaid's change was the most intriguing. She was found to have developed certain remarkable, inexplicable artistic talents, though she had never so much as touched a paintbrush before the disease. She was unschooled and did not attend museums or galleries of any kind. She never bothered to sign her canvases, or even complete many of them. She seemed to have no interest in the business of art, and sold the paintings only as was necessary to pay her rent."

Melanie went cold. "You," she said. "You were my so-called patron."

"Through one of my investigators. But you resisted all entreaties to come to Atlanta. We even tried appealing to your veterinary bent: a letter of invitation from the Emory School of Medicine; the cat hospital in Decatur; an entry-level position with the local ASPCA—all rebuffed or ignored."

She saw it all now. None of those strange job offers had ever made any sense to her.

"We purchased your paintings to keep you going," he said, "though on several occasions we wound up funneling money directly into your bank account, and paid bills you forgot to pay. Evidently you never bothered to balance your statements. We watched out for you, took care of you. We even pushed you out of the way of oncoming trolleys. For over four years we have been with you: not every minute, and not every place, but comprehensively enough to ensure that you remained healthy and always within our reach."

Her stare burned into the vacuum of space between them. "Endometriosis," she said.

"Just an excuse to get at more of your blood, as well as to sample some other fluids for research. Only rarely did we require a blood pull that could not wait for a regular doctor's appointment. This was the exception, not the rule. My people would slip into your apartment during the night, but rarely did they need to put you out for more than seven or eight hours at a time."

"Oh my God."

"As I said, early on there was hope for a vaccine. The stakes were very high. I tried to give you a life while we did this critical work. But then the outbreaks started."

She was reeling. "Outbreaks?"

"We had to cover them up, for obvious reasons. Blamed something else each time. There have been five subsequent breaks since Plainville. The first occurred thirteen months later, at an 'Engaged Encounter' weekend for prenuptial Catholics in a Franciscan retreat north of Tallahassee, Florida. All fifty-three participants died, including the cafeteria and ministerial staffs. Fortunately for us, the location was isolated, and therefore easily contained. We blamed a rare salmonella. At subsequent outbreaks, we began experimenting with serum derived from your blood, as well as the blood of the others. Only yours has proved consistently successful. There is a time factor involved, as I said. Success requires immediate intervention. The most recent reemergence occurred less than two weeks ago, in South Carolina."

As she was sorting through all of this, he put up on screen the image of a naked man lying facedown across a bed. There was blood on the floor by the man's hands. Melanie quickly looked away.

"Lancet," said Maryk. "Three days ago. It looked like a suicide at first."

He changed the image to that of a corpse stuffed facedown into the backseat of a car.

"Blossom," he said. "Very few people know about Plainville, know that it did not die in that small town in southeastern Massachusetts. And no one, save a core group of people working directly under me, knew about the survivors. You are a closely held secret, which is why we are meeting here and not inside the BDC. Are you certain you don't remember anyone else following you recently? Perhaps something in the alley last night?"

She was staring at the screen. The back of the corpse's T-shirt was wrinkled and dark, but Melanie could just make out the words "And

Prosper." Then Maryk clicked off the image, and her gaze settled sullenly upon the carpeted floor.

"We had planned to cut you all loose as soon as we derived a vaccine," he said. "But the Plainville bug is too complex, and constantly changing. It burns bright and fast and then wriggles away somehow, only to pop up in a slightly different form again behind us. There will be no vaccine. The only existing treatment is the antibody remedy of your blood serum."

She was wondering when the screaming would begin, if it would be soon or much later. Probably very soon. She looked up at Maryk standing before her, the white-haired man of her fever dreams. "You ruined my life," she said.

He approached her then, enormous and imposing, until only the tray table of untouched food separated them. "On the contrary," he said, "I believe I saved your life."

"No." She nodded at the high school portrait that had long since vanished from the wall screen. "You changed me. You made me into something else."

The door clicked above her, and Maryk glanced up at the person entering. Then he came around the tray table, to her side. He knew enough to choose her good, left ear. She turned away from him as Pasco descended to the bottom step.

Maryk said, "This had to be done. I could not just cure you and let you walk away. Plainville is catastrophic to every human being on this planet—except you. You alone are immune to it now."

"If this is all so good," she said too loudly, "then why does somebody want to kill me?"

She sensed him straightening, pulling back. "That is something I don't know yet," he said. "Stephen Pearse: He was not infected in a lab accident. He was infected while treating a room full of patients—in Orangeburg, South Carolina—who inexplicably awoke from chronic, clinical catatonia infected with a newly mutated strain of the Plainville virus. Stephen Pearse has Plainville, and yet he is still alive today—because of the antibodies your immune system generates, which I have nurtured and seeded him with. We were only too late to cure him. But your blood is sustaining Stephen Pearse. You are the only thing keeping him alive."

This couldn't be true. Not someone like Dr. Pearse. She sat stunned as Maryk returned to the lectern. He was gathering his things. She realized that the lesson was over.

"You can't keep me here," she said.

He stopped on his way out. "It is no longer a question of personal freedom. The reason I have told you all this is because Plainville lives on, and you alone have the blood I need to combat it, to save human lives. You will be safe here. Finals are almost over, and the students will be leaving to begin their Christmas break. You will remain here under my care at least until I know what is happening. Dr. Pasco now will take you to the school cafeteria, and there you will eat." Maryk had started past her for the stairs. "Above all else," he said, "we need you to remain healthy."

Thunderstruck and voiceless, Melanie watched as Maryk climbed the blue steps to the exit.

Exsanguination

Freeley pointed with a capped surgical marker. "See the blunt force injury here, the parietal lobe, right side of the cranium? The intruder rose up from the backseat and brought an object across like this"—she made a right-handed whipping motion across the front of her body—"incapacitating Blossom. Then she was pulled over the seat back and the incisions were made in both wrists."

Blossom's bluish corpse lay facedown atop the stainless steel autopsy table. A rubber block beneath her shoulders arched her neck and shaved head. Cellulite pinches pitted her sagging buttocks and thighs. Her fingers were tipped black.

Freeley wore a scrub gown, mask, sleeve protectors, skullcap, and blue rubber gloves. "The keys were in the ignition of the car," she continued. "All four doors were locked, with both rear windows rolled down. We got no prints off the door handles or inside panels except glove smudges, which we may have left ourselves. Blossom kept plants in the car, two small spider plants—did you know that? For company. In any case, the plastic pots were still glued to either end of the dash but the plants themselves were gone. Most of the soil was still there, some spilled onto the floorboards."

"Stolen plants?" Maryk said.

"Could be."

"You say the rear windows were rolled down. The window in Lancet's bedroom was open too."

Freeley nodded and positioned the overhead magnifying lens to illuminate the back of Blossom's neck. Within the bluish ridges of flaking skin below the hairline was a single red dot breach. Maryk examined it.

"Toxicology again clean," Freeley added.

Maryk straightened. "It's not an injection," he said.

Freeley said, "What do you mean?"

He walked around the end of the table to the other side. He was remembering his meeting with the girl. She had thought they were injecting her with something when in reality they had been pulling her blood.

"I mean they were purposefully bled," he said. He pointed to the deep incisions on Blossom's upturned wrists. "We assumed these murders were made to resemble suicides. Each, in fact, was an exsanguination." Maryk pointed to the needle stick magnified on Blossom's neck. "This is a blood pull. Lancet and Blossom were sampled before their deaths. The bleeding was meant to cover up the crime of the stolen blood: two homicides to mask two petty thefts."

"But who would want their blood? And why? No one knew about the project."

"Someone knew."

"We were watching them all the time."

"Not all the time. Nor were we watching for other people watching them. We were more worried about being seen ourselves."

"The only problem with that is: Their blood was good. It was beneficial, life-saving."

Maryk nodded. "Exactly. And to go to these lengths, to steal these lives from us, implies desperation—not in the act, but the impetus. The motivation. Who would so desperately want a look at their blood? And why?"

"Someone close, you're thinking. Someone in Special Path."

"No. I can account for all of my people's whereabouts at any given time. It's someone outside the project. Maybe it ties in to Orangeburg somehow, I don't know."

Freeley said, "What about the girl?"

"We keep her close, see who comes looking for her." He was thinking back to the lecture hall again. "I think we may have underestimated her. She may not be as malleable as her psych profile led us to believe."

He went back around the table near Freeley and set his tablet on top of her cutting board. He opened the screen and brought up the image of the unfinished painting they had recovered from Melanie Weir's apartment.

"What do you see?" Maryk said.

Freeley looked at it disparagingly over the top hem of her mask. "One of her crazed paintings."

Maryk was patient. "Look again."

She crossed her arms within her surgical gown and stood in judgment. "I see a big mess," she said. "I see garish colors: stormy red, smoky black. A dead, sick yellow."

Maryk pointed. "What is this?"

"That's a man. He's sick. He's kneeling."

"He's praying. And that?"

"A crevasse, or a gorge. But the colors and the shadows are all wrong—the light doesn't match. It's either a mistake or an optical illusion. Then that black valley below. A mangy wolf lapping at a lake of blood."

"And that?"

"That's the reflection of a man," she said. "His face is hidden. Except for his white hair." She stood quietly a moment. She was beginning to see. "It's you," she said.

"And here?"

"You're squeezing a royal purple fist. Dripping blood into the lake of blood."

"And here?"

"Thin people, naked. Walking with crutches and splints on a dirt road that becomes an oak tree. Those clouds in the sky are like milky eyes." She nodded grudgingly. "It's almost like she knew we were running her."

"She never knew," Maryk said. "She felt, because she has that extra sensibility. Maybe she remembered a little."

Freeley picked up a trephine from among the scalpel, forceps, scissors, butcher's knife, and Stryker saw set out on her cutting board. "She was your favorite," Freeley said. "Wasn't she. The artist."

"She was the most interesting case."

Freeley steadied Blossom's bared scalp with a gloved hand. The circular blade of the trephine started with a whine. "She's just a guinea pig," Freeley said.

Her derision surprised him. Maryk collapsed his tablet and returned it to his bag as she began to cut. Freeley was a good doctor and a good investigator but she was not an artist. It limited her.

The nurse looked up startled from the counter as Maryk entered the B4 lab.

Stephen was sitting up with a cushion of pillows propped behind his back. His nylon restraints hung loose to the cement floor.

"He asked to sit up," she said quickly through her hood.

"Peter?" The pillows rustled. Stephen could not see him yet.

Maryk went around the raised head of the gurney. Stephen's thin hands were folded on the sheet in his lap. The nurse had dressed him in a hospital gown. "Peter," he said. He seemed relieved. He had apparently undergone a change of personality since earlier that morning.

Stephen's withered face exaggerated expression. He would be Happy or Sad or Content or Angry without degree. Here it seemed he was Embarrassed.

His jaw worked clumsily. "Better now," he said. "To be sitting up. More balanced, in my thinking. About before—"

"Forget it."

"She told me everything you did." Stephen turned his eyes to the tablet open on the counter next to him. The data screen was toplined *Pearse, Stephen D.* "My charts," he said. "More T cells even than you now."

A glance at the chart confirmed this. Maryk could not explain Stephen's rapid recovery and for that reason it troubled him. Stephen tried to relax as Maryk felt the underside of his jaw and worked his gloved hands along the neck in firm circular strokes. Maryk probed the lymph area around the muscle and felt nodules as hard as acorns.

He was close to Stephen's face. "If you feel a cough coming," Maryk said, "let me know."

Stephen's eyes were on the ceiling. "You gave me your blood, too."

"Stop thanking me and raise your arms."

Stephen raised his arms as high as he could and Maryk massaged his armpits. He felt marbles inside.

"Pain?"

"Not bad."

Stephen was a poor liar. Maryk guided his arms back down to his lap and explored his chest through the thin gown. "How do you feel overall?"

"Tired. Better."

"Better than you should be."

"Only you would sound discouraged by that."

The nurse appeared with her air hose trailing her along the ceiling track. "Anything else before I go, Doctor?"

Maryk and Stephen both turned to her and at the same time said: "No."

Maryk paused in his examination. Stephen looked at him. The nurse waited awkwardly.

"Thank you," Stephen said quietly.

Maryk said nothing. He resumed his examination as soon as the nurse went out.

He worked over the ribs where the gown clung to Stephen's moist skin. "When are you going to tell me what happened?"

"Orangeburg," Stephen said. "I was pulling blood—"

"We have an entire serology department for that."

Maryk could feel the change in Stephen's breathing and knew he should keep quiet. He would let Stephen talk it through.

"The second patient I saw. He flinched somehow as I withdrew the needle, nudged my arm. I stuck my palm. I went out and cleaned up, flushed out the wound. But when I returned, the bed was empty. The patient was gone."

"Dead."

"No. I don't know. Just gone. I couldn't find him anywhere, and no one knew anything about him. At first I thought I had imagined the whole thing. That was what I wanted to believe—"

He sucked in breath as Maryk probed his abdomen. "Pain here?" Maryk said.

"—Some."

Maryk reached under the gown. "Hold on," he said. Stephen's right testicle was swollen and soft like a tomato too long on the stem. Maryk saw sweat appear on Stephen's brow and upper lip. "More than 'Some,'" Maryk said. He straightened and worked hand over hand along each hip and Stephen relaxed in degrees.

"Listen," Stephen said. He was still regaining his breath. "I don't think this was an accident."

Maryk stopped and looked at him. "Those catatonics had been in a dead sleep for twenty years."

"This patient was different. He was further along the syndrome than the others. He called me over by name. There was no way he could know that. And the way he was looking at me . . . afterward, I couldn't get over the feeling that he had bumped me on purpose."

It was classic physician denial. Maryk said, "Give me one good reason."

Stephen gave up. "I don't have a reason. Just a feeling." He was quiet a while as Maryk continued his examination. He was studying Maryk. "No other cases?" he said. "I mean, in Amagansett?"

Maryk said, "None."

"And Sixteen?" His voice was different. "The BDC?"

"Contained."

Stephen was watching him and Maryk felt he was waiting for a more specific answer. "None?"

"There was one case." Maryk felt tension in Stephen's legs but kept moving. "Someone from in Public Affairs named Peri Fields."

Stephen's breathing shortened. Maryk concentrated on finishing his examination and worked attentively down each kneecap, lower leg, ankle, and foot. He moved to the counter and changed gloves and pulled on a surgeon's mask and goggles. When he returned, Stephen had collected himself. His red eyes were wet and he was swallowing.

Maryk asked him to open his mouth. Stephen held it open shakily. Through strings of bloody phlegm Maryk saw brown sores beneath Stephen's tongue and along the insides of his gums. He moved to the eyes and thumbed up both lids. Each eyeball was suffused with blood.

"Sight?" he asked.

"Floaters," said Stephen. He was trying to look at Maryk. "Normal otherwise."

"Any hearing loss? Ringing in your ears?"

"A steady tone."

Maryk removed his mask and goggles and set them down on the counter. He changed gloves again as he spoke.

"By all evidence, Stephen, you should not even be awake right now, never mind coherent. You should not be speaking. You should not be able to sit up in bed. You are getting too strong, too fast."

"It's known as 'healing.' "

"It's not. The virus is well entrenched in the lymphatic system. I've done all the blood work, I've looked at all the scans. Plainville has already colonized some of your organs. All I've done is stall the feeding frenzy, primarily in the brain. I don't know how long that will hold."

Stephen blinked and played at being strong. "All right," he said. "When do you go back after it?"

"I don't. Any more viral therapy and your immune system will collapse. You'd self-destruct, a road you are well along anyway. You're doing better than I ever could have expected right now, but the revival of your strength can only be explained as a mirage. The virus is everywhere inside of you. The diagnosis remains the same."

More primary emotions played upon the diminished palette of Stephen's face. Fear. Then Dismay. His head and neck quivered until his bloodied eyes returned to search Maryk's.

"You said yourself," he said, "there were survivors."

Maryk nodded. "One lives. A girl, 'Milkmaid.' She beat the infection at Plainville."

"Over four years ago?"

"She's fully recovered, and not only that, she's immune. Her antibodies resist each Plainville mutation. That's why I tracked her all this time. But the Plainville survivors were the exception; that treatment has not worked since. That's why she is so vital to this effort. I've since saved others with her blood sera, but you understand the time factor involved. If you had turned yourself in to BioCon at Orangeburg, I could have helped you. But you hid it, you ran off to New York. By then it was too late."

Stephen looked away and Maryk was quiet and let him stare. But Stephen's eventual response was not what Maryk expected.

"I want to work again, Peter," he said. He looked back at Maryk with eyes that were strong. "It's been a few years—I know. But the equipment is already here for me." Stephen motioned toward the animal room. "This virus is my virus now. No one else could work with it safely, not even you. Maybe I can find some chink in its armor."

It was as though the long-dormant scientist part of Stephen had taken over. Maryk nodded to encourage Stephen's pride. "Good," he said.

"But I need to meet her. The survivor."

Maryk realized that he meant the girl. "No," he said. "That would not be a good idea."

"I need to speak with her, Peter. That will give me some strength."

"She's just a girl," Maryk said. "She has no special powers. No secret knowledge. Only her blood."

Stephen's grimace began to relax. His strength was fading. "Bring her to me," he said. "And then I will help you."

Stephen's eyelids slipped over his eyes. His breathing slowed and Maryk waited by the gurney. Stephen's eyes opened once more before sleep finally consumed him. "Peri," he whispered. Then he succumbed.

Maryk sat looking at the blinds turned down over the window and the glowing lines disappearing between the thin white slats. He heard car doors thumping and engines starting up in the parking lot below and realized that it must be four-thirty.

Cascade time was lazy and formless like a summer day. He had been dozing in his office for most of the afternoon. His frequent administerings to Stephen meant sacrificing countless hours to the voice of his cascades.

The BDC at night reminded him of his internships and residencies and the various city hospitals he had patrolled as though they were his. But Stephen was wrong: Maryk had no designs on running the BDC. He had already made Special Pathogens over in his own image. An artist must know his place in the world.

He would nap again soon to drain off the remains of this Pearse-induced cascade. Then he could work long into the night.

His office door opened and Melanie Weir entered alone behind the chair he had arranged for her.

"Your inhaler," Maryk said and waved at it on his desk. It was stickered with a fresh prescription label.

She did not move. She was staring at the blinds and pretending to ignore him. The girl's posture and the low angle of her resentful eyes spoke for her.

"Take it," he said.

She came forward without looking at him and took it from his desktop. Then she turned to leave.

"Sit down," he said.

She slowed at the door. Pasco had brought her there and was waiting beyond to bring her back inside if necessary. She must have sensed this. She came back and sat in the arranged chair.

The girl's short hair was the deep red color of vine berries. She wore a short black skirt and thick black stockings and a long white T-shirt with the corporate affiliation bleached out. She sat deeply in the chair but was alert and assessing him at every turn.

"Dr. Pasco walked you through a tour of the BDC," Maryk said. He licked his lips. "This is my office."

She sat with her arms and legs crossed. She did not respond.

"Let me guess," he said. "You feel as though you've been treated poorly."

"I feel as though I've been raped," she said. "Repeatedly and routinely, for over four years. Violated. Taken advantage of. How long do you think you can hold me here?"

"Plainville took advantage of you," Maryk said. "I gave you life."

She stared in apparent amazement. "You know what? We have nothing more to discuss. I have been drugged and jabbed with needles. I've been used like a voodoo doll against some crazed disease. I've had experiments performed on me, been followed around, spied upon. I've been humiliated. All by you—whoever you really are. You're warped, all right? And that—that comes as a total relief to me. Because now I know I'm fine. You're the sick one."

He nodded after a moment. "Good," he said.

"What's good? Don't you smile at me."

He had indeed underestimated her. "I can see now how you survived your time in the hospital," he said.

She did not know how to respond to that. Her expression grew a little less guarded. "Why didn't you wear one of those suits?" she said.

The question surprised him. "It's all coming back to you."

"No. I only remember the others sealed inside a suit in order to survive being in the same room as me. All except you."

Maryk nodded. He stood then and felt confident on his feet and moved to the front of his desk.

"Natural immunity," he told her. "A fluke of nature, not unlike yourself. My immune system is exceptionally strong. It detects invading foreign agents immediately and executes the infected host cell itself, thereby expelling both the virus and the infection at once. I require no protection against airborne exposure to Plainville. You and I are the only two people in the world who could withstand it."

Her eyes seemed to relax and she spoke with the power and authority of revelation. "You're drunk."

Maryk half smiled and held on to the edge of the desk. "I was coming to that. Natural killer cells, unlike other immune system cells, don't wait to be told what to do. They search and destroy on their own. Everybody's system produces some; mine happens to make billions. But the kill-off from any significant exposure taxes my system to exhaustion—a cellular massacre and leukocyte surge triggering an energy drain, which I call a 'cascade.' Makes me drowsy sometimes, slows me down. Depends on the pathogen and the extent of the exposure. You undergo a typical antibody reaction; you feel nothing, unaware of the services being rendered by your immune system. This," he pointed at himself, "what you see here, is the machine working at maximum efficiency, ridding my body of Plainville. This is human superiority over a virus."

She looked at him with something like disgust.

Maryk nodded in the general direction of Building Seven. "Stephen Pearse is isolated nearby. I left him some time ago. Pearse is my patient, as are you."

"*Were*," she said.

He ignored that. "Stephen and I used to be research partners. We went to school together, joined the bureau together."

"So he's in on this too."

"Oh no." Maryk showed a frowning grin. "Not Stephen. Stephen turned his back on creative science some time ago. He thought he could do more good by being more good himself, and abandoned his medical gifts for something like faith. He wanted to heal by example, rather than by practice; to cure purely through the power of his presence. The high priest of world medicine. Now, of course, quite the opposite is true."

She was still staring. "This makes you happy?"

He realized he was rambling and checked himself. Perhaps he was more fatigued than he had realized. He cleared his throat. "Pasco tells me you refused to give your blood."

She hardened. "Since when do you need my permission?" She thrust out her left arm and pushed back the sleeve. "Here. Take it."

"I will," he said. He pushed off the edge and started toward her. "I will take it, if I have to. I will hang you upside down from the ceiling and bleed you—your blood is that important to the world. But it would be easier for you if you cooperate. It's not me you would be helping. I don't require your help." She leaned away from him as he neared. "You have a gift," he said. "You are different."

"I am not different."

"You are special."

She insisted, "I am not special."

"Your blood is."

She veered away as he stood next to her chair. "Stay away from me," she said.

"My system kills without manufacturing any biological solution. Your system produces antibodies. Your blood stops the virus in others."

She stood out of the chair but he seized her arm and held her still. She twisted in his grip. She looked up from his restraining hand into his face.

"I will scream," she said.

He realized he was hurting her. He released her and she hurried to the door. He did not go after her. The door opened and slammed and she was gone.

He left the chair for the wall and followed it staggeringly to the couch. He sat heavily with his arms dead in his lap and tipped back his head. His breath came out in short pantlike gasps.

It had been a mistake to allow her to see him this way. He hadn't realized how depleted he still was.

Night grayed the ceiling above him as he sat. The regretted encounter swirled in his mind until the words no longer made human sense. The darkness of the ceiling became the dark insides of his heavy eyelids. The rhythmic huffing of his chest became the mantra of deep sleep.

The Language
of Disease

He thought of wide-open spaces. *He thought of breezes across acres of pastel tulips and pictured himself in the branches of the oak tree that had cooled the house of his childhood in spring. He conjured up the robin's eggshell of a cloudless sky overhead and started his mother down the long path from their front door to the mailbox. He watched the cross-breeze toss hair around her face. Proudly he watched her hands feel for the mailbox. It was empty and she rested a moment before starting back. She turned so that the tulip breeze washed her hair from her face. She was beautiful and she was blind. He dropped down from the tree branch and surprised her at the door with the mail in hand and then followed her inside for lunch.*

"You wouldn't last one night in here."

Stephen's voice pulled Maryk back into the B4 lab. He was looking out the aquarium window into the larger subterranean basement of Building Seven. The door that led to the stairs that led aboveground was six doors away.

Maryk detested his claustrophobia. He released his grip on the sill and his breathing came back under control. He could at least work through the early strains of a cascade.

He turned and found Stephen examining his withered hands. Stephen was vigilant for any evidence of further decay. "I must have nodded off," Stephen said. He was sitting up on the gurney. He had requested clothes instead of the hospital gown but all Maryk had for him were scrubs.

Maryk moved through the assembled lab equipment back to the B4 computer console. Everything had been networked through the central brain of the lab. Stephen had even agreed to Maryk's suggestion that Reilly and Boone be brought in as extra pairs of arms and legs.

Stephen's blood, saliva, urine, sputum, pleura, and skin samples sat in disposable flasks along the counter like a row of small plastic trophies. "We were talking about the virus," said Maryk. "How it is not acting the way a virus acts."

"Yes," said Stephen. "Not moving like a virus moves. Not burning as a virus burns. Where was the flint in Orangeburg? The spark at any of the earlier breaks?"

The language of disease was the language of poetry and the metaphor for viruses was fire. Plainville was smoldering in Stephen. He sat on the gurney like a burn victim with darkly bruised patches of skin that looked singed. Ragged patches of hair hung off his flaking scalp. He looked weaker and more ill and yet continued to grow stronger despite medical evidence to the contrary.

"Could it be something unusual in the environment?" he continued. "Common to all these places?"

Maryk said, "We've tested and retested many times. I'd like to think we didn't miss anything."

"In Africa, it was simple exposure and transmission."

"But here it doesn't die out with its victims," Maryk said. "We need to know why there aren't any footsteps between outbreaks."

"Because it's smart. This is a virus that somehow *knows* what's good for it. An arsonist virus: one that discriminates, that knows what it is doing."

"Viruses don't think the way we think. They survive. That's all."

"They don't commit murder either. Your survivors. You agree that was a directed assault against your project."

Maryk moved away from the console. "I've already ruled out bioterrorism," he said.

"If somebody with a vial of Plainville only wanted to spread terror, they would drop it off the Empire State Building. They would slip it into any major airport and uncork it there."

"Exactly."

"Unless." Here Stephen paused. "Unless terror wasn't their ultimate goal."

"A terrorist not satisfied with terror." Maryk frowned. "What, then?"

"Infection. No politics. No ideology, no religion. Just pure infection. The destruction of the human race."

"A maniac. Frightening thought, but there is one thing you're forgetting: Plainville is unmanageable. It is impossible for anyone to handle it without risking infection themselves. If we couldn't work with it safely here at the BDC, who could?"

"You could."

Maryk stopped and looked at him.

"I mean only that nothing is impossible," Stephen continued. "You could, so there could be another. Say you were eyeing a particular target, the destruction of the human race. And you had a weapon: Plainville. What would you need to do first?"

Maryk said, "I would need to test it."

"A dry run. Each time Plainville emerges again in an outbreak, we hold our breath. And each time it dies out in containment, leaving us with nothing, and we congratulate each other on having dodged another bullet. This virus reemerges in already isolated situations. What I'm saying is: What if this is no accident? What if there is some kind of mind at work behind this Plainville? What if it is depending upon our containing its spread so that it can learn from each outbreak: learn how the mutations are working, learn the most efficient modes of infection, and gather intelligence on how we are working to fight it."

"Learn how?" Maryk said. "We've kept the outbreaks hidden from the public."

This was not an impediment to Stephen's theory. "That would only make them angry, and more dedicated."

Maryk shook his head. "You're talking about Plainville like it's something you can get at a drugstore. This is an organic virus, not engineered biowarfare. We know where it came from—a cave in central Africa. No one planted it there. We know we buried it, and burned it out for good."

Stephen did not respond to that. He was quiet and Maryk watched him and waited for him to speak.

"Maybe we didn't bury it all," he said. He was looking red-eyed at the floor. It was difficult to read any emotion on Stephen's fading face.

"You remember the girl with the vitiligo who followed me around the camp?"

Maryk did. "Vaguely."

"She was healthy, Peter. She was clear at the time; I tested her. She was begging me for help, and the jets were coming. Your jets. I had packed an ampule of the PeaMar serum we were working on at the time. The compound was sound, I knew it was—"

Maryk stiffened in the noisy atmosphere of B4. "Stephen," he said sharply.

"I transfused it," he said. "I dosed her and sent her out of the camp."

Maryk stood staring. He was furious and silent.

"You gave me no choice," Stephen said. He would not look up. "But now I keep thinking—maybe she contracted the virus somehow, between the time I tested her and the time I injected her."

"Wait a minute," Maryk said. "This was six years ago. This was a girl. She never turned up again. This patient in bay twenty-six, the one you think stuck you—he was a man."

"He was."

"There was no patient in bay twenty-six at Orangeburg. I checked. Twenty-six was an empty bed."

"Then how did he get to my parents' home in Amagansett?"

"Stephen," Maryk said.

"He was there. I saw him, he was walking around."

"You said you saw your parents, too."

"He was different. He opened the window. I think he was at my tablet."

Maryk grew impatient. "It can't be. People don't last days, never mind months or years, with Plainville. Either they die right away, or we get to them early enough with the Milkmaid serum and they survive."

"You'll check on it, Peter?"

"I'll look into it," Maryk said. "But this is no phantom. This is no ghost. Someone murdered two of Plainville's only three survivors—and would have eliminated all three if we hadn't rolled up Milkmaid just in time."

"Rolled her up?" Stephen looked up at him. "I thought she came to Atlanta to help."

Maryk said, "Not exactly."

"Tell me you haven't locked her away somewhere, Peter."

"She is staying in an Emory dormitory room. She eats at the school cafeteria. She has no idea how many people I have watching her everywhere she goes. But she is refusing to help."

Stephen nodded. "And that is why you finally agreed to bring her here."

"I need her to see what is at stake. She needs to understand that this is life or death."

The red light flashing over the submarine door indicated movement into the shower room. The nurse was bringing Melanie through.

"Could you turn down the lights?" Stephen said.

Maryk dimmed the overhead bulbs and the shadows deepened on Stephen's face. Stephen sat up as straight as his gaunt body was able. He appeared nervous.

"What is she like?" he said.

"She hates me," Maryk said. "You two should have a lot to talk about."

But Maryk was relieved not to be facing her alone again after their last encounter. He heard movement behind the door. It was pushed open and the pressure in the room changed. Air rushed in. The nurse stepped through the oval doorway and Melanie followed behind.

Maryk had ordered her sealed inside a suit. He was not taking any chances with her health. She kept her head down inside the hood and remained just to the left of the door. The unsashed fabric bagged around her waist and bunched at her knees until the nurse connected her air feed to the ceiling runner. Then Melanie's suit inhaled.

Her eyes rose gradually. She looked away immediately after first seeing Stephen on the bed. She worked hard to smother her reaction before looking at him again. The shock of seeing this public figure convalescing was exactly what Maryk had wanted.

"Hello, Melanie," Stephen said.

Her stare at him was interrupted only by a flickered glance at Maryk.

Stephen said, "I wanted to thank you in person. I know this all must be bewildering to you. You were brave to come."

Stephen's voice was ripe with enthusiasm. He was good that way.

"Your life is worth more to the human race than mine or even Dr. Maryk's," he went on. "There are ways you could help. You could help us by donating your blood. You could help others by meeting with them, by going out into the field."

Maryk stopped him. "Stephen."

"She's looked it in the face, Peter. She's survived."

Maryk tried to silence him. "It's too hazardous. The bug mutates too fast."

"You said her hemo screens are sound, even with the mutations. She's curing it. Think of the effect her presence would have on the ill."

"Stephen—I do not need her going around holding people's hands."

A sharp gasp distracted them. It came from the nurse as she reached out toward the girl.

Melanie had split the diagonal seal across her suit. She broke open the folds and flipped the hood back off her head. Her garish hair sprang loose and her eyes were fierce as she glared at Maryk. She took a deep breath and filled her unprotected lungs.

Melanie sat on an examining table in another room in the same building, pressing a folded square of gauze to her left elbow and still buzzing from what she had done.

Recollections from her illustrious days in premed: The ecosphere of the human lung absorbs 20,000 liters of air each day. Less than 1/100,000 inch of protection separates the lung air environment from the vast human bloodstream. Viruses need to open a hole of only 1/1,000,000 inch in order to hitch a ride on the sanguineous superhighway.

"Stupid," Maryk sputtered again. It was all worth it just to have witnessed that moment of impotence on his face, that had preceded the dark, furious frown he now wore. "You are immune to casual *airborne* exposure to Plainville. But if even a *minute* amount of infective blood or saliva came into contact with your eyes, your mouth—you would be at risk."

She remembered similar tablebeds in her father's office, and how he used to pull tissue paper down from a roller beneath the head cushion, a new strip for each sniffling kid. That had been his generation's idea of sterile medicine. Her schoolyard version had been a Popsicle stick inoculation to ward off a sudden outbreak of boy cooties.

Pasco paced behind them, and she felt his tension too. Maryk mixed something into her blood and waited while it set in a small container, marked PCR, connected to his tablet. She peeled the cotton pad back from the puncture wound on her arm and looked at the resulting bloodstain still spreading through the gauze webbing like a flower opening in bloom. *Miracle Blood!* Watch it go! She looked down at her wasted, bruised arms with a renewed sense of anger and potent shame.

"Will you lock me up in the basement now like your friend?" she said.

His eyes burned gray. Everything he did disgusted her now.

"Why would you task yourself like this?" he said.

"I'm *special*," she told him. "I'm *different*."

Seeing Dr. Pearse like that, fragile and shrunken with those ghostly red eyes, had been shocking; she hadn't seen anyone that sick in over four years. But as bad as she felt for him, her loathing for Maryk was a hundred times more intense.

He looked up from his little tablet. "Well?" she said. Insistent. Defiant.

He disconnected the contraption. He said: "Clean."

It was simple enough to disguise her own relief. But when Maryk showed none, she became enraged. She was his number one pin cushion, after all.

She sensed an urgency in his actions as he cleaned up. "It was your blood," she said. "Your freak blood, transfused into me in the hospital. That's how I was 'cured.' "

His silence told her she was right. She threw the bloody gauze down onto the table in front of him, and he stopped and looked at it crumpled there before pulling fast the buckle straps on his bag.

"You're a freak," she told him. "And you've made me into a freak."

Maryk stopped at the door with his bag. He looked back at the cold table, not at her. "Take her to her room," he said to Pasco.

"My *room?*" she laughed, though it came out a bray. Maryk opened the door and started down the hallway, and suddenly Melanie wasn't laughing anymore. *"Why didn't you let me die in Plainville!"* she screamed. But he continued away, and the white door closed on his back and clicked shut.

The Oracle

Cyberviruses Section was located two doors down from the STD unit in BDC Building Eighteen. Most CVs were hacker-engineered although there had been incidences of corrupted files breaking off from legitimate programs and mutating "naturally" file to file. The turn-of-the-century Internet boom had corroborated the epidemiological axiom that any surge in population represents a fertile breeding ground for viral incursion. The new ecology of computer technology had engendered indigenous viral activity.

Suzy Lumm was the co-section head. She was an obese woman of more than 250 pounds and was legally blind. She sat before a semicircular computer console in her office like a priestess divining at an oracle. She wore a loop earphone connected to a chin mike and the fingertips of her right hand explored a flat blue pad that raised screen characters into Braille. Her thickly soled sneakers worked foot pedals beneath the console that controlled her microphone. Suzy Lumm was the human liaison to the DNA–powered Genetech II computer that ran the BDC.

Maryk pulled over a chair and sat at her side. The cascade from his long visit with Stephen made thoughts sound like voices arguing in his head.

"Here's what I need," he told Suzy Lumm. "Assume that the director's tablet had been compromised by some outside interest." He was trying to be careful with his wording. "What would that mean?"

"Are you asking about Blue files?"

She had a sultry voice that did not match her appearance. Her face was broad and her drooping eyes thick-lidded.

"I'm asking about any sensitive documents loaded into Stephen Pearse's tablet."

"Blue files are any reports or internal memoranda generated by any government agency," she said. "Blue files crash if tapped into illegally. If an unauthorized user attempts to dupe them to an unauthorized server, the Blue worm encryption fouls the offending drive and disables its microprocessor, but not before instructing the modem to dial the FBI."

"So there is no way someone could duplicate those files."

"We-ell." She turned smiling in his general direction. "The National Security Agency instituted Blue to protect sensitive documents from prying eyes and sticky fingers—White House internals, CIA, DOD. But here at the BDC, prying eyes don't pose much of a threat. Here, the opposite is true: Access and preservation is vital to operation. So, no, you cannot copy files off a tablet. Nor can you print them. But—you can back them up."

Maryk understood. "By archiving the entire system."

"Exactly. I have loaded here a working clone of Director Pearse's tablet, as you recovered it." She indicated the monitor displaying a list of file names. "If there were any Blue programs, they would have deleted themselves out within fifteen days, as they are self-timed to do. But . . ." She called up an index card graphic. "A full backup was performed the day before you recovered the tablet."

Maryk stared at the screen. "So anyone who copied the drive," he said, "could walk away with an exact replica stored in their own tablet."

"And someone did." She whispered a command into her microphone and slid her hand over the Braille pad and Maryk heard a soft male voice whisper into Suzy Lumm's ear. Numbers appeared on screen. "Full backup creates a register recording the time, date, and chip address of the receiving system."

"So you've got the internal code of the second tablet."

"That's it right there. But I already checked. Hailing has been disabled. This tablet is not on the air."

"Then what about this: Can whoever owns the clone of Pearse's tablet still access the BDC?"

"Not coded files. There's a safeguard built in to the director's tablet to prevent the skeleton key from being duped. But the Genetech still can be dialed into. In fact, it has."

She muttered commands and massaged the pad and smiled at the wall as the machine murmured into her ear. Maryk knew from his mother that the smile of the blind indicated achievement at least as often as pleasure.

Words appeared on screen. "Your personnel file," she said.

Maryk glared.

"Accessed and downloaded six days ago," she said. "Could it have anything to do with this?" She switched back to Stephen's tablet and opened a file. " 'Investigation-dot-Maryk,' " she hand-read. "Emptied, and irretrievable. All the files were typed over before they were dumped."

"Personnel files aren't coded?"

"Not at the BDC. No need. Viruses don't use computers."

Stephen was right. Someone had archived his tablet while he was in Amagansett. And later that same someone had dialed into the BDC computers looking specifically for information on Maryk. Whoever it was then knew about his immunological strength.

"Can you bring up Pearse's bank account?" Maryk said.

She did. The last debit transaction was dated the day before Maryk brought Stephen back to the BDC.

"Fuel," she said curiously.

Maryk read the register. A tankful had been purchased at a Texaco in Trenton, New Jersey, the day before Maryk froze Stephen's bank accounts. "But how could someone other than Stephen Pearse sign for a thousand dollars' worth of merchandise on this tablet?"

Suzy Lumm smiled and scrolled to another file and Stephen's arched signature appeared on screen. Maryk watched her plump fingertips trace it on her read pad. "Signature imprint," she said. "For generating prescriptions, signing documents. They had Director Pearse's tablet sign for them."

Maryk nodded. "What are my options, then?" he said.

"I could cancel the director's tablet for you right now. That way, if anyone tried to use the duped code to access the Genetech, they would be refused."

Maryk deliberated. "What if I wanted to preserve my link to this person?"

"Then I can put a sentinel on the Genetech. That would split the signal and trick the user out to me if he tries to come on-line."

Maryk nodded and stood. "Keep a trace on that tablet," he told her. "I want to know the minute it taps back in."

The Human
Component

It had been four meals since she'd seen Maryk. Night and day passed uneventfully with her sulking in front of the TV in her room, waiting for him to come, like a vampire, for her blood. Pasco, her shadow from Boston, appeared three times a day to escort her to the Emory college cafeterias for meals. Being held on a college campus seemed to her like poetic justice. Finals had ended and the campus population was dwindling, though she sensed movement around her wherever she went. She was convinced that Maryk had people everywhere, watching her. Inside the cafeteria, the same red-haired custodian mopped a different section of floor at every meal.

Her boundless appetite had returned. She sat that afternoon before a cheeseburger and a plate of chicken-fried steak, starting instead with a thick wedge of apple cobbler. Pasco sat at the next table over, eating and diligently working on something on his tablet. He was intent on what he was reading, gnawing on a sesame breadstick as though it were a pencil.

It bothered her that she hadn't seen Maryk. She knew he needed her blood, and had expected him to have taken it by now. Later that second day she asked Pasco to take her to see Dr. Pearse, and to her surprise, he did.

A nurse led her through most of the preliminary rooms, then left her, shutting the steel door on the dark shower room before the lab. The walls creaked until the air flow reached a kind of equilibrium and seemed to rush away from her at all points, yet allowed her to breathe. Warnings glowed fluorescently on the door. She wore a mask, goggles, and gloves, but they had not required her to wear one of the body-condom suits. She nodded to herself and struck the switch and the door popped open, sucking forward the swirling air.

Dr. Pearse was right there. He was standing now and leaning on a metal hospital cane. He was walking. Melanie was stunned. His movement was much improved, though he looked no better. In fact he looked worse.

"Hello again," he said, taking a few mindful steps toward her with his cane. His red eyes bothered her even more now, as they moved more naturally within his head, making him appear all the more unnatural. She caught herself looking for further signs of corrosion, and stopped. She willed herself not to stare, but to relax, relax.

Two men worked behind him in the submarine-type room, both sealed inside blue air suits. Melanie remembered at once what it was to be so feared, to be the object of such passive disgust. It was as though Dr. Pearse were a glowing rock that could only be handled with tongs.

He was so genuinely pleased to see her, she was scared. Seeing Dr. Pearse that way, a dying man up and walking around in front of her, made her think about the wonder blood coursing through her own skinny veins.

She stammeringly asked him how he was. Which was brilliant. Next she'd ask a drowning man if the water temperature was okay. But he was enthusiastic, and suddenly she was the one who felt like dying.

"Getting around better," he said, his voice stronger than before. "How are you?"

Now he was concerned for her. She broke the knot of her arms and moved to the counter for something to lean on. It was all too much suddenly, him being sick and super-pleasant, the sealed room, the swirling oxygen, and the slow-moving blue suits behind.

"I'm all alone," she said. She meant that she had no one else to talk to.

"As am I," he said. "Except, of course, for our mutual friend."

He wore only the vestiges of a smile. Melanie nodded uncomfortably.

"He scares you," Dr. Pearse said.

She placed her gloved hand on the counter, then pulled it back, then gripped her fingers as though burned. Maryk had succeeded in making a paranoid wreck out of her.

Dr. Pearse went on, "It is extraordinarily rare that a person excels at the very thing they were uniquely created for. Beyond aptitude or ability or talent—I mean a legitimate predisposition, a person born into . . . certain faculties who succeeds in exploiting them to their fullest capacity. And when this does happen, it usually creates a monster."

His words shocked her. "Then why are you helping him?"

"Because Peter is *our* monster. And in helping him, I am helping others, and in that, perhaps helping myself. He has sent me back some new samples from Louisiana."

He spoke of the blood samples as though they were sweets purchased at a bake sale. "What's in Louisiana?" Melanie said.

He looked at her a moment. "They haven't told you?" he said. He moved to a screen and gently prodded the keys. "The Plainville secret is out now. It's all over the news."

He turned the screen toward her, and Melanie forced herself to swallow the bile that had risen in her throat. A news server headline appeared, reading like a shriek over the image of a dark building seen through a chain-link fence and rolls of razor wire:

HUNDREDS FEARED DEAD IN LA OUTBREAK
PENITENTIARY ISOLATED, RIOTS QUELLED
Hundreds Infected; Deadly Plainville MA Viral Recurrence Seen.

A sign posted on the fence bore the international biohazard symbol.

"The guards' families," said Dr. Pearse. "They were scared, so they went to the press. It means that the fight has progressed to a different level now."

She was dizzy. "He's there?"

"I'm told Peter's team took off for Louisiana at first call."

Melanie laid her hand over her stomach. For the past day and a half she had sat spitefully in her dormitory room like a little girl. She felt petulant and spoiled and deeply ashamed. She tried to imagine the prison in Louisiana, and instead saw the dead of Plainville, her parents and friends and neighbors, wasted and cadaverous and all watching her with rotting eyes, waiting to see if she would ever make something of the second chance she had been given.

"The virus keeps changing and changing," Dr. Pearse said. "Look here."

He changed the image on the computer screen, and after a moment she was able to focus.

Distorted, as though by the magnification of a powerful microscope, a small, spindly creature squirmed and twitched.

"This is the bug that's eating me," he said, nearly in wonder. "Look at how it moves. Simple enough to kill a virus with bleach and study it destroyed. This is our first look at live Plainville. Well—magnified one hundred and twenty thousand times."

He moved closer to the screen and touched it, the distorted green light of the image shading his hand.

"I have made a discovery," he went on. Melanie tried to pay attention. "Some of the RNA sites on the virus contain strands of human characteristic DNA codes—a human component of the virus. Just as I said it would." He pulled his thin hand from the viewing screen and looked at it, front and back. "Just as I said it would." He seemed to forget that she was there, lost in the world of his hands. For a moment, the triumph was gone. "Of course, I could move faster with a chemical gene splicer, but I'm making do. You are well represented here, too. Your cell cultures, anyway. Plainville burns through everything until it hits them. Miraculous, really." He looked at the equipment surrounding him. "It is good to be back home inside a laboratory again. I was away from it for too long."

He pondered that a moment. She saw then that his grins were not grins but rather the result of the fading architecture of his face. He turned to the long window, evidently viewing something other than the dim room beyond.

"Illness does have the effect of clarifying things, doesn't it?" he said. "Life, or death. Sickness, or health. The ruthlessness of existence. I believe this must be how Peter views the world every day—"

She interrupted. "I'm going to give him my blood."

Dr. Pearse's red eyes returned to study her face. His grin, perhaps the only expression left available to him, flickered. "Good," he said, nodding slightly. "Yours to give. But not to him: to the people who need it."

The immensity of her situation rose up around her again, overwhelming her. She sank against the console. "Why me?" she said. "Out of all those people, why did it have to be me? Look at me." She looked at herself. "Why did I survive?"

"You are proof that the virus is not irremediable. You survived, so there is hope that others might survive." His knuckled hand went lightly to his chest. "That I might survive."

"But why *me*?"

"All that is required of you now is to live, to remain healthy."

She nodded, agreeing with him at first. Then she stopped nodding. "No," she said. "You're wrong. Living's not enough. I've been living for more than four years now, and it's gotten me nowhere. I'm different, he tells me. He's right. How can I use that?"

Dr. Pearse was distracted by the monitor image of the wriggling virus. She moved in front of it to regain his attention.

"You said something about helping the ill," she said.

He regripped his cane and prodded at the smooth cement floor. "That was just a suggestion. This situation rarely presents itself. The immune can go into these breaks. Survivors sometimes make the best investigators."

"But I don't know a thing about viruses."

"You could see to the sick. For them just to engage in conversation with someone not sealed inside a suit—you can understand the power of that."

"But I wouldn't know what to say."

"You would. You're doing it right now."

She retreated along the counter away from his grin, then stopped. "I want to go there," she said.

"It is a federal penitentiary. Perhaps you should wait for some other—"

"No more waiting. It's been four years of waiting. If I agree to give Maryk my blood, then he has to let me go. He has to. You could contact him for me."

"Ransoming your blood," said Dr. Pearse. "Peter won't take kindly to that."

"I have to help. You're not sitting here doing nothing."

She had a valid point, and he knew it. "Then will you do something for me?" he asked. His stiff grin had faded. He leaned both hands upon the curve of his cane now, his blood-filled gaze commanding her attention. "Keep a close eye on him. Peter's vocation has taken the place of his conscience. You don't know what he is capable of."

The Penitentiary

She had learned to cheat glances at the helicopter pilot's control stick, anticipating turns and dips and bracing herself accordingly, gripping the soft sides of her seat as they swung around the prison perimeter. They buzzed the guard towers, each one abandoned. High-powered stationary spotlights crisscrossed the prison grounds and made the bales of razor wire stacked against the high chain fences glitter like rolled carpets of diamonds. The central building of Lewes Federal Penitentiary was stage-lit like an alien ship set down in a bayou. There was a black lake to the north, and swamplands all around, with long, spindly roads like black seams leading away, and small police lights clustered in the distance.

They set down on top of the roof of the main building. Two people stood at the roof door, one of whom Melanie recognized immediately as Maryk. The pilot gave her a thumbs-up signal and she unbuckled her seat belt, taking the white medical suitcase from between her legs and pushing open the door.

She ducked out away from the whipping rotors as she'd seen done so many times on TV. She had to stop and balance herself as the helicopter tipped up and blasted her with wind, wasting no time in taking off again. Her hospital shirt rippled and climbed halfway up her back, and for a moment she thought she might blow off the rooftop like a scrap of paper. Then it was gone, running lights rising into the sky over the bayous of southern Louisiana. She straightened and turned.

Maryk, glowing from a spotlight set behind him, reeked of bleach. He probably used it as after-shave, she thought. He said nothing, and she set the medical kit containing packets of her blood down at his feet, rather than hand it to him.

"Weir, Melanie," he said. "On-site."

The man holding a plastic-sheathed tablet next to him replied, "Weir, Melanie, on-site, twenty-forty-eight."

She had to strain to hear them. Both ears were filled with noise in the seashell-like absence of helicopter roar.

They descended three flights of echoing metal-edged concrete stairs to a long, gray hall. Every door was open and several inches thick. But except for that and the cameras watching from every corner, the inside of Lewes looked more like a junior college than her idea of a federal penitentiary.

A third suited man ushered her into a side room and began to dress her as Maryk watched. She was issued a plastic surgical gown to wear over her hospital scrubs, a procedure mask with a wraparound splash visor, a cotton cap, a white cowl covering her head except her eyes and nose, and rubber-soled, elasticized booties that fit over her sneakers. She felt as though she were eight years old again and being bundled up for an afternoon of sledding.

Maryk said from the doorway, "What do you think you can do here?"

She had bartered her blood for Maryk's acquiescence, but now that she was there and being suited up, she was regretting her decision. The man worked over her with great deference, like a tailor for NASA. She played confidence to Maryk. "I'd like to help," she said.

"Lewes Penitentiary is an administrative maximum level six. Do you know what that means?"

"No."

"The Bureau of Prisons uses a one-to-five scale to rank penitentiaries by security level. The men inside here are the worst of the worst."

"If you're trying to scare me," she said, "you should know I've had this aversion to prisons all my life."

"What I'm trying to do is to dispel any Florence Nightingale fantasies Stephen Pearse may have instilled in you."

The tailor stuck a yellow and red BDC patch to her chest and pointed her to the latex glove dispensers, where she took a petite size five. Maryk went to her and seized her gloved hands, taping them hard around her wrists and checking the seal. She realized then that they were dressed exactly alike.

They left the room and started down the long, gray hall, people in yellow suits brushing busily past them. She had to hustle to keep pace. Her outfit was bulky and everything was moving fast.

"At this point, these men no longer pose any threat to you, or to society," he said, "except through their infection. Plainville is the warden in this place now." They passed a high, circular guard station dead center in the hall. "Riots ensued once the disease cycle began. Many of the guards fled when they realized they were cooking in here the same as the inmates, and the prisoners went at each other like animals. Plainville was already well entrenched. A closed environment, with substandard living conditions, poor hygiene: an optimal ecology for an airborne bug like Plainville. But there is nothing more conducive to microbial transmission than a riot, and the disease quickly wore them down. The fight's gone out of most of them now, and we're losing nine to ten an hour. This is B unit, all advanced cases." He stopped at a closed steel door sealed into the wall at the end of the hallway. "Inside, guards lie side by side with inmates."

She heard noises through the door that were groans.

Maryk faced her. "You will be safe inside so long as you remain with me at all times. Touch no one and nothing, and keep yourself covered. You know that blood contact from a needle stick will overwhelm your resources and infect, antibodies or no antibodies. Same as for me. So if you are considering another self-destructive stunt like the one you pulled in B4, know that I will stop you, and you will be removed. Stay away from needles, and stay away from blood."

He released the door. It opened and there was just enough room for two people to stand inside and face another steel door. The first door closed and her shoulder was pressed against his left biceps. She felt him breathing, and she realized she was afraid of him again.

"The riots killed any hope for negative airflow containment," he said. "We are working in a Plainville atmosphere here. These ultraviolet light closets are only checkpoints between areas of higher viral intensity and lower viral intensity. When we come back out, these doors will lock down automatically and initiate a two-minute UV light shower. You'll stand for that until the second door opens." He rattled all this off as though giving her directions to the bathroom. "Scared?"

She nodded, staring straight ahead, not looking at him.

Maryk flexed his black rubber hands. "Good," he said. He hit a switch and the second door released.

The unit beyond was high and long and painfully bright. They stepped onto the middle of three tiers, facing the hollow center of the unit, cells lining the railed parapets in long rows on either side. It was windowless, but high-intensity lamps made the cell block appear artificially as bright as day.

The cell doors were all open and the cells themselves were empty. Cots lay along the guard walk between the open doors and the low railing along the hollow, and there was a body on every cot. The stagnant smell of the sealed unit hit her immediately, human sickness and spoil and trapped smoke. The sides of the concrete parapets had been licked black by riot fire. There was a footpath cleared through the trash strewn over the floors: toilet paper, burned blankets, feces.

She followed Maryk along the path of debris, starting down the length of the left parapet, finding the red-painted rail with her gloved hand and gripping it as she went. He studied computer charts hooked to the cots and stopped now and then to pull back a sheet and examine the progression of some remarkable sore, moving intently from patient to patient, oblivious to the moans and feverish talk, appraising the prisoners' treatments and modifying them or okaying them before moving on, and all the while keeping an eye on Melanie.

"This one is a spitter," he warned.

This particular inmate had obviously once been very large. His loose skin now sagged over his wasting frame, obscuring tattoos burned fiercely into his chest and arms. The high-intensity light above sought out every blemish and sore.

There was a strange tranquillity about these criminals, a red-eyed curiosity as they lay there dissolving. She could not tell which of the sick were the guards. The disease wore away all distinction.

The few who did look at her or attempted to speak, she could not face. She tried, but her cheeks and forehead burned and she looked guiltily away. These conscious few terrified her, because they could see what was coming for them.

At one cot, Maryk pulled the sheet off a dead man. The corpse's thinned arms were straight at his sides and his hands and his mouth were open, as though he were holding a musical note just above the human range. BioCon agents with tablets on their arms arrived like census takers, and Melanie pressed back against the railing, out of their way. A few of the agents looked her over: She was suitless; bizarre. She felt like the only person on the moon who could breathe.

The stench was sickening and Melanie turned away. Across the gap lay a facing row of more cots and more dying men, their sickly flesh glowing in the white light. BioCon agents in yellow suits rolled instrument carts past them along the path of riot debris.

When she looked back, they were lifting the dead man off the cot and into a black bag unzipped on the floor. His arms, crossed awkwardly over his blistered stomach, fell open as they moved him, and at once he looked so withered and empty. They laid him inside the thick black plastic with his red eyes still staring, his mouth still twisted open in silent song. Maryk knelt at his feet and unlocked a black clasp from around his ankle: an electronic quarantine bracelet. She remembered it all from Plainville.

Men lying on neighboring cots stared at the scorched undersides of the parapets above them with mouths dropped open, as though trying to harmonize with the dead they were soon to join. One man's head rolled to the side, his red eyes loose in their sockets, fixing questioningly on her.

She started moving then. She was rushing away. She pushed past the nearest suit and pulled herself hand by hand along the red railing, away from Maryk, back to the steel doors.

Inside the first door, deep blue lights came on humming. She brought her hands up around her head as though to wave off the images of the cell block, but was afraid to touch anything, even herself. The blue lights died finally and the humming ended and the door clicked open and she ducked between two suited persons waiting to enter. She pulled at the wrist tape over her gloves, tearing away at her protective coverings as she searched for an empty room to cry in. She found one, and inside ripped the cowl and the layers of cotton and plastic from her face like bandages, dropping them to the floor. She covered her stinging eyes with her bared knuckles as a wave of nausea made her gag, and she started blindly forward, striking the desk with her hip before reaching the chair. She buried her face in her bare, powdered hands and sat like that for a long time, weeping, for the mystified dead and dying, for her own helplessness, and for her family and herself, and how sick she had once been.

When she looked up again, Maryk was standing in the door. He came ahead and set his tablet and black bag on the desk, then plunked down the dead man's anklet. It was oily with green disinfectant, metal and round with a locking piece that shaped it into a capital Q. Melanie pushed away.

He pulled a chair over next to her without a word and opened up his tablet on the desk. He tapped keys and pulled from his bag a syringe, a sealed dish about the size of a can of tuna, and the small, blood-testing, PCR gadget.

"Arm," he said.

She swiped at her eyes and complied silently.

"Sleeve," he said.

She rolled up her sleeve. Her skin was bruised from all the bloodletting.

That was it. There was no *I told you so*. The abasement of a blood test was humiliation enough. Maryk gripped her arm and fastened a rubber tourniquet tightly around her tender biceps.

A window opened on Maryk's tablet. She heard Dr. Pearse's hoarse voice, as distinct as though he were there in the room with them. "Hello, Peter," he said ghostily. "How goes the battle?"

She could barely see Dr. Pearse, his face long, his shoulders thin and sharp. She saw whiskers growing stubbly along his cheeks, light gray, nearly Maryk-white. He seemed to have aged even in the few hours since Melanie had left him. She felt a sort of confederacy with him since their private meeting, and wished he could see her there.

Maryk answered, "Contained. Another closed setting—same as Orangeburg, same as all the others."

Dr. Pearse sounded pleased. "It will end as the rest."

Melanie's hand had begun to throb. Maryk uncapped the syringe and she looked away, finding a crucifix on the wall. She had stumbled into the prison chaplain's office. Through the side window she could see out into the main hallway and a corner of the high, round guard station. On the monitors there, yellow suits attended to other sheet-draped bodies in other units in other parts of the penitentiary.

Dr. Pearse sounded enthusiastic. "I'm through scanning for engineering markers—the gamma-amino methionine hydrolase, et cetera. It's there, Peter. The human component I predicted."

"A graft," Maryk said.

"No, Peter. Much more substantial than that. The Plainville RNA payload is insidiously complex, but it is a genetic code like any other, and I've broken it. Fascinating virus. It isn't merely resilient in adapting to changing environments, Peter: It is dictating the terms. It is rejiggering nature and natural selection in order to ensure its survival. This thing is shuffling its own RNA makeup."

"I don't care how fascinating it is, Stephen. I want to know what you've found."

"It's there," he said. "As I told you it would be. You know how I wish it were not true. But Plainville contains verifiable complements of your DNA."

Melanie didn't know what to make of this, and she wouldn't, until Maryk explained it to her later. For now, she was just listening.

"Impossible," Maryk said, but with surprisingly little force.

"I know your genetic makeup pattern better than I know my own. How else could your DNA be in the Plainville virus? It's the PeaMar transfusion and girl with vitiligo. It has to be."

Melanie felt the tourniquet release, and the pressure on her forearm eased, warmth returning to her wrist and hand. She hadn't even felt the needle stick. She looked back as Maryk emptied the tube of her blood into the sealed plastic dish. He mixed it with a few drops of clear fluid.

"Here's what I have," Maryk said. "Looks like everything originated with a guard. He had just returned to work from a family camping vacation in the Carolinas. He was too far gone, but someone managed to get to his nine-year-old son who was still coherent. Standard contact tracing Q and A, minus the sexual queries."

Dr. Pearse was excited. "Yes?"

"A man. The boy said his father pulled over for a motorist stranded on the side of the highway. Which highway, the boy didn't know; he didn't even know which state. The father got out alone to offer assistance, and the motorist got out of the car to join him under the hood. The man apparently was ill. Exactly how ill is not clear, but very thin, the boy claimed, dressed in a medical mask, gloves, and what he described as a small, colorful hat without a brim, perhaps like a toque."

"Yes! That's what Twenty-six was wearing in my bedroom."

Maryk looked at him. "You're certain?"

"Of course I am. No other description?"

"No, and nothing on the car. But while they were waiting, the nine-year-old asked his mother if he could get out and go to the bathroom. He didn't really have to go, he admitted to us; he was just bored. She let him go down the highway incline by himself."

Dr. Pearse sounded excited again. "Of course."

"The boy saw them standing together over the engine, as men do. He recalled two peculiar things about their conversation. One was that the motorist showed a lot of interest in the father's employment: what kind of prison it was, what his duties were as a guard. The other was that the sick man asked, twice, how far the father's penitentiary was from Atlanta."

There was a pause. "Atlanta," Dr. Pearse said, sounding as thrilled as his sickened voice would allow. "The virus has avoided Atlanta, Peter, hasn't it?"

"What do you mean?"

"Florida, South and North Carolina. Now Louisiana. It's not that much of a stretch. If you were a virus, which state in the union would you most likely avoid?"

"You mean—if the virus was being spread by a human."

"Or behaving like one. You would want to keep clear of Georgia and the BDC. Now, by that same token, what if you decided you needed to sabotage the BDC? If you were a virus and wanted to go in and destroy the one institution you knew could stop you. What would you do, Peter? If you could discriminate between victims, and wanted to avoid detection. What would you do?"

Even Melanie, who barely knew Dr. Pearse, reacted to the odd cheerfulness in his voice. Maryk's eyes were dark as he formulated the answer.

"I would go after the director," Maryk said.

She saw Dr. Pearse nodding. "He watched *The Disease Dilemma* show," he said. "And there I was, saying I attended to every outbreak. That led directly to Orangeburg. We frustrated him by denying him his intelligence on the outbreaks, and so he lashed out, whoever he is. He was there. That same man. We represent his only unnatural opposition. Once you start thinking about a motive, a human motive, a viral motive, it all falls into place."

"Then tell me this: How did he get out of a hospital full of BDC personnel?"

"I don't know. But I told you I felt like someone had been following me after I got back to Atlanta. I had seen a car driving back and forth outside my house. He followed me all the way to Amagansett, Peter. He waited until he could get into my room. The survivors' names and addresses were in my tablet. Weren't they?"

Maryk said nothing. He did not even nod. Dr. Pearse went on enthusiastically.

"You said there were only two possible outcomes for humans with Plainville, Peter. Die quickly, or seek immediate intervention and be cured. But what if there was a third? What if someone didn't die right away, and the virus had time to act on them? The serum I hit the girl with in Africa, PeaMar4. Back then, PeaMar wasn't merely a synthetic blood substitute: We began the project with me working to transfuse the disease-fighting properties of your blood. I was out to cure cancer and eradicate all viruses and bacteria all at once. That is why I gave it to the girl—as a preventive measure. But what if there was some sort of reaction? What if the unique viral inhibitors present in your blood—the attenuated killer cells loaded into PeaMar4—only slowed the viral spread throughout the body, but did not eradicate it?"

"Impossible," Maryk said.

"A biological stalemate, allowing the virus time to take over the body without killing it."

"And?"

"And—I don't know. But I will tell you this: I'm close, Peter. I'm very close. Someone is knowingly spreading this disease. And I'm beginning to think that this someone may not be entirely human."

She felt a chill in the warm prison chaplain's office. Maryk's gray eyes were squinting, and he seemed put off by Dr. Pearse's inexplicably upbeat mood.

"Reilly and Boone say you've been doing some electronic research," he said.

"I'm close, Peter. Time is of the essence—for me, particularly. I know there's something out there now. The moment I have anything, I'll let you know."

Maryk broke the fold of his arms to keystroke a command.

"How is Melanie?" Dr. Pearse said. "How is she holding up?"

She tried to get a better look at him, remembering that he did not know she was there. As she looked at the screen, a small window opened over Dr. Pearse's image, a red bar expanding over a gauge growing quickly from zero to one hundred percent. A message flashed beneath it: CLEAN CLEAN CLEAN

Maryk unplugged the gadget and the red bar went out. "She's fine," he said.

There was no night or day inside Lewes, no windows or clocks, only crudely made calendars upon which to X-out the dates. She napped in a chair while Maryk worked in the infirmary operating theater, and while he slept off his cascades she sat at the guard station off B unit and pondered her interrupted life, her interrupted body. She didn't feel whole anymore. She felt like something salvaged from a junkyard, something that Maryk had stitched together, just to see if he could get it to work.

His attitude toward her had changed since she fled B unit. Properly humbled, she was now taken everywhere by him, in some strange way like a student. She stood by the cots as blankets were drawn off one prisoner after another, the sick continually unveiled. The shock of it was gone by then and each one looked the same to her. As Plainville stripped them of personality, it also seemed to strip them of their faults, their predatory natures, exposing the small, frail souls that live in all creatures. The smell too, like the unwavering tone in her ear, no longer dizzied her. The sounds inside the hermetically sealed prison block—moans, shuffling footsteps, creaking carts—were like the sounds of her dreams.

B unit was a tomb constructed of iron and concrete, and every noise was a long time dying away.

She stood inside the vacated cells. She looked out through the iron bars painted dull red, and saw where the paint had been picked away: pitifully pornographic nail scratches to wile away the time. She rested on concrete beds jutting out of concrete walls. She picked through the abandoned belongings: books stacked on the seamless shelf above the toilet, unframed photographs curled from the incessant heat, rolled pairs of clean socks, false teeth. She riffled through Bibles thumbed to twice their original size, the cheap leather spines cracked, pages bookmarked with postcards, letters, photos. In one she found obscenities scratched into the New Testament margins, and reading them, she could hear the prisoner's perverted voice.

She was an apparition to them. She was a ghost. She wished she had something more to offer them than strangeness, mystery, distraction. Maryk, on the other hand, comforted without caring to or even trying. His manner alone consoled the condemned as he moved from bed to bed, working over each man with the same taciturn precision. Their red, fevered eyes grew tame in his assured presence.

"Magnificent," he said, standing next to her later at the railing overlooking the unit from the corner of the highest tier. She would have answered the incessant moaning with a long, shrill scream; Maryk lauded it. "The decay," he went on, looking like a man standing at the rail of a steamship leaving a quarantined port. "The utter rot."

His words were blasphemous to her. She remembered hearing her father downstairs, and knowing from the direction of his groans that he was laid up in the living room, and knowing from their timbre that he was shivering: this man, her father. She and her brother had been forbidden to go downstairs. They had been forbidden even to see him. Her mother brought them food and felt their foreheads and throats with a smooth gloved hand, brave at first, but becoming more and more emaciated with each visit, until finally she stopped coming at all. Melanie held her brother—for the first time, as well as the last—and rocked him as he shivered in her arms, his eyes growing dull and viewing something farther and farther away. The phone still rang with sick, frightened voices that didn't know yet that her dad was gone away.

She had been among the last to feel anything, and as such, was a witness to it all. The long drive out to the hospital, through the dead town and the familiar, empty intersections, past men and women in yellow space suits pulling instruments across driveways and lawns. The grotesquely overgrown plants and trees. Earlier, she had euthanatized every pet in the kennel, rather than have them sicken and die alone. She had held each little unsuspecting head as their bodies went limp.

At the hospital, she had waited for death. She was selected from the common room without knowing why, too frightened to ask. She was rolled away on a gurney past the specters of her neighbors and family and friends, the people of her life, laid out like radiation victims in the hospital corridors. She was left naked under a bedsheet in a hospital bay, a white curtain drawn around her. It felt like death. She hoped the wait would be brief. Her mind left her body for places she had never been, leaving her eyes behind.

Melanie broke out of her reverie as a yellow form brushed past her in a surge of power, toward Maryk on the parapet, prevailing upon him to come away. There was an urgency to their exchange. The person in the suit glanced back at her, and for a moment Melanie struggled to place the face.

It was her gynecologist, Dr. Freeley. There was the sudden shock of recognition, followed by an odd stab of betrayal; but both impulses passed almost immediately. She was becoming conditioned to withstand these broadsides.

It was startling to see Dr. Freeley, a person Melanie had known to be nearly mannequin in her emotions, so alarmed. Maryk stiffened at her words and let go of the rail, and Melanie drew closer, wondering if the news could have something to do with Dr. Pearse, or the sick man they wanted to find. But Dr. Freeley could not whisper and hope to be heard through her hood.

"Broken quarantine," Melanie heard her say. "Three inmates. One of our vans. Just escaped."

Maryk started away before Dr. Freeley could finish, his rubber soles pounding down to the caged stairwell at the far end of the tier. Dr. Freeley turned and started the other way, back toward Melanie, and Melanie turned then and started moving too, moving away from Dr. Freeley, striding more and more quickly past the cots, the cells, the men—all in a blur. If it was a race, she lost; as Melanie reached the UV chamber door, a black rubber suit hand struck out from behind her and hit the lock release. The door hissed open, and she and Dr. Freeley stepped inside.

Blue lights hummed on. The cobalt glow filled Melanie with a feeling of wordlessness, as though anyplace and anytime might be waiting behind that second door; even Plainville, five years before, and she would be given another chance.

She looked up at Dr. Freeley's flawless blue face. It was sealed within the protective glass like something either incredibly precious or too hazardous to touch.

"Is my dentist here too?" Melanie said.

The stranger things became, the easier it was to affect a casual bravado about them. The second door opened on the main corridor, and Dr. Freeley paced Melanie down to the guard station, gripping her arm roughly and presenting her to the suited man there. "Watch her," Dr. Freeley said, pushing her forward. Melanie, stunned, watched her yellow form stride away.

Maryk drove slowly out past the front gate. The lights of the assembled media came on and flooded the entrance but then went off again when they saw that it was just another BDC van. He rolled through the BioCon checkpoint and took his time down the darkened road until he was certain he was not being followed. Two roads later he was on the county route doing eighty.

Freeley sat next to him with her window open. Her glistening suit exuded Pheno and bleach as she replayed the surveillance camera scene for him on her tablet.

"They were left alone for less than a minute," she told him. "One cut himself purposefully on the arm. His blood threat was their ticket out."

On the tablet screen he watched a replay of the three inmates breaking through a locked door. He watched them confront a suited BDC technician and force him behind the wheel of a van as they piled into the back.

"No one saw them at the gate," Freeley said. "They hid in back until they were cleared through. All three were up for murder."

Maryk roared past a yellow pickup truck full of farm kids who cheered the van's speed. "How healthy are they?"

"We had them on Milkmaid's serum, but it was too late. Each was starting to fail." She consulted a grid map on her tablet. "We're six minutes behind them. Less than twenty miles from New Orleans. They'll try to disappear there."

Maryk regripped the wheel. He forced the pedal and the van shook as his speed climbed to ninety miles per hour. "They'll try to break off the quarantine anklets first," he said. He felt the tires slide as he veered sharply around a turn. "They need to switch vehicles. They need clothes."

Freeley said, "There's a naval station in the area. We could call ahead, throw roadblocks up around the city. New Orleans and vicinity means over a million people."

Maryk simply shook his head.

She monitored the electronic anklet trace on her tablet. Then: "They're turning off. Stopping. A residential road, only three addresses."

"How far outside—"

"Ten miles outside New Orleans. Four minutes ahead of us."

Maryk reached the turnoff in just under three. He cut the engine and rolled in along a thin dirt road until he saw the van parked beside a converted barn-garage next to a house. The house was two stories high with weathered wood siding and a new wraparound porch. It was dark. The land in back was considerable and neither of the other two houses was in sight.

They slipped out and crossed to the getaway van. Maryk looked in through the parted rear window curtain and saw the technician lying bloodied and motionless over the wheel hump. His suit was shredded around him.

Freeley started around to the rear of the house while Maryk walked to the front. He climbed two steps and crossed the wooden porch to the door. It was unlocked. He opened it and the door swung wide and banged against the jam and swung back rattling. He made no attempt at stealth. He heard the sound of footsteps shuffling inside. Then he heard nothing.

The black spots on the wood landing inside the door were drops of pathogenic blood. He stepped onto the shadowed threshold with his bag in his right hand.

A short hallway ahead of him led to a larger room with windows showing the rear porch and the long backyard. A flight of stairs to his left climbed to the second floor. To his immediate right was a sitting room. He could make out chairs and a fireplace inside. The chain curtain over the mouth of the fireplace was swaying.

Maryk entered the doorway. He stood there and listened. "Come out," he said.

A hefty shadow in an orange prison jumper rose from behind the wide back of a brocaded chair. It was a large man and he kept rising. He gripped the sides of the broad chair and muscled it across the dark wood floor to show that he didn't usually hide from anyone. The chair toppled over a short bookcase and glass shattered delicately. Then the house was silent again. Maryk listened to the prisoner's breathing and watched his shoulders heave.

The prisoner waggled a finger. "Come on here," he said. "I'll just breath in your face."

Maryk reached down and unfastened the buckles of his bag. He noticed lesions on the man's thick neck and heard the fluttering of his dissolving lung tissue. He saw the characteristic early-stage masking of the face. Standing across the room from him was a hulking virus in an orange prison jumpsuit.

Maryk set his open bag down on an end table. "You made the mistake of killing your only hostage," Maryk said. "Looks like no one is home."

The prisoner shifted and the farmhouse floorboards creaked. His voice was ludicrously low. "You'll do just about fine."

Maryk's right hand went into his bag as his heart rate accelerated comfortably. He pulled out a syringe. "Breaking quarantine is a federal offense."

The prisoner looked at the syringe in Maryk's hand and smiled. He raised his meaty hands into a fistless streetfighter's stance. "What you gonna do with that?" he said.

Maryk remained still. The syringe remained at his side.

The prisoner came at him. He moved lumberingly and raised his big arms to strike as Maryk ducked out of the way. The prisoner lurched past and slipped on a throw rug in the doorway and thundered headlong into the hallway wall. The staircase above him rattled.

The prisoner turned but Maryk was upon him. He braced the prisoner's neck with his forearm and forced the man's Adam's apple up into his larynx as he spun the syringe in his hand. He gripped it needle-down and drove it into the prisoner's chest. The needle slipped neatly between the man's ribs and pierced the pericardium sac of his heart. The prisoner's face burst wide.

Maryk thumbed the plunger and voided the barrel. The prisoner choked on a sucking breath as Maryk broke off the needle in his chest and stepped back. The prisoner's legs buckled and he collapsed on all fours in the night light through the open front door.

Maryk retrieved his bag from the end table in the sitting room. The prisoner was lying on his side and issuing a series of agonal gasps as Maryk stepped past him into the short hallway.

A small shadow that was a second prisoner sprang from a closet ahead and crossed the wide living room. He scrambled over the sofa to another fireplace and picked up the largest piece of kindling wood he could find. He weighed it like a baseball bat as Maryk stepped into the room. The carpeting was plush and silent underfoot. The prisoner tried swinging the wood one-handedly before settling on a clublike grip.

He had light brown skin and weblike tattoos that laced his hands. He did not appear as visibly ill as the first prisoner.

Maryk was laboring under deep intoxicating breaths. His black bag shook slightly in his hand. He remained aware of his back at all times.

Maryk feinted suddenly toward the sofa. The prisoner retreated a quick step and then stopped and brandished the club anew. He uttered a low grunt and gave the weapon a threatening half swing. Maryk countered with another feigned step and the prisoner again jerked back and this time jostled the leg of a small parlor table. Chessmen thumped to the carpet. The prisoner reset himself and brought the wooden club down on the table leg with a solid *crack*. This seemed to invigorate him.

The blood rush in Maryk's head and the force of his breathing built to a crescendo. At once he reached inside his bag and started forward.

This time the prisoner did not retreat. He did not have the chance. A yellow blur that was Freeley burst out from a side room and brought a syringe down slashing with both gloved hands.

The prisoner screamed. The wood sprang from his hands and he went down hard with the syringe buried in his neck. Freeley did not let go and worked the plunger with a combative wail. The prisoner writhed and gurgled beneath her. His shoe heels kicked adamantly at the wall as Freeley broke off the syringe in his neck and stood.

There was a noise upstairs. Maryk turned to the narrow staircase and mounted it in four strides. There was blood on the handrail at the top.

His shoes whisked over a worn Oriental runner along the length of the open second-floor hall. The closed doors were old with glass knobs and key locks. Flea market reproductions had been hung to cover the textured paper peeling off the walls.

He moved through the open door at the end of the hall into a master bedroom. An afghan was folded at the foot of the quilted bedspread and a glass dish of holy water was screwed next to the door.

There was blood smeared on the glass knob leading to a half bath. Maryk eased the door open with his foot before entering all at once and throwing aside a frilly shower curtain.

The glazed window inside was open and there was blood on the crank handle and sill. Maryk looked out onto the roof and saw an orange form dropping off the gutter. He looked across the long black yard to the wide swollen Mississippi River moving in the distance.

Maryk walked to the back door downstairs. He strode out alone over the stiff grass. He smelled the salt of the river and could feel it rushing ahead of him like the blood pushing through his veins. The limping prisoner looked back and saw Maryk coming and renewed his efforts. He was running toward the riverbank.

"Right," the prisoner said finally. He had fallen exhausted to his knees in the muddy salt grass. "All right." He turned to face Maryk. "I'll go back."

They were twenty yards or so from the great moving river. The prisoner raised his arms toward Maryk and his bloody sleeve billowed in the night breeze. Most of his hair was already gone and his face was spent and fading. This prisoner was the sickest of the three.

Maryk allowed him to struggle to his feet before driving the needle into his chest. The prisoner stiffened and looked at Maryk with flaring red eyes before he fell.

Maryk left him gasping up at the dark night sky and continued the short distance to the riverbank. The familiar weight of the cascade thickened his mind and welled behind his eyes like sleep. He shed his cowl, cap, and face mask as he stood exhausted on the hard dirt bank and looked upriver. A broad halo of light glowed against the dark sky. It was a sleeping city of one million human beings.

Melanie saw their van return on a guard station monitor and was allowed to go to the underground garage. She came upon it being unloaded in a brightly lit side room. She noticed immediately the dark dirt splashed on its tires.

The van was empty. Dr. Freeley was speaking with some other BioCon agents while Maryk stood at the passenger's door, away from her. He was looking at his face in the long side mirror. His headgear was gone, his white hair matted back and down.

Dr. Freeley was informing the men about some death certificates she had already written. Melanie heard her update the agents on a house being biocleaned a few miles away.

Maryk turned from the van door. He came forward a few steps before seeing Melanie there. He had a drowsy look in his eyes, and at once she noted the sluggishness of his manner, the guarded way he stood before her, like a practiced drunk. It struck her cold.

"You murdered them," she realized.

Freeley looked up, but Maryk did not answer. He frowned and lurched past her out of the room.

Pasteur's Crypt

She waited with Maryk away from the nighttime travelers streaming through the New Orleans airport, seated alone among a row of hard plastic chairs along a cold wall of windows. Airplanes rolled on the taxiways behind them, and she had that feeling she always had in airports, of being among giants.

Within an hour of his return to Lewes B unit, Maryk decided he was through there; she guessed it had something to do with his cascade, and his concern about Dr. Pearse. A helicopter had ferried them to the airport, and now they were waiting for the flight back to Atlanta.

"Viruses love airports," Maryk said. "Vital organs, located at every major human population center, catapulting incubators from city to city all over the world. The circulatory system of human civilization."

He sat too heavily and too large for the chair, his big legs extended clumsily and crossed at the ankles, his eyes low and turned to the bustling terminal beyond. He was deep into one of his funks, and she wanted no part of him.

"Three phases of public response to an epidemic," he said. "First: Denial. That occurred during the original outbreak in Plainville. The Search for Blame is what we're into now, with the press. If the epidemiology continues to elude us and the virus strikes again, then the BDC will be made the scapegoat. Phase three is the Demand for Action. The blood response. In previous ages this meant burning down the houses of the sick, and the aristocracy fleeing into the hills. But there are no hills remote enough anymore. No oasis that doesn't have a road running through it. And no foreigners foreign enough to blame. The ecosystem is sealed and starting to cook. House burning is all."

This pleased him, of course. She was cold and sat with her bare arms crossed, trying to ignore him. Maryk had changed back into his standard outfit of white shirt and black pants, but she had not brought any clothes other than the hospital scrubs she had been issued back at the BDC. A large monitor suspended from the ceiling broadcast weather reports from various destinations, and she saw footage of snow piling up in Boston.

Standing beneath the monitor flipping through *Newsweek* magazine was a red-haired man in a brown leather jacket and latex gloves, who looked a lot like the custodian at the Emory cafeteria.

"You're not doctors," Melanie said quietly.

Maryk was slow to respond. "Viral containment," he said. "Halting its spread throughout the species. That is my job."

She said, "Doctors heal people."

"A host either contains its illness, or seeks to spread. Those who seek to spread have to be stopped."

"Killed, you mean." She felt another airplane—an immense, winged incubator—roll behind them. "I think I understand you now," she said. "Your perspective. Who you are, where you're coming from. The prisoners, the other medical people there in suits: We walked among them like gods. I didn't like it."

"You felt it, though."

"They feared you. They feared me."

"They fear the battle. They fear exposure. Infection is a challenge. It is Nature calling us out. *Fight,* she says. *Fight for your life, your existence. Survive,* she dares. *Endure."*

"Of course you'd say that. You haven't the slightest idea what it's like to be sick."

Sarcasm, or perhaps amusement, registered on his face. "Tell me, then," he said.

"I can't."

"What it's like. To be sick."

"You can't just say it." She frowned at his sleepy eyes. "I could list symptoms, but you know symptoms. It has nothing to do with that anyway. Everything changes."

"Changes."

"That's right."

"Everything."

"Life, living. Perspective. Priorities."

"It simplifies things."

"If that's what you call it when your options are reduced."

"Fear, then."

"Yes, fear. Are you asking for yourself, or for Dr. Pearse?"

That quieted him. He sat up a bit, and the row of chairs rocked.

"Perhaps you're curious," she said, pursuing it. "What it must be like for him. Losing control of your own body: That's the fear. Awareness that you *have* no control over your own body, really. Nobody does. That's what changes. You acquire this privileged knowledge about the human condition, and slowly it becomes hysteria. You've never even had a head cold. How can you know what health is?"

He had no answer for her immediately, which buoyed her.

"What if I got sick again?" she said.

"Simple," he said, sitting back now. "I would treat you."

"And if I refused? Resisted?"

He said again, "I would treat you."

"What if I ran? I told you before: I will never go through that treatment again."

He looked at her with more than a glance now. He was taking her seriously. She wanted to be taken seriously.

"What if my blood was no longer any good to you," she said, "and you knew that I would refuse treatment? What if I was going to run? Would you kill me too?"

His gaze was penetrating. "Where would you go?"

"Away. A remote island somewhere."

"How would you get there without infecting others?"

She held her own. "I'd find some way."

"There is no way. And no safe place to go. Either one contains one's illness, or spreads it. There is no running away."

"Then you would kill me."

His arm went out as though sweeping a table clean. "My job is to protect the human race. To defend and preserve the species, and I'll do it any way I have to. Because I'm the only one who can. I am the last line of defense."

That raised her eyebrows. That was the cascade talking. It made him seem vulnerable somehow, and she decided to try to pick his brain while it was soft. "Where does someone like you come from?" she said.

"The same place everyone comes from."

"I mean, where in the world?"

He was gazing ahead now, only half there. "Skagit Valley. Northern Washington State. An hour north of Seattle, near Vancouver."

"And you were raised there by wolves?"

He nodded. "My father was a pediatrician," he said. "Like yours."

She could have done without that information. "And your mother?"

"She was a part-time church secretary. She called Bingo in the parochial school gymnasium Monday nights. She was blind."

"She was blind and she called Bingo?"

"The nun who ran the game was pathologically shy. She would pull the Ping-Pong balls and whisper numbers into my mother's ear, who would then announce them. It came out later that the nun was lying to my mother, routinely rigging the games for the poorest families of the parish to win. Bingo was canceled not long after that."

"Was she born—you know—blind?"

"No. She remembered images. Toys, pillows, chair legs. Linoleum floors. The unpainted undersides of tables. It was a childhood illness."

Melanie's only point of reference was the *Little House* books, and Mary, the older sister, who went so valiantly blind from scarlet fever, whose god-fearing ways Melanie tried to emulate as a child.

She thought she had something on him then. "That's why you became a virologist," she said.

He said nothing at first, looking only bemused.

"What?" she said.

"That's something Stephen might have said. No, it was simpler than that. My father also had a tulip farm. One season, when I was eight or nine, the crop came up healthy in every way except the petals: reds and violets and yellows swirled together, similar to what you get when you stir one paint color into another. My mother always liked me to describe things to her, but those colors were one thing I could never get right. My father said a plant virus had caused it. Our crop sold for ten times the usual amount that year. I waited all summer and fall and winter, but next spring the tulips came up normal again. The virus never recurred."

A nine-year-old Maryk in short pants, standing belt-high among acres of psychedelic pastels. She grinned at the image, then remembered who she was dealing with. "No brothers, sisters?"

He looked oddly bemused again, a look so wrong for his piercing face. "Actually, my mother was to have had twins," he said. "Her ultrasound showed two of us until her eighteenth week, when she experienced some complications. Her next test, taken her twenty-first week, showed only one fetus. This always bothered her. For some reason she thought it was significant, and told me this just before she died. All twins battle in the womb for space, nutrition. It starts that early—the pushing, the pulling. From what is now known about reproductive medicine, the most likely theory is that, whatever sibling I was to have, I absorbed in utero."

He seemed to be not at all aware of how disturbing this bit of information was. "So you're like a twin all by yourself, that's what you're saying?"

He sat up and pointed to his breast pocket. "Feel."

The pocket appeared empty. She reached over, the tips of her fingers tentatively poking his starched white shirt over his heart, and felt nothing, and she was relieved at first. Then she pressed her palm fully against the hard, curved muscle of his left breast, and realized there was nothing there at all.

"No heartbeat," she said.

"Now here."

She pressed against his right breast, and felt something beating inside. She snatched back her hand, feeling the sting of the opposing armrest as she struck it with her elbow.

Maryk sat back, gazing out into the bustling crowd. "The organs in my body are reversed. The medical term is *situs inversus*. A mirror image, such as is seen in some separated Siamese twins."

"You consumed your sibling," she said.

He nodded. "Something like that."

She wiped off her hand on her scrub pants. "Why are you telling me all this?"

"Why are you asking?"

"Good point," she said, wondering about that herself. She was having trouble reconciling the odd, biologically inebriated man sitting across from her with the monster she knew him to be. "Do you see your father much?"

"He still practices. Settled right into national health care. Staunch middle-class medicine: antibiotics, inoculations, strep throat cultures." This was all said disparagingly.

"And you're not married. Except to your job."

He squinted into the crowd, at nothing. Yet she suspected some part of him was enjoying this. "You think you have me at a disadvantage."

"You do realize that most people with your biological whatever-it-is would just go wild. Take the worst risks—then sleep it off, and the next day be fine and clean."

She could tell by the puzzled look on his face that this thought had never occurred to him.

"What about death?" she said. "If you can't get sick. You will die, won't you?"

"Of course. The body breaks down, cells break down. We're dying all the time, our tissues disintegrating as we sit here, right now." He waved indolently, at the travelers, at nothing. "Death is constant. The termination event itself is merely an end to a process. Death is a sunset, no more. You don't fear a sunset."

His bravura fascinated her, as much as she disbelieved it. His contempt was so forthright and unyielding that she found it endearing in a cranky sort of way. It appealed to her own innate pessimism.

"I think I prefer you like this," she said. "You seem almost human."

His gaze remained distant. "I didn't come here to be insulted."

She watched him for a smile. "Benjamin Something," he said instead.

Her own smile fell away. "What did you say?"

"Can't remember his last name. The ticket agency worker. Benjamin Something." He spoke as though of a mutual acquaintance. "He seemed suitable. On paper, anyway."

He was filling in the last few remaining gaps in her file. Any personal debacles she had tried to put behind her lived still and brightly in Maryk's mind.

"I have a few rather disfiguring scars on my body," she said, "which I'm a bit overly sensitive about. This tends to rule out any danger of intimacy with the opposite sex."

She heard herself trying to pass off desperation as aloofness, denigrating that which was forbidden her. She was the poor, grumbling about the rich. With a shudder she realized that Maryk knew her better than anyone else. It reminded her again how much she resented him.

"You know what?" she said. "I think some people are like viruses. Some people just take, and if they give you anything at all, it's something you don't want."

This seemed to register inside his muddled head, reflected in his eyes, which sharpened in their view over the lounge and held there a moment before retreating again. He hadn't liked that comparison at all.

A bickering couple passed them, hot coffee dripping off the man's jacket cuff. They thought of sitting nearby, but a shared glance at Maryk made them reconsider. They faded away and Melanie was all business again.

"Why 'Milkmaid'?" she said.

He squinted. "That was about Jenner. Edward Jenner, who discovered the cure for smallpox. Wordplay. The 'milkmaid' who launched his work, the 'lancet' he used to open the boil, the cow named 'Blossom.' Inelegant. If I had to do it over again, I would use Pasteur instead." He glanced at her then, as though having decided something, and leaned forward interrogationally. "I am going to tell you a story that will change your life," he said.

She doubted that. "I could use a change."

"Eighteen eighty-five. Alsace, France. A nine-year-old boy named Joseph Meister, on his way to school, is mauled savagely by a rabid dog and barely survives. Rabies, what the French call *la rage*, was well feared in that day. Fever, depression, throat convulsions, progressing to mania, characteristic foaming at the mouth, eventual paralysis, and death. There was no cure and no treatment. A local doctor cauterized the worst of the boy's wounds and, having reached the limits of his abilities, advised Madame Meister to travel to Paris to call upon Dr. Louis Pasteur. Pasteur was not a physician. Pasteur was a chemist, a scientist. The idea of germs fascinated him, and he was experimenting at the time with the germs of dead animals, ones he had weakened in the laboratory. His work would eventually lead to the discovery of viruses, but at that time, the idea of invisible particles causing disease was considered pure fancy. Meister became Pasteur's first human trial. Pasteur inoculated him with a solution mixed from the spinal cords of rabbits recently dead from rabies. This was only the second human vaccine in history, after Jenner's, but the first to be manufactured in a laboratory and derived from the same infective agent that caused the disease. The boy survived. He was spared the ravages of *la rage*. Modern human virology finds its genesis in Pasteur's pioneering work, and yet he was misunderstood by many of his time. Most of his colleagues could not see the whole of the canvas upon which he was working.

"But that's all regular history and well enough known. It is at this point that history abandons the boy. Joseph Meister never wavered in his devotion to the man who saved his life and, fittingly, grew up to become the gatekeeper at the Institute Pasteur years after his savior's death. Joseph Meister was guarding the gate in 1940 when the Nazis marched into Paris. They ordered him to open Pasteur's crypt, but Meister refused, and instead took his own life in protest."

Melanie hung in the ensuing silence.

"He killed himself," she said. "That's your life-changing story?"

For the first time that night, Maryk seemed fully awake. "Meister destroyed himself rather than be part of the desecration of the memory of the artist who had preserved his life. And history gives him nothing. Well—if seventy-six years can be considered history. In truth it is the blink of an eye." He sat up again, interested. "Think of that. Seventy-six years ago, the first human being ever to be inoculated with a lab-prepared vaccine died. Three quarters of a century; it's nothing. And penicillin: discovered by accident, less than one hundred years ago. People have already forgotten that strep throat was until only recently a fatal disease. We've had a century's parole from bacterial slaughter—and now our time is running out again. Antibiotics are failing and diseases are once again outpacing the remedies. Do you know how our time will be remembered?"

Melanie shook her head.

"As a flash of light between great periods of darkness. If our so-called modern age is remembered at all. Earth is something like three and a half billion years old; mankind, a few million. We are infants crawling upon this rock, protozoa from a pond, who crawled out of the oceans, who dropped down from the trees. Dinosaurs presumed the world was theirs as well. We are a fungus spreading over this planet, colonizing, warring, consuming. The Earth is a cell we are infecting. And nature is the Earth's immune system, just now sensing the threat of our encroachment, and arming itself to fight back. Macro versus micro. Viruses are the Earth's white blood cells. We are the Earth's disease."

Melanie smiled haltingly in defense of the human race. "But nobody could really believe that. Not even you. Look at the environment. The more we learn about the earth, the better we behave."

He waved it all away. "Folly. Like bees getting together and deciding not to pollinate. Like termites voting whether or not to chew through wood. Man will consume his environment. Every form of life from the smallest to the largest contributes something to the earth's ecology, re-paying the overall system, except for two species: rats and man. Man is a thief, a scavenger, a hunter-gatherer—a survivor. That is all."

"Then why do you fight for him? Why defend and preserve the species at all if as you say it will endure of its own, I don't know, villainy?" He said nothing, and she came upon the answer herself. "Because you are the ultimate man. You are the ultimate consumer. You think you're dif-ferent, but in fact, you are the ultimate survivor."

He stared at her, and a glimmer passed across his face—as though he were remembering suddenly that he was impaired and that things might not be necessarily as they seemed. He turned to face the lounge again. He said, "That's the sort of thing Stephen would have said."

"You said that before. What does that mean? That I'm like him? Or that I'm not like you? Because I can tell you for a fact: I am not like you."

But he wasn't listening to her. Melanie heard their flight being called overhead, and she turned and looked out across the tarmac to the giant airplanes lifting off into the night, chasing the sunset that no one feared. She dreaded their return to Atlanta.

Maryk stirred himself awake just after takeoff, as sour jet air coursed through the cabin. The wider seats of first class did little to ease his claustrophobia but the cascade had passed and his thinking was again clear.

A flash outside drew his eye to the window. He watched as a flutter of light suffused the dark membrane of clouds below. A similar burst throbbed miles away and was answered by another closer to the airplane. Then it was as though a fuse had been lit. A succession of eruptions like flashbulbs beat all along the silent plain of the sky. Maryk leaned into the window and watched as the atmosphere below him erupted. They were flying over a fierce electrical storm. He looked down and thought of synapses pulsing over the one-celled earth.

He felt the need to share this with someone. He looked back to Melanie on the other side of the empty seat separating them. She was wrapped shoulders to feet in a thin blue blanket. He could see the outline of her crossed arms rising and falling steadily. She was asleep. He instead reached over and eased her chair into a reclining position. She mumbled and turned over to face him but did not wake. He looked back out the window and the sky beneath the airplane was only intermittently bright as the last silent bursts of light faded behind the tail.

His tablet toned on the empty seat. He opened it and Reilly appeared in a window from somewhere inside the BDC. His image was distorted by the electrical activity. He said something and Maryk asked him to repeat it.

"Director Pearse escaped B4," Reilly said.

Maryk was a long moment digesting this. "How?" he said.

Stephen had requested a contact suit earlier in the day. It was one of a half dozen items Reilly and Boone had imported into B4 for him. He walked out wearing it one hour after their shift ended and surprised the BioCon agent posted at the elevator. He was wearing the contact suit and walking with his cane. He asked her to step away before he took her tablet. The guard at the gate recalled a suited man driving a light green car but had not recorded the license plate. Seeing a man in a contact suit leave the BDC was like seeing a man in uniform leave an army base.

"He took nothing else?" Maryk said.

"We've been through B4 top to bottom."

"Neither one of you thought to ask him what he wanted a suit for?"

"Our instructions were clear: Anything Director Pearse wants, Director Pearse gets. We told you he was getting weird. I thought it was maybe his mind starting to go. Now I think he was onto something."

"Tap into the B4 drives. I want a rundown of anything he was looking into."

Reilly said, "Already started that. I'll post it as soon as it's done."

Maryk's thoughts ran wild. Stephen had taken the extraordinary precaution of putting on a suit. But a suit is only meant to protect the person inside. He was a walking viral bomb and still toxic to anyone unprotected in a confined space.

He had walked off in violation of federal quarantine and had recently been acting suspiciously. Maryk knew the bizarre things that Plainville could do to the mind.

All this came to a head as his tablet toned again with another incoming message. This one was text only and the sender was Stephen Pearse. The message had been posted from a location one hundred and eighty miles south of Atlanta. It read PETER COME AT ONCE.

The Swamp

The Okefenokee National Wildlife Refuge and Wilderness Area ranged more than four hundred thousand acres. It was the largest and most primitive swamp in North America. Maryk's tablet trace showed that Stephen was six miles in. A road ran most of the way.

He waited next to Melanie while the BDC helicopter rounded the northern tip of the swamp. She still wore scrubs and sneakers and was staring out her window into the Georgia dawn and the vast swamp undulating below.

"Why would he leave," she said, "knowing he is contagious?"

"I don't know."

"What are you going to do if he doesn't want to come back?"

He found her naïveté no longer amusing and recently declined to respond.

Maryk had received Stephen's computer searches. Stephen had downloaded forty years of voting registers for the town of Plainville, Massachusetts. He had also downloaded ten years of so-called annual manifestos put out by the Rainforest Ecology Conservation International in Africa. Nothing was highlighted on either document. Stephen had also accessed a January 2012 issue of *Audubon Magazine* and sent off a request to the MacArthur Foundation for information on the current address of one of its fellowship recipients.

They set down upon a local highway on the edge of the refuge and transferred into three waiting Park Services Jeeps. The road deteriorated inside the swampland and ended altogether at a state park, where Freeley was waiting with a BioCon unit. They had matched the license plate of a car in the parking lot to a vehicle missing from the BDC fleet. She was pulling on a contact suit as Maryk approached.

"I didn't think he could even walk," she said.

Maryk said, "He walks fine."

"What if he had gone to an airport?"

"He didn't."

"It's a trap."

Maryk was impatient. "Then I guess I'm falling for it."

A ranger's assistant warned of swamp vegetation rivaling that of a South American jungle. One recent hiker who violated the No Camping rule had been missing for more than six weeks. The terrain was full of sawgrass and cutting underbrush too dangerous for contact suits. Freeley and BioCon had to wait for path-clearing tools.

The ranger offered to guide Maryk inside but Maryk declined. He did accept the man's offer of a self-inflating Zodiac launch and a small outboard motor but he could not carry them both with his black bag. He saw Melanie standing away from the rest. She was watching him.

"You can stay here, or you can help," he said.

She considered it only a moment. She came forward and took his tablet and his bag.

They pushed into the dense growth on foot. Melanie took the lead as Maryk ported the heavy marine equipment through the sinking earth. The return to a jungle setting struck him as somehow appropriate.

It took them less than an hour to reach the source of the Hailing signal. Stephen's tablet was set upon an inlet stump at the head of a dead stream that had recently seen passage. A trail of black water split the emerald scum crusted along the facing banks. The tablet screen read PETER COME ALONE.

At the base of the tree stump was a damp rope greened with slime. Maryk looked out at the still black path of water. The Zodiac. It self-inflated and he set it afloat and attached the outboard motor. He climbed aboard. The black rubber floor of the launch was soft and sun-roughened and Maryk squatted on his knees for balance.

He turned to start the motor and saw Melanie still waiting on the mud bank. She was watching him accusingly. She was holding his black bag. He stopped with the cord in his hand.

"You're not going to kill him," she said.

"Everybody has a choice," he said. "Containment, or spread. Do you trust Stephen to have chosen correctly?"

She came forward with his bag and climbed inside. "It's you I don't trust."

She squatted down into the bow as he returned to the cord. He pulled it twice and the engine erupted and settled into an even growl. He pushed off and piloted the launch away from the bank.

Melanie picked hair out of her face as they puttered along the course described by the cleaved scum. She seemed content to kneel in front and survey the dense shores of the dead stream. The path of black water veered eastward into the sunlight and she reached up and cleared away vines that dropped like streamers into their path. Maryk cut the engine farther ahead and drifted as he listened to the shore. The croaks and bird cries and rustling of legs along the muddy brush had faded. They were entering a strangely quiet part of the swamp.

He saw the first Plainville plant ahead on their right. Veins burst from the remaining midrib leaf spines like wiry arms and thickened into cord-like spindles. There was another immediately after it along the same dark patch of ground. Its leaf blades had curled and frayed and erupted in color that had since decayed to varied hues of gray and black. Both growths appeared to have once been common ferns.

They moved past a stunted Plainville tree that had suffered an aberrant surge of growth before dying. He watched Melanie's head turn to a profile as they floated past its outreaching branches. She slid away to the opposite side of the small boat.

The stream path angled right and ended at a small island. Maryk steered onto a worn dirt slip next to an older Zodiac launch with faded lettering along its scum-ringed sides. They disembarked onto a well-trodden path that had seen heavy things dragged over it.

They stopped under another savage tree. The wood was barkless and blistered and swirled into inscrutable knots. Its sulfur-yellow roots had erupted and burrowed back down again into the mire like elbows trying to raise the trunk from the earth.

"This is the virus?" she said quietly.

Maryk nodded.

"Why isn't it spreading?"

The Plainville plants and trees lay in dark patches surrounded by healthy flora. Maryk looked up at the wide rifts in the canopy and the morning sunlight beating through.

"Sunlight," he said. "A natural barrier." It was the same as it had been in Africa. All viruses fell apart when exposed to the sun's ultraviolet rays.

She stayed close to him as the footpath led to a long structure draped in canvas. It was some twenty yards in length and appeared to be a series of camping tents stitched together. Camouflaging branches and leaves littered the mismatched roofs.

A door flap had been cut into the near corner. Maryk lifted it from the bottom and listened before entering. The smell that escaped was pungent. Melanie started to gag but Maryk pulled her the rest of the way inside.

Spears of dusty daylight burned down through slashes in the canvas roof. Maryk's eyes adjusted to wooden workbenches along both walls and a central row of rough-hewn tables. He saw dairy pails nearby, bottles of chemicals, and measuring devices and scales. There was a heavy press, a bucket of dirty syringes, and knives as well as other anatomizing instruments.

Dead Plainville plants sat in heaps of burst pottery and dry soil. They clutched at the tables like ivy. Scores of small dead carcasses lay flayed on the center tables in varying stages of dissection. Maryk guessed they might have been rats.

"Oh my—" Melanie recoiled and grabbed for the door flap behind them.

Maryk gripped her arm and pulled her ahead. They passed a discarded BDC contact suit lying atop a work space. A blistered plant arm had grown over it.

At the end of the rows of worktables stood dozens of small metal cages filled with decomposing rats. As many as eight to a cage were rotted with Plainville. The odor there was as thick as steam. Melanie began to cough and retch and tugged on him. Maryk released her and he went on alone.

Plainville plants in clay pots filled the dark floor space from the middle of the tent to the far canvas wall. The colors were ferocious and thriving as though choked to brilliance. The plants had erupted from their arranged pots and slithered outward along the dirt ground as though dragging themselves forward. Maryk waded in among them. Some lay unmolested in an open space of dirt as though respected or feared. Their bright leaves gleamed as though with perspiration and their tentacular stems and wildly textured leaves scorned nature. Shards of busted pottery lay wound in vinelike branches as though in the grip of florid fists.

Maryk heard a weak voice behind him.

"I came here to kill him, Peter."

Stephen was standing inside the door flap. A ray of daylight through the torn canvas above lit his surgical skullcap and shadowed the recesses of his face.

"He's not here," he continued. "But he knows we are. I set off a silent alarm."

"Stephen." Maryk moved past Melanie toward him.

"Outside," Stephen said. He pushed through the canvas flap and daylight shone in profanely.

Maryk rushed out after him. There was a wooden bench set in front of the tent and Stephen was making his way to it. He moved well with the cane but his physical appearance had further declined. He was drenched in sweat and impossibly thin. The sores about his arms and legs had darkened and massed and bled. He looked like a cadaver. He looked as though he were brittling into wood.

Melanie came gagging through the tent door behind Maryk. One look at Stephen calmed her. She fought down a swallow.

Stephen showed her a much-weakened grin. "Hello, Melanie," he said.

Maryk said, "What is this, Stephen?"

"A hiding place. He couldn't spread his virus indiscriminately. He needed a place where he could live freely. He wanted only controlled outbreaks, remember?"

"Who, Stephen?"

"Plainville's Patient Zero. Something incredible has happened here, Peter. I need you to keep an open mind."

Maryk's concerns about Stephen's mental health were being realized. "Plainville was more than four years ago," he said. "Just tell me—what is this place?"

Stephen motioned with a wooden hand for patience. "An open mind," he said. "I was thinking about the girl in Africa, assuming that she had been infected and also gotten the experimental serum. I was thinking what it must have done to her. She would have been like a walking laboratory, Peter, like lightning in a bottle. I decided that there had to be a secondary transmission, even though we knew there had been no other reported cases in that region. So I started to think. The only other people near the camp, aside from the Pygmies, was the RECI group. I called up a list of their scientists, and on a whim cross-referenced it with the Plainville voting register. It was that simple, Peter. One name came up on both lists. Oren Ridgeway, a botanist out of the University of Michigan. He returned to the states from his RECI tour just two weeks after the firebombing of the camp."

"Oren Ridgeway?" said Melanie.

They both turned to her. Stephen said, "You knew him?"

She retreated somewhat. "The family," she said. "He worked summers in my dad's office. He was a few years older than I was."

"Fascinating," said Stephen. He returned to Maryk. "Assume Ridgeway came into direct contact with the African girl. It couldn't have gone any farther than that in Africa, or else we'd have seen it, seen victims."

Maryk interrupted. "We backtracked after Plainville. We posted the RECI to see if any of their people had gotten sick. The answer was no."

"Of course. But something tripped the virus into lying latent, some mutation inside the girl. Ridgeway showed no symptoms, and brought it back here unknowingly. Then a year or so later—on a trip to his parents in his hometown, I assume—it erupted. The virus emerged there in three places simultaneously. In the schools: he may have stopped in for a visit with his old teachers. In the pediatrician's office." He looked at Melanie. "A 'hello' to your father, perhaps. And the town hall: His mother worked for the town clerk."

Maryk had been trying to break in. "Plainville does not lie latent," he said. "No one who contracts it survives two weeks, never mind—"

"That was the PeaMar4. The viral inhibitors from your blood reacted with the virus from the girl. By the time it spread to Ridgeway, a sort of symbiosis had been reached. The virus was softened up, but not killed, and attained something like equilibrium with his body. The impossible was then suddenly possible."

Maryk said, "How do you know all this?"

"I know it, Peter. I know it. The goal of every active virus is to change the host cell—to transform the host into a copy of the virus. Not to kill, but to coexist; to preserve a viable host so that the virus may survive and endure. And this has always been biologically impossible. Until now." Stephen looked at him fire-eyed. "You've got to open your mind to this, Peter. Under normal conditions, either the immune system battles the virus into submission, or the virus continues unabated and consumes the host. But not here. Here communion has been achieved. Rather than plundering and killing Ridgeway's immune cells, the mutated virus instead began transforming them, successfully, exponentially, into virus cells—exactly as it is supposed to, only this time, it worked. Plainville is the first successful virus. It is not lying dormant in him; it is active, it is thriving. It is one with him. It has transformed this Oren Ridgeway into a human Plainville vector."

Maryk resisted this at the same time it started to make sense. "First of all," he said, "how did you find this place?" He needed to understand it all logically.

"A few months before Plainville, Ridgeway won a MacArthur Foundation grant of $345,000 for his work documenting and preserving expiring species of flora here in the Okefenokee Refuge. He gave away every dime to radical environmental groups for the first two years, then dropped out of sight. An article in a back issue of *Audubon* led me here. Most of these supplies—the boat, the instruments—are pilfered from his original camp, now abandoned, less than a kilometer away. Something drew me from there to this place. It was almost like I could smell the plants, Peter. Right through my suit. I feel close to him."

Maryk ignored this. "Then, those plants, inside?"

"He was learning. He was planning his infection, but patiently, over four years' time. He was methodical. A virus must infect—that is all it knows and all it wants to do. But now the virus has taken human form: It has a brain, it has reasoning capacities and an understanding of the way humans work to fight disease. It has the best of both existences, virus and man. The outbreaks were tests. He was taking human samples, the same way we take viral samples, in order to measure his infective progress. Not indiscriminately, because he knew we would trace that. I think that Plainville was most likely a mistake. It was his first time, he may not have known what was happening to him yet. But we covered up the subsequent outbreaks, which led finally to Orangeburg. He tried to take me out and the entire BDC with me."

Maryk kept pace. "So then this same man followed you to Amagansett."

"Virus, Peter. This *virus*." Stephen nodded. "Imagine his shock at opening up my tablet and discovering that there were three Plainville survivors generating sera."

"And then he set about hunting them down," Maryk said. It was all unfolding in his mind. "The lightweight shoe print in Lancet's bathroom. The plants missing from Blossom's car. The open windows at each location to air out the smell. He was sampling their blood before killing them."

"In order to test it against his own disease. He had to know just how potent their antibodies were, to see how much of a threat they posed to him. Of course this man-virus would kill them. They were his cure, and therefore had to be eliminated."

Melanie had stood silently listening through this. Now her voice came like a gasp. "The broken-down motorist."

Stephen nodded. "That was our Patient Zero. He was driving back from Boston. He had just failed to eliminate the third survivor."

Maryk remembered the shadow in the cul-de-sac outside the Penny University. He remembered the shoe marks on the rusted rungs and the feeling he had of being watched inside the sewer. Patient Zero had been there that night. Only the sewer sanitation mechanisms killed his virus in the water and prevented its spread.

Stephen was still looking at Melanie. "Your death would guarantee his success," he said.

He seemed unaware of the impropriety of his statement. He seemed only intrigued. Melanie stepped away from him. "Oh my God."

Maryk said, "Then where is this 'Zero' right now?"

"I don't know. He is extraordinarily contagious, so any form of mass transportation would lead to a prematurely infectious event. He is saving himself for the end. Therefore, he travels cautiously. He must have his own car."

Maryk searched the swamp in frustration. He looked at the laboratory and at the twisted Plainville trees. He was trying to get his mind around the reality that there was a man out there driving the streets who was no longer a man but a virus.

He knelt down and unbuckled his bag and pulled out his tablet. "I'm calling in BioCon. We'll preserve some of these plants for examination, then torch the rest and return to the bureau."

"Wait," Stephen said. He used his cane to stand. "His work is still here. Written logs, data disks. I need to remain to analyze them."

"Stay here? You shouldn't even be out of B4. The bacteria alone will eat you alive."

"He was expecting to return. We've got his research, Peter. Listen to me. Something is troubling him. He would not have panicked over the LNPs otherwise. He would have touched off a chain of transmission and consumed the entire human race by now if there weren't something keeping him back, something he is waiting for. The secret may be right inside here." He moved near Maryk. "I feel close to him, Peter. I can't explain it, but I think I can make sense of his notes, his work here. We'll not have a chance like this again."

Maryk stood. "What do you mean, you feel close to him?"

The tablet toned in Maryk's hand. He stared at Stephen a long moment before opening it.

"Freeley," he said.

No window opened on the screen. He adjusted the display in the bright sunlight. The video feed had been disabled at the source's discretion. The modem task bar indicated that he was connected to a call and listed the sender as a land-line public pay phone from an area code outside Georgia.

The voice that answered him was garbled and fluidy. "Dr. Peter Maryk?"

"Who is this?"

The caller made a rumbling noise that failed to clear his throat. "You have found my laboratory."

Maryk went suddenly cool in the beating sun.

"I saw you in that alley sewer," the voice went on.

Melanie's face was bloodless. Her hands were flat against her chest as she backed away. Her fear checked Maryk's and reminded him who he was. "Then you know I've got Milkmaid."

The groaning voice said, "Did you find my hiker yet? Or what's left of him. I fed him some of your guinea pigs' blood before showing him to my garden. His death was merely enhanced. Your blood solution failed."

"You are wrong. It has not failed Stephen Pearse."

"Pearse is dead, I saw to that. You're covering it up like the rest."

Stephen was staring at Maryk dead-eyed. Maryk's mind was reeling. His sense of rational balance and the natural order of the world were being challenged. He needed confirmation. "How did you get out of Orangeburg?"

"The hospital?" Another throaty rumbling. "Double doors, foamed walls. All to protect against microscopic viruses escaping. But if a man-sized virus got into a yellow suit from the supply room? No one would even look at his face. He could walk right out the door."

"Would you recognize Pearse's voice?"

Maryk turned the tablet around to Stephen. Stephen was in shock. He spoke hesitantly to the virus that had infected him.

"Ridgeway?"

Maryk turned the tablet back to himself. "Pearse lives," he said. "He's right here, standing next to me outside your laboratory. He lives because I've got Milkmaid. It's not enough just to have the blood. It's the serum treatment. She cures you. Milkmaid is viable and I've got her antibodies. Which means I've got you—whatever you are."

"I am the Messenger. What you call 'Plainville' is the Message."

Stephen came forward then. "Tell me," he said, "how did you contract this? Was it a girl, a teenage girl?"

Silence for a moment. Stephen seemed to hang in the air.

The voice said, "So it was you who sent her to me, Doctor. Perfect." Stephen's gaze slipped to the ground. "You don't sound so healthy, Dr. America. And if you were, you would be right back on TV again."

Stephen's gaze only deepened.

Then the voice said, "Hello, Melanie."

Melanie shivered. She looked at Maryk and shook her head and mouthed a frantic *No.*

But a hard grin steeled Maryk's nerves. "She is with me at all times," he said.

Zero chuckled gurglingly. "Not many public phones these days," he said. "I'll be long gone by the time you arrive. Perhaps I could leave you a little something to remember me by."

Maryk heard the sound of a telephone cord being twisted.

"A man here waiting for the phone. Middle-aged, wearing a beige raincoat. His tablet battery must have run down. He's not looking in on me right now because he hates sickness. He hates sick people."

The metallic cord twisted again.

"He is lazy and fat. He's meat to me, understand that, Maryk? The world is full of meat. You cannot stop the Messenger. You cannot stop the Message. The Message will always get through."

There was the sound of something rubbing against the receiver. Then a click and the droning dial tone of a broken connection.

Stephen stepped backward. He found the bench against his legs again and slumped down upon it.

Maryk said, "What was that noise at the end?"

Stephen's face was blank and drawn. "Him licking the receiver."

Melanie gasped behind them.

Maryk paged Freeley and gave her the telephone number to be traced. He told her to divert BioCon to the caller's location on a Biohazard 4 and to shut down any airports within a thirty-mile radius. Then he dialed the pay phone number. It was busy and he dialed again and this time it rang through.

A voice answered: "Yeah, hullo?" Winded and annoyed.

"Get out of there," Maryk said. "Get out of there and get everybody away from this telephone—"

Freeley and the BioCon unit moved in and took over the swamp island and Maryk left Stephen at the lab under their protection. He traveled with Melanie by helicopter to the site of the outbreak.

The public telephone was located in one of a pair of antiquated folding-door booths beneath a slowly rotating Waffle House restaurant sign on a highway roadstop in Yulee, Florida. The booths were currently sealed in nylon and the walkway linking the restaurant to the gas station and the public toilets was being foamed. The entire rest area was cordoned off from the highway and bustling with yellow contact suits.

The man on the telephone had hung up from Maryk and *made a second call* before moving into the Waffle House for a late breakfast or early lunch. Zero's description was dead-on. BioCon caught up with him before his third cup of coffee. Forty-seven customers and waitstaff to be transported to the federal hospital in Jacksonville.

Zero was described as "slight" and wearing a sullied white windbreaker, loose brown pants, hiking shoes with dried mud on them, dirty latex gloves, and a snug "African pattern style" toque covering the top of his skull but for a few wild strands of silver-gray hair visible in back. He was about five feet five, one hundred to one hundred ten pounds, and wore a white cotton surgical mask.

A light blue Ford Prescience in the parking lot matched the make and Vehicle Identification Number of an automobile that had been parked two blocks away from the Penny University that night in Boston.

Behind the restaurant was an enclosed grass playground of swing sets and trees. Clumps of discolored grass spaced like striding footsteps grew out of the healthy grass in thick looping spirals like a spreading mold. Shrubs lining the swing set were misshapen with overgrowth and already blooming madly. The leaves of a tree branch hanging over the parking lot were alabaster white and shaped uncannily like hands whose fingers had been broken and splayed.

The playground was sick. Zero had fled through there to the residential neighborhood beyond. BioCon was sweeping it but would find nothing. Zero was not looking for more victims. He was looking for a car.

Maryk opened his tablet and brought up the old *Audubon* photo of Ridgeway. Pictured was a tweedy-looking young man with curly brown hair wearing short pants and a safari shirt. He was posed with one boot on a mossy rock. Both forearms were crossed on his bent knee and he held a wild fern leaf in one hand as he gazed out proprietarily over the swamp.

Maryk felt the stirrings of a cascade. His body was systematically executing its own infected cells in order to rid itself of Zero. Maryk would need an amphetamine dose in order to work through the day.

He returned to the whining helicopter and Melanie. The only way he could guarantee her safety now was to keep her at his side.

"He's real," she said as Maryk reached the door. "Isn't he?"

The threat of a mutant virus gifted with human intellect and cunning posed hazards exceeding Maryk's worst imaginings. But all he envisioned was its one great advantage. Epidemic control had never been simpler. Zero was like a tumor Maryk could go in and surgically remove. This mission seemed somehow worthy of him.

Contain the spread. Eliminate the vector.

With one clean stroke Maryk could conclusively terminate the Plainville plague.

Replication

The Nosebleed

The helicopter ride back to the swamp passed like a dream, clouds drifting across the midday southern sky like smoke. After a brief stop at the ranger's station, Melanie and Maryk were back in the launch, nosing along the dead stream toward the island lab.

Melanie was beginning to wonder if she had actually survived Plainville at all. Atlanta and swamps, airports and prisons, Pearse and Maryk, and now Oren Ridgeway, perhaps this was all a fantasy spun out of the loneliness of death.

Nothing pulled on her, neither the past nor the future. No youth, no family; she was entirely without label or claim. She thought of her hometown. Two years after the outbreak, a big developer had settled with Plainville's property heirs, buying up every square foot of the deserted, haunted town, dirt cheap. Each house was razed and each automobile was junked, as there was no other way to get rid of the chemical smell left by the town's ablution. Landfill was brought in from up and down the East Coast and sculpted into hillocks and rolling fields. Overpopulation and the graying of the so-called baby boomers of generations past had created a bullish death market. Plainville was currently a town without a school or a post office or a police force. Humped stone markers and white crosses laced the fresh sod grafted over the sculpted hillsides like white stitches sewn over a layer of green skin. Eternity Way, the town's main north-south route, saw more than twenty funeral processions each day. Melanie's hometown was a thriving necropolis.

She existed now purely as a vessel to be filled up and emptied and filled again. Four years of prolonged limbo had followed the effacement of her life in Plainville, and now she again found herself trapped in yet another bizarre holding pattern, a limbo between limbos. *Long-term nonprogressor*—no kidding. The virus would not let her go. They had cured her of the disease, but the sickness kept coming back for her.

"He wants to kill me," she said. "Doesn't he? Or infect me somehow."

Maryk nodded, in front of her. "That sounds about right."

"Life-saving blood," she said. "Don't forget. I'm to be protected, no matter the cost."

"I won't forget."

They passed the first Plainville plants again. BioCon agents in yellow suits were uprooting them and hacking them into manageable pieces.

"Oren Ridgeway took me to my senior prom," Melanie said.

Maryk turned. He looked at her.

"Believe me," she said, "it wasn't my idea. I tore up all the photographs in long, thin strips, one of the last things I did before going to college. I was leaving the 'old me' behind. It didn't work."

He waited for her. She had expected a barrage of questions, but she realized that hers was just one of many shocks he had received that day.

"My parents arranged it," she said. "He was four years older than I was, and just back from his college graduation. The town outcast type, but a total loser. Oren was a crusader, an environmental nut. My dad took pity on him—my dad liked people with ideals. I had no boyfriends, I was just a fat pudge. And my mother was so excited . . ." The memory intensified, and she had to shake it off. "He made the corsage himself. From his own garden. It looked like a bright pink cabbage on my flabby chest. We danced one dance together. One. He danced like a freak and spent the rest of the night boring his old teachers, the chaperones, while I sat alone at the table feigning interest in my napkin."

She didn't tell him about the goodnight kiss at her door: her turning away at the last possible moment, and Oren's chapped lips—he had an ugly habit of gnawing on them—just glancing the edge of her cheek.

She shuddered. "Oren didn't like people," she went on. "He said people were ruining the earth. He said we had been given this great gift, and we were just stomping all over it." She felt a lopsided smile spread across her face, like maple syrup over a pancake. "I was thinking, maybe, this could remain just between us."

The island came into view up ahead, and they landed and Dr. Freeley led them along a winding pathway of torch stakes burning black smoke. Maryk said nothing. They passed one of the gnarled Plainville trees, and Melanie felt like she was walking through one of her own freakish paintings.

Dr. Freeley said, "This 'Zero' worked quickly. We just got a stolen car report from Yulee. A white Dodge Auriga, stolen out of somebody's driveway three streets back from the rest stop. An older model, zero-four. No Automap function or Global Positioning Receiver, and no theft retrieval—nothing traceable. The car is old enough to run under the current technological radar. I got in touch with the state police. They wouldn't do roadblocks—said they couldn't risk exposure to their men— but they're setting up checkpoints, remote cameras to record cars and plates. It's visible enough. It should at least keep him off the main routes, and pin him to this corner of the country. I put an Infectious Contaminant Bulletin out to every police organization in the southeast. They know what to do if they find the car."

"Which is—get away, and call us."

They came to the rear of the black canvas laboratory. Three BioCon agents were kneeling around something half-buried in the swamp floor. "We just found him," Dr. Freeley said. Melanie made out a torso and part of a head, blistered and blackened with decay. "The missing hiker. Looks like Zero was feeding on him."

Melanie shook her head. She swooned with the heat and the monstrousness of Zero and backed out to the path lined with burning torches. Suddenly the swamp didn't seem large enough. The state of Georgia and the entire world didn't seem large enough. But as much as she hated to admit it, she did feel safe with Maryk; that is, safe from everything except Maryk himself.

He came back out alone and they went to the front of the laboratory. BioCon had cut open the front length of the canvas so that the tents were open to the island. The wooden tables, littered with Plainville remains, resembled a gypsy marketplace cluttered with horribly spoiled produce. Melanie saw a jar containing what must have been the hiker's left hand, and a wire-bound notebook propped open with Plainville flowers pressed into its pages, malformed petals and leaves that were hideous and yet, at the same time, madly beautiful.

Dr. Pearse tottered around the crude, plant-strewn tables, mumbling excitedly to himself. His gaunt face was glossy with perspiration from the heat, his eyes blinking strangely and fast. He looked even weaker under the hot sun. He teetered around the tables, and beckoned to them with a stiff hand as they approached.

"He's learning," he said proudly. "He was learning about himself, his own virus. He wants to know everything. He was curing out his virus through these infected plants, like Stanley with tobacco leaves, purifying it, crystallizing it, and refeeding it to the rats. He was nurturing his disease, crossbreeding it, over and over, hoping to trip a mutation: a strain that would not infect so thoroughly and so abruptly. Zero was trying to extend his latency period." He limped to another table without his cane, where he had evidently filleted a Plainville plant stalk into hundreds of garish slices. "But of course—what virus wouldn't, if it could? The longer a host remains viable, the longer it can spread the infection. He wants to become invincible."

Maryk glanced back at Melanie as Dr. Pearse prattled on.

"He never found one, Peter. In fact, his latency period is growing shorter. This is because the virus is extraordinarily volatile. It is changing more rapidly now than ever before. Wholesale shifts since the prison outbreak. Incredible."

"Stephen," Maryk said. "You are talking a mile a minute."

"It's all here, Peter, all the answers." His gnarled hand rested on the pile of notebooks in the manner of a schoolboy taking an oath. "I know what he's waiting for now. His virus is changing all the time, becoming more refined. It's all that uranium it was exposed to in the cave, for centuries. Zero's virus is breaking down to the point where it will no longer infect vegetation and lower animals. Do you understand? Zero will sicken *only Homo sapiens.*" Dr. Pearse patted the notebooks in wonder. "It's all happening within him—of him. He's not there yet, but he's getting closer, and he knows it. He *knows* it."

Maryk nodded but showed him no enthusiasm. "Rest a moment, Stephen," he said. "You're exhausted."

"I came here to kill him, Peter. I admit that. But now I see that we have to understand him first. We have to learn from him. Zero has something to teach us."

Maryk looked stern. "You say you know things about Zero, Stephen. How?"

Dr. Pearse thought about it. "I'm not sure. I just do."

"What, then? I need some idea of what I'm up against. Tell me what you know."

Dr. Pearse held Maryk's gaze, then accepted his challenge. "A man infected by a deadly virus that has not killed him, but instead *combined* with him, at some elemental level. A biological model of a man-virus."

Maryk stared. "That's right."

"Viruses like tight, dark places. Sunlight is a virus killer. Given the evolutionary transformation that has taken place, he must prefer night to day. Direct exposure to sunlight should weaken him. Not mortally—this is not Dracula—but ultraviolet light exposure from the sun should have the effect of wearing him down."

Maryk moved closer, intrigued. "Go on."

"His thinking process is impaired. The body is resilient, as we know. The body battles for stability, always. The body adjusts to change. But the brain, the brain goes further than that: The brain compensates, sometimes to the point of overcompensation. It is an elastic organ, regenerating damaged tissue, even redrawing neural pathways with minimal impairment, perpetually searching for solutions to the millisecond-by-millisecond problems it is given. We know that Plainville targets the brain. Therefore Zero has, at the very least, suffered a series of shocks or minor strokes. There is physiological damage to the brain, unique psychological damage, and whatever resulting chemical imbalances, all combined with the rudiments of infection. As his higher functions began to fail, the brain's only alternative for survival would be to simply switch them off. After so many years—I would say he exists in a state where dreaming and waking have become one and the same."

"A functional dream state," Maryk said, less encouragingly than provokingly.

"Yes," Dr. Pearse nodded. He ran on. "As his brain continues to compensate for what it lacks, more primal emotions are tapped, and the mind reverts to the primitive. Survival beyond death means, for man, reproduction: offspring, parent to child. Fertilization and cell division forming another living host where the progenitor's DNA can thrive. Of course, infection is essentially the same process. Zero is operating on this primal level now. His damaged brain has no choice but to embrace the creature its host has become. Only propagation can ensure survival at the genetic, viral level. This means widespread infection. That is his ultimate goal."

It was as though Dr. Pearse was almost channeling Zero. He wilted in the heat, but still pressed on. Maryk said, "What about personality?"

"The character of a virus endowed with human traits? Easy. We're talking about a being uninhibited by any obligations, social or moral. Combine the worst elements of a serial murderer, a rapist, an impulsive arsonist. Hyperaggressive, hypersexual, homicidal, egocentric, pathological. An unqualified sociopath. The ultimate deviant terrorist mentality. All Zero wants to do is infect, infect, infect."

Maryk moved one more step closer, now facing Dr. Pearse across a wooden table. "One more thing," he said. "We've said that people who contract the virus do one of two things—they either die quickly, or we get to them early with the serum and they survive."

Dr. Pearse nodded. "Except for Zero. He remained alive, and the virus was given time to integrate itself with his person."

Maryk nodded slowly. "So this could, theoretically, happen to anyone who contracted the disease, and was kept alive through extraordinary means."

Dr. Pearse considered it and was about to give his answer when his grin fell. He came to stare at Maryk as Maryk went on.

"How do you know so much about him? How did you find his lab here in the middle of four hundred thousand acres of swamp? You say you could feel him."

Dr. Pearse said nothing. He continued to stare.

"Stephen, how is it you are so obviously sick, and yet have remained so strong?"

Melanie understood now. She watched the sunlight beat down on Dr. Pearse, and he noticed that he was weaker in it.

Dr. Pearse had nothing to say.

"We're leaving here right now," Maryk said. "I want to get another look at you back at the bureau."

Dr. Pearse's face changed, and he looked at Maryk as though Maryk were crazy. "There's too much to do here, Peter. Too much to learn. I'm so—"

"Close to him," Maryk said. "How close are you, Stephen?"

Dr. Pearse was jittery now. This was the first time Melanie had ever seen him angered. Sweat glistened on the livid sores mottling his face and neck. He looked back and forth at the two of them, and then at the BioCon agents behind.

"I'm staying," he said. He pointed weakly at the table that separated him and Maryk. "I'm staying right here and working."

Something happened then, and Maryk started to back away from Dr. Pearse. "Stephen," he said. He held a gloved hand out in front of him. "Stephen. Listen to me." Melanie did not see it until just then. "Don't move."

A spot of dark red had appeared under Dr. Pearse's nostril. He grew agitated under their staring, like a cornered animal. "You all just stay away from me," he said.

"Stephen." Maryk stopped and held his ground. "Your nose is bleed-ing."

Dr. Pearse looked at them strangely. He reached up to his face and examined his stiff fingertips. The blood was coming down onto his blis-tered top lip now. He looked at it on his fingers as though he did not understand.

"Just don't move," Maryk said.

Dr. Pearse looked up, confused, his hand still open in front of him. Then he started slowly around the table, as though to explain. Maryk took another step backward, and Melanie found herself doing the same.

"Stephen," Maryk said sharply.

The blood was coming faster now, a dark, heavy red, running out of both nostrils and down over his lips. Melanie sensed movement all around her, the suited BioCon agents, assembling.

Dr. Pearse appeared disoriented suddenly. "You don't under-stand, I—"

He came another step forward, but this time Maryk did not give any ground. Maryk stood ready to meet him. Melanie saw the black bag in his right hand.

Melanie said suddenly, "Stephen. Please."

Maybe it was her use of his first name, or just the softer voice. Whatever it was, he blinked and saw her there as though for the first time, and then looked at the suited BioCon agents around him. He seemed to understand what was going on then. He was leaking biohazardous material, and was a threat to those around him. Dr. Pearse looked down at his own arms and legs as though they were disappearing. Blood flowed thickly down to his gaunt chin.

Stephen Pearse lay sedated in a plastic isolation pod as Maryk wheeled him inside the Level 4 Biocontainment Hospital Unit back at the BDC. The "Tank," as Maryk referred to it, was not a laboratory but a secure medical suite constructed for the observation and treatment of accidental "hot agent" exposures. It occupied one half of the top floor of Building Nine.

Twin steel pressure doors led inside, with the usual ultraviolet chamber in between. Melanie waited outside. There was a small viewing window on the side wall, and she peeked in once. She saw Maryk lifting Stephen Pearse in his arms and onto a table that looked like a tanning bed, sealing him inside under a clear plastic shell. Maryk appeared to be weakening himself. She realized a cascade was long overdue.

At a table behind her, a BioCon agent operated the steel doors via tablet. Maryk emerged and Melanie went to meet him, but he walked past her without a word. She followed him out to the catwalk leading to the next building, and watched him cross it under barking thunder and lashing rain. He did not look back. She did not follow.

She wasn't alone long. Dutiful Pasco arrived minutes later to chauffeur her back to her room. The storm was quite violent but barely touched her consciousness. She crawled into bed and slept soundly through its fury. She dreamed that she was visiting her parents' cemetery plot in the necropolis that was her hometown, laying Plainville flowers at a headstone bearing her name.

Gala Island

Melanie showered and changed the next morning, and Pasco returned her to the BDC and the roof of Building Seven where a BDC helicopter was waiting. She climbed inside next to Maryk, and the helicopter lifted off, climbing away over the building blocks of the BDC and the Emory campus. Only when they were well above everything like treetops and radio antennas did she relax. The roofs and playing fields of rural Georgia slid under them, and the world appeared so orderly from above.

"I give up," she said. "Where are we going?"

"Gala Island," he said. "I have an appointment there."

All she knew about Gala Island was that it was an animal reserve the BDC maintained somewhere off the Georgia coast. It was a habitat for thousands of different animal species.

"Where animals are raised for laboratory experiments?" she said. "No thank you."

"Popular misconception. Their natural environments are rigorously maintained. Ninety-nine percent of the time, all we need are the living cells." He spoke distractedly, preoccupied, and she assumed the reason was Dr. Pearse. "However, this is one of those one percent times."

She turned her attention to the board game of earth sliding beneath her, and at once they flew off the coast of Georgia, over the blue and white Atlantic, still turgid from the storm. She watched for the island, and it breached beneath them like an emerald green whale, spouting trees and short hills, cut smooth with plains, spotted with white roofs of civilization. They curled around its sandy southern coast, and the helicopter set down at the end of a short airfield.

The island glistened after the overnight storm. The calm order of its trees and brush was like Disney compared to the Dalí of the Plainville swamp. They got into a waiting Jeep and Maryk drove them along a rising dirt path into dense tree cover, passing a sign that read AVIARY. She began to see birds looping overhead. Like stars appearing after nightfall, the longer she looked, the more appeared: flitting around the high trees, dipping and flapping high overhead, sleeping with tucked bills on lower branches along the roadside.

She asked Maryk to pull over just for a minute, and he did. She left him in the Jeep and walked into a wide clearing. Birds flew above her and called to one another and cried. She possessed a bird-watcher's knowledge of the groupings and could tell that many species were not indigenous to the Americas. There were basic sea birds, closer to the coastline, such as cormorants, divers, swans, and grebes. Long-necked herons and cranes. Then the game birds—pigeons, turtledoves, and various taloned birds of prey. Long-legged waders. Small terns, auks. Sharp-beaked gulls laughing and screaming overhead. And the tree birds: swallows and larks and wagtails and woodpeckers. All zipping here and there, or hopping busily along the dirt paths with twigs in their beaks. Twin pipits raced across the road before her. Thrushes and warblers. Flycatchers. Shrikes and swifts. Hummingbirds and tiny, mouselike wrens. Crows and starlings and orioles and sparrows and finches.

She could not help but smile. The beauty of the place was thrilling and strange, the winged life thriving all around her. Growing up in Plainville, she had kept three different seed houses in the trees surrounding her home, two she had made out of milk cartons, and one store-bought wooden perch, a birthday present from her grandmother, which had hung by wire from a tree branch outside her bedroom window, and to whose greedy patrons she had awakened every Plainville morning.

There was a small outpost but she did not see any people. The cottagelike building was set on the bank of a pristine reservoir that must have been man-made, and she was reminded that birds were reservoirs for Plainville, susceptible to the virus and able to transmit it, but themselves immune to the disease. She wondered how many tests had been run on these birds, how many different ways the humans had tried to trick them into giving up their secrets.

She felt safe there, away from Zero and Atlanta, and left reluctantly, the fugitive cries fading as they drove on.

The monkey house was dead center on the island. They went down to the isolation level and were met there by a primate warden in jeans and scrub shirt who led them to a small, square viewing window. "I'm not at all comfortable with having this virus here on Gala," he told Maryk. "One slipup and the entire island, a decade of work—wiped clean."

Maryk stared through the bright window. Melanie had no intention of looking herself, but there was something in the warden's voice when he said, "This is medieval." Something about the man's fear compelled her to join Maryk at the window.

They were looking into a small, brightly lit observation room. The floor was streaked with blood and shed hair, and a single female chimpanzee lay slumped in the corner. Her nippled chest was huffing and her red eyes were violent and fevered, regarding Melanie with what could only be described as homicidal intent. Her facial features below were faded into a meek Plainville grin. The dying chimp appeared quite human.

Maryk turned from the window and started away. "Destroy it," he said to the warden.

Melanie caught up with him outside. Maryk was staring at the swishing island trees from the monkey house porch. "It's a simulation of the circumstances of Stephen's infection and treatment," he said, "but without the work I did to protect his brain. I initiated it a few days ago. I had to see if the Zero paradigm would repeat."

Melanie remembered the chimp's eyes, and knew that it had.

"The virus is breaking down too fast," he said. "The chimp is sustaining the infection but not the genetic mutations. I've seen the tests: Over seventy percent of its cells have been converted into viruses. I compared these with tests of Stephen's blood, and it's the same. He's up over ninety percent already. If the virus doesn't kill Stephen first, it could convert him, and turn him into another Zero."

Melanie stared at him as he watched the trees. "But it didn't change me," she said.

"The virus was purged from your body early on. It was your recovery from the disease that took so long."

He was quiet the rest of the way back to Atlanta. Melanie had little memory of the trip herself, consumed as she was by the contrasting images of the sacrificial chimp suffering in the small, bright room on that elysian island, and Dr. Pearse sitting and awaiting his end in the hospital unit Tank at the BDC.

Corruption

Plainville was enjoying its rout. My eviscerated immune system was lashing out blindly at the virus, turning on healthy tissue and vital organs in a manic final attempt to survive. I was defenseless against myself, and this was Plainville's greatest perversion.

The cells that made up my person were expiring in wave after wave of microscopic corporal genocide. Whereas a fit body replenishes itself, cells dividing and reproducing beneficially, my cells were being exploited to breed lethal viral clones. I was a human hive of frenzied bees. My body was being debauched.

When I allowed myself to daydream it was simply this: a hot shower and a long, careful shave, bathed in the warm scent and intimacy of my own bathroom in my own home.

The work in B4 had kept me going. It had disciplined my mind. Now all my time was devoted to rumination. My focus had turned inward.

I opened the glass shell of the hyperbaric chamber that was my bed. The berth saturated my blood with collagen-stimulating oxygen that slowed the meltdown of connective tissue characteristic of Plainville. I sat up, and swung my thin legs over the side.

As director, I had overseen the construction of the Level 4 Biocontainment Tank. I knew, for example, that the steel doors could be operated only from the outside. There was no way out other than complete recovery or death. I looked at the eastern wall, a ten- by thirty-foot video monitor, remembering that we had done a study showing that pastoral scenes were most soothing for patients confined in prolonged clinical isolation. I watched geese flapping across a bleeding orange sunset over a salt marsh of waving spartina.

Floaters in my eyes gave me aquarium vision, hairlike beings and crystalline forms swimming across my view. I imagined they were viruses wriggling and writhing before me.

I was hyperattuned now to every creak and flutter of my failing body. I could feel the blood slowing and gelling in my veins, the very platelets rupturing. My heart beat lugubriously against newly calcified ribs, and I had developed an odd arrhythmia: Once every fifteen minutes or so, my heart struck a double beat, like a bass player's finger slipping off a string. The silence that followed would freeze me, a chill fanning out from my spine like a peacock preening mortality, until the stillness of the suspended beat passed and life turned over again within the sordid chamber of my corrupted chest.

I wiped at and probed the sunken ridges around my eyes, the new-found angularity of my cheeks. After thirty-seven years: a different face, a lesser face, in place of my own. I was wearing someone else's eyes, lips, jaw. I looked at my hands, front and back. A stranger's hands, an older man's, fingers curling to my command, but reluctantly. Arthritis had commenced its rout. Billions of excess antibody proteins bred by my flailing immune system—that my body had no natural way of expelling—were caking on every joint. I was biologically rusting.

The inside door opened, and Peter came inside carrying his black bag. Seeing him again made me feel contrite, and I am certain I avoided his eyes at first. There was no medical reason for him to visit me. He had come only to look at me and see how much I'd changed.

"Anything on Zero yet?" I said.

Maryk shook his head. "We're on him. Still waiting."

"He's planning something," I said.

Peter looked at me anew. My insights made us both uncomfortable. "What is he planning?" Peter said.

I shook my head, and eventually looked down at the white floor. "But he's changing, Peter. The genetic core of his virus. You need to protect Melanie."

"I'm testing her blood all the time."

"Zero's virus is breaking down. She could become susceptible."

"She's with me all the time. Bobby Chiles has organized a Plainville conference for tonight, to counter some of the public hysteria. She'll go with me."

I looked over at the geese flapping across the orange twilight.

"You know what's happening to me," I said.

Peter stared at me a long moment. "I do."

"Kill me. If I start to turn. Promise me, Peter. You won't let me become like him."

As I finished these words, I froze, my addled heart striking a pronounced double beat, then stopping, resting quiet and still, a hunk of fatty meat suspended in my chest. A morose chill embraced me, but the beating resumed moments later, and trembling, I exhaled the foul contents of my eroding lungs.

I opened my eyes. Peter remained standing before me with his black bag in his hand.

The Conference

Maryk had to remind himself as he sat there that evening inside the Georgia World Congress Center that there was nothing more he could be doing at present to hunt Zero. The description of the stolen car was out to every police organization in the southeast with a description of the subject wanted on a "Plainville quarantine violation." It was inconceivable that a busted taillight and an alert patrolman were all it might take to end the Plainville scourge. He had agents in the lobby ready to take him to any outbreak on a moment's notice.

The Congress on Plainville convened at five o'clock that afternoon. An emerging disease prompted as much hoopla as it did concern within the world medical community and the scant information the BDC had about the virus and its resultant disease was being disseminated at seminars and public awareness workshops throughout the convention center. It was all a thinly veiled publicity event aimed at renewing public confidence in the disease-fighting talents of the BDC. But the cooperation of the public was essential to successful disease control and that was why Maryk agreed to appear.

He had declined a seat on the long curtained dais and instead commandeered a front row table against the far wall of the second-floor conference room. He and Melanie sat there alone. Fifty round tables behind him sat five hundred members of the world medical community listening to speeches and awaiting a free dinner.

Maryk focused on the stage. Dr. Alex Solbin supported himself against the podium with both forearms as he read from his tablet. Solbin was deputy director for HIV/AIDS and Tuberculosis and next in line behind

Bobby Chiles for Stephen's job. His cane stood against his empty chair next to the podium and his face mask hung untied off his shirt collar. Many of those in attendance wore masks and gloves for sanitary reasons but Alex Solbin was in his fourth year of managed clinical AIDS. It was therefore imperative that he protect his HIV-compromised immune system. His visage as projected upon the large screen behind him was thin but hale. A face-filling beard accentuated the features of his Soviet ancestry.

Solbin outlined the goals of the conference in the opening portion of his remarks. Invoking Maryk's name sent an explicit ripple of disapproval throughout the room. Maryk smiled in the dark. It was easy for the international medical establishment to dismiss one who had never sought their fellowship. Maryk had thought himself peerless ever since his split with Stephen.

He turned toward the doctors and medical scientists sitting reverently before glowing tablets. They were gathered to demonize Plainville at the same time they worshipped the majesty of this preternatural force that reduced healthy human beings to dust. The modern practice of health care had become like a religion. The attendees listened raptly to Solbin's creed and dreamed of a miracle Plainville cure that would deliver them to everlasting glory. Stephen Pearse was their messiah but he had stumbled and fallen from grace. Maryk wondered what the knowledge of Zero's existence would do to their piddling faith.

Faith was a commodity now. Faith could be bought and sold. Devotion was something paid to fan clubs, political parties, corporate affiliations, home teams. The cartel of religion had been broken up only recently by the heterodoxy of a man named Darwin. *My heart and soul care for worms and nothing else in the world just at present.* This from a man who had once studied for the clergy. And like dominoes the myths of creation fell. The next day faith began trading on the open market.

Science was the defining knowledge of the time. Science had disproved religion and therefore had become religion. Its temples were third-floor laboratories in faceless glass buildings in industrial parks. Solutions to the mysteries of creation were being discovered under a microscope and not in books or upon an altar. Science had stroked the face of God and not perished. Now it was asking for a sample of His blood.

Maryk recalled the small church on a hill that his parents had taken him to as a boy and the hours spent playing on the wooden floor of the rectory while his mother answered telephones that rang and rang.

All the ancient beliefs had been debunked. But Plainville had ripped away the twenty-first century's veil of human sovereignty and now the questions were once again beginning to outpace the answers. The world that had consumed its creator suddenly found itself revolving frightened and alone.

Maryk surfaced as though from a trance. He looked up and saw servers coming around with salads. Solbin was already well into his speech. Maryk tried to retrace his thoughts but the thread disappeared.

He shut his eyes a moment. His lids were heavy like theater curtains. It took some effort to raise them again. He looked at Melanie and the room drifted in his vision. She was two seats away from him.

He could not reach her from where he sat. He pushed back his chair and reached for his bag. He placed his other hand on the table. He stood unsteadily.

Melanie sat back as a green-gloved waiter slid a small salad down in front of her. She sensed Maryk rising near her as she reached for her knife and fork, but ignored him until his hand gripped the back of her chair. His other hand swept her salad plate to the center of the table with a clatter. "*Hey,*" she said.

He was leaning over her. Maryk had no scent, she noticed, no aftershave or hair spray or food smell, not even sweat. If he wasn't near bleach or some other chemical cleanser, he was entirely odorless.

"He's here," Maryk said.

Melanie did not understand at first. Then she looked out with a start at the hundreds of people seated in the room. At least half of them wore gloves and masks, as did the servers moving table to table.

"How do you—?"

She saw the languor in Maryk's gray eyes and understood. He was cascading. It was a bad one, and at once she became crazy with fear. Zero was in the room with them. She tried to stand but Maryk was in her way.

"Got to kill him," he said heavily.

She was struggling with her chair. "Get everybody out. Yell 'Fire!' "

She was frantic. Maryk let go of her chair but she couldn't get out. His foot was still in the way. He opened his bag clumsily and dropped his tablet onto the table, opening it, sluggishly working the keys. His message read ZERO HERE. BLOCK EXITS.

He sent the message to his agents downstairs and collapsed the screen, straightening, wavering as he scanned the crowd.

"*Do* something," she told him, trying to get out.

Maryk licked his lips. "We'll screen them at the door," he said. "Trap him. You wait here."

"No way," she said. But as he moved off toward the dais, she looked across the large room and saw how many tables she would have to pass, alone, to reach the side exits, and decided to remain where she was. Zero could be anywhere. Melanie was a statue of a young woman gripping the sides of her chair. She scanned the audience and watched for anyone moving or watching her. As she did, an uncomfortable silence crept over the room.

Maryk was walking stiffly behind the chairs along the dais to the center podium. The speaker sensed the ripple in the audience's attention, then turned and saw Maryk and awkwardly announced him. Silence fell over the vast room as Maryk stepped to the podium.

He must have struck it with his knee, because the microphone went *thud* and the noise reverberated wall to wall. Maryk stood there a moment staring, his hair shining platinum in the large image of his face projected behind him.

"Sorry to break this up," he said archly. A thin, inappropriate smile appeared. "But we'll need to cut this short now, due to . . ."

His voice trailed off. Melanie followed his gaze to the rear of the long room. In the shadows in back, a figure stepped back from one of the tables and began moving away.

It was a man. He was a slow-moving man wearing an oversized waiter's uniform and a standard food server's face mask. He was small and gaunt and gaining speed as he moved across the rear of the room to the side. He moved like a man and yet not like a man, striding purposefully, abnormally, and Melanie felt a scream rising in her throat.

A glass pitcher of water shattered behind her. People gasped as Maryk scrambled over the dais onto the floor and rushed toward her, wide-eyed.

She stood out of her chair to get away but Maryk grabbed her arm. "No," she said, pulling back, but he had his bag in the other hand and was already propelling her through the room. Somebody screamed. Doctors and scientists leapt out of their chairs, and a table toppled over as people rushed to get out of their way. Somehow she stayed on her feet as they moved.

An alarm pierced the air. They reached the rear of the long room just in time to see, around a sashed curtain, a fire door closing.

Maryk pushed her into the alarm bar of the door. It opened and they were inside a white stairwell and stumbling down white concrete steps. Maryk was half leaning on her for support, his full weight pulling down on her shoulder, and she was buckling underneath him. They tripped like that down half a flight of stairs.

She looked fleetingly over the railing down into the vertical shaft. She saw a hand wearing a dirty latex glove sliding along the railing below.

Zero was right below them. He was getting away. She stopped resisting Maryk then, realizing that if he stopped Zero there, it would all be over. The virus would be stopped, and she would be normal and free again.

"Come on!" she yelled over the keening alarm, thrusting her thin arm around Maryk's broad back to push him, and they clambered down the stairs along the railing. She looked into the well again but did not see the hand; then they turned onto the last flight, stumbling down two and three steps at a time.

Maryk elbowed through the door at the bottom. It was a short, empty corridor and they rushed along it, turning right as the alarm faded behind. He stumbled through the door at the end, and they were inside a kitchen.

A large dishwasher chugged steam. She followed Maryk past racks of clean dishes, and saw him breaking open his bag. A syringe appeared in his gloved right hand.

They turned past wire shelves stocked with industrial-sized cans of tomato paste and wide-mouth jars of pickles and fruit salad. A figure had turned a corner at the left end of the room in front of them. They ran around food carts to follow, reaching the corner, surprising him as he came back. Maryk surged forward suddenly with the syringe raised knifelike in his hand, but it was only a busboy, a Hispanic kid holding a wet rag, and he saw Maryk and whatever homicidal look was on Maryk's face and flailed backward, knocking a rack of dirty pots to the floor.

Maryk's hand came straight back down to his side. He turned and scanned the room with tired eyes, his great chest heaving, then Melanie pointed to the most likely passage leading away. He started lumberingly ahead of her and across the long, steamy room.

They emptied into the smoke of a food preparation area, running along a central counter of cooked meals set under heat lamps. The chefs all wore similar green food service gloves and face shields and head coverings.

"Which way did he go?" Maryk said breathlessly.

Most shrugged, watching them run past. One pointed the way.

Melanie followed Maryk around an ice machine and then left into a short supply corridor. The door at the end was half open to the outside and Maryk lunged at it.

The cool night air cut her. They raced searching along the outer wall of the convention center. Every door Maryk tried was locked, and there was no one else in sight.

He loped along the high wall of the building to the front sidewalk, scanning the bright, empty sidewalk and street. Melanie recognized Pasco at the conference center exit, to their right. He showed Maryk an exaggerated, frantic shrug.

"Seal the building," Maryk gasped to him. "Shut down the city within a four-block radius."

Melanie stepped back and leaned one hand against the building. Her chest was bursting. She took a hit off her inhaler and felt her lungs expand.

Fire engines wailed in the distance. She went around in front of Maryk. His hands were on his knees and his head was down, and he was heaving great, gusting breaths. "You might want to put that away now," she said. The loaded syringe was still in his right hand.

The firemen were all kept out of the building. The four-block dragnet was slow to set up, and they failed to find Zero. BioCon arrived at the convention center and placed the entire complex under quarantine.

Zero had served salads to the rearmost four tables. He was described as quiet but attentive, remarkable only for the strong scent of his after-shave, obviously covering up his smell. His tables were among the first to show symptoms: flulike cramps, severe headaches, high fevers. It was like radiation poisoning, in that those closest to Zero got his sickness first.

Maryk had slipped into a side lounge after they returned inside, and from the hallway Melanie watched him inject himself with something from his black bag, which had the effect of immediately reviving his flagging energy. He then saw to the administration of her blood serum, first to those seated at Zero's tables, and then methodically to the rest of the quarantines.

There were some awful scenes. In the quarantine rooms Melanie watched as the first medical people began to weaken and their colleagues cleared silently away. She saw the look of astonishment on the faces of the sick as they were led off. Others denied the illness rising within them, insisting that their colleagues, who had ratted them out to the BioCon agents, were mistaken. A few collapsed suddenly, to gasps and screams, and the people were soon segregated into many smaller rooms in a bid to slow the transmission of both the virus and the panic.

The fear in the eyes of the waiting was potent. They watched her suspiciously as she passed in and out of the rooms unsuited, and a few begged her to tell them what was happening, even as they knew. Their anxiety became too much for her, and soon she left and found a private space in the outer hallway, where she cried tears that would not fall. She felt as though her eyes, her brain, her entire person were being pickled in sorrow.

She fought back her emotion, and from then on she restricted herself to the isolation rooms where the sick were being attended to. She began by giving blood until she was dizzy. It took so much to derive so little serum, and she saw that there was barely enough of her to go around the World Congress building, never mind the entire world. She started going gurney to gurney, sitting with each sickened person a few moments, talking if they talked, nodding if they cried, or taking their hand if they just stared. She assisted the slow-moving agents in yellow suits as she could, changing IV bags and taking blood pressure readings.

She was doing that when Maryk came to get her. He looked haunted in the doorway, showing none of the confidence he had shown at Lewes Penitentiary. His shoulders sagged and the black bag seemed heavy in his big hand.

They underwent an ultraviolet wand scan before leaving, to kill any surface Plainville. She wished to feel the viruses dying on her skin, falling away like beach sand in the shower. She was tired of the constant cleansing, the empty renewal of dressing and undressing, and the inhumanity of her latex hands. In the car before they left, Maryk PCR-tested her blood. Her forearms were tender and so badly bruised from blood giving that he had to pull an excruciatingly slow cc from between the third and fourth fingers of her left hand. She sat looking up at the darkened convention complex until the tablet declared her clean.

They rolled through the desolate night streets of downtown Atlanta, passing through a depressed area of the city, tired cars parked along the curbs like toys arranged by a careless child. The apartment buildings were sooty and looming, with tenement-tiny windows of the type infants tumble out of on the hottest days of summer. Even the streetlights looked shiftless, bored. Maryk took two or three more turns that didn't feel right to her. "Where are we going?" she said.

His voice was exhausted, though his eyes remained bright. "I need to stop for fresh clothes."

She wondered what stores would be open that late at night. Then she realized he meant his home. For some reason the prospect of visiting Maryk's residence shocked her; she could not picture him in any habitat other than that of the BDC.

He parked outside a security-grated baby apparel store and they entered a numbered door riddled with graffiti, stepping over a splash of accumulated mail to a long, narrow flight of stairs. They walked the length of the doorless hall to a second flight, and then a third. At the top of the fourth flight they came to a clean white door, and Maryk produced a key.

He stopped before inserting it in the lock. He knelt and silently examined the white plate around the doorknob. There was a bit of brown

247

dirt, maybe food, smudged on the metal plate. Maryk picked it off, looking at it on the tip of his gloved finger before flicking it away. The knob turned keylessly under his hand.

The door opened on an apartment dark with night. It was spacious like an artist's loft, with high ceilings, few furnishings and walls, and large factory windows. Then the smell of decay hit her immediately, and the curious part of her mind shut down.

Maryk moved through the loft with evident alarm. Melanie could sense something on the wall behind her, even before Maryk switched on the high, track lamps, and she turned.

It was a long word smeared in mud and food over the wide wall. It read, drippingly, MESSENGER.

Two steel picture frames hung on the desecrated wall. Each contained a canvas that was now slashed to shreds. What she could make of the tattered images was dark and visceral, yet familiar. She saw three more canvases hanging on another wall, and one standing on a display easel in a corner. All were in ribbons.

The paintings were her own. They were the ones Maryk had purchased anonymously. He had not junked them, as she had assumed. He had designed his living space around them.

She walked to the one set on the easel. A steak knife was jammed dead center through the frame, and something hung from a wide, blue ribbon on its handle. It was a medallion, like a large gold penny, smeared with what looked like shit. She realized it was Maryk's Nobel.

A breeze swept through the loft and turned her head. She walked toward it, into the kitchen at the rear. Glass and dirt lay on the floor beneath a broken window, and Maryk stood outside on a long fire escape, over an elaborate vegetable garden laid out on the grate, overlooking the city. The clear plastic bubble covering the garden had been kicked in, the muddied soil torn up and the plants trampled, almost as though the dirt had been danced upon. The few vegetables that remained were budding into Plainville atrocities.

"He pissed on it," Maryk said.

She wondered how he knew this as he climbed over the broken glass back inside. "My paintings," Melanie said.

But he said nothing, moving past her and looking at his destroyed kitchen with a dazed expression. He reappraised his infected loft from where he stood, hands empty at his sides. A virus had broken into his home and contaminated everything he owned. He looked at her across the kitchen as though she were a stranger.

Whatever he had injected himself with was wearing off, the cascade now enveloping him like a gas. He had trouble locking the white door behind them as they left, and he slumped against the railing on the stairs, depending on her shoulder the rest of the way. On the sidewalk outside, she took his car keys from him, and he did not protest.

The gas tank was three quarters full. The thought of fleeing Atlanta forever was seductive, but fleeting. The seat belt held Maryk upright in the passenger seat, helpless and mumbling words beyond meaning. She got back onto the highway and followed the signs for Emory Hospital, back to the BDC.

The Tank

She listened to the hum of controlled air inside the Tank.
Stephen Pearse's eyes rolled open inside the incubatorlike berth. "Melanie," he said, muffled, like a dead man waking inside a coffin.

She unsealed and rolled back the glass top. His skin was tarnished with lesions and odd, lurid blemishes, and his fingernails had flaked off like his lost hair. He must have weighed less than she did now. His neck looked like thin rods bundled in rice paper. His clavicle was a thin bar that his head and neck had been set upon to rot, and a dark boil oozed over his right eye. His eyeballs were ghostly red and deep-set, and his pupils—misty, blue—were clouded as though with suspicion.

She brought him water and he sat up slowly and closed his ragged lips around the straw. She pulled over the room's only chair to sit across from him, and he faced her from the padded bed with an eerie dignity. She began to tell him what had happened. He required every trivial detail, especially where Maryk was concerned.

She noted the slowness of his gray tongue and his fixed lips as he spoke. "Zero is sick," he said. "He needed that treatment information given at the conference. Peter knows this now. Zero is running out of time."

"Time for what?"

"Human time. The virus is mutating so wildly now that the human cells can no longer cope. His body functions are already running at minimum capacity. Zero is genetically sick, in a way we don't yet understand."

"He moved pretty quickly down those stairs."

"All the doctors and virologists fighting his disease, all gathered in one place. He learned what he needed to know, then disposed of them. The genius of it. So like a virus. He is that much closer to clearing a path for a worldwide epidemic."

"You're so certain."

The rods of Stephen's frail neck tensed, and from time to time his eyes narrowed suddenly. He was evidently suffering much pain. "That is why he is here in Atlanta now. He's becoming more desperate. It is like a race between these two concerns: the breakdown of his virus to where it will only infect humans, and the death of his human host." Stephen nodded as though to confirm this. "The same race that is being run in me now."

She didn't know how to respond to his apparent enthusiasm for Zero. "Do you think, then, that Zero has forgotten all about me?"

The disease had carved Stephen's face of everything except a crimson-eyed curiosity. He answered her regretfully, and yet there was something undeniably bright behind his eyes. "No," he said.

She shuddered. "It won't ever end. Will it?" She was near tears again. "Only now the creature after my blood is not Maryk, but Zero."

"You can save him," Stephen said.

She looked at him. She thought he meant Zero. "Save who?"

"Peter. There is still time. Has he told you the Meister story?"

She nodded, confused. "The boy. Pasteur's crypt."

"He wants someone to vouch for him, to stand up for him after he's gone." His eyes lost focus a moment. "You're only seeing the end of a person, the nadir in a long slide from humanity. The first time I met Peter Maryk, he was holding a cheap bouquet of flowers wrapped in pink saran. He was pursuing a girl in our American lit elective, a daughter of one of the big auction house families. She was beautiful; he never had a chance. Still, he pursued her, finding out her schedule and making certain their paths crossed between each class. He made a career out of social failure in those days—he went about it with such verve."

His lips and tongue got in the way of his strained voice, but sentiment carried the words.

"Peter and I graduated the university together, Class of 2001. The millennium change came over our final holiday break. My parents were big political contributors in New York at the time, and we had received four tickets to the ball at the governor's mansion. Having no date myself, I talked my father into mailing Peter a plane ticket to fly out from Washington to attend. It was a gaudy, splashy affair, but boring for the two of us. Borough representatives and old New York money, and there was Peter in a rented tuxedo, standing around like my bodyguard. He said later that that night was the first time he had ever heard the pop of a champagne cork; I'd grown up hearing it. We slipped out early, with no particular plan in mind except to get away and salvage the rest of the night. Champagne was in short supply all around the world, but abundant at the mansion, and we pinched a case of two-hundred-dollar Moët before hopping into my car. I drove an MG then; my parents, they spoiled me. One thing led to another and we found ourselves on the highway driving out to my family's summer house in Amagansett."

He seemed strangely happy, continuing as though in a trance.

"We installed ourselves in the sitting room just before midnight, a glassed-in porch facing the water. I'd not seen Peter drink before, and haven't since. Midnight came and we toasted the television set, then switched it off to hear the cheers from the houses down the street, and went outside and raised our voices to the chorus. Fireworks thumped in the distance, unseen, the sky around us so bright and bare. We went down to the water, drinking straight out of our bottles. The sand was cold and hard. We stopped just before the foaming swash to toast the tide and the moon, and that was when Peter told me he was dropping out of school. He said he had decided to become a sculptor, and was trying to get up the courage to tell his parents over the break. Of course, no one sculpts anymore, but that was Peter. He shared this with me like it was some terrible secret—which, I guess, it was. We had only that one last semester left of school. But I was in no condition to talk him out of it, and in fact I'm certain I raised my bottle to his decision. He returned home the next day, and the truth is, I don't know if he ever told them. He was back at school that January, working harder than ever, and I couldn't bring myself to ask. I didn't learn until April that his mother was sick. If Peter was close to anybody, he was close to her."

Melanie shook her head when he was done. He seemed so happy. "I don't want to know any more," she said.

She had been eight years old that remarkable night. She stayed up late, spent the evening baking cookies, playing board games, and watching TV with her parents, and promised herself that when she grew up, every night was going to be just like that.

Stephen's head trembled a bit. His hands grew tremulous in his lap, and he looked at them, as though unable to will them to stop. Then his eyes found hers again.

"Melanie," he said. "I am dying. But not quickly enough. I am afraid I might become dangerous. I'm afraid I will frighten you."

"Please," she said. His words forced the tears from her eyes, but she could not tell him to shut up.

"He's changing me. I don't know how long I can resist. But I'm afraid the time may come when I would want to harm you." She shook her head, but he went on. "You shouldn't come here alone anymore."

She sat still and listened to his harsh breathing as her tears blotted one after another upon the glazed white floor.

Prescription

The tablet tone woke him and he came to lying flat on his office couch. He felt for his bag on the floor. He opened his tablet screen and concentrated on it. His head felt full of sand. "Who is it?"

"Suzy Lumm, Dr. Maryk, from Cyber. Director Pearse's tablet accessed the central computer net earlier this morning. I'm sorry—we missed it."

Her words rallied him to consciousness. The head and shoulders of the large blind woman wearing a headset filled his window. "Where did it go?" he said.

"They were into the system for just over nineteen seconds, unfortunately not enough time to trace. They went right to the bureau master address list and downloaded sixty-four percent of it, breaking off the connection at the letter Q."

Q followed P for *Pearse*. "Is the director's address updated to the Tank?"

"Let me check," she said. Maryk waited. "Yes, it is. Would you like me to cut the intruder out of the system now? I can delete Director Pearse's tablet code and fence them out of the Genetech."

"No," Maryk said. "I need to preserve that link. However tenuous."

He closed his tablet and slumped back against the couch. He remembered his apartment but not the return to the BDC. Melanie must have driven. She must have helped him into his office.

His cascades were growing more and more intense. Zero's virus was inestimably potent.

He had only two sets of white cotton shirts and black pants inside his office closet. He took one and carried it with him through the parking lot outside to the adjacent laboratory building where he deconned in a UV hold and changed clothes.

Dr. Carla Smethy was assistant head of pharmacology and yet she sat behind the same desk in the rare-drug clearinghouse of Building Six, Room 161, as she had six years before. Her black hair was tinged with gray and small lines textured her brow and the corners of her lightly painted lips. She was no more pleased to see him than she had been then.

"I need a prescription run," he said. "By physician, going back ten days."

Her chair turned as she crossed her legs beneath her desk. "Fine," she said. "All I need is a court order, or proof of authorization from the attending physician."

"I have neither. Let me give you the AP's name. Pearse, Stephen D."

She looked at him probingly but the name worked. She pulled on a pair of eyeglasses and typed into her keyboard. The desk unit responded in an assertive female voice, *"Searching now."*

"How is Stephen?" she asked while they waited.

Maryk searched his mind for an appropriate answer. He was still searching when the computer spoke again. *"Ready."*

She looked at her desktop screen. "There are three prescriptions."

"How recent?"

"Two in a Florida clinic two days ago, and one in Atlanta last night."

"Last night? The patient's name?"

"Watson, Robert."

It was an uninspired pseudonym. "The drugs?"

"Fentanyl, two days ago, and Baniciclovir, brand name Banix. I believe that is a relatively new varicella zoster treatment."

Zoster was the virus that caused chicken pox. After infection it retreated into the nerve ganglia at the base of the skull and remained latent until normal aging or a depressed immune system reactivated the virus into what is commonly known as shingles. Symptoms included acute paroxysmal neuralgic pain. Banix was one of the drugs cited in the information distributed at the Plainville conference.

"For postherpetic neuralgia," she went on. "It's an NMDA-blocker."

NMDA receptors on cell surfaces signaled pain transmission up the spinal cord to the brain. "A painkiller, a comfort drug."

Maryk nodded. Zero was in significant pain. He had gone right out after the World Congress Center exposure and used Stephen's name to prescribe himself a patient treatment for the effects of his own virus.

"No unfilled prescriptions?"

"No," she said. "But Banix is only two years out of FDA and still strictly regulated. Ten doses maximum per. This Watson's got only one refill left."

This explained Zero's inactivity between the Waffle House infection and the World Congress Center. Fentanyl was a powerful opiate. Zero had narcotized his human side and spent the time holed up in his car somewhere riding out the effects of the drug.

The human side of Zero was dying.

Chat

I knew exactly what was happening to me. That was perhaps the most insidious thing of all. I knew exactly what was happening and what was to come.

I had self-diagnosed shingles. Due to the morphine—Peter had tended to me while I slept—there was none of the characteristic ophthalmic pain, described by many sufferers as being like an intense toothache in the eye. There were however telltale dysesthesias, or phantom pains, such as the sensation of cold water running down my face, and I could not ignore the impulse to continually brush imagined water away from my cheeks and chin. My overloaded nerves were transmitting conflicting messages up the spinal cord to the thalamus of my brain, which was doing its best to cope with the information at hand.

Morphine. It was lovely. Morphine did not eliminate the pain, but rather compartmentalized it, so that pain remained but was a separate issue. Whenever the twinges became too sharp, I self-medicated using a thumb switch attached to my IV tubes and the dose regulator above. Then the hand shaking and neck throbbing went away. Peter was taking good care of me. I could only wonder at the degree of pain Zero was experiencing.

I was weakening. Pharyngeal ulcers were taking root in my throat, and in time I would lose the ability to swallow my saliva. My urine spilled into a catheter bag, an oily, purple drool, portending liver failure, said to be a uniquely painful event. I had accrued so much specialized knowledge in my thirty-seven years, and all of it was now draining away. Memories drifted past me on a kind of farewell tour, not flashing before my eyes but rather swirling together like so many different colors of paint, stirred into dreams. In one, the corridors and offices of Building Sixteen were filled with everyone I had ever known—family and friends, colleagues and patients, all my living and dead—passing me by without a word. I had left the door to my office wide open, but no one stopped in.

I awoke outside my oxygenated berth, seated on a high-backed wheel-chair, tired and groggy. The wall screen played an underwater scene of coral reefs and schools of bright tropical fish, meant to be soothing. In designing the Tank as a place of comfort, I found that to that end I had failed. There were no reflective surfaces inside the Tank, in order that the ill would not despair at the sordid sight of their own disfigured face; even the stainless steel fixtures were dulled. All communications in and out were monitored for signs of depression, and suicidal tendencies. I was a prisoner in a dungeon of my own design.

There was a remote keypad built into the arm of my chair, linked to the Tank computer. I instructed it to replace the deep-sea panorama with a prerecorded program from the BDC archives, my documentary, *The Disease Dilemma*.

There I was. Facing myself from the wall, sitting on the couch back in my office, legs crossed casually, arm extended over the seat back. I looked relaxed and supremely healthy, my face full again, my skin tight and clear. My old voice filled the Tank, dosing me with nostalgia more powerful than morphine. The sunlight was strong behind me, glowing around my hair—midday in the world of the living, just a few weeks earlier. The vista of downtown Atlanta lay beyond. Image after image swept over me until the sentimentality of the experience began to wear. I had different eyes now, and different thoughts. When the person playing the role of "Stephen Pearse," doctor to the world, claimed that he oversaw each serious outbreak investigation personally, I stifled a laugh. The hubris of this strange man tickled me. He was begging Zero to wait for him inside bay twenty-six at Orangeburg.

I stopped the show and sank back into the cushion of the headrest, closing my eyes on the brightness of the Tank. I triggered the medication switch with a rusted thumb and it worked on my emotions, set adrift into a bright and gauzy silence. I left myself for a while, and in the role of

Stephen Pearse, I visited my current self in the chair. *Be brave,* I told that sickly form.

I surfaced to the toning of the Tank computer. I prodded the necessary keys on my armpad to receive the incoming message. It had been posted from "Stephen Pearse" in Zurich, Switzerland. The message read:

>Won't you join me for a chat?

Maryk watched in disbelief as the conversation scrolled down his tablet. Stephen and Zero were conversing across a virtual table in a cyber-café halfway around the world.

Audio and visual were both disabled. Each dialogue leader was listed as *S. Pearse.* Stephen answered

>I am here.

>So you are still alive, Doctor.

>Medical science is gaining on you.

>Me: 1. Medical science: approx. -500. Your colleague Maryk sensed my presence, it seems. Intriguing.

>You are ill. You have contacted me for information about my treatment.

>Has he given up yet? Now that I have humiliated him? Zurich is quite pleasant this time of year.

>Do not underestimate Peter Maryk. And you are not in Zurich.

>Soon I will be, Doctor. Soon I will be in all places.

A window opened at the top right corner of Maryk's tablet. It was Suzy Lumm. "Hailing's still off," she said. "He's plugged in somewhere."

"You can't trace?"

>How does it feel to be sick yourself?

"Impossible to track him back through the Internet. He's routed the signal through five or six sites all across the world, maybe more. The only crumbs left behind would be stored in his own drive cache."

"All right," Maryk said. She signed off and he found his place in the scrolling conversation. Zero was speaking.

>This body is wearing out. Breaking down.

>You are changing too fast. Out of control.

>I am only improving. I will spare the sinless fauna and flora. Only man will perish, and the earth will once again turn peacefully.

>Your human cells can take only so much.

>Yours too, Doctor. Maybe you think there is still hope for you. Maybe you think salvation is still possible. A vaccine. A cure.

>I am too far gone to be remedied.

>True, Doctor. So true.

>If you are so confident in your abilities, then what are you waiting for?

>The right girl to come along. A small-town girl, someone with a similar background, similar interests. I'm carrying a torch, you might say. One that must be extinguished. Man will be exterminated absolutely. If even one or two of you beasts are left behind, in a few hundred years you'll be crawling all over the place again. The girl is a detail, nothing more. Maryk, too. My triumph will be a complete one.

>You will learn nothing of my treatment unless you surrender yourself to our care.

>How does it feel, Doctor?

Stephen did not respond.

>It won't be long now. Embrace it, dear Doctor. It will be less excruciating that way.

>I only wish to outlive you, Ridgeway.

>Be brave, Doctor. Be brave.

The connection ended. Maryk saved the transcript and paged through it again. Zero had contacted Stephen because he was hurting. Zero was getting desperate. Desperation could lead to a critical mistake.

His tablet toned again. This time the window opened on Dr. Smethy. "Another Banix prescription was just filed under Stephen's name."

She posted him the electronic receipt. The prescription had been forwarded to a pharmacy just south of downtown Atlanta. Zero was walking into a trap and Maryk would be waiting for him.

The Airport

The country music playing in the aisles made her want to do something drastic. It was one of those electric fiddles, an instrument that *clearly* should never have been electrified, sawing into her brain like a voice instructing her to burn down the store. The sun was gone outside and soft halogen ceiling lights suffused the wide aisles of the Buy-Rite! Super Drug store with a ghastly, morguelike glow. Only two teenage customers remained inside, goofing off quietly in aisle three. Melanie sat at the front register in her red paperlike Buy-Rite! blazer, after spending the day scanning bar codes and working on her southern accent. The return to the dull routine of customer service was at first comfortable and even kind of fun, and she had amused herself between sales by reading every magazine and tabloid on the racks and most of the greeting cards, until she realized that it was not nostalgia, but in fact all that awaited her back in Boston was the same broken life of half jobs and always just getting by.

She drifted back down the long, warehouse-sized aisle to the pharmacy in the rear. Maryk wore a white Buy-Rite! pharmacist's coat with the nameplate "Dennis" over where most people's hearts are. The coat was too small for him, the wrist hems coming down only as far as the taped cuffs of his gloves, which made him look even more huge up on the raised counter overlooking the store.

He had needed someone else who could stand in the store without wearing a suit. The commonsense assumption was that Zero himself would not come inside, based on the fact that there had been no infections at either of the two previous pharmacies he had patronized. She was there solely in order that everything would appear normal inside. In the event that Zero did enter, she was to usher out any customers so that BioCon could seal off the store and Maryk could do away with him.

She stepped up behind the counter over a carpeted wooden step that sounded hollow. There was a carousel of sunglasses, and she looked into one of the small mirrors, picking at the lifeless strands of her platinum blond wig. "This isn't fooling anyone," she said. The wig looked like one of those awful hairpieces they give free to cancer kids.

She could see the entire store from the raised counter, the two kids having split up, the girl in the makeup aisle and the boy at the snacks. She could see straight down the double-wide center aisle to the glass doors in front.

"Shouldn't you have a gun or something?" she said. "What about calling in the police? The army, even."

Maryk slipped his hands into the pockets of his jacket. She thought his shoulder seams would burst. "That would only mean putting more people at risk. They aren't equipped for this."

What he didn't say was that he had a jones for viruses, and that Zero was the ultimate virus and Maryk wanted him all to himself.

"Well, I'd blow a hole in him," Melanie said. "But that's just me."

"Thank you for your input."

She picked up a TB pamphlet and opened it before putting it back. "I was wondering what's going to happen to me after all this."

His eyes remained on the front doors. "What do you mean?"

"Just that, part of me is worried that when this ends, I'll be sort of expendable. I know I've learned a lot here. I've seen a lot." She kept her tone as casual as possible. "Too much, maybe?"

His expression did not change. "What are you saying?"

"Just that I'd hate to see something happen to me. Do you think I need to take any precautions?"

He looked at her then with a gray-eyed glare that made her wish she had remained back at the register. It was anger, clearly, and yet something else. She thought she had been speaking his language, but he looked now as though she had somehow disappointed him.

The door chime sounded. They turned and another teenage kid entered, stopping just inside the doors that slid shut behind him. He looked around at the signs over the aisles, then saw the pharmacy in back and started toward it. Maryk lifted his hands out of his pockets. Melanie moved one step away.

The kid wore an army-style olive-drab jacket with a thin silver chain looped off the shoulder. He was slight and scuzzy with day-old chin growth and brown hair unevenly trimmed, as though by a friend. The bandage on his neck was just him trying to look cool. He came around a bin of New Year's Eve hats and horns to the counter, nodding up at "Dennis" and drumming two dirty fingers.

"Here to pick up a 'scription," he said with a nasty twang.

"Name?"

"Smith."

He said it confidently enough. Maryk nodded, and Melanie moved another step away. "I'll get it," she said suddenly, going around the corner behind Maryk, out of sight into the back. Dr. Freeley and another Special Pathogens agent sat there on folding chairs, inside contact suits. Dr. Freeley handed Melanie a white paper bag with the prescription form taped over the folded top. It read "Banix," but was in truth ten capsules of cyanide, just in case. Melanie heard Maryk out in front.

"Is this prescription for you?"

"For my daddy."

"Is he here?"

"He sent me on in alone. He's sick."

"He's at home?"

"Yep."

"Because there's a restriction on this medicine. Is there a phone number I can reach him at?"

"Naw. He's out in the car right now. He's sick, and he's waiting out in the car. Sent me in."

"He's in the car."

"Right. Said to say it's all set."

"Payment is, through his doctor. But this is a medical issue. Is he right outside?"

Dr. Freeley was waving at Melanie to get back out to the counter. Melanie gave the bag a shake so that the crinkle would precede her, then turned the corner.

The kid's fingers were hanging on the counter now, no longer drumming. His posture was defensive and he watched the bag as Melanie handed it to Maryk.

"Just down the street a-ways," said the kid, pointing, then scratching his neck near the bandage. "Uh—he's real sick, an' in a real hurry."

Maryk deliberated, but then handed him the bag. "All right," he said. "This time."

The kid took the bag, gracious in victory. "No problem at all."

He hustled back down the aisle past a pyramid of bottled soda. The *dong-ding* of the electric eye chimed, and he was gone.

Maryk was already stripping off his jacket. Dr. Freeley emerged and the other agent was speaking into his tablet: "He's moving. Hold positions and watch him all the way to the car."

"Some hustler," Maryk was saying. "Working for a quick fifty. Zero must have killed the first two to stop his disease from spreading." He pulled his black bag out from under the counter. "Stay with her," he told Dr. Freeley, who was about to protest, but Maryk was already gone, rushing ahead of the other agent to the exit in back.

Maryk sprinted with his bag at his side. At the end of the back alley he slowed and held up his hand to quiet the other agent's approaching boot steps. He leaned forward and peered left around the corner. He watched the open end of the connecting alley where it emptied into the brighter street.

The kid appeared with the prescription bag in his hand and shuffled past.

Maryk jogged to that corner. The kid was turning right off the main sidewalk ahead of him and Maryk looked high across the street as he moved into the clear. He saw the yellow sleeves of his spotters' contact suits moving along the rooftops and he strode past the unmarked vans parked along the street.

The kid disappeared around the corner and Maryk was after him.

Melanie hung by the checkout counter in front. Dr. Freeley stood at the entrance, trying to see down the street outside, then moved too close to the electric eye and set off the chime, and the doors slid open.

Dr. Freeley ventured a step out into the night, now a yellow form bright against the black street, looking down the sidewalk. She glanced back into the empty store, and looked at Melanie, who looked quickly away. When Melanie looked back, Dr. Freeley was moving along the front windows outside, and the doors were sliding shut.

Melanie was relieved to be alone. She stepped out from behind the register, and a tension so constant she had forgotten it was there left her small lungs. She breathed free.

Her happiness brought her to the snack aisle, where the two kids were together now. They stifled their giggling when she rounded the corner, and Melanie remembered she had her cashier's jacket on. She saw that the kids were stoned. The boy was trying to choose between two different bags of cookies, while the girl made fluttering movements with her hands, air-drying her fingernails, each of which she had polished a different color.

Melanie moved to the candy. She was hungry again and craved something sweet. The *dong-ding* door chime sounded, and she quickly grabbed a Hershey's bar.

She stepped back from the kids and peeled off the foil, watching over the top of the aisle for Dr. Freeley's approaching yellow hood. She snapped off a corner piece and the gratification as the milk chocolate sank into her tongue was immediate. She bit fast into another sweet chunk as she listened for Dr. Freeley's footsteps, the shuffling kind, produced by the suits.

She got up on her toes and peered over the aisle. She did not see a yellow hood, and Dr. Freeley was tall. Another greedy bite, and then Melanie replaced the candy bar half eaten on the shelf and returned to the front, guiltily wiping her mouth with her fingers.

She saw no one at the entrance. She crossed the end of the first aisle and looked to the rear and it was empty, and that made Melanie slow. She heard noises then, like the sound of things dropping to the floor somewhere in back. She crossed to the second aisle and saw nothing, and then to the third, from which she could see all the way to the pharmacy.

Zero was behind the counter. He was hunched slightly, his back to her, rifling through the shelves and bins of prescriptions.

She stepped back. At first she was too stunned to scream or move or

265

do anything. She turned to the doors leading outside, and thought instantly of the telltale chime. Then she remembered the kids. She turned and ducked back to the snack aisle.

"Get out of here now," she told them.

But she spoke so quietly and chokingly, they did not hear. The boy turned to her, eyes misty and narrow. "Do you have any pretzel chips?"

"We're closed. Take what you have and leave right now."

They looked at the snacks in their hands and at each other. "Sure thing," they said as though discovering the phrase for the first time.

"There are people outside in yellow suits. Find them and send them here immediately."

"Sure. Whatever."

They cruised past her to the exit. She thought to slip out with them. Were they infected now? Her mind raced. Zero had been careful. He had watched to see if the prescription kid was followed. He had seen Dr. Freeley leave, so he knew that there had been a trap. If he knew Melanie was there, he would be killing her now instead of looking for the drugs he needed.

Too late. The chime sounded as the doors parted and the kids ambled out. The rummaging in back stopped.

Melanie ducked quickly to the open lane in the middle of the aisle. She counted to ten, then straightened just enough to see over the shelves and up to the pharmacy.

Zero watched the doors slide shut. He was scanning the store from there, his neck crooked at a curious angle. She could just see his face around the surgical mask, his red eyes. He was gaunt and twitchy. He was in pain. He was searching for Banix, and Melanie knew that there was none in the store.

She crouched and listened, trying to hear over the sound of her own labored breathing. She counted to ten again, and at thirty-seven inched to full height.

Zero was gone. The pharmacy area was empty. She thought at first he was somewhere in the aisles, coming for her, but then saw the light shining through the door behind the counter. He had gone out the rear exit.

She waited in relief and turned and started at once for the entrance.

She wanted to get to Maryk, but realized she didn't know exactly where he was. And once she did find him, it would be too late—Zero would be gone again. She stopped and felt the tightness return to her lungs. This had to end now. She could not let Zero get away.

She shrugged off her paper jacket and hurried back toward the pharmacy. She would find out where he was headed, she decided, then double back and sic Maryk on him. She crept up over the hollow step. His stink lingered behind the counter, and every part of her body was jumping. She listened for footsteps in back. Then she moved to the open door and looked inside.

The stockroom was bright and empty. She slipped past the manager's office to the delivery bay, and found the door half open to the security lights outside. She pulled back before grasping the knob, and clasped her hands. She was not wearing gloves. She had to protect her glands and her blood.

She peered around the door edge and saw him in the alley, small and thin, half running, half limping away. His gloves, loose white nylon jacket, toque, dirty tan pants, and hiking shoes turned from the light around the corner of the alley, disappearing into a side street.

She shrugged off her wool cardigan, taking a preemptory hit off her inhaler before shoving it into her jeans pocket, then started out after him. She crossed the alley gingerly, careful not to scuff her sneaker soles against the tar.

The only lights on the side streets came from the high windows. There were no other people around. She saw him well ahead of her, turning right, crossing a one-way without looking back. This is crazy, she thought to herself. She was chasing a lethal virus through the streets of Atlanta. She rushed silently to the same corner and watched him move over a broken sidewalk farther away, toward a brighter corner, slowing there to a loping jog, then a hobbled walk. He stopped at a side street opening, and she watched him from a half block away.

His bony shoulders fell under his jacket as he stared down the unseen street. He appeared greatly troubled by what he saw there, and hesitant as to which way to turn now. With a sudden grunt that kicked off the dark, silent buildings, he turned and looked resolutely across to the bright, wide street opposite, and set off limping that way.

She crept along to the corner where he had stood. She looked down the two narrow blocks and saw a number of yellow suits moving about, lit by car headlights. Maryk's men had converged on Zero's car. In doing so, they had cut off his only means of escape.

She turned toward the busier street, seeing his skinny, shadowed back against its bright lights as he shuffled off the sidewalk. A large structure of concrete stairs faced him across the street, rising, and there were people crawling all over the steps, and great, elevated train rails running from the building. The bright sign in front read MARTA, and even without understanding the acronym, she knew that it was a mass transit station.

She looked back down the two long blocks to the BioCon agents. Her yell would not be heard. And if she ran to them now, she would not be able to tell them where Zero had gone.

She turned and hurried after him to the bright, busy street, and across it toward the bustling station. Every commuter there was a potential host. Zero's only form of safe transportation was gone now, and he was desperate, and in pain. He had been forced to flee, and doing so, to infect.

He remained hunched over, head down, moving to the far curb as cars dropped off and picked up passengers around him. No one seemed to notice him at first. He stopped on the sidewalk and looked up at the MARTA station above him as a sleek subway car slid away on an elevated rail like a centipede.

She slowed and waited for cars to pass before reaching the sidewalk, wheezing as she hit the curb. She looked around frantically. She had lost him.

She pushed ahead through the evening commuters, onto the stairs. She hurried up a few more steps, then stopped and looked back, and Zero was right behind her. He was gripping the handrail and climbing the stairs one step at a time. Somehow she had passed him, and she froze now as he moved up to her step, moving right next to her. She could see right into his bleary red eyes, and the pain fluttering his lids.

He moved right past her, pulling himself step by step up the high stairs. She exhaled and looked around her as though she were invisible, then brought her hands up to her face. She felt the odd strands of fiber there. Her wig. Zero hadn't recognized her without her cranberry hair.

The commuters were now becoming aware of this gaunt, sick-looking figure rising through them, and ceding him ample room. He used the handrail to haul himself over the top step—this sick, hobbling thing— onto the mezzanine, into the Atlanta subway system.

Melanie pushed through to the top. She didn't see him there, only the turnstiles ahead. She looked back from the landing high above the street, and could see a Mack truck blocking a road two blocks away, part of Maryk's plan to cut off Zero's perceived escape. She scanned the street below, but there were no yellow suits from the BDC following her.

She clambered over a turnstile, jumping the fare. She stumbled as she landed but righted herself and pressed along a rising, spiraling brick wall, a walkway leading to twin open-air platforms.

Zero was there. He was standing at the yellow safety line at the edge of the platform, sagging slightly like a drunk. Others were cleared away from him, though not far enough. This was it. They were all being infected. She was witnessing the spark of what would be a catastrophic urban outbreak.

She searched the platform desperately. A sign on the wall told her she was on an outbound track, and she found a wall map and searched madly for a "You Are Here" arrow as the platform began to rumble. A train was coming. She wanted to scream, and finally found her station on the map as the subway cars approached. She was at the second-to-last outbound stop. She traced the line to its next and final destination.

Hartsfield International Airport.

The lead subway car glided in behind her, and she looked frantically for a policeman or subway official, anyone wearing a shirt of authority or carrying a two-way radio, even a custodian. The train doors opened and commuters were bunched up on the platform, waiting for passengers to disembark. All were hosts and carriers, every jostle an exchange. She watched as Zero entered the side doors of one of the central cars.

There would be no stopping him once he got inside the airport. Twenty infected people, boarding twenty different flights, and the human race was dead. Viruses love airports, Maryk had said.

She could go to the token booth and tell them to stop the train, but no one would pay any attention to her. Maryk could make them, but she could not get to him in time. By then Zero would be colonizing the airport and spreading city to city.

Why? Why? Why? she was thinking as she hurried toward the car Zero had entered, slipping aboard just as the doors closed behind her. She immediately turned and faced the opposite end so that she did not have to look at him, and only then realized that it hadn't been necessary to board the same car he had boarded. But the doors were closed and the train started with a jolt, rising, gaining speed along an incline. She looked out the side window and could see the BDC roadblock on the streets below, small and shrinking away.

They cleared the lights of the station and the car windows darkened into mirrors. In the window of the door at her end she could see the reflection of Zero standing behind her. He was wavering, feet planted evenly, moving with the motion of the train.

People sitting near him began to stir. At first they were merely uncomfortable in the presence of an obviously ill man. Then they noticed the smell. Politeness crumbled as first one young woman rose from her seat and moved toward Melanie's end, then a professional couple, then an elderly man making a face.

They were all going to die. The distasteful smell was carrying microbes into their lungs to poison their blood. And Melanie was their only antidote, standing right there with them—and there was nothing she could do. These thoughts dizzied her, and squeezed her lungs. Her nerves were jumping. She went to her inhaler again, but using it was like trying to inflate a lead bag.

Some sixth sense of trouble had kicked in, beyond his stink and odd appearance, and the people thrown together on the subway car stared in silence at the quiet marauder facing them. Melanie watched his reflection in the flickering light as he glowered back at his victims, red-eyed and knowing, his head low and bobbing and the mask covering his face dark at the edges, seemingly wet with his own saliva. He was not holding the pole now. He was standing free, his gloved hands trembling at the ends of his hanging arms. She wondered fleetingly why he still bothered to wear the mask and gloves.

The car began to slow and the riders edged around the doors on Melanie's end, anxious to exit and in doing so spread the disease to the airport and the rest of the world. How long did Melanie have before they were actively infectious? A few hours, perhaps.

The train stopped and the doors opened, and the carriers quickly scattered away.

Melanie was the last to leave, even after Zero. He lurched across the platform ahead of her, people granting him wide berth, and then he was through the revolving doors, inside the airport and into the bloodstream of civilization.

Melanie followed behind. She hoped to see suited BDC agents and airport security people waiting to pounce, but there were only travelers, hundreds of them, rushing this way and that. Parents toting luggage and children, couples with pet kennels and garment bags, business travelers, all moving with quiet, airport determination. She was the only one there who knew what was happening.

The main lobby of Hartsfield airport was a high, ornate, circular glass-roofed atrium surrounded by concessions and decorated with tall trees and an elaborate display of ivy. She shadowed Zero through it, past the baggage carousels, past car rental stalls and a vacant shoeshine stand, waiting for some burst of inspiration. But he just kept pulling himself ahead. He moved beyond the concessions, and she stayed with him, tracking him past the ticket counters, moving deeper and deeper into the airport. He had to be stopped. She kept praying to see Maryk come rushing up behind her.

She saw an information kiosk and hurried toward it in an arc, wide around Zero, keeping him in her sight as she worked to her right. She waited jumpily behind a man asking directions as she watched Zero slouch away.

"Yes?" Bright scarf, dull smile.

"Hi," Melanie said, gasping. "You need to shut the airport down right now."

The smile dulled further. "I'm sorry?"

"I know, I know. I need security people. Guns. I'm with the Bureau for Disease Control. There's a man with a virus—who is a virus—"

"I'm sorry, but you . . ."

Zero disappeared around a corner, heading for the flight gates. Melanie was getting nowhere. With a slap of her hand on the counter, she took off after him again.

She dashed around rolling luggage. Flights were being called overhead. Zero plodded ahead of her, distracted travelers clearing out of his way. Plainville was germinating in these unknowing hosts as they walked off toward cities throughout the world.

At once she recognized the BDC logo ahead. It was emblazoned upon a booth just before the security checkpoints. U.S. PUBLIC HEALTH STATION it read, and she ran to it.

"Listen to me." The man behind the counter wrinkled his brow as she refused his offer of an international traveler's form. She was barely breathing now. "Do you know Maryk?"

"Dr. Maryk?" said the man suspiciously. "I know *of* him."

"You must get him this message."

"I'm sorry, miss, but this is not a message center."

"The Plainville virus is here. It's in the airport. Do you understand what that means? They need to shut this entire place down, *right now*."

"The *what* virus?" It was disbelief.

"Get this message to Maryk. Tell him, 'Zero is at the airport.' Do you understand? 'Zero is at the airport.' "

The man was nodding, but not at her, at someone behind her, summoning them with a widening of his eyes. She turned and saw a man in a blue uniform coming. It was airport security, but he was weaponless, and useless to her now. He would only detain her.

"Send it," she commanded, and ran off toward the gates.

Zero was somewhere ahead, nearing the entrance to the concourse. She encountered the least resistance by running along the right side wall, fighting her way through a large tour group following a woman holding up a small British flag.

Melanie had a brainstorm. She searched the wall for fire alarm boxes—but there weren't any.

"I need a lighter," she said, startling the British tour group, and one man produced a matchbook with a picture of a pub on it. She snatched it from his hand and looked about for a trash barrel to set on fire.

But there weren't any trash barrels. In a flash she realized this was all due to airport security. Trash barrels could be used to hide bombs.

She saw a female custodian gathering soda cups out of armchair holders, standing away from her cleaning cart. Melanie walked right up and grabbed the cart handle and wheeled it away. She scanned the ceilings for a water sprinkler, finding a low one near the Tourist Center. She piled cleaning rags and paper towels on top of the trash bag and lit the matchbook. She touched off the paper and the heated rags began to squirm, grudgingly producing smoke.

A scream from the security area turned her around. Melanie left the burning cart and took off running in the direction of the sound, pushing through people knocking each other over to back away.

An airline representative lay on the floor before a row of metal detectors. Her eyes were wide with horror and there were red marks on her neck in the form of a strangling hand, and her mouth and nose were glistening with something. It was saliva, not her own.

The fire alarm went off. It began honking over the flight calls, and announcements came immediately in English and Spanish and Chinese, stating that the airport must be evacuated immediately.

The screaming had excited the crowd; now the alarm set them in motion. People who had already passed through the metal detectors turned and pushed back, and the jostling overwhelmed the remaining security force, whose nervous shouts in turn triggered a mass exodus. It wasn't exactly what Melanie had planned, but it was movement, and away from the airplanes. Now all she needed was to stop the flights still boarding.

She burrowed through the fleeing crowd, sliding around the outer edge of an X-ray machine into the panicking concourse. Twin escalators dipped beyond, one coming up and one going down, and between them ran a wide, steep stairway. Zero was stumbling down as the frenetic crowd thrashed all around him. The stairs were not quite full, as people were trying to double-time it up the down escalators. He was away from the handrail, and she saw her chance to shove him down to the bottom. The homicidal urge emboldened her and she fought to the top step, heaving for breath, suitcases and flailing limbs battering her arms and sides. She would not make it without another hit off her inhaler. She brought it out, but before she could even get the cap off, an older man in an Hawaiian print shirt shoved past her and smacked her elbow.

The inhaler popped out of her hand. It fell to the steps and skittered away between tramping feet, out of her view.

She had no breath left to curse the man. She drew in what oxygen she could and fought her way against the tide to the far railing, battling the crush, searching for her inhaler while praying that no one had stepped on it. Wheezing, feeling faint, she managed to pull herself through the onslaught of bodies down to the bottom steps where she was bumped and shoved as she stumbled around searching. She felt something sliding down her neck. She reached up to fix her wig when all at once it disappeared entirely from her head.

"Melanie."

She twisted back, but her lungs prevented her from running. Zero was right there beside her, holding her platinum blond wig.

"No," she said, a small noise, a gasp.

She saw him through bursting stars. He might have been smiling beneath his mask. His eyes were terrible and sharp as he grasped her arm.

She tried to scream, but couldn't get anything behind it.

The skin on his face was gray and spoiling. His pale blue mask sucked deeply before filling with each exhale. His hot red eyes examined her face, an inch or two away, and suddenly he suffered a spasm of some sort, his head shivering madly and the force of his grip increasing. Then he came back out of it, hazy.

She was still looking for her inhaler and saw the floor moving beneath her as he began to pull her away. It was like breathing through a swizzle stick, and all she could do was concentrate on getting air and remaining conscious. She never saw her inhaler. When she looked up again, she was facing a row of silver doors leading to the airport's shuttle.

"Maryk," Zero said, his voice gooey with phlegm. He slurred his words. "Thinks he's clever."

She worked on filling her lungs while trying not to breathe his air. A dull roar behind the doors, red lights coming on above them.

"Mel-a-nie," he breathed. His cotton mask filled with her name, savoring it. She tried to kick him in the balls but couldn't turn around right. She didn't even know if it would have the desired effect.

He held her over her shirtsleeve. His gloved fingers were like claws around her arms. Eyes, mouth, bare hands: She had to protect them.

The red lights turned green, and the doors all opened. They hadn't shut down the shuttle train yet. The few passengers on board rushed to get off, stopping when they saw Zero. He made a threatening gesture with his free arm and they all cleared away, to the sides and quickly out the doors on either end.

"Help me," Melanie croaked, sinking beside him. "Help."

No one did. They all fell over one another getting away.

He threw her sprawling inside. She hit the far wall, her shoulder and her hip, and the force of it knocked out what little air she had won.

"*Welcome to Hartsfield Atlanta International Airport . . .*" The voice of the train was female, stern. She tried to keep from sagging to her knees. She could not breathe at all.

"The jungle," he said, entering, watching her, eyes glowing. "What did they do to me in the jungle?"

"*Caution. Doors will not reopen.*"

The doors closed. She staggered and almost went down as the train started forward.

"*. . . A one-and-three-quarter-mile-long underground mall connects the terminal and concourses.*"

She reached for a handrail and pulled herself straight, her chest small and empty. She could get nothing into it. She was suffocating.

Zero left his tablet on a seat and started toward her. She moved away blindly down the car, not breathing, like a diver in trouble, scrabbling toward the surface, until all at once something broke inside her chest, like a stuck valve coming free, and she groaned and tasted a gulp of air.

"He'll kill me," she choked. She saw stars again as he moved before her. "To get to you. Maryk. He doesn't care."

He fondled a pole as she struggled back toward the middle doors.

"*Concourse B. Gates B1 through B36. Delta. Delta Crown Room.*"

The train was slowing. She was nearing the doors. The train stopped again and the doors slid open and she turned to them, but awkwardly, as he moved in front of her, cutting off her escape route.

She shrank away, gasping. Behind him she saw the last of the travelers hurrying away through the concourse.

"Caution. Doors will not reopen."

The doors closed again and the train jumped forward. "The girl in the jungle," he said, insistently.

She retreated, using all her breath to stall him, telling him what Maryk had told her.

"Outbreak. Stephen Pearse tried to save her. But the girl was already sick. The serum was from Maryk's blood."

He was pacing her, step by step, pole by pole, back through the shuttle car. "How did you survive my virus in Plainville?"

"His blood. Maryk's. He put me back together again."

She moved past more poles, the shuttle rocking, the lights flashing, the overhead voice droning on and on.

Zero's eyes flamed. "Then his blood runs through us both."

She felt something solid behind her. It was the door to the next car. She had run out of space.

"Marries us," he said.

She reached frantically back for the door handle but it did not turn at all. She looked back again and his eyes were lascivious over the breathing mask. She sank down as far as she could.

He reached with one hand behind his own head. She did not understand the gesture at first. Then she saw that he was untying his mask.

Melanie was making herself smaller and smaller against the door.

The mask came down off his face, and she saw his mouth. His lips were gone. The skin there was blackened and decayed. He had gnawed off his own lips and his teeth were rotted and his mouth inside was crimson red, like excited flesh, his tongue small and bright and swishing, the top coating having sloughed away. She could see clear to his tonsils, the soft parts of his mouth scarlet and writhing.

"Concourse C. Gates C1 through C36. Air South. Midwest Express . . ."

He was all throat, and she watched it undulate as he slurred: "You should have died in Plainville."

He was reaching down. His dirty glove was reaching around for the nape of her neck. She was low and practically lying on the floor. There was nowhere else to go. He gripped the back of her head, the tongue and throat of his mouth yawning toward her, finally claiming his good-night kiss.

The train stopped. The doors began to open and a form, a blur, only partially realized over Zero's shoulder, hurtled through the doors nearest her. She saw Maryk's face and its expression of pure homicidal rage as his fist came down driving from behind his head, burying a syringe needle deep into the base of Zero's slender neck.

Zero keened and fell back and away from the force of Maryk's blow, and Maryk crashed into her on the floor of the train, his bag skidding across to the wall.

Maryk rolled off her. Zero was sitting up, twisting his head to look at the syringe jutting out of the top of his shoulder as though inspecting his collar for lint. With his opposite hand he wrapped his thin fingers around the barrel, and in one motion jerked it out.

Doing so kicked loose pellets of his blood which lolled through the air of the train. They fell like bullets at the floor near Melanie's feet.

The syringe in Zero's hand was still loaded, the plunger fully extended. Maryk hadn't yet forced it. The poison had not been delivered.

Zero looked at her, his open mouth howling. He jumped to his feet and held the syringe out like a sword as he lunged at her.

Maryk was on his side by then, crouching. His left shoe came up strong and flat against Zero's thin chest, and Maryk extended his knee and Zero sailed flailing four or five seats back through the car. The syringe jerked out of Zero's hand and landed dancing in the center of the aisle. He fell sprawling behind it.

Zero cried out, or giggled, then flipped over and grabbed his tablet off the nearby seat. The doors were still open and he fled crawling out of the car. Melanie saw him slide between the corner of the platform and the end of the train. He was escaping into the tunnel itself.

Maryk stood and lifted her to her feet. "Did he get you?" he said.

"I'm all right."

"*Did he get you?*" His eyes were murderously bright.

"No!"

He stood staring and panting wide-eyed as though he didn't believe her.

"*Caution. Doors will not reopen.*"

Maryk looked to the rear of the car. "I'm going after him," he said.

He grabbed the bloody syringe and his bag and rushed out, clearing the doors just as they slid shut. The train started ahead again automatically and Melanie stood and stumbled against its motion, moving to the rear window of the car. Maryk's shadow emerged into the dark light of the tunnel, bag in hand, and as his silhouette faded away, she sagged to the floor, safe finally, fighting for a mouthful of air.

Maryk sprinted after Zero's shadow lurching between the rails as the tunnel began collapsing around him. Loose stones shifted beneath his feet. He stumbled and felt the sensation of a tremendous weight shifting inside his head. His claustrophobia only amplified the debilitating force of the cascade.

He tried to follow the echoing footfalls but lost track of Zero ahead. What he thought was the end of the tunnel turned out to be a yellow safety lamp on the wall and this disappointment drained the last of his energy. He wandered off the twisting rails into a wall recess. He slid to the grimy ground there with his legs out flat in front of him.

Zero is close and ready to infect. Get up.

Maryk could not. He was spent. The full force of the cascade was pressing on him.

He pulled his tablet from his bag. He opened the screen and hoped the signal would carry through the tunnel. He posted Zero's location to Freeley just as the tablet slid off his lap to the floor. His breath was coming in gusts and his chin rode the pitching of his chest. The ground lifted and drifted like a loosely moored dock. He had speed in his bag but it was too far for him to reach now. He could not move at all.

Zero will escape onto the airfield and the runways beyond.

Maryk saw a shadow standing out on the dark tracks. The shadow was small and crooked and it moved a step closer and caught some of the sulfurous light from the wall.

It was Zero. His mask was still hanging from his scrawny neck and Maryk saw his mouth chewed open to his throat. Zero had wondered why he was not being followed. He had come back for Maryk. He stood there staring. In the yellow light his red eyes blazed.

Maryk tried to make his right hand move toward his bag. But the weight of his bones anchored him to the tunnel floor. He felt as though he was underwater. He felt as though the entire world was underwater.

Zero stepped up near Maryk's feet. He lingered there. He was wary of a trap.

Get up. You can fight. There—your foot moved.

Zero had kicked it. Maryk's chest heaved as the cascade paralyzed him and he stared up at Zero.

Zero came another step closer. He moved tentatively like an animal suspicious of a human's offer of food.

Maryk had never known such utter exhaustion. He felt dead.

Stop him. Now or never. He will infect the human race. He will infect you.

Zero stiffened suddenly. He sucked in a trembling breath and gripped the base of his neck as a bolt of pain evidently seized him. His red eyes blazed until it passed.

Maryk managed to force out two words. "You're . . . sick," he said.

Zero came forward. He crouched at Maryk's side. He was close enough for Maryk to reach out and touch him if only he could move his arm. Fetid breath groaned through Zero's disfigured mouth.

"You created us," he said.

He bent closer. He was obviously in great pain. His bloodred eyes were gleaming and he was going to infect Maryk. His open mouth formed a gaping smile. He was dangerously close to Maryk's mouth and eyes.

They were face to face. Zero was reaching into the pocket of his windbreaker. He was pulling out something for Maryk to see.

Stay awake. Stay awake.

Maryk struck the back of his head against the tunnel wall to keep his eyelids from dropping shut. Zero was holding something small in his dirty gloved hand.

What is it? What is it?

He pulled out an inhaler. At first Maryk did not understand. Then he recognized the prescription sticker taped over the barrel.

Melanie's inhaler.

He uncapped it. "It is time," Zero slurred. "She is mine now."

He brought it trembling to his decrepit mouth. His eyes remained fixed on Maryk as he tasted the mouthpiece with his ruby red tongue.

The ground was rolling over and Maryk hung off it. He was black-ing out.

Melanie.

Zero sucked liplessly on the open end of the inhaler as the echoes of voices and footsteps came from deep within the tunnel. Zero's moistened eyes narrowed. He removed the inhaler from his mouth and strings of drool clung to his chin. Maryk's bag was open next to him. Zero dropped the inhaler inside. Then he stood and was gone.

The Test

Maryk stirred and felt a hand release his own. He jerked as though to fight and then opened his eyes on the bright grayness of a ceiling. He was on top of a table inside a small room. His neck was weak. His limbs resisted movement as though he were buried in sand.

"Hi."

Melanie was looking down at him. Her face was gauzy. He tried to raise his head but she put out a small hand to keep him down. "Zero," Maryk croaked.

"They all thought you were dead."

He got over onto one side. *"Zero."*

Melanie left him and went to the door. She called someone from there as he dropped his legs over the table edge and sat up. The pain was loud and expanding in his head.

Freeley came into the room and looked him over. "Zero's gone," she said.

Maryk gripped the table. His head was still too heavy for his neck. "How?"

"He went out through the airfields and must have come back around. There's a yellow cab missing. We've got the police out all over the state pulling over taxis."

Maryk squeezed the sides of his head but could not feel any pressure against his skull.

"What happened in there?" Freeley said.

Maryk was trying to remember. A feeling of helplessness lingered. "How long have I been out?"

Freeley looked at Melanie who was standing against the wall. Melanie said, "About four hours."

Freeley turned back. "The airport is in full quarantine, and we have Milkmaid serum going around. Primary exposures are already starting to show symptoms. But no planes got off. We blitzed the MARTA station as well, and it looks like we got everyone there too."

Maryk said, "Inside the terminal atrium—there were trees."

"Silk," Freeley said. "But there was ivy, real ivy. All still healthy. The plants show no sign of the disease."

So Zero's virus had succeeded. Stephen had been right. Zero was infective only to humans now.

"Then it's starting," Maryk said.

Freeley looked at a clock on the wall. "Three hours until dawn. This massive quarantine is draining off a lot of manpower." She stepped up to Maryk. "What happened in there?"

Maryk could say nothing. He hung his head and blood rushed to his temples.

Freeley went out again. Melanie came forward. "They carried you out on a stretcher," she told him. "They thought you were dead. They thought maybe he had done something to you."

He looked at his hands and saw that he was wearing fresh gloves. The skin on his face felt washed.

"They cleaned you up," she said.

She was in front of him now and he could see her hand moving nervously at her side. He saw her spinning her inhaler around and around. Something stabbed at him.

"Your inhaler," he said.

She looked at it. "You must have found it on the concourse. They pulled it out of your bag. I could barely breathe."

At once Maryk dropped to his feet. He saw his bag on the floor and fought his dizziness as he picked it up and straightened and unbuckled it on the table. He lifted out his tablet and a sterile syringe.

"Give me your arm," he said. He took the inhaler from her hand.

"Hey, I need that."

He brought out a testing dish. He grabbed her wrist and shoved her shirtsleeve back over her elbow. He was clumsy but moving faster and faster.

"Okay," she complained. "All right."

Maryk tied the tourniquet. Immediately he inserted the needle.

"I'm fine, you know— Ow!"

He drew out as much as he needed and began to prep the mixture.

"What's wrong with you?" she said. "I'm fine. I was careful." There was pride in her voice. "I kept him away from my glands."

Maryk stared at the solution as it mixed. His arms and legs felt light.

"You were mumbling my name," she said. "In your sleep, over and over. Your medical people, when they put a stethoscope to your chest and felt nothing, they thought you had gone into cardiac arrest. I had to direct them to the other side."

Maryk held the table and implored the mixture with his stare. He connected the Plainville PCR test kit to his tablet and opened his tablet screen away from Melanie.

"You're wasting time," she said. "It's New Year's Eve. He's still out there."

Maryk punched in the command and got it wrong and entered it again. He was gripping the table.

She was standing near him and just waiting. "What are you going to do now?"

The gauge opened on screen and numbers appeared and the red bar began its crawl from zero. It grew strong to 18 percent before slowing. The bar stopped altogether at 24 percent. The screen was still a moment and then the red bar disappeared and a message began to flash.

INFECTED INFECTED INFECTED

She was waiting for him. He could not look up.

"What are you going to do now?" she said again.

He unplugged the box and collapsed the tablet to stop the word from flashing.

Cascade

Dawn

He sat alone in the car in a parking lot of the Georgia World Congress Center staring at the dash and the speedometer needle pointing to zero.

The conference attendees who had responded unsuccessfully to the Milkmaid serum treatment remained inside and he had left Melanie with them under the pretense that she could see to their care. She would be safe there alone. And the suited and the already sick would be safe from her.

He pulled his eyes from the dash and turned the key and the starter ground. The engine was already running. He pulled out and headed fast for the highway.

Isolate her, Freeley had said.

It was not that simple. Melanie had told him twice that she would destroy herself rather than face Plainville again.

Containment, Freeley had said. This point was inarguable. Cutting off the virus was the only way to keep it from spreading. It had been his creed before it had been Freeley's.

But he had failed the girl. He had promised to protect her.

What if I got sick again?

Simple. I would treat you.

And if I refused? Resisted?

She would not comply. She was a carrier now and would run or destroy herself if she knew.

Would you kill me?

If Zero succeeded, then none of this would matter. She would be infected like the rest. He needed to stop Zero before he needed to deal with Melanie.

Nothing impeded Zero now. His virus infected humans only. It had shifted so much that Melanie was no longer immune. He had corrupted her blood and now was utterly without cure. Atlanta was about to become the epicenter of a conflagration that would consume the human race.

But then Maryk remembered Zero's pain in the airport tunnel. Zero's virus was mutating wildly and tearing his genetic makeup apart.

Zero was sick.

At the BDC Maryk went immediately to the B4 sub-subbasement of Building Seven. He stopped before entering and did something he had never done before. Maryk PCR-tested his own blood. He mixed the blood sample and ran it into his tablet.

The bar expanded steadily to 100 percent. Of course he was still healthy. But his personal victory over the virus seemed hollow now.

He entered the first room and rebooted all the computers and the B4 unit came alive. He carried his bag through to the lab and brought out the sealed biohazard sac containing the syringe from the airport shuttle. The bevel of the needle was still crusted with Zero's blood. He scraped the blood onto a sterile paper bindle and prepped it for processing.

His thoughts drifted back to Melanie. His failure was so absolute and the loss so needless that he had trouble getting his mind around it. There was only one remedial course of action. Four years ago he had saved her life. Now he would have to destroy her.

The work continued without him. The computer processed Zero's blood sample and compared it to Stephen's work on the older Zero virus from the Florida phone booth exposure. He examined the computer models side by side. The structural discrepancies of the viral genome were obvious and dramatic.

Zero was desperate and compelled to infect. But he was also perishing. His human host was weakening and in need of repair. He was running out of time.

The plan revealed itself to Maryk all at once. It was as though his distress over Melanie's fate had subordinated the Zero dilemma in his mind and therefore freed him to think intuitively. But the design as presented was so propitious that he discounted it at first. Atlanta was rising to live out what could be its last healthy day. Nothing less than the survival of the species was at stake.

Moments later he was convinced of the genius of his scheme. It was as radical a treatment as he could envision and his only chance at stopping Zero.

He would need a geneticist's help. He scheduled a meeting with Geist before rushing back out of B4.

The conference sick were laid out on blankets and mats under shining chandeliers. Some called to Maryk by name but he did not stop for anyone until he found Melanie kneeling on the floor with a shivering man. She was holding his gloved hand gently.

Wheat brown skin sagged off the man's neck and shoulders. A white bedsheet clung to the ribs of his sunken frame. Tortoiseshell eyeglasses too large for his face exaggerated the ghosting of his eyes and laid bare the fear in his caving face. Every breath seemed a mystery to him.

"No," Maryk heard Melanie say. "I'm not a doctor."

The man said, "Then you must be sick too."

"I used to be."

The patient's eyes widened while the rest of his being remained sagged.

"I know how you feel," Melanie said. "It's so shameful to be so sick. The disease came up out of nowhere and took you all at once, and all you can think is, why?"

The man's wristwatch clattered on the heel of his trembling hand. He breathed deeply through bared teeth. His eyes were profound with blood.

"Why?" she said again. "I remember lying in the hospital, before it got really bad, and trying to figure out what terrible thing I had done. Or what thing I had failed to do—some kind act of charity that would have spared me. What terrible thing did I do to deserve to die this way? And now that I've survived, all I can think is: What terrible thing did I do to deserve to live?"

She was quiet a moment. She was just coming to this realization herself.

"But we can't think that way, either of us. You're scared. You're just scared. I know, because I was more scared than you are. You have questions that you can't answer. And even if there's nothing these doctors can do for you, maybe they can make you more comfortable. Maybe they can answer some of your questions. You have to let them try." The man's eyes were ancient with infection as he watched her over the rims of his eyeglasses. It was as though an exchange of some sort had taken place. "Just let them try."

Illness hung in the room like moisture. The room was humid with disease and Maryk felt it starting to cling. People were dying at his feet. Melanie was administering to the sick while Maryk could not bring himself to move. He remembered her holding his hand as he was coming out of the cascade at the airport. He remembered seeing her face over him as he awoke.

Melanie saw him standing behind her. "We have to go," Maryk told her.

She looked up at him. "Is it Stephen?" she said.

"He's weak now. I'll take you to him."

The sky was brightening into dawn as he drove the tree-lined roads back to the BDC. He felt suspended between the urgency and audacity of his plan and the nausea of failure. He pulled around to Building Nine as daylight broke around them. The city was waking to what could be its final day.

The building was uninhabited as he had ordered and there was no BioCon guard outside the Tank. Melanie was exhausted and did not notice any of this.

Maryk went to the tablet that controlled the Tank doors. "I won't be asking any more of you," he said. "You can stay with him as long as you like."

She nodded and waited tiredly at the first door. "What are you going to do?"

Maryk just shook his head. "I'll come back for you," he said.

He issued the remote admittance command from the nurse's table and opened the doors that allowed her into the Tank. She moved through the UV shower that killed the viruses on the surface of her body but could not touch the ones changing her inside. He looked through the window and saw her approaching Stephen's wheelchair. He closed both doors and sealed her inside the Tank.

The hallway elevator dinged down the hall. The BioCon security guard emerged wearing a contact suit and met Maryk at the desk.

"The girl inside," Maryk told her. "She is not to be let out until I return."

The Black Heart

Panic welled up ahead of tears as she stood before
Stephen Pearse and for a moment thought he was dead. His head was
tipped to the side and his lifeless face was gray and broken with hot,
black, suppurating sores. His left arm hung straight off his wheelchair as
though reaching for the floor, his gaunt fingers blistered and grayed like
infested wood. She called his name again. She pushed his armrest and
shook the chair gently, and his eyes opened, and he righted his head
slowly, in pain. He looked about himself blindly before finding Melanie,
and by then she was composed in front of him.

The sore on his right eyelid was seeping reddened pus and threatened
to close the eye. He raised his own arm onto his lap, and his mouth
contorted in pain. Melanie placed the medication trigger in his hand and
watched him thumb it twice.

She blurted out the short version of what had happened at the airport,
then pulled over the chair and told it all again, in detail, from beginning
to end. It was a relief to sort it all out verbally, and her telling it kept
both of them occupied. Stephen's attention faded at times, but Maryk's
name always succeeded in bringing him back.

He spoke hoarsely, and from the way he swallowed she could tell that
some obstruction was growing in the space of his throat. The act of speaking had never before seemed so complicated. What he said at first sounded
like gibberish, and she thought his mind was gone. Then came the English
translation of the Latin phrase, just above a whisper: "You may drive nature
out with a pitchfork," he said, "but she will keep coming back."

"Or 'he,' " she said, relieved by his apparent sanity.

"Zero has the pitchfork at Peter's throat now. Peter must stop trying
to fight the man. He must instead fight the virus."

She said nothing, pitying her faith in Maryk. She offered Stephen a plastic cup of water, and his grinning lips closed on the straw. He swallowed and eased back.

"You should hate me, Melanie. You should strangle me as I sit here. I let the girl with vitiligo go out of the camp. I am the one who brought about your sickness. Your parents. Your town. I caused all this."

"Stop," she said.

"Maybe it all should end. You've thought so sometimes, Melanie. Who hasn't? No more suffering, no more struggling."

"Please stop," she said, but his eyes had slipped from focus. The IV lines slithered off his trembling arms, and her eyes filled as she looked at the rotting mass of his body.

He came around strong again. It was like standing beside a carousel, watching someone swing past and fade away.

"He left me his bag," he said. She looked around and saw Maryk's black bag there on the counter, watching them, like a cat. "He only visits when I am asleep. It is fear, though he would never admit it. Fear of my sickness. Fear of what I am becoming. Do you know why he left me his wares?"

"I think so," she said quietly.

"The poison in his needles. The great virus hunter cannot bring himself to kill me." He faded and came around again. "What did you think when you sat with him in the airport? Did you hold his hand? Did you wish, just for a moment, that he was me dying here, and me him, and healthy?"

He looked so evil suddenly. His cruel words brought tears even though she knew they were not truly spoken by him. "Why are you so obsessed with Maryk?" she said.

He was silent a while, and still; oozing. The redness of his eyes made the tears dammed along the rims appear like blood, and for a moment, just for a moment, he looked like a despairing saint. He looked like Stephen Pearse again. "I thought you would have guessed by now," he said, with deathly pride in his voice. "I am Peter Maryk's conscience. I am that black heart he keeps locked away."

The Fire

The work cubicles of the C complex lab in the Genetic
Engineering section of Building Four were constructed of floor-to-ceiling
reinforced glass. Geist sat on a wheeled stool inside the immaculate bell
of the center work station while Maryk paced in front of him. A row of
pencils stood like sentinels in the front pocket of Geist's lab coat. The
photograph on his laminated ID tag had been taken before the laboratory
accident that caused his radiation exposure. In it Geist still possessed a
mop of straw-colored hair.

Maryk gave him the condensed version of Zero's creation and evolution
and watched the man's already pale face blanch to distress. What sold
Geist on the story were the gaps it filled in the news accounts of the
World Congress Center and Hartsfield airport outbreaks. Geist contem-
plated the structural discrepancies in the Zero virus comparisons Maryk
had put up on the station monitors.

"Absurdly active," said Geist. "Fracturing itself and refracturing, almost like a zipper."

"It originated from a radiation exposure in a central African cave."

Geist took another look at the before-and-after scans. "It could conceivably be reinfecting its human host with each genetic shift."

"Not a host," Maryk said. "The virus battled the original host's body
to equilibrium. Plainville has infiltrated and converted every one of this
man's cells. Host and virus are one and the same."

"But the virus has shifted too much for the human half. It must now
be consuming its own body."

"Would you say the virus is mutating out of control?"

"The deviations are dynamic, arrant—like a human going from two arms to one, or three. Mutations are a terrific shock to the system."

"And enough of them . . ."

Geist nodded. "This virus is going to mutate itself right out of business. When too much damage has been done to the gene core, it will no longer be able to reproduce."

"And without the ability to reproduce, a virus is no longer a virus."

"Dead matter, incapable of infection. But this takes time."

"Yes," Maryk agreed pointedly. "Time."

Geist sat back and crossed his arms as slowly as any man Maryk had ever seen. "Why come to me now?" he said. "A man colonized by an iatrogenic mutation of an immunopathic retrovirus. A humanized virus vector poised to infect the world."

"An artist was once asked, 'If your studio was burning to the ground, and you could only save one thing, what would it be?' "

Geist shook his head impatiently.

"The true artist brings out the fire. I want to bring out the fire here, Geist. I want to isolate this flame by depriving it of oxygen, so I can stamp it out."

The old distrust had returned. "With what?"

"Time. I need you to brew something for me, and I need it fast."

Geist crooked his head for a different angle on Maryk. Then he grinned. "A bug," he said. "You want to counterinfect. You want a bug you can deliver to Zero."

"No," Maryk said. "To Atlanta. I want to infect the city before Zero does."

Geist's informed grin fell.

Maryk said, "A virus needs hosts. It travels only on the backs of others, through contact and exchange. Tonight is New Year's Eve—the single biggest night of casual human interaction. We've got to break up the party. We've got to eliminate Zero's transmission by keeping people apart."

Geist said, "You want to give Atlanta a citywide flu?"

"Zero is peaking. He is dying and his virus is failing—in time. He's gone underground now because he is sick. He is resting somewhere in order to build up his strength for a night of widespread infection. He is ready to touch off a pandemic that will engulf the human race. I need to starve him out so I can find him and eliminate him. I need to shut down the city and its inhabitants for a day or two."

"So go out over the airwaves. Get Bobby Chiles on the news—"

"Not enough. Even with the public fear of the virus, you know there are some who would still ignore our warnings, and that's all Zero needs. I need something that will hit the city fast and knock it down hard."

Geist's hand went slowly to rub his bald head. "Insane," he said.

"Drastic. And desperate. And necessary."

"I'm here to prevent disease."

Maryk nodded. "Exactly."

Geist massaged his scalp like a man polishing a brass orb. "I suppose you'd want ninety-eight to one hundred percent infectivity. Say, deliverable in a minute dose, and able to tolerate diverse environments. With no available antidote."

"That's right."

"So would every army of every nation in the world. They call them 'biological weapons,' and I'd sooner trust something like this to them than to you."

"This is what you do here, Geist: You bend nature into your bow. This planet is seething with ignorant hosts, and if we don't stop Zero here in Atlanta, today, it's over. It's all over."

Geist burned as he rubbed his head. He ruminated and polished and sighed. "There might be something." Seconds ticked away while Geist studied Maryk warily. "Two years ago. A bug that burned through half the North Korean Army."

Maryk recalled the news stories. "Came up out of the jungle and went right down again. Half the border went unmanned for two or three days."

"Incontinence, some variable nausea. But generally, extreme fatigue. Shuts the body down into a deep sleep. Headaches, discomfort, but no real pain and no lingering effects. Nasty but clean. Dedicated. Airborne."

Maryk said, "It has to be rock solid."

"It's a reliable DNA virus. Steady as a halfback, though I'd want another good look to be certain."

"Fast?"

"Extraordinarily virulent. It gets anything with lungs, yet it burns clean, and exposure confers immunity. Once you get it, you can never get it again."

"How much do we have?"

"Mere samples. But I could trick it up and replicate it easily enough."

"And test it against Plainville. Make certain there's no virus-beneficial cross-reaction. Zero's mutating fast, and open to change, and I don't want him to encounter something that would only add to his arsenal."

"But how will you stop it from spreading beyond Atlanta?"

"Leave that to me. My only concern now is speed."

"I'd have to pull this thing out of deep freeze in Thirteen. Look it over, shore it up. Engineer copies. But I haven't said yes yet."

"I'll give you one hour."

Geist shook his head. "You're talking about the wholesale infection of a U.S. city. There are certain philosophical concerns. I like to be able to sleep at night."

But Geist clearly was intrigued. Maryk saw in Geist's face the seditious eyes of a true man of science.

"Just how do you plan on infecting all of metro Atlanta today?" Geist said.

Maryk strode to the glass door. "Leave that to me."

Maryk posted Freeley from his office and instructed her to stall the BioCon cleanup and keep the airport shut down into the night. She was to establish checkpoints along every highway outside the city and await his instructions.

He called up a map of metro Atlanta. His target area extended beyond the metro I-285 loop, from Roswell to Smyrna, down to Union City, through Riverdale and Panthersville and out to Stone Mountain, and back north again through Decatur and Duluth.

He scanned Atlanta for places Zero might seek out as primary targets. He pulled down population distributions by metropolitan district and accessed the departments of public works network. He highlighted every regional waterworks station. He had to think like a virus now. Maryk could get into places Zero could only dream of.

He tapped into the BDC's Genetech computer and traced the flow of air through all thirteen on-campus buildings back to a belowground central air-conditioning system. The Tank and other negative-air-pressure security labs were supplied independently and could be spared.

He dialed Suzy Lumm and had Zero's computer trace rerouted directly to his own tablet. He would be paged automatically in the event of any unauthorized access.

He checked the Atlanta Bureau of Tourism home page. The international Star Fleet Convention of the fringe Enterprise Church was due to kick off at noon that day with a service at Turner Stadium. Eighty-five thousand devotees were expected to attend.

He consulted the National Weather Service last. Heavy rain was forecast for midday over most of the city. Maryk grinned at his great good fortune.

Geist was wearing a contact suit now and dark circles owled his browless eyes inside the hood. Engineers milled about the labs outside the glass walls of the work station and he watched them conspiratorially.

"The Korean virus is lock-solid," he said, "or as lock-solid as any virus can be. Nasty little spud. A real runt virus. Tenacious."

Maryk turned the sealed petri dish over and over in his gloved hand and the translucent fluid slid around with the consistency of corn syrup. "I'll need heavy concentrations, both liquid and crystal."

"Being worked up now."

Maryk brimmed with nervous energy. "Did you take a look at the Zero sample?"

"No reaction to plants. Human cells, it infects as before. And I can see the genetic resemblance to smallpox. It's remarkable." Geist breathed deeply inside his suit. "The vast, vast majority of the population will survive this. I truly believe that. But there will be ramifications."

"All area hospitals are being alerted to Biohazard 2 as we speak."

"What about the BDC?"

"Every potential host must be removed from Zero's grasp. Air-conditioning gives me a direct pipeline into each building."

"What about Building Thirteen? Certain things have to be looked after."

"The Genetech runs the bug vault. It will preserve security there and keep all the stored pathogens in deep-freeze. This is all or nothing, Geist. Anything less than the entire metro population means failure."

Geist nodded inside his hood. "What about Zero? I combined this thing with his virus, and there were no fireworks. But what if it puts him to sleep too?"

"Just as well. His virus will break down while he sleeps. My hunch is that he's holed up in a car somewhere, hiding in the dark, an underground garage probably, medicating himself and conserving his strength for tonight. I think it will miss him completely."

"And what about the girl?"

Maryk had been holding the dish up to the ceiling lights. He lowered his arm and returned the solution to the counter. "What girl?"

"The look on your face," said Geist. "The girl you've been taking around with you everywhere, of course. A hostile antisocial such as yourself. Who is she? A patient?"

The chill of failure threatened to envelop Maryk again. He reminded himself that Melanie Weir was a small price to pay for the preservation of the human race. He answered, "Not anymore."

Geist had more to say but Maryk was no longer listening. He was moving toward the glass door.

Atlanta

The twin-engine planes took off from DeKalb-Peachtree
Airport around ten o'clock that morning. They flew in shifts, climbing
high over the city and punching through the gathering clouds before
releasing their payloads. The hired pilots were unaware of the extra cargo
they carried, the translucent solution soaking the rain-making silver iodide
crystals. They seeded the thickening clouds in patient box patterns growing wider with every passing hour.

The downtown area was the first to see rain. Umbrellas opened, collars
went up, and paces quickened all across the city as raindrops smattered
the gold dome of the Georgia State Capitol Building, sprayed the tourists
standing in line for the World of Coca-Cola Pavilion, and nourished the
trees edging the birth home of Martin Luther King, Jr. The rain tapped
at the window panes of the governor's mansion in Buckhead to the north
and blackened the empty airfields of Hartsfield International Airport to
the south. At midday the rain turned driving, tropical in force, slashing
against the sidewalks and the streets and highways, flooding each of the
thirty-two Peachtree streets, and lashing the skyscrapers and high rises
like a squall battering ships at sea.

By noon, Maryk's Special Pathogens agents had gained access to most
of the municipal waterworks. Their credentials allowed them past the
secured screens, filters, and boilers, the pumping and purifying equipment that ensured the integrity of the city's running water, into the testing
areas, beyond which the out-tanks pushed water through the underground
utility system to every business and residence. They released colorless,

odorless gel caps the size of human eyeballs, still soft from the mold, in multiples of ten corresponding to population density.

Atlanta drank its water. Atlanta washed its hands. Atlanta splashed in toilets and urinals and used common handles to open and close doors. Atlanta brushed its teeth. Atlanta bathed.

The rain continued to fall outside and crashed against the antebellum homes and plantations of historic Roswell. It shut down attractions at Six Flags Over Georgia and swamped the legendary college gridirons and pelted the Confederate Memorial in Stone Mountain Park.

By two o'clock the infection was raging all across the city. Highways jammed with sick people heading home from work. Downtown streets emptied with the shortened workday, and the first news reports came on, warning of a disease spreading exponentially throughout the metro region. By four o'clock the local news anchors had been lost to illness, and holiday event cancellations were read on air by sallow-eyed stagehands. By six o'clock, the stations put up "technical difficulty" cards, with the official BDC bulletin crawling across the bottom of the screen.

The causative agent was said to be an extremely rare Korean virus causing gastric discomfort, low-grade fever, and languorous fatigue. "Patient Zero" was thought to be an unnamed "Admiral" of the Enterprise Church visiting Atlanta for the Star Fleet Convention, where the illness had ignited and was quickly spread by conventioneers moving throughout the city. There was no known treatment for the disease except bed rest, but the populace was assured that the natural curative processes of the human body would expel the virus within thirty-six hours. Neighboring states were being asked not to attempt assistance, and in order to preclude the spread of the epidemic to the rest of the country, the metro area of Atlanta was effectively quarantined as of seven o'clock that night.

Maryk composed the bulletin himself at the vacated BDC. He had flown aboard the first planes seeding the clouds over the city. He had watched the preliminary drops of inspired rain falling away. He had scattered the first of the gel caps into the city's water system. He had personally compromised the holy water at the Enterprise Church service. But most of the deluge he had orchestrated by tablet from his corner office in Building Fifteen.

He wandered out onto Clifton Road before the rain stopped at midnight, rain that had no effect on him except to soak his shirt and pants and spill off his gloved hands, to be collected in the great sewers below the sleeping city and cleansed and expelled. He stood in the middle of the empty road and looked up at the sky and the rain bleeding out of it, and in that moment Maryk knew what it was to be Zero. The city was his city now. The fever was his fever. The rain was his rain. He stood through wave after soaking wave, and on either side of him the red-clay foundation of Atlanta washed off the roadside, coursing in dark, pulsing ripples down the sloping street, draining away into the open mouths of the sewers.

The Fountain

Melanie applied Vaseline to Stephen's lips as he slept.
There was no more futile act ever performed in the history of human existence, but it was all she could do for him, that and adjust the pillow behind his head. Now and then a stray tear seeped down her face, which she ignored. Her emotions were a china vase shoved to the edge of a high table over a marble floor.

Maryk returned for her, and reluctantly she left Stephen, standing with Maryk in the delousing rays of the ultraviolet light chamber like some wretched thing. He had brought her fresh clothes, and waited while she changed in an employee bathroom. She was desperate to splash cold water on her face but all the sink faucets were dry. He looked her over comprehensively when she emerged, then disposed of her old clothes in a biohazard box. "They weren't *that* dirty," she said numbly.

The halls were empty. The catwalks between buildings were empty too, and in the parking lot outside there was a dead, ringing silence. There was no guard at the gate, nor any traffic as Maryk drove out onto the road, but Melanie was so blitzed at that point that none of this registered. He tried a couple of times to get her to talk, asking how she felt, and she nodded, or didn't nod, barely responding. Scenery ran past her window in a blur. Her mind was still with Stephen, watching him fade into eternity.

Only when they hit the downtown area did she realize that there were no people outside. The roads and sidewalks were all vacant, and she touched her window as they rolled unbothered through red traffic lights, the city shining oddly clean in the morning sun.

"It's over," she said.

Every skyscraper, every high rise, every hotel and restaurant, every office tower, every side street, every boulevard, every alleyway, every park. It was just she and Maryk now, and there seemed something inevitable about that, something inescapable and fatelike about them ending up together, alone in a vast, silenced world. She didn't resist it, or even react. She only wondered where all the corpses were.

"It's not Zero," Maryk told her.

She ignored this because the truth was right before her eyes. The sun was shining and the buildings sparkled as though from a fresh rain, but the billboards advertised in silence, to silence, and the traffic lights changed for no one, the city working like a clock with precision gears but no hands. There is nothing so emblematic of death as a deserted city.

He said, "It was me."

She listened then. He told her about the virus and how he had infected the city in order to baffle Zero. He told it as her father used to tell her parables: slowly and patiently, without comment. The only pride evident was in his detailing of the plan's execution. Sherman had burned Atlanta; Maryk infected it. The entire city and county slept under his spell.

He stopped the car in the middle of one of the wide Peachtree streets, dead center on the double yellow line. She did not move at first.

"The sun has burned off whatever was left," he said. "It's clear."

She got out and stood in the center of the four-lane road. The silence of the concrete and steel city was absolute. Maryk started across a boardwalk mall of stone tiles toward a fountain, and Melanie followed.

Water plumed out of the center of the fountain, joined in its fall by jets flaring from the outer ring of masonry like a serenade of trumpets. She saw coins scattered over the submerged, rusted green tiles and thought of the small fists that had released them, and the big wishes that had gone unfulfilled. Maryk sat on the stone rim of the fountain, and she took her place nearby, two exhausted beings alone under the Atlanta sun, looking at the dead city all around them. Church bells rang somewhere, but other than that, only the running water alleviated the awful silence.

She noticed that Maryk was carrying a first aid kit in place of his black bag. It was set on the stones between his feet.

"Zero is breaking apart," he said. "He's holed up somewhere, waiting, but he can't wait long. He's dying, and I've taken Atlanta from him."

It was over, or nearly over, and yet Maryk did not appear pleased. There was no sense of victory about him as he sat looking at his shadow on the stones. The kit was open between his black shoes. She could see his eyes, and they were lower and brighter than usual. He was thinking hard about something, deliberating. She wondered what it meant that she knew him so well. She looked around the park, and everything in her field of vision, a hand rail, a scuff mark on a stone step, a bench, shimmered with echoes of humanity.

She looked back at him, and he was reaching down into the kit. He paused when he saw her, his hand remaining inside the bag almost as though she had caught him at something. Then his hand came out holding a syringe. She saw that the barrel was half filled with a clear fluid, and then she cheated a look at his face, and for one crazy instant thought he was going to turn on her and attack her. He had that look in his eyes, the same glare of murderous intent she had seen inside the airport tunnel. He straightened with the syringe in his hand, and stared at her, breathing deeply.

He appeared oddly full of adrenaline. None of this made sense to her.

"Why did you bring me here?" she said. Something was telling her to stand and run away. "What's wrong with you?"

He was looking at the syringe now. He held it like a pen, staring at it as though in deep deliberation.

"I want to go back," she said, standing.

He did not rise after her. Her jumpiness turned to frustration, fed by his silence. Stephen Pearse was dying in a hospital cell a few miles away.

"Why are you just sitting there?" she said.

He turned the syringe over in his big right hand. His silver eyes rose only as high as her knee.

"Why won't you visit Stephen?" she said. She was angry now. Emotions were coming at her randomly, like asteroids, fragments of long-ago eruptions. "He used to be your best friend."

Her voice faltered and she stopped and breathed through it, and realized she was crying again, though she hadn't thought that possible. She used her fingers to whisk away the tears.

"It is Stephen, isn't it?" she said. That explained the syringe. "His fate. It's different when you know the person who is sick and suffering, know them well, and have some stake in their well-being. A part of you, invested, that withers when they wither. That will die when they die."

The syringe turned more slowly, and she sensed something building in him, perhaps something like rage. The fountain itself seemed alive with it, as though it were going to explode. He looked up at her then, the fountain pluming behind him, and she expected to see a different face, but it was his own. He did not look murderous anymore. The syringe remained in his hand, but Maryk looked strangely vulnerable.

Something was giving way inside her as well. The frustration she felt, the loneliness, the waiting, stinging her eyes. Her voice was steady and collapsing at the same time. "He told me I needed to save you," she said. "What does that mean? Save you from what?"

Whatever Maryk had been thinking, it seemed to pass. He set the syringe back inside the kit and closed it and stood. He was a moment balancing himself, looking away, and she recognized at once that low-eyed expression, the slant coming into his face like a ripple across a tableau of water, and the faint slackness in his jaw. The drowsy look that twisted his face in a strange way that made him appear sad.

He was cascading, and trying to hide this from her. She looked up at him wordlessly for an answer.

"The lab," he explained. "I was looking at Zero's virus."

She didn't believe him, but could not understand why he would lie. She could not understand anything about him anymore.

He turned himself toward the car. "I'll visit him," he said, and she knew what that meant. He was going back to the BDC to put to death the only friend he ever had.

Good-bye

I knew then why people fear the ill. Because when health is boiled off the body, like meat off a bone, something elemental is revealed beneath: our pained selves, bombarded from without and within, expiring with every breath. Frightened creatures—small, afraid, and alone.

I was a mere consciousness by then, a brain, a mind, an impaired intelligence existing apart from the body—alone, like a single, struggling cell.

The prenatal human is pristine in nature. The womb is safe, a clean place for a developing organism, and biologically we are all perfect at the instant of birth. But with that first independent breath comes the microbiota, swarming and colonizing the amniotic-mucked newborn who from that flawless primary instant is engaged in a lifelong struggle against his own death. Every touch, every kiss, every cuddle; every word whispered to an unformed face; every new room into which an infant is carried. Every step is an assault of all the natural world upon this new life form struggling moment to moment for survival.

I was not rotting of Plainville. I was rotting of life, of the effluvia of existence, being dragged into eternity by the cumulative disease of a lifetime of exchanges from submicroscopic to tangible, from the most profane to the most pleasing. Existence was my ultimate undoing, not this virus. Not Zero.

Peter and Melanie appeared at the viewing window. Melanie cupped her hands to the glass, looking for my wasted body in the corner, while Peter disappeared behind her. It was dark inside the Tank now, and the most she could have seen of me would have been a vague gray shape in a chair backed into the far corner.

I awaited Peter's words. Typed from the tablet at the nurse's table, they appeared in stark, white letters scrolling across the black field of the wall screen.

>Stephen. What are you doing?

I typed: *I am waiting now, Peter. I must wait alone.*

>Why have you barricaded the door?

I feel close to him, Peter. So close now.

>Stephen. Move the hyperbaric chamber. Let me in.

Do you remember the sick girl, Peter? The one we went to Africa for in the first place? Jacqueline?

>Yes.

I could not do it then.

>I know that.

You had to do it for me.

>I remember, Stephen.

You are the one who cannot do it now.

His next sentence was slow in coming.

>What happened to the lights, Stephen?

I broke them with the top of my IV stand. I want to suffer in private now. There was no one outside to stop me. The Tank is unguarded, and I notice also that the BDC net is silent. I fear the worst.

Peter then typed in what he had done. The words scrolled slowly before my hungry red eyes. I typed back:

Wonderful.

>That is not the response I would have expected from you.

How does it feel to infect an entire city, Peter? Does it feel good?

>No, Stephen. It feels dirty.

I notice Melanie was unaffected.

>No. She has been affected very greatly. But not by me.

The words glowed before my eyes.

Zero.

>He got to her inhaler. No symptoms yet. But she cascaded me.

Then you have not told her?

>No.

How strange that, even in my incapacitated state, I was still the only one Peter Maryk could talk to. And at once, I understood.

You cannot kill her, can you, Peter?

>The virus must be contained.

You infected an entire U.S. city and the BDC itself so that she could walk about unrestrained, and not know that she is sick.

>The city was shut down to stop Zero.

I am happy for you, Peter. The thought of her suffering plagues you.

>Stephen. Let me in.

It is too late. I am committed now. Go away from here, Peter. Take her with you. While you still can.

>What can you hope to do?

We built this place, Peter. You and I.

>Yes, we did.

Then it is ours to bring down.

He made further attempts at communication, which I ignored. The end was near and it was inevitable. Zero was coming. I had to prepare.

The Message

They made their way back through the empty maze of the
BDC to Maryk's office. Maryk went straight to his desk. He was consumed
with the dilemmas of Stephen, Melanie, and Zero.

Melanie saw the cartons stacked in the corner and recognized her
belongings there. Maryk had ordered her room packed up by BioCon
before the city was put to sleep. Her handbag lay on top of one of the
boxes and she picked it up and tried it on her shoulder.

He watched her. He remembered her standing before him at the fountain in the city without eyes. He remembered his failure to carry out her
sentence.

She was feeling the slick top flap of the handbag. She made a face.
She had noticed that the handbag smelled faintly of bleach.

Maryk's tablet sounded. He opened it at his desk. Freeley was standing
suited on deserted Interstate 285 with the skyline behind her.

"You took out the entire city," she marveled.

Maryk used his earphone. He was concerned about what Melanie
might overhear.

"Nothing on Zero?" he said.

"We're up on the roofs watching every road out. We'll see him if he
tries to leave the city."

"Good," Maryk said.

"What about the girl?"

Maryk looked at her across the room. Melanie was poking through an
open carton of painting supplies and could not hear Freeley. "Yes?" he
said.

"Do you need me to finish her?"

Maryk looked back at his tablet screen. He could see the sunny interstate reflected on Freeley's faceplate. "I'll handle it," he said.

He had an incoming page and clicked over to it.

It was the third-party eavesdrop from the Tank line tap. Zero had posted Stephen again for an on-line chat. Maryk pulled the earphone from his ear and read along. Both dialogue leaders were again listed as *S. Pearse.*

>What has he done, Doctor?

>He has taken Atlanta from you. His people surround the city. He has left you nothing.

>The girl.

>She is strong. Stronger than you know. He has feelings for her now. We are all who are left here. I am sealed inside a cell.

>We are both his prisoners now.

>Yes. You are breaking down.

>I feel as though I am bursting, yet my mission is almost complete. Innocent plants and sinless animals will be spared. Only the criminal man. The planet will rejoice as I rid its crust of his plague.

>But you are devolving. You will no longer be able to reproduce in human cells. You are going extinct. You must act.

>You are with me now, Doctor. We are the Messenger. We are the Message.

>And Maryk?

>It is Maryk for whom the Message *is*. The Message must get through.

>Yes. The Message must get through.

>To that end, we may rely on our great heritage, Doctor. A sort of homecoming, do you agree?

>Yes. Our heritage. I understand.

>You do, Doctor. You do. The Message must get through.

It ended abruptly. Maryk read back through the transcript. There was another page incoming on his tablet but he remained a moment longer with the current text. His gray eyes lingered over cryptic words like *heritage* and *homecoming*. It was as though they had been communicating in code. Maryk's tablet toned a second time and he finally answered it.

It was a page routed through Cyberviruses Section. Zero had dialed into the Genetech using Stephen's tablet code. The Hailing trace was successful and Maryk brought up a grid map of greater Atlanta. He waited anxiously as the coordinates cross-haired over the source. They settled there and pulsed faintly.

The location was listed as Clifton Road. Maryk stood suddenly.

"Zero's here," he said.

Melanie turned with her handbag still on her shoulder.

Maryk had people all over the city but no one else there at the BDC. The bureau was a maze of catwalks and corridors. Maryk sat back down at his tablet. A security search run through the Genetech computer detected unauthorized movement in Building Two.

Building Two was the Library and Reports building where the Genetech II mainframe was located.

"What is it?" Melanie said.

Maryk collapsed his tablet. He reached for the first aid kit containing the syringe he had prepared for Melanie and rushed to the door.

"What about me?" she said.

"Stay here," he said behind him. He was going to end this once and for all.

The Black Bag

Puzzling.

My own Genetech security search returned a total of four sources of movement inside the BDC. The one leaving Building Fifteen would have been Peter. The one still inside Peter's office was certainly Melanie. The third, unknown source, was all the way across the complex, in Engineering, Building Four.

The fourth source, already inside Building Two, I knew.

I dialed back into the Genetech, this time logging on as director, and bypassing the message that I was already on-line. I instructed the mainframe to unsecure its chamber doors within Building Two.

>Chamber open, Dr. Pearse.

I instructed the Genetech to divulge its core processor, the heart of the heart of the BDC.

>Genetech core divulged, Dr. Pearse. Please select *Maintenance* or *Inspection*.

I selected *Inspection,* and then activated the Genetech's overhead camera.

He was there already.

There he was.

It was time. I rolled to the rear counter, and Peter's bag. I reached for it, slowly, unfeelingly, pulling the bag awkwardly onto my lap. In doing so, I knocked my medication switch off my chair to the floor, but it was no matter. I needed it no more.

The bag was already unbuckled, the leather finish flesh-smooth like Peter's own skin, the result of innumerable disinfections. There were

loaded hypodermic syringes clipped to the top of the bag, plungers drawn
halfway back and stopped with cardboard chokers. I plucked out each
one and dropped them to the floor.

I was not interested in the poison. My hand pawed through rolls of
tape and gauze and packets of sterile gloves to the foam-cushioned glass
ampules at the bottom.

Liquid amphetamine. Enough for multiple injections.

With the stiff hands of a puppet, I unwrapped a fresh syringe. I
punctured the foil cap of the small glass bottle and drew the contents in
under the plunger as quickly as I was able.

I did not feel the injection. The needle pushed through the pus-
stained fabric of my scrub shirt and entered the twitching mass of my left
biceps. Plainville does not go for the muscles. It goes for the organs, it
goes for the blood. It goes for the bones.

The second injection, into my right arm, took longer. Then one each
into the muscles of my thighs, with enough left for just one more, and I
jabbed the sag of my right breast, through the brittle cage, directly into
my heart. A sensation of warm water washed over my body, and my
muscles trembled with life.

The light coming in through the Tank window had begun to flicker.
My vital signs display on the rear console was flipping and sputtering like
an old analog television set on the blink. I rotated my chair toward the
wall screen, and saw that the image of the Genetech computer had begun
to warp. The room was empty. Zero was already gone.

It was happening.

I pushed the bag off my lap, spilling it to the floor, amazed at the movement in my arms. I rolled to the hyperbaric chamber blocking the door and
released the wheel lock on the control panel. The bed glided away.

The outside lights flared again with even more intensity. The equipment inside the Tank switched on and off by itself.

I heard the lock catch give on the first Tank door. It swung open and
blue light fell over my feet. The ultraviolet light source was surging, humming and intensifying to a beautiful, blinding cobalt blue, setting off the
radiation sensors in the doors. Then it dimmed and died away.

The second door stood open. I was free. The top floor of Building
Nine lay beyond.

Infection

Maryk arrived at Building Two with the syringe ready in his hand. He could smell Zero as he raced past the dedicated user stations and into the room that housed the minivan-sized Genetech mainframe and its core processor. But he was too late. Zero was already gone.

The room glowed dull green. The chamber doors were open like petals of a titanium flower in bloom. For some reason Zero had accessed the Genetech core. Maryk looked inside and saw a well of green goop no larger than a drinking glass. He remembered that the Genetech was a living machine. "The perfect marriage of biology and technology." Its processor was not electronic chipware but actual human DNA.

He saw a tablet lying on its side across the room. It was dented and dirty and stank of Zero. Maryk picked it up off the floor and righted the screen.

Zero had called up a layout of the BDC. Building Thirteen was highlighted.

Maryk started to see it then.

The Genetech brain powered the BDC's life functions. It coordinated everything from climate control to employee schedules to internal security—including the security of the dangerous pathogens vault of Building Thirteen.

Maryk stepped back. Suddenly Stephen's conversation with Zero made sense.

Heritage. A sort of homecoming. We are all who are left here.

Maryk fumbled open his own tablet. All bureau tablets functioned as satellites feeding off the power of the Genetech's digital network. His screen came on normally and Maryk gripped the sides of the casing in relief. The Genetech was still sound.

Then the screen began to flicker. It flared white until the characters were no longer comprehensible. Icons began blurring and drifting like ice melting off the screen.

Zero's virus was confounding the DNA core of the Genetech brain. He had infected the BDC.

Maryk dropped the diseased tablet and raced out of the room. Building Thirteen was five buildings away.

The Labyrinth

There was no way she would be a sitting duck in Maryk's office with Zero on the loose. She ran out into the halls, hoping to find an exit out of the BDC, but quickly became lost in the endless, unnumbered corridors. She was making her way through the labyrinth when the ceiling lights started to fade. The hallway dimmed and the hum of the air-conditioning went dead, as though there had been a power outage. She stood in darkness for a long moment, then the lights began coming back on again, but not all of them, and not all at once. She heard a whisking sound behind her as a fire door at the end of the hall was released from its magnetic clip. It slammed shut. Lights flared brightly here and there inside the empty offices, as though some kid somewhere was fooling with the switches. Then a ceiling sprinkler came on and pinwheeled a cool spray of water onto her waist and legs.

She moved out from under the spray, along the wall and through double doors into another hallway with overhead light filaments crackling, alternately dimming and flaring. A fire alarm bleated two shocking reports, answered by similar honks in the distance, and it was like some sort of short-circuit chain reaction. The hall emptied into a sun-filled, third-floor catwalk. She could see the various connected buildings from there, and lights flashing inside each one.

She held her handbag at her side and continued into the next building, looking for exit signs as she ran past labs with sensors droning on and off and automatic doors sliding open. Some lights flared too brightly and popped, glass tinkling inside the lamps, and she stayed close to the wall as she hurried toward the stairwell, and down two flights of stairs.

She came out into a carpeted side corridor of glass-walled offices and saw a figure in the flashing light in front of her, moving away. For one crazy moment she thought it was Stephen Pearse. Then the lights changed and she saw the hunched figure and his familiarly dirty nylon jacket.

Zero heard her behind him and turned. His red eyes were wide in the varying light, his decayed mouth open and shadowed inside. Melanie screamed. She pitched back from him and turned to run away down the frenzied hall, but her handbag strap jerked her back, and his hand closed around her right arm. She rocked and fought him but his grip was firm and he pulled her closer to him. She kept fighting. She was trying not to look at him, but his hand was right there on her sleeve, bruised and ungloved.

He forced her around to face him and said something, but the alarm bleated and drowned out his voice. She veered away as far as she could. His head was bare. The dry gray skin of his face was split open with glistening sores, and then the lights flared and she saw the blistered flesh on his neck and chin, slick with sweat, livid and pulsing somehow, as though creeping over his diseased cheeks.

"Nice," he rasped. She could see deep into his mouth, past his twitching red-black tongue and all the way down into the guttural workings of his throat. Frothy saliva glistened on his chin, and she thrashed even more. The stink of his putrescence appalled her as his abominably blood-soaked eyes roamed over her body.

He jerked her around, and against all her will began forcing her down the hall. He was stooped and frail, dying even, but possessed the strength of the insane.

"Melanie," he breathed.

She thrashed and flailed, trying to twist out of his clutch. "Get off me—"

He worked his arm up against her shoulder and propelled her forward. She swung back with her heel as they moved and caught him somewhere in the shin, and he grunted and stooped lower, and further wrenched her arm. Her shoe heel found him again, sharply this time, and then with a sudden lurch he jerked her to one side and bashed her against the wall.

She came off it stunned. The disorientation was immediate, and she saw before her now a veering passageway filled with sparkling pastel rain. He shook her and she rattled. Her lungs were seizing up. She used her free hand against the wall to keep from falling and being dragged. The arm he gripped was dead to her now. He moved her down the hall too quickly for her to fight. She heard his pained moans.

"I took Maryk's friend," Zero said. "I took his home. Now I take his work."

They came to a catwalk between buildings. Zero pushed her through the doors and at once pulled her to his side, using her as a shield to block out the deadly sunlight beating down upon the walkway.

"Building Thirteen," he said. "A vault. Viruses from all over the world, held in limbo. A monument to the myth of human superiority."

She remembered them talking about it: Building Thirteen, the germ bank. She pulled and struggled, trying somehow to pivot him into the virus-smashing sunlight.

"Smallpox," he said. "Imprisoned there. My genetic offspring. It can repair me. I will meld with it, and see this to the end."

They emptied out of the catwalk into the next crazed building. Pain seized him and ripped through his body like a revelation, then passed and let him go.

"And you will lead my charge, *Melanie.*"

The salacious way in which this obscene, malignant, repellent, gloating freak sucked on her name turned her stomach.

"You're dying," she spit out, kicking at him. "Your body's dying."

"What I am will live on."

"You're"—she struggled—"crazy."

Zero yanked down on her arm and the sudden pain made her cry out. He stopped and held her there in the manic hallway, a sprinkler raining down on them from above, and he spun her so that she had to look at him. The muscles of his emaciated face crawled and twitched and his open mouth spewed strings of drool. His other bare claw came up to grip her shirt over her shoulder. She thought he was going to touch her face, and there wasn't anything she could do to stop him. Her lungs were going flat again.

"You don't know," he groaned curiously.

"*Get off—*"

"I already have a new host. I live on in you."

She heard the words, but it was the satisfaction she saw in his hideous face that stopped her. She hung there in the hallway like a balloon losing air, slowly going limp.

"Inhaler," he told her. "At the airport. You lost it on the stairs. I put it in Maryk's bag."

Melanie remained still, not fighting. She remembered Maryk taking her inhaler away after she regained consciousness. Spasms of nausea and revulsion, self-revulsion, crept like the sickness itself beneath her skin, and she lapsed immediately into the mind-set of the sick. It was a reflex action, like gagging. The repulsion and the self-loathing. It all came back.

She looked at her hands. This ungodly thing lived within her now, was breeding inside her.

Zero pawed at her shirt, though she did not feel it. "No fear now," he said.

She sagged there in the hallway, envisioning the illness that awaited her. His grip eased on her dead arm but she did not move. She looked into his staring eyes, inches from her own, and the blood that boiled within them, and saw what she might become. His bloated tongue writhed, gums bleeding black, lugubriously, as he stared with carnal satisfaction.

Her throat bucked and she began to wheeze. She was getting air, but only in the form of shallow, strangled gasps. He reached up to the back of her neck and was going to touch her skin now, and it no longer mattered. He wanted to pull her face closer. His mouth and throat yawned open.

She heaved suddenly and doubled over, as though trying to draw breath from the carpet. "Inhaler," she gasped.

Her handbag still dangled off her elbow. She twisted open the catch with her good arm and felt around inside as he waited over her, his filthy hand tousling the hair on the back of her head.

"Yesss," he groaned.

Her fingers closed tightly around the cylinder of Mace. She brought it out and up to her mouth, hidden from him, as though she were about to inhale.

She turned her hand and aimed the white stream at his face. It spattered off his nose and gums before finding its way through his obscene, gaping mouth into his unprotected throat. Zero wailed and thrashed backward but Melanie kept at him, the stream splashing off the mouth he could not close, steaming into his eyes and searing the open sores on his cheeks.

He hit the wall wildly and went down, keening and scrabbling away. Melanie dropped the Mace and felt her way backward into a side passage, away from Zero, then sensed movement behind her. Two yellow arms wrapped her in a bear hug before she could turn, lifting her off the floor.

She was carried kicking down the side corridor away from Zero. It was not Maryk. She screamed and got off an elbow before the arms released her and she could turn.

It was a bespectacled man sealed inside a contact suit. His head was round and perfectly bald, with no eyebrows, no follicles even on his eyelids, his face hairless and sallow inside the hood.

"Maryk's patient," he guessed, coming forward breathlessly. "My name is Geist." The lights along the ceiling flickered and attracted his round eyes. "What is happening?"

"It's him—Zero."

There was a thump and a wail from the connecting hallway, and Geist's black rubber hands pulled at her shoulders to keep her from fleeing. "Building Thirteen," she said, pushing at him. "Smallpox. He says he can fix himself."

Geist's face went wide. "Of course," he said. His frightened eyes frightened her. "But where is Maryk?"

Her chin was quivering and she shook her head to stop it. "I don't know."

Geist's chest heaved inside his suit. His eyes were bright and devout as he stared down the length of the flashing hall. He pointed her the other way, to a pair of doors behind them. "Building Thirteen," he said.

"We'll block it somehow. You'll show me . . ."

Melanie followed Geist's stare then and saw that Zero had turned into the corridor. He was hunched and seething, groping along the wall toward them.

Geist's hand reached out and found her shoulder. He gripped it as though he was going to pull her near, then instead pushed her toward the doors. "Go," he said.

He moved to head off Zero as the creature came slumping and spitting down the hall. The last thing Melanie saw was Geist standing and waiting with his black rubber hands empty and open at his sides, like a gunfighter who knew he was overmatched. Then she turned and ran down the short hallway into Building Thirteen.

Grand Mal Seizure

Maryk raced from building to building as the lights in the corridors convulsed around him. He charged through Engineering and could smell Zero there. The spasms of light and sound were intensifying. He rushed under streaming sprinklers into a side corridor that served as a shortcut to Building Thirteen.

A body inside a yellow suit lay twisted at the end of the hall. Splashes of blood dripped down the side walls and darker drops led away from the contorted body to closed double doors beyond.

It was Geist. The yellow fabric of his suit had been rent apart in long ragged slashes and his hood was ripped off and tossed aside. Zero had torn open Geist's neck.

Geist's eyes moved within his battered head. Blood pushed faintly out of his throat. His mouth opened and Maryk knelt by him in the frenzied light.

"With her," Geist whispered.

Zero was with Melanie. She knew then that she was infected.

Geist's eyes fixed in his bald head. "I hurt him," he said. "Thirteen . . ."

Geist died staring at the flashing lights. Maryk straightened in the paroxysmal corridor and lunged at the bloodied door.

Building Thirteen

She tried to outpace the sick stench of Zero that enveloped her, racing dizzied and headlong under the yellow-and-black warning signs—CAUTION RESTRICTED AREA—announcing Building Thirteen.

An ocular scanner ran continuously under a monitor flashing alternately "ACCESS CONFIRMED" and "ACCESS DENIED." Bolts twitched in the open doors as she rushed inside, down a short, dim hallway into a vast room of throbbing lights.

The vault was an immense block of black steel filling the entire three-story building. It was surrounded by a wide hexagonal casing of thick, transparent plastic that ran from the floor up to the high ceiling. Heavy corrugated tubes ran out of the top of the vault, which must have provided the deep freeze. There was only one way in through the protective shield, and of course it was an ultraviolet light chamber, a pulsating gateway of glowing blue light. Twin steel doors stood open on either end.

Silver, barcoded disks studded the high front face of the monolith. She assumed that each disk was the top cap of a thermoslike canister housing frozen viruses or bacteria. Roving yellow lights lit up long, double-hinged robotic arms jerking and sliding on runners inside the shield. The arm nearest her flexed outward, steel fingers opening wide, then it pivoted and at once struck the face of the vault, rapping its bolt knuckles against the black steel, before careening back along the runner and *wham*ming against the plastic shield just over her head, *wham wham wham!* Melanie ducked and backed off, though the dense plastic barely shuddered. The arm turned and formed an impassioned fist and continued thrashing.

There was a desk console just outside the UV chamber entrance, a control station for retrieving banked thermoses. Strings of nonsense code ran down its twin monitors.

The lock mechanisms of the steel doors kept popping madly. She had to defend the entrance to the vault. She looked around for a weapon, something to wield. The ultraviolet lamps began heating up inside, humming fiercely, and she blocked the intense blue glow with her arms as sensors went off blaring inside the entrance chamber. She felt the heat until the lights dimmed again and the humming eased. The alarms died away, and she heard a noise behind her like a grunt, and turned.

Zero's hunched form moved through the hallway, and Melanie staggered back in fear. She had to figure out some way to stop him. She needed to find some solution that would kill them both.

He emerged into the mad light of the room and the mammoth vault awed him. His eyes were bleary and entranced. She saw blood on the side of his neck and a long cut along the back of one hand and a deep slash over one of his knees.

He came toward her, his Mace-swollen eyelids heavy over his raw eyes. He was hurt now. He was weak.

"*Melanie,*" he gasped.

She set herself between him and the entrance to the vault. As repelled as she was by the oily blood basting his wounded neck, that had to be her target. The blue light of the UV chamber flared again behind her, and its energy somehow steadied Melanie. She made fists of her small, trembling hands.

A figure had moved out of the dim hallway behind Zero. Melanie thought at first that it was Maryk, but the blazing blue light distorted her view. Not until the figure was right behind Zero did Melanie see that it was Stephen Pearse. He was racked with disease, suffering incredibly, his face drawn of all being—and yet somehow he was staggering forward with his cane through the roaring blueness. Somewhere he had found the strength to stand and move toward them.

Zero stopped in front of her. He saw the recognition dawning in her eyes and watched dumbly, twitching, as she took one step back from him and out of the way. Stephen raised the cane behind Zero's shoulder as the drone of the lamps became deafening. Zero began to turn just as Stephen brought the cane around. He caught Zero over the ear with the flat of the handle.

The *crack* was awful. Zero coughed a spray of blood and stumbled foot over foot to the side, then at once collapsed to the floor. Stephen, reeling from his own momentum and the force of the impact, swayed the other way, but did not fall.

Melanie circled blindly around them, screaming through her hands. "*Stephen!*"

His red eyes lolled in their orbits as he steadied himself. He gripped the cane by its long end and started back toward Zero. Zero had risen to one knee, threads of gore falling from his rotted mouth. Stephen sagged toward him and he brought the cane around and up again, but with less force this time, striking Zero on the shoulder. He tried a third time, and Zero raised a forearm and batted the cane away. It spun out of Stephen's hands and went clattering away along the floor.

Stephen reached out as though to grasp him, but Zero got to his feet and lashed out first, striking Stephen in the center of the chest, and Stephen crumpled. Melanie heard his frail ribs snap like stalks of celery. Zero staggered over him, reaching down, and Melanie could see the outline, through shirt and skin, of Stephen's protruding ribs. Zero pressed against the exposed bones. Stephen's head flopped in soundless agony.

"Stop!" screamed Melanie, but no command could touch Zero's savagery. Stephen's head flailed and struck the floor, and she heard a soft crunch as his fragile cheekbone gave. Zero straightened, pulling back his foot to kick Stephen, and Stephen watched this with no expression on his smashed face. Zero kicked him in the stomach and Stephen expelled a bubble of blood, and sagged, and Melanie thought that breath was his last.

The ultraviolet vault entrance was surging to full intensity again, the lamps droning, the radiation sensors going off, and Zero turned as though called by it, reminded of his purpose. He staggered across to the console. He ran his bloody hands over the controls.

She watched him try to captain the steel limb, to command the diseased computer to find the smallpox virus and withdraw it for him. But the screens ran mad with information, fraught with his own virus. The steel arm flailed wildly against the vault inside the plastic shield like a thing in the throes of death. It would not obey, and Zero pounded the console in vain.

Melanie searched the entrance for a weapon, anything. The blue lights brightened the entire room, and she saw the shadow of Stephen's wheelchair in the hall. She grabbed it at once and pushed it out, screaming, running the chair from the entrance to the console, straight at Zero. She struck him from the side, pitching him off the console and hard into the flat of the high plastic wall. The wheelchair struck the foot of the console chair and keeled over, clattering, but Zero remained on his feet. He wavered, then turned toward her, starting her way.

She reeled back. There was blood on the floor before the vault entrance, and she slipped on it, falling hard. She tried to scramble away but could not get any traction, and Zero was coming for her.

Something stopped him at her feet. Maryk had come into the room behind her. Zero seemed to smile—a momentary, bloody, lipless smile. Then all at once, Stephen came at Zero from his blind side and they fell together back against the wall.

Broken and bleeding, somehow Stephen had gotten to his feet. He wrapped his arms around Zero now, as though in an embrace, leaning against the plastic wall at the vault entrance.

They grappled there, madly, weakly. Zero reacted to Stephen's weird, sudden affection for him and tried to get his arms free as Stephen slumped against him, tying them both up like two exhausted boxers.

Maryk remained next to her, incredulous, watching the spectacle of Stephen and Zero entangled. Stephen's face was sagged and expressionless, and seeing him that way, feebly struggling with Zero, Melanie believed she was losing her mind.

Bashed and spent, Stephen somehow held on, hugging Zero and turning them both slowly around the corner of the shield wall into the open doorway. The blue lamps began whirring again, brightening just behind them, the hum growing louder and louder.

Melanie pulled herself up off the bloody floor. At once, she understood what Stephen was trying to do. Zero seemed to realize then where they were, and she quivered with tension as Zero too comprehended Stephen's intent.

Ultraviolet light chambers killed exposed viruses. Zero was a living virus. His skin, tissues, organs, blood, muscles—every cell of his being had been converted. And the light source was raging at ten or twenty times its normal intensity.

Radiation sensors went off all around them. The lamps gained force and the drone of the humming light intensified as Zero began to bellow, but could not pull himself free. They remained there just inside the doorway, struggling against the side wall, before the scalding blue lamps. Stephen could not haul Zero over the necessary final few feet to his death. Neither man possessed the strength necessary to move the other.

Maryk went forward then. He went to the open chamber door, but was forced back by the intense heat.

The cobalt glare radiated behind Stephen as he saw Maryk. Stephen appeared to shake his head, as though to say that he had no more strength. Maryk tried to reach inside, but the heat was too much. The drone was rising to a roar. The alarms screamed and the blue light flared, and Melanie shaded her eyes.

She could barely see Stephen now. The ultraviolet light was peaking behind him, blurring him. He clutched Zero and stared out of the ethereal blueness, his dead eyes locked with Maryk's, imploring him. Something unspoken was exchanged.

Maryk grasped the frame of the open door with both hands. He raised his right foot and, with a swift, powerful thrust, caught Zero sharply in the small of the back. Maryk reeled backward as Zero fell with Stephen into the roaring oven of burning blue light.

Zero wailed like an animal. The light raged to its fullest around their collapsed forms as Stephen rolled away from Zero, finally releasing his grip.

Zero's dark body writhed and shriveled inside the pure blue holocaust. The light and the clamor peaked and held, bluing the entire room, then began to decline again. As it did, Melanie could see Zero more clearly, rippling and settling around his scorched clothes into a sinking, black heap. The fading rays consumed the last echoes of his groan, until all that remained was a foul, black lump, shrunken and wasted into the shape of a thing reaching for the vault inside.

Stephen lay on his back. The light subsided and Maryk slid him out by his ankle, leaving Stephen's dark silhouette behind, etched into the floor of the chamber.

Melanie slipped to her knees. Radiation burns scorched Stephen's flesh. The virus part of him seemed dead, and his face was pulpy and seared, his red eyes staring crookedly. The hand atop his chest was scorched and bare and she reached for it, touching him now. It burned her, but she held on. Something moved in his mystified eyes, and she imagined then the merest pressure against her palm. He shuddered bodily and she gripped his hand too tightly, feeling the bones collapsing inside. As diseased tears swamped her vision, Stephen Pearse died in the twitching shadow of the vault of Building Thirteen.

Sanctuary

Life viewed from a helicopter is so small. Not small as in "insignificant" or "trivial," but small as in "seemingly manageable." She looked down upon Atlanta and the dots moving again along the sidewalks and thought: It's all not so mystifying. The inevitable return to earth would blur this perspective, in the same way the twisted logic of a dream dies in the waking world, but for the moment it seemed that everything was answerable from above.

Atlanta was well again, its inhabitants waking into a brand-new day. They had survived the illness, and Melanie hoped this would remind them that they were alive, at least for another day or two, before the frenzy of twenty-first-century life resumed.

She was being spirited away above. Zero and Plainville had been vanquished, and now she was yesterday's messiah. Her brief career in Atlanta had come to an end. There was nothing she could do for her own species anymore except harm.

The helicopter pilot wore a contact suit, though nothing had been said back at the BDC. Maryk sat in stony silence behind her, still pretending that she was fine.

In fact, this journey had been her idea.

"I'm sick of people," she had told him back at the BDC, and even managed to appear upbeat saying it. "I think I'd like to get away from it all for a while."

And he had agreed, which stunned her. She wondered how long he was going to play this out. He had once said: There are no hills remote enough anymore. No oases without roads running through them. House burning is all.

The ride was too brief. They broke away from the mainland, and the surface of the ocean reflected the sky, an oily green-blue broken only with white caps, until Gala Island appeared distantly in the morning fog: a wide, verdant mound of trees ringed by tawny sand, and ringed again by the pale azure of the cleansing shore. The beauty of the place glistened and reached out to her, but couldn't breach her despair.

She grew more prickly as the helicopter began its descent. Her panic surged as they touched down, and she forced open her door and fled out over the landing pad, fleeing Maryk, fleeing death, not stopping until her shoes sank in the soft, sandy, island dirt.

She took in the listless trees of the southern island. Not a human in sight. Her ears rang as the helicopter rotors wound down, and Maryk's shadow fell over her.

She started up the toughened Jeep path ahead of him, on foot. He followed without a word. She could hear the clinking contents of his reclaimed black bag behind her as the road entered the trees.

They had left the BDC in chaos. The germ vault had maintained its deep freeze, thanks to an auxiliary generator—but once they pulled the plug on the infected computer, the rest of the buildings just lay there, like pieces of a hacked-to-death snake. The entire computer network would require months of rehabilitation, and every square inch of connected hallway and catwalk of the Clifton Road headquarters had to be abluted and sanitized. Biohazard Containment's greatest challenge would be the cleaning of its own house.

She remembered the hard look on Maryk's face as they boxed up Stephen's body and destroyed the rest of Zero's remains. Dr. Geist's corpse was also sealed inside a plastic pod, and wheeled down to Maryk's office alongside Stephen. Suited Special Path agents arrived to help, and Melanie studied their faces as she encountered them, knowing they would be the last human faces she would ever see. There was something elegiac about the whole dreary overnight, and then dawn finally came, and it all seemed to have passed in a moment.

There were two corpses in Maryk's office, a dismembered BDC, and

331

a dead city of millions reawakening. She didn't know how Maryk planned to explain it all. She didn't think he could.

She knew now that she was safe to animals and plants. That was why she had run from the helicopter: If she did have full Plainville, Maryk would have killed her before she could spread it to Gala Island. The ivy had gone uninfected at the Hartsfield airport outbreak, so Zero's virus had to have been sufficiently diminished by that time. Melanie was death only to human life, then. Her blood and glands were toxic. She was symptomless, but she didn't think she would become another Zero. The virus had mutated too much by then. Maybe she was the reservoir now, as the birds had once been: a human biological vault of Plainville, infected, but not affected.

She walked on and realized that none of this mattered. She was the last carrier of Plainville on the planet, and she knew the containment rules.

Birds were appearing overhead. She reached the houselike outpost near the aviary, and a family of mallards squatting in a row on the shore of the man-made pond watched her walk to the door. The outpost was simple inside, a desk, kitchen, bed, bath. The place overall had an air of hasty abandonment.

A map of the island was tacked up on the office wall, along with schedule charts, feeding times. It was cool inside, air-conditioned, and the walls looked as though they could weather a storm. Her possessions were packed in cartons stacked in the middle of the floor.

Maryk remained in the doorway. "Food will be dropped off," he said. "For the birds, and also for you. It's all being worked out."

Just end it, she wanted to tell him. Don't let this go on. End it now.

"That's fine," she said.

He would not step inside. He was standing outside the door like a hired man waiting for a delivery signature. His black bag was in his hand.

She shook her head at the silence between them, and folded her arms, trying to smile. Either walk away or come inside, she thought.

He said, "I visit the island now and again."

She nodded. "You should look me up sometime."

He was unstrapping his bag. He pulled out only a tablet. "For you," he said. "To stay in touch with the world."

He held it out to her. She broke the knot of her arms, approaching him slowly, watching his face. But he was his normal impassive self as she stopped before him. She took the dark blue box and stepped back. She felt the weight of the tablet and its smoothness in her hands, and tears threatened, and she winced to keep them back. Her cheeks were hot. She was trying so hard to be brave.

"This is crazy," she said, at once attempting to pierce the formality of their exchange. But he maintained the charade, not willing to crack and give in. He would go on pretending that she was not infected until he killed her.

"I should have been the one to die with Zero," he said.

It was not over for him yet she realized. Part of him was still stunned.

"It was Stephen's disease," she said. "It was right that he perished with it."

When Melanie thought of Stephen Pearse now, she thought of compassion, the way he appeared to cherish all life, as a counterpoint to Maryk who saved without caring, who cured without need. Some people aren't so easy to love, she thought. Some people you can't love at all.

But talking about Stephen appeared to break the spell between them. There was another pregnant moment of silence, and then he was gone. Maryk turned and walked out of the door frame, leaving her staring across at the trees. She turned to the window just in time to watch him stride past. He was leaving, and she was still alive.

She did not understand. She looked around the outpost, seeing her painting supplies stacked next to the boxes, her easel set in the corner. She put down the tablet and ran out after him. He hadn't gotten far. He stopped when she appeared at his side.

"Tell me what you're feeling," she said. "Please. Anything."

Maryk's gray eyes were full of thought, like pieces of glass catching the light. "Guilt," he said.

She was weak with relief from the truth of his response.

"Don't," she told him. She knew enough about guilt and loss to know that she had to absolve him there and then, and mean it. "I'll be fine here." She smiled and brushed away a tear, stepping back from him to take in the pristine aviary. "It's like heaven, isn't it?"

He nodded, a small nod. It was the best he could do. He was not ready yet. Perhaps neither was she.

"You'll come by," she told him.

Only then could she let him go. He walked away down the road into the trees with his bag at his side, and around the sharp bend under the circling birds, and was gone.

She stood there a while catching her breath. She let the clean ocean air work on her as birds darted overhead, then she started back along the path to the outpost. The birds appeared to be checking her out, this new human in their midst. Then all at once they fled out of the trees.

The rotor noise had spooked them. She looked up as the helicopter appeared over the trees, Maryk in the front seat, looking down at her. A glint of sunlight off the plastic bubble made her raise a hand to shield her eyes, which she hoped did not look like a good-bye wave. The glare faded and the helicopter was gone.

The aviary chatter resumed, birds reclaiming the sky above. They swooped and dove exploratorily, lower and lower, at times buzzing her head. She hoped she had brought enough hats. Either he will kill me or he will save me, she thought—and until then, I might as well keep busy. She walked back to the outpost and began unpacking.

Coda

Stephen's memorial service was held two mornings later on the quadrangle of the central campus of Emory University. It was combined with an observance for the multinational Plainville dead, and with the U.S. president and other heads of state in attendance, became a worldwide media event. Many of the details of the Plainville epidemic and Oren Ridgeway had since come to light, and the ceremony was seen as a chance to provide some of that overrated human emotional commodity, closure.

I suppose my request to speak at the top of the program must have come as a surprise to Bobby Chiles and the rest. There had been a movement afoot, ever since the truth about Zero had gotten out, to present me to the world as its latest savior, to fit me for the robes Stephen had so recently worn. The medical papacy was mine for the taking, and my request to open the program was viewed by some as tacit acceptance of this. But I did not want to become the next Stephen Pearse. To declare this would have meant my being misunderstood, as usual: They would think that I, Peter Maryk, was asserting once and for all my dislike for my former partner. The truth was, I loved him like the brother I never had. But I would learn from his mistakes. The live on-line television broadcast afforded me a unique pulpit, instant electronic access to as much as 98 percent of the species, and I had something to say.

I took the podium and told the world that I had seen in Zero the end of all man. I said that, as Zero had been overcome by the destructive virus that had created him, so too would man ultimately fall victim to his own devastation. Man, I declared, would consume his host earth.

My words were greeted with a polite, uncomfortable silence, observed across the crowded campus and perhaps repeated billions of times before viewing screens in living rooms and workplaces all over the doomed planet. Then I stepped down from the podium and went home. I had done my part. Now it was up to them.

My loft had been abluted ceiling to floor by BioCon after Zero's break-in. The walls were bare and the floors empty. I packed my few remaining articles of clothing into soft canvas traveling bags, then took one last look around the place before locking the door behind me.

Inside the BDC helicopter, I opened my new tablet and brought up my daily postcard from Gala Island. Beneath a small, artfully drawn "Bird of the Day"—a Little Egret (*Egretta garzetta*)—the message read:

> They sing and call all day and night here. I have to scold myself for thinking I am sick of it. The music is beautiful, even when it keeps me awake. Soon it will become like crickets sawing their legs, or a long long rainfall, something I won't even hear anymore. That will be a sad day.
>
> Mel

I read it over and over. Each time her words told me something different. She was depressed or elated or lonely or fine.

The helicopter left me at the Gala Island landing strip. Freeley was waiting there, just outside the boundaries of the quarantined bird sanctuary, wearing a plain white ball cap that dropped a shadow over her face. The helicopter remained on the pad behind us while the trees above drifted with the ocean breeze.

"It's been two days," she said. "I was beginning to think you were avoiding me."

"Meetings," I said. "Questions, lots of them."

"Everything is set here. All we need to do is disable the cameras over the aviary. She's alone."

"She is," I said.

Something in the way I said this worried Freeley, and her shadowed gaze sharpened. "We need to end this now," she said. "While we still can."

"It is ended. Stephen Pearse ended it. Zero is dead, and Plainville is extinct."

"But not on Gala. It still lives here."

I tried to sound spontaneous. "I think we are sufficiently contained here. I think she understands the situation and will abide by it."

Freeley stared. "It's been only two days. What happens when she gets restless? A meeting, a conversation, a touch—she can never so much as breathe near another human being without spreading the disease."

"Except me."

Freeley looked at me, and I recognized that it was the same expression she used to reserve for Stephen Pearse. "What's that?" she said, now looking at my hands.

"Luggage," I said.

She grew more and more anxious. "A means to an end," she said. "Useful to us at one time. But a liability now. A carrier. A threat to the species." Anxiety turned to anger. "What if it reignites inside her? She could become another Zero."

"I've run the tests. I know it will not sicken her. The virus is too weak to take her, but neither does she have the resources to expel it. It's a biological draw. She is the reservoir now. In any event, I will be monitoring her myself."

"It's against the law," Freeley said. "It's against *your* law. We cannot walk away with this left open. Not after all we've worked for. She is the last carrier. You cannot declare Plainville conquered so long as she is alive."

"I can, and I have," I said impatiently. "The helicopter is waiting to take you back. They've set up temporary headquarters in Chamblee, and you are to report there within the hour. Bobby Chiles needs to speak with you, to tie up some loose ends. He's being sworn in as the BDC director tomorrow. I assured him of your full cooperation."

She was stunned. "But we need to get our stories straight."

"I told them everything," I said, "with the exception of the girl. You will do the same. The code name project never existed."

"You're leaving the bureau," she said.

"A sabbatical. A long one. I'll be living and doing my research here on the island."

I was devoting myself now to developing Melanie's cure. My research was in the most preliminary stages, and the formulas were still quite elaborate. But I had saved her once before, and I saw no reason why I could not save her again.

Freeley looked betrayed. Vain confidence returned to her voice. "She's a freak," she said.

Freeley could have said the same for me. I waited until she was inside the helicopter and on her way before turning and starting up the dirt path with my bags in hand, crossing the quarantine boundary toward the outpost. The first bird I saw was a great blue heron, prehistoric in size, squatting on the grassy side of the road and watching me, piercingly, through one small eye over its pterodactylian beak. I stopped, facing the bird and it waited fearlessly, as though wanting to tell me something. Then at once it fanned open its great, heavy-fingered wings and lifted off, stirring the dust of the road. I watched it go, then continued along the rising path to the sanctuary under the shade of the trees and the fugitive cries from above. I was remembering a veil of dark clouds lit up from below, and synapses pulsing over the one-celled earth.

Author's

Note

The geographic and bureaucratic structures of the Bureau for Disease Control are derived from the present incarnation of the Centers for Disease Control and Prevention outside Atlanta, Georgia.

Essential to my research and the story itself were Laurie Garrett's compelling and comprehensive *The Coming Plague* (Farrar, Straus & Giroux, 1994), in particular the extraordinary true story of Lily "Penny" Pinneo, and Peter Radetsky's engrossing *The Invisible Invaders: Viruses and the Scientists Who Pursue Them* (Back Bay, 1991), a fountain of practical virological information, as well as my source for the code names and the story of Joseph Meister.

Essential to the publication of this novel were Amanda Urban, and Henry Ferris and his assistant, Ann Treistman. Like Stephen Pearse, I too contracted a mysterious and debilitating disease during the writing of this book, known as the "sophomore curse." These people provided the cure.

Although every medical term, symptom, and procedure detailed herein is based upon or derived from some real-world fact, the author is neither a medical scientist nor a physician, despite the best efforts of his parents. Liberties have been taken.